In Awe

In Awe

Scott Heim

Scott Heim (signature)

HarperCollins*Publishers*

Grateful acknowledgment is made to Gordon Sharp for permission to reprint lyrics from the songs "Gift of a Knife" and "Playtime" by Cindytalk, words by Gordon Sharp, © 1988.

HarperCollins books may be purchased for educational, business, or sales promotional use. For information please write: Special Markets Department, HarperCollins Publishers, Inc., 10 East 53rd Street, New York, NY 10022.

FIRST EDITION

Designed by Elina D. Nudelman

Library of Congress Cataloging-in-Publication Data

Heim, Scott.
        In awe/Scott Heim. —1st ed.
            p.   cm.
        ISBN 0-06-018687-9
        I. Title.
    PS3558.E4527I5   1997
    813'.54—dc21   97-1505

97 98 99 00 01 ❖/RRD 10 9 8 7 6 5 4 3 2 1

This book is for Eryk Casemiro
and for Michael Lowenthal

FOR INVALUABLE ASSISTANCE WITH THIS BOOK,
MY GRATITUDE TO THE FOLLOWING:

James Ireland Baker, Fiona Hallowell, Robert Jones, Michael
Lowenthal, Louise Quayle, David Rakoff, Jamie Reisch, Scott
Savaiano, Gordon Sharp, Sherri Weiss, and M. Elizabeth
Woodbury. For constant inspiration, Elizabeth Fraser, Robin
Guthrie, and Simon Raymonde. And, always and always,
Carolyn Doty.

March of the Zombies

Boris Appleby
Date of Birth 10/26/78
Lawrence West High School
Lawrence, Kansas
Grade 11

Submitted for consideration
to the annual Douglas County
High Schools in the Arts contest
1995–1996 season

Chapter 1

At midnight the undead rose from the earth. Of the three zombies, the boy made it out of the ground first. His fingernails clawed at the black soil that foamed around the gravestone. One arm struggled forth, another, then the shoulders and neck. Slowly, his face emerged, hints of white skin gradually visible, like a drowned boy surfacing from the cold depths of a lake. It had rained since his burial, and his exquisite struggle made soft sucking sounds. In the distance he could hear a barn owl's lamentation. And the thunder, like a warning.

The boy pushed up, fists on the ground stamped firm by the gravedigger's boot. He could feel the spiders weaving webs in the seams of his clothes. The worms on his wrists like gray bracelets, biding time until their burrow into flesh. For now he didn't mind. The boy fought harder, sloughing off the earth. His knees, ankles, feet.

Body cleared at last, he crouched to brush the loamy residue from the headstone. The capital B of his first name, the following four letters, the surname given by unknown parents who'd orphaned him fifteen years ago. The dates *1978 to 1995. Rest in Peace.* The boy stared, uncomprehending, then stood to wait for the other two.

The young woman was next. It seemed as though she'd practiced months to meet the challenge. Her movements were graceful, her resurrection smooth as ballet. Soil peppered her eyelids, her scarlet lips. She shook her head, nuggets of damp earth falling from her hair to reveal the blond beneath. In the moonlight her face was pale, beautiful, smoldering. She still appeared girlish, years younger than her thirty-two. Her ankle twisted in the mud. She kicked her shoes away and lumbered barefoot toward the south end of the cemetery, where the boy waited. When she saw him, the memories registered, and she offered the chilly gift of her arms until they fell around him in a fusion of love and exhaustion.

Last was the old woman. As with her friend, death had made her gorgeous. The two days of rest had gelled her beauty, proved it true. Her silvery hair, ribboned with vermilion and gold, had tumbled free to curtain her face and shoulders. They'd buried her in white, the fluted dress a shock against the cemetery's shadows. The old woman took her time, clawing through grass and clods of dirt. She tore petals from a spray of roses that someone, feeling sorry for such an elderly soul, had placed at her grave.

The woman heard her friends approaching and looked up. Her eyes were like gray slate, reflecting their vacant faces. A crimson petal clung to her thin shoulder. She reached for their hands, and the rest of her removal came easy.

At last they stood together. Tens, hundreds, thousands of skeletons rested unbreathing beneath them. Grave markers held still on all sides, headstones against the moonlit horizon like razorblades embedded in the soft black flesh of earth. Somewhere another night bird murmured and mourned, heralding their ritual of revenge. The time had arrived, time to repay the years of torment, the sorrow and suffering. Their impatient and unbearable hours of sleep over, the trio joined hands and formed a circle. They were ready at last.

The March of the Zombies had begun.

Suffering Box

1
August

*D*arkness waits for them. It waits
with purple thunderheads and wet ivy shadows and spangled air
gone blizzardy with rain. It will wait forever if they let it. At last
they give up, shield their faces, walk out: past the hospital's automatic doors, glass sliding open and whipping shut, and into the
parking lot.

Sarah holds one of Harriet's hands; Boris, the other. They crane
their heads toward the storm and its hot adhesive threat. Five-
thirty—the close of afternoon visiting hours—yet it seems like
dusk, the bruised sky bandaged with clouds, the inky water falling
slow and sugar-thick. They didn't remember umbrellas. Behind
them, in his bed, Marshall still sleeps, spinning numb through a
black consumptive dream. "Fading," the doctor told Sarah. He said
the word in a surly whisper, with Harriet out of earshot, and for a
long, long time Sarah heard it, *fading, fading,* its two-syllable echo
rattling in her head.

The sky shakes and shakes and blankets every car with the same gray shade. Here, a pickup with a flat front tire; there, another sporting a rear-window tableau where a widemouth bass leaps to snag a fisherman's spinnerbait. Rows of Kansas license plates: blue numerals superimposed over gold shocks of wheat. From the slippery distance, a storm siren initiates its wail. The stereo tympani of thunder; a cicada's flat drone; the wind's hissing rip against the shaggy dropseed grasses. But conquering these sounds, conquering the cars in the lot and rain on Sarah's face, is the odor. It slams into them, unrelenting, heavier than the antiseptic memory of Marshall's hospital room, the hot rubbery macadam, the floral hint from the storm's onslaught. It is a scent Sarah should easily pinpoint, like bananas or blood. Yes—there—spray paint. A smell of high school art projects from years back, spray-painted plywood sculptures she and Marshall giggled over, turned in for measly B minuses.

She tightens her hold on Harriet's hand and feels the older woman's ring pressing its nugget: a junk-store pigeonblood ruby, Marshall's gift from some Mother's Day or birthday past. Sarah brushes her lips against Harriet's fingers, lets her hand fall, and fumbles in her bag for keys. A change in the air's current suctions leaves between her feet. The echo of the warning siren ceases; within that stillness, Sarah looks at her car.

Boris stops. Harriet stops, the wrinkles on her forehead deepening. They have seen it, or rather comprehended it, first. Boris steps closer, breathing an unintelligible monosyllable, and Sarah moves beside him. It is her Volkswagen, and although it remains positioned as before, now she barely recognizes it. Its red color, changed; its beetle shape, altered. Sarah drops her fingers on the side door, gradually clenching them into a fist, the knuckles shiny-white and hard as cherry stones.

She walks around the wreckage of her car, each step cautious and rabbit-soft. Only hours before, she drove south of town to pick up Harriet; she stopped at a filling station for five self-serve gallons and added a bottle of multivitamins, for Marshall, to her bill. She and Harriet and Boris had whiled the day at her best friend's bedside and she should be devoting her thoughts to him, Marshall, not this. This practical joke, this artifice or mistake. Hammers or crowbars or wrenches have bashed the doors' midsections, have spider-webbed the windshield, dented the fenders. A star-blast cavity, evidence of a boot kick, has ruined the passenger-side headlight; the sideview mirror bears a deep meniscal crack. But these wounds seem less noticeable under the painted words. The vandals used black, blue, and white, scar colors against the red. Letters overlap parts of other words, some words misspelled, trailing off the sides of fenders or breaking at the angles of window frames. Sarah reads what she can: GUTTERSLUT. HOMO. AID'S VICTIM. BITCH IN HEAT. FOSSLE. FAGGOTS. SMELLY OLD CRAZY GRANMA. QUEERS. She rounds the back end of the car and studies the other side. PROSTI-TUTE. LOOSERS. PANSYASS. STUPID CUNT. ROTING FLESH GRAY-HARED BITCH. COCKSUCKER. TRASH MOTHERFUCKERS.

The siren blares again, pizzicato bursts warning, warning. They stand poised in their separate places, circumventing the gashes and dents and broken glass. The aqueous black of the asphalt rises and ripples around them. Boris shuffles forward, nickels and dimes and pennies jangling in his pocket. He takes Sarah's arm as though she needs steadying. "I'm okay," she says.

But Sarah knows she isn't okay; knows she should worry about repairs or the identities of the culprits. Instead she wonders what her heroines would do: those victims in horror films, women who run screaming through the woods or the empty spirit-dark house, arms pinwheeling the air, only to be corralled by the murderer. Alone and headspun with fantasy, Sarah sometimes pretends to *be* those girls. But now, as she opens the VW's door, those dramatics seem improper, wrong. Her best friend is dying; his mother stands trembling beside her; and Boris too, her meek and innocent comrade. Marooned in reality, far from dreams of movies, Sarah only stares. The T's on PROSTITUTE mock, meant for her, lowercase crosses wedged between the surrounding capital letters.

The sweat from Boris's palm threads down her arm. Sarah inhales another breeze of paint fumes, steps closer, places her foot on the seat to brush away the shards of glass. Then she slides behind the wheel; Boris takes the back, leaving the passenger door open. The rearview frames him: strawberry-blond bangs, evening-sky eyes. PANSYASS, they wrote. HOMO. His gaze links with Sarah's, and she looks away.

The rain pounds in warfare across the lot, but Harriet doesn't yet join them. She is growing older and older, Sarah knows, but still she is lovely. There was a time when she would con Sarah into cutting her hair, Marshall's hair, but now he no longer requires that and Harriet has abandoned haircuts. Years ago she suffered an illness too; hers, however, took a definite shape and lodged steadfast within her body, and through radiation and surgery the doctors healed it. These days Harriet feels fine, but there are always errands, always hospital steps to climb. She wears her old tennis shoes, blue, decorated with bluer heels and toes and tongues, unsoiled and untattered still. The same pair she used to wear loyally while on shopping trips with her son and Sarah.

Harriet reaches into her purse. She confiscated Marshall's camera, days earlier, from his room. Now Sarah watches as his mother leans closer, laboring over zoom and focus. The mantle of trees begins its slowpoke sway. Harriet disregards their warning, striding away for panoramic views of the damage, the automatic advance whirring feebly, the flash sizzling. She snaps final shots of the car's tail end—*eight,* Sarah silently counts, *nine*—that red chrysalis containing the engine. Wet wind loosens Harriet's hair from its bun. It falls across her face, silvery and frizzled as filaments from a scouring pad. She shields the lens with a cupped hand and leans with a stiff-limbed curtsy into the car.

Sarah twists the key in the ignition: a shudder and a cough and at last the frustrated rev, choking like something battered and maimed, but alive. She can smell the sickness on her hands, her clothes. AID'S VICTIM. They have been friends for as long as, as long as . . . In a box at home she keeps a valentine he sent nearly twenty years back, in eighth grade. Just last month, his shred of hope obliterated, he gave her his crystal that was supposed to heal. Now it dangles from the rearview, metronomic, dappling color on Sarah's and Harriet's faces, a section of Boris's between them.

Storm clouds make gray whipcord scars against the deepening blue. They fall low and then lower, and Sarah feels as though she is moving the car through sky instead of land. On the radio, the announcer reports northern Kansas hailstones as heavy and round as baseballs. "The storm's a monster and it's headed our way, folks." The wipers draw semicircles on the icy lace of the crushed windshield. Sarah stares through an unshattered corner, beyond the downpour, to the narrowing road. Out there, other cars swerve and tap their brakes, a red Morse code anticipating the flood weathermen have prophesied. Tree branches buckle and churn; a hunched figure shields its head with a newspaper, racing to a parked car.

Sarah leaves the blacktop for a narrow country road. She drives ten, twelve miles away, clouds emptying over the miniature Lawrence in her side mirror. Birds rocket above the box elders, into the blurry air. The minutes wobble past, silent, uneasy. No one speaks, the graffiti words like layers of black tape crossing, recrossing their mouths. On both sides of the car, the ditches slope away to puddles the dangerous width and depth of ponds. For one second, Sarah imagines twisting the wheel, careering herself and her comrades to a watery death. Rescuers will find the wreckage, unable to discern which part of the demolition resulted from the crash, which from the vandals. They will be the same who have pointed and whispered about her, about Marshall. About all of them. GUTTERSLUT. TRASH MOTHERFUCKERS.

Glass litters their feet like jewels of rock candy. Its ghost dust lies across the dashboard; wedges in the waterstained seats of ocher foam. Back at Harriet's house, Sarah will help prepare more meals for Marshall, soups filled with green and yellow vegetables, bitter herbs, which, according to a twenty-two-dollar book Harriet bought, will boost immunity. Now the older woman's face tilts toward her, and her voice hammers the tense silence. "I reckon they knew it was our car?"

Rain runs in mirror rillets and Sarah feels it licking through the window cracks. They pass a pasture where Hereford cattle huddle together, a glossy russet-red. A farmhouse's handmarked sign, over-turned, spells WATERMELON/CANTALOUPE into the mud. Ahead is the junk store where, years ago, Marshall bargained with the owner over Harriet's ruby ring and, some time after that, a handpainted music box for Sarah. And now its CLOSED sign, its triple-bullet-hole window, its black front door boarded with splintered table legs. Sarah speeds but understands there is no escape: lightning can scissor the hood at any second. They can float away with the water. Any swift, miraculous thing can happen.

"Those words," Harriet continues, "they were referring to us. Right?" The insults, Sarah knows, are words Harriet has never used. Only this afternoon, someone has seared them, permanently, into her vocabulary.

Ahead, people have parked beneath an overpass, taking shelter. Their cars and pickups seem spotless, unharmed. The wrecked VW trundles past, Harriet's farm—and yes, Marshall's too—looming somewhere in the dusky periphery. "I think so," Sarah answers, the rain's percussion nearly smothering her voice. "Yes, that's us."

The omen, the unheeded warning, the initial drop of poison. Until today, Sarah maintained hope. *Maybe,* she thought, *just maybe* . . . A part of her still believed everything would remedy itself: their world polished, balanced. Perhaps, by wishing, she could detain the terrible accelerating click-click of suffering. But today she sees her mistake. There are body shops undaunted by the evening storm, and she knows she should stop, should shell out her wallet's meager contents for a mechanic to purify and erase the damaging words. But Sarah keeps driving. She and Harriet and Boris, she imagines, will make their way around town in this manner for the rest of the summer, throughout the coming autumn. They will drive the ruined car after Marshall's death, as part of the slim funeral procession to his grave, even after.

The townspeople, Sarah knows, will grow to expect it. They'll hear the rumble and chug and look up, bearing witness to the monster's rackety cavalcade through the wet streets, its trio of "misfits," its "freaks," crammed inside. The painted words will smear in a purplish stream as they pass. And after two weeks, three, perhaps a month, their injured presence in the town will become a constant, a staple. The people will stop pointing and jeering. Sarah and Boris and Harriet will drive, somber but strangely cavalier. Their fists clenched, their bodies tensed with purpose. All eyes focused on their stormy destination.

2

September

With autumn the days grow darker and in darkness comes the rain, insistent and slow and narcotic, the town's punishment. The streets flood at night and crumble by morning. Leaves fall early, brown by the month's herald, dragged down by the chill and the wind. At night the breeze blows from the southwest, bearing a candylike hint of apple cider from the orchards of McIntosh and Red Delicious that border Lawrence. But mostly the smell is rain. People stop smiling. In stables horses whinny and in kennels dogs howl, as animals do before tornadoes or quakes, their voices harmonizing to interrupt sleep.

The Kansas River is a wound, carving the town in two. The storms have made it furious. It pounds and laps and breathes pale yellow mists. A pair of university students have been reported missing since the advent of fall semester, and a headline in the newspaper blames the river: FLOODS SUSPECTED IN GIRLS' DISAPPEARANCES. The townfolk whisper otherwise, trusting no one.

Midnight means curfew at Sunflower Youth Home. Boris clicks off the lamp, stretches out, closes his eyes. He focuses on the river and rain, their bastard clash, and can't sleep. The muggy darkness persists, tightens at his throat, yet he clutches the blanket closer. He's replaced the Sunflower blanket with one swiped from his last foster family, the Mercurochrome stain still spotted on its trim, their house's soapsud smell pasted to its fleece. Boris breathes the scent and feels everyone drifting off around him. Nearby, his roommate, Carl; the other twenty-two teenagers whose rooms divide the hallway; the pair of night counselors who sleep in adjacent beds. He senses them losing consciousness, oppressive waves stilling, dispersing, leaving him alone at last.

Boris pictures Sarah and Harriet and, between their sorrowed faces, Marshall. He tries to replace his thoughts of today's funeral with the missing students. He imagines the discovery of a body: it will happen, he's certain, soon. He dreams hunters in camouflaged hats and coveralls, stamping through the woods at the north side of town. One hunter, scanning the bushes and mulch heaps for deer, will spy something strange through binoculars. One shotgun will drop; another, and another. They'll find her face peeking forth from piles of leaves, her buttermilk eyes watching them, flesh the color of a peeled potato, dried blood against her frozen lips. Boris catalogs the details: a church bell's chime in the far distance; secretive crackle of the grasses; scavenging arc of birds that ache to gnaw at her knuckles and toes. Starlings' songs trapped in her unhearing ears. Wasp stings the last bitter flavor on her tongue.

His room lies at the hall's darkest end like a secret fairy-tale chamber. On the inside, though, it is ordinary to the point of severe, no Sleeping Beauty castle or Bluebeard lair. He arrived that first day with two suitcases, a photo album, the Dr Pepper he'd bought at the bus station. He slurped its remainder through a half-gnawed straw and withheld a wince at the assigned room. He still hates it. Like all others at Sunflower, it consists of white-painted walls, enclosed by a spackled ceiling, unornamented except for a single gold crucifix above each bed. Posters, photographs, or cork boards aren't allowed. There are two closets, two dressers, two desks with matching chairs. Boris has learned snippets of history by reading his desktop's ballpointed graffiti; the knife nicks from legions of past orphans and runaways, underage arsonists and shoplifters. Delinquents, black sheep, thieves! He has heard the stories, the gossip. In the room directly above sleeps a girl who, when ordered by her mother not to attend junior prom, slit twin verticals in her wrists with a carpet knife. Down the hall, a boy who attacked three friends with a rubber mallet. Once upon another time, more than a decade ago, even Sarah was here, captive during her own damaged and vaguely criminal adolescence.

Boris claims the dresser on the left. Unlike Carl's, its bottom drawer has been rigged with a lock. He keeps the key taped to the inside of a Bible, a pocketable New Testament with a cover the color and texture of a lime. Sunflower supplies one Bible per tenant, but Boris only opens his to retrieve the key. He's revealed its whereabouts to Sarah and Harriet, telling them they can uncover the drawer's contents "in case I'm murdered, or become the target of a terrorist's bomb, or mysteriously disappear from the face of the earth."

Carl sleeps, eyes and mouth closed, his ribs visible above white boxers. He's a freshman at the high school, two years younger than Boris, but could pass for much older within the miserable light. It fans from the mullioned window to illuminate the never-shaved blond hairs above Carl's lip. The lashes, bristled like a bat's. He shifts, moving his head from view, and Boris, privacy assured, edges from his bed to extract the Bible from under the mattress. Digital numbers on his nightstand clock glow a burgundy 1:04—Sarah's not due for another fifty-six minutes—so he tiptoes to the dresser and inserts the key.

Crammed inside the drawer is the Suffering Box. Boris considers it a masterpiece, a first-rate sculpture Sarah made nearly fifteen years ago while still a Lawrence West senior. It resembles a small crib, two feet long, one foot wide, its sides constructed with ribs of wood, animal bone, wrapped clumps of chicken wire. Inside rest more bones, unthreaded needles, glass shards, feathers, rosebush thorns, and various mementos from the distant and recent past. One month ago, Sarah presented it to Boris: "An early happy birthday." She stipulated only that he keep it safe and continue adding to its contents, just as she'd done over the years. "It's like an ongoing work," Sarah told him. "Use it. Stuff some sort of reminder in the box." She included her final items—one of Marshall's translucent blue hospital bracelets, a palmful of finger-nails she'd clipped from his hand—and surrendered them.

At the bottom of the Suffering Box are pieces and bits of Sarah's earlier life. Locks of hair; class rings she and Marshall once wore; a torn-but-retaped photo of a boy swinging a tennis racket. They serve to add slight tints to a monochrome past she doesn't readily divulge. In another of the box's photos, a teenage Sarah grins sheepishly, displaying a deeply charcoaled portrait of Marshall. She wears a tight blouse, too much makeup, henna-yellow pixie curls at the cheeks. The words on the picture's reverse read "Grand Champion, Douglas County High Schools in the Arts Contest." Sarah insists that everyone but a few select boys, back then, hated her guts; still, Boris figures she must have earned notoriety for her artwork. She grabbed first place in the very competition Boris hopes to win this year.

Instead of visual art, Boris plans to enter *March of the Zombies*, his horror novel-in-progress. The pages he's scribbled thus far are crammed together with his diary between the Suffering Box and the right side of the drawer. Boris will build the narrative around Sarah, Harriet, himself; he originally intended four characters, but after Marshall, he narrowed his scope. The plot focuses on their tribulations, the most horrifying and terrible hours from their pasts. A fatal accident turns the protagonists into zombies. They lurch from graves to prey on all who have abused or ostracized them. Instead of inventing these scenarios, Boris figures, he'll base everything on truth. Besides detailing his own experiences on pieces of school notebook paper, he'll collect letters from Sarah and Harriet, notes of confession categorized with a gigantic red *S* or *H* above each page.

Carl stirs. Boris shuts the drawer, then waits a dozen seconds before reopening. For last year's arts contest, he entered a not-quite-autobiographical short story about a foster kid torching his various sets of pretend-parents' houses. He was new to Lawrence then, recently dumped by another host family, and all his effort received was a participant's ribbon. The contest awarded students who'd entered paintings, poems, tapes of songs they'd composed; grand champion trophy went to a chubby girl who'd once called him "faggot" during class. Her sculpture of a ferocious phoenix soaring from papier-mâché flames still towers in the vice principal's office.

Boris adds today's funeral pamphlet to the box, the outside light spangling on the words inked at the page's top border:

MARSHALL DAVID JASPER

JUNE 3, 1963–SEPTEMBER 15, 1995

On the reverse, a pastel of heavenly sunbeams seeping through stained glass accompanies a poem included at the church pastor's urging. Boris slides the slip of paper to the box's corner, yet it seems out of place: for here, top of the pile, perhaps even more hush-hush than Sarah's photos and memories, more than his novel, is Boris's shrine to Rex Jackson.

Rex. How can Boris possibly describe him? Months back, when Sarah asked him, he couldn't. "Oh, god. Rex. Um, he's, um, beautiful." Rex, Boris's most mammoth crush, attends his same school. One year ahead of Boris, but light years away from ever knowing the extent of his love.

The first time he saw Rex he felt splashed with cold champagne. Boris, newly transferred, was heading for algebra; shop class seemed Rex's destination, as in place of books or pencils his hands gripped a hammer and a sheaf of sandpaper. Rex walked with the clumsy swagger of a drunk. Scrapes dotted his knuckles like dribbles of strawberry jelly, and mudstains browned his jeans. At the far end of the lockers, an argument between two stoners elevated to a fight, and Rex's bored face rose toward the ruckus. Fluorescent light graciously haloed him. Boris saw the beauty there, its sharpness leaching away each of his senses like a sweet syringe until he felt so puny and stupefied he nearly fainted. A girl bumped the book from his hand. In the time it took to lift it off the floor, Rex had vanished.

Later that day, Boris glimpsed him, *him,* again. Rex clicked like a jigsaw piece into the mold that Boris, after brief years of boy watching, had begun to develop as his "type"—tall, skinny but broad-shouldered, somewhat uncomfortable amid his surroundings. Hair so black from a distance it resembled paint, from superclose possibly licorice, although Boris hadn't, and still hasn't, attempted that proximity. Disarming green of his eyes. Big ears. Big hands and feet. Best of all, a smooth, almost Roman nose in the exact center of his face. To some, Rex's nose might be considered too large; for Boris it's heaven-sent. He dreams of touching it, clamping his lips down, tonguing the runneled cartilage.

After two weeks of eying him, Boris inaugurated his collection. When Rex fumbled a butterscotch disk tossed by a female admirer, Boris waited until he could safely snatch it up. He slid checkout cards from the back covers of library books, Rex's left-slant signature repeated in different inks. Boris lingered outside classrooms, learned his idol's schedule, risked tardy slips. He pocketed leftover screws from Rex's shop project; pieced-off sneaker tracks of dried farm mud; a brown paper towel dampened by grimy hands. The R. JACKSON nameplate hung from its hook on the gymnasium Ping-Pong tournament board? Nabbed by Boris. The smiley-face sugar cookie Rex neglected to eat during cafeteria hour? Stolen from the trash and canvassed in a cellophane bag.

Boris even found fresh Magic Marker scribblings of lyrics from metal bands' songs on Rex's gym locker. He tried transferring them mirror image to a tissue with careful dabs of spit: THE FIRE IM FEELIN WILL TAKE ME TO HELL/IF YOU WANNA FOLLOW BABY, JUST . . . the rest is unreadable.

The Rex collection started months ago, long before Sarah gave him her bone and chicken-wire box to house it all. Now, September, the rain rises and falls and strips toast-colored leaves from the trees. Boris lords over his bottom drawer with the devotion of an evangelist. The Suffering Box, *March of the Zombies* and its preparations, everything he's lifted and scraped and assembled of Rex. There has to be something to desire, right? Something to live for? Rex surely wouldn't dream of speaking to spindly, girly-boy Boris. But the slim possibility that maybe, just maybe Rex could, keeps Boris going.

When he met Sarah and Harriet and Marshall, he'd been anchored at Sunflower less than a month. He had memorized everyone's first and last names. He knew, from his bedroom window view, when lights went off and on in the neighbors' homes; the schedules for their postal deliveries and dogwalkings. This time he didn't worry about getting attached, for he'd no doubt seen the last of the foster families. Stuck: this halfway house, this Sing Sing, the last stretch of a foster-home tunnel from which turning eighteen would free him. Boris didn't argue when the supervisors gave orders. He washed dishes, folded stacks of laundry. Twice a week he volunteered, like the other kids, for community service. Among the less glamorous stints were lawn mowing at City Hall; repainting storefronts; nosing for trash in riverside bushes after the July Fourth celebration. These tasks were assigned to the runaways, the mom beaters and botched suicides, the teen hooligans who collected misdemeanors like postage stamps.

But they let the foster kids choose their duties, and Boris chose hospital work. Tuesdays and Thursdays, after school, he'd make a beeline for Lawrence Memorial, homework books at his side, earphones roaring twin splinters of sound into his brain. He noticed the women his first week there. What outcast doesn't notice another, their gazes crashing head on with equal degrees of admiration and contention, as if being a misfit is a contest? Yet Boris, at school, felt too shy to approach anyone. The two women waited in the hallway where he cleaned, the wallpaper a sherbety glow behind them. The older woman looked like an overdressed sparrow. She sang to herself, glanced at the clock, and sang some more, slightly louder this time. The younger woman's foot kept perfect fox-trot rhythm, and she held a plastic bowl the size of a spittoon. Peanuts in their shells: Boris could smell them, could hear her munching. Her T-shirt showed a still from *Psycho*—shower head drizzling water, as seen from below—but while Boris loved horror films too, he couldn't muster the courage to approach.

She saw him staring nonetheless. "I'm Sarah, she's Harriet." Something soft swirled behind her eyes and made Boris feel that she recognized him, foresaw his future. She pointed at his greenbristle broom and dustpan. "Have some peanuts. You a candystriper, or the janitor?"

The sound of an alarm clock, beeping; someone's ragged cough. "Neither," Boris said. "I'm a foster kid."

Later he leaned beside the window in the hospital room, nibbling a fingernail. Harriet stood at her son's shoulder, guiding the paper cup to Marshall's lips, stroking his hair. When Sarah made introductions, she relayed information she'd already gleaned in the hallway: Boris was new to town, and lived at Sunflower, "like I did, the early eighties, all those centuries ago."

Marshall wore a patch over one eye. An IV trailed its umbilical into one forearm. Beside his bed were seed catalogs, equestrian magazines, a European travel guide with a cover photo of a half-naked, ponytailed boy. "Howdy," Marshall said. His face looked inhuman, buttery, and seeing him smile and speak was like watching a painting spring to life. "How's Sunflower? When I was around your age, I used to sneak there to see Sarah. God, I sound old."

When Boris opened his mouth, only a stutter fell out. He cleared his throat and grinned back at Marshall. "It's not so interesting there, now. I'm like an inmate. Only the supervisors have a new name. They call us CINCs. Children. In. Need. Of. Care. It'd be cooler if they pronounced it 'kink.' But they have to say 'sink.' So until someone takes me in again, I'm a CINC. But I'm nearly seventeen, so no one's going to take me now, right? They'll wait for me to graduate, then I'm history."

"Well," Marshall said. There was an uncomfortable silence. Harriet looked at Marshall, back to Boris, back to Marshall; at last she selected a horse magazine and resumed her humming song. The melody clashed with the trapped-animal shrill of the air conditioner. "Well, Boris," Marshall said, "it's a rare day when I get guests beyond the queen and princess here. And nurses, I can't forget them."

The room smelled of incense, which Sarah explained as an herbalist's blend of healing aromas, concocted to overpower the hospital odor. "It's illegal here," she said, "but the nurses are certain me and Harriet are witches-slash-lunatics, so they leave us be." Harriet laughed at that. Boris laughed too, then stopped when she stopped. He looked out the window: A woman pushed a double stroller; trees stretched back to more trees; a rake rested teeth up, its handle knotted with a checkered necktie. A gardener unrolled strips of new lawn like carpet, roweling parallel swaths of green with a silver implement that reflected up to Marshall's window.

When Harriet left for the restroom, Marshall's voice smoothed to a whisper. "It's what you think it is," he said. He explained how he wasn't *that* sick, not yet. He would get to go home tomorrow, maybe; he just needed to regain strength. Boris chewed his fingernail a millimeter deeper until Harriet returned. Yes, there would still be time outside the hospital for Marshall. And then more time in the hospital. And then, and then.

"Look at this kid's red hair!" Marshall told the women. He pointed at Boris with his exposed arm, the IV wiggling its tendril. "And up close there—the eyelashes and brows are nearly blond. Boy, you'd make a pretty girl." As a child, Boris would stomp weeping from the room at comments like that. But not now. He already liked these people. And the guy was *dying*.

They spent the remaining visiting hours talking, talking more. Soon Harriet pat-patted the chair beside her son's bed and Boris, a buzzing warmth spreading through his chest, took the seat. They all shared slices of an apple and four paper cups of peppermint tea. Harriet hummed a new song; Boris, recognizing it, joined in. At some point, Sarah reached to take his hand. "Re what you said about no one wanting to take you?" she asked, and Boris shrugged. "You said, 'Who'd want me, right?' Well, forget that. We'll take you." She indicated Marshall and Harriet with a nod of her head, then touched her thumb to his chin. "It's official. You're ours now."

Boris, sleepyhead, planned to wait for 2 A.M., for Sarah's horn signal to whisk him away. Instead he dozes off, his bed a skiff sailing toward dreams of Rex he fruitlessly struggles to dream. During sleep, a procession of mosquitoes steals through the open window. In a matter of minutes they do their damage, divebombing for skin Boris's sheet has left uncovered. His ankles and shoulders and forearms redden with welts. He wakes to the metallic whine of a mosquito, screaming in the hollow of his ear, sniffing his fragrant heart.

The room brightens with what at first seems like lightning, electric strobes that make the stark surroundings clarify, blur, clarify. . . . Boris feels confused, as though he's woken inside a tornado. He swipes the bangs from his eyes, stretches, leans near Carl's bed. It's just the digital clock that flashes. Has a storm passed? Yes, he hears the trampoline shudder of thunder. He counts out sixty bursts of the clock face. The power loss has reset the time, 12:00,

12:00, but he's certain it's close to two, precisely two, or somewhere past.

Some nights, after her late shift at the truck stop/convenience store on the interstate, Sarah kidnaps him. They tour Lawrence with the aimlessness of sleepwalkers. She'll lure him out by standing in the parking lot, tossing twigs against his window, as the demon does in one of her favorite horror movies. Hearing nothing tonight, Boris jolts to his feet in the fear she's abandoned him.

He looks out through drizzle and the fronds of a weeping willow. The Volkswagen sits in the lot, alongside a supervisor's car and a Sunflower transport van. There is Sarah's shadow, waving through the shattered windshield. Boris hoists the window higher to maneuver his body through. Here, nothing's locked from the outside: People can't enter, sure, but as Carl informed him once, some stipulation of law prevents the supervisors from bolting kids in. He shrugs his body past the pane, shuffles through the lot—a cricket stops chirping, a pickup in the street varooms past, did someone see?—and grasps the door handle. The spray-painted QUEERS splits apart, then rejoins on the slam.

Streetlights sear white-dot mirrors on the windshield, kaleidoscoped through the crushed glass. Sarah backs out and speeds away, her single unbroken high beam sending a glimmery beacon through the rain. Her side window, obliterated by the vandals, is now a taped-up square of cellophane; through it light glints, green and eerie, in her hair. "Have I got news," she says, targeting her eyes on the road. "Police found one of the missing girls. The same day as the funeral, and they find one of the bodies."

"What else do you know?" Setterlike, Boris shakes the drizzle from his brow. "Where was she? Was it on the news? What happened?"

"I just heard it on the radio. She washed up way downriver. Dead, that's all I know."

Boris fights the urge to click on the car's tinny radio for more information. Sarah usually keeps it blaring (the college radio station; one of Marshall's handpicked music tapes), but tonight, silence. And whereas she sometimes smells of gasoline or the sausage cooker from the convenience store, tonight's scent seems more like liquor. Boris knows her mind isn't on the dead girl. He squints, attempting to read any emotion in her face. "Are you doing okay?"

"It's warm in here," Sarah says. A double pause, and then: "Am I doing okay. Really, I'm not feeling much. It would have been different if he hadn't taken so long. Wasn't like a murderer slipping in to stab an otherwise healthy and expected-to-live-fifty-years-more sort of person." She half-grins, pleased with her answer. "I guess I felt more way back when. About the time he first told me he was sick."

She points to the side door, and Boris cranks the handle. Water beads seep through the crack and blow across his shoulder and forehead. The wipers squeak their rubbery swath, stamping leaves and June bugs further into the flotsam at the windshield's bottom. Rhode Island Street, New Hampshire, Massachusetts, Vermont; the VW meanders up the central hill toward the university, humming on the incline, the headlight swinging its white finger over the houses. Some brood darker than others, their electricity snuffed by whips of lightning. But the campus glows brighter, lampposts dropping white umbrellas of light before the science and humanities buildings, the history museum. The Kansas Union shines brightest of all, its glassed-in marquee exhibiting posters for upcoming movies, fliers offering reward for the missing students.

Sarah eases down into the campus drive's twenty-mile-per-hour limit; turns for the road to the central bell tower. KANSAS UNIVERSITY MEMORIAL CAMPANILE, a sign reads. Ahead, the structure raises its illuminated tip to the froth of clouds, a landlocked lighthouse in the rain. "Marsh loved this place," Sarah says, and Boris agrees. He knows what goes on here after dark. Men abandon their cars, then disappear into oak and cottonwood shadows. Two sidewalks branch like arteries from the bell tower's cement oblong, one leading near cars parked beneath a canopy of trees, the other following a footpath down to a shaded valley between the Campanile and the football stadium. Scattered in that valley are various bushes, sycamores, and mulberry trees, all interlocking arms. But no walk lamps, no light whatsoever. Just men, hidden in darkness: Boris imagines heel-toe footsteps, rustlings, the soft minuet of laughter.

Not long before Marshall reentered the hospital, he brought Boris and Sarah here, explaining in the voice of a tour guide the secret locations where he once cruised, all the sequestered nooks for sex. Two sores showed through the charcoal hair on Marshall's arm, rose-violet dots under the Campanile's light. "This way," he said. Sarah strolled, then skipped ahead, asking question after question. Boris wanted Marshall to detail his experiences, but was too embarrassed to ask. Since then, in private, he's imagined boys below the campus trees, their eyes watching his approach.

A police car moseys past, the officer inside regarding their jumble of graffiti, and Sarah momentarily parks. Next to them is a red Mustang with a figure behind its wheel. Boris is too bashful to look. At the bottom of the hill below, further from the bell tower and heavily shrouded by trees, lies Potter's Lake. It betrays its name, more a pond than a lake, speckled with lily pads and cattails, ramparted by a small brick bridge. During the day, students kiss there, toss bread to ducks. At night everyone avoids the place. According to story, a philosophy major once drowned in Potter's. Every year, students reestablish the rumors: "Weird choking sounds can be heard there at night"; "I saw a figure lurching from the water," et cetera.

"This place isn't seeing much business," Sarah says. "Marshall used to like it here best when it rained. Bad weather brought out the real die-hard junkies." Around them, the sidewalks look caramelized; Sarah backs, concentrating, from the parking spot. "I'm not going to be one of those friends who'll preach and preach to you. But listen. Marsh knew someone who was attacked with a baseball bat here." She turns off Campanile Drive, steers away from campus. "Too boring tonight. Let's head north. See how far the water's risen."

The car fills with a strange silence. Boris, unsure how to break it, watches the world from the window. There, as if through tinted lenses, the southeastern glow from the fairgrounds, the Douglas County Carnival currently in town. Its lights stretch skyward, opalating the bank of thunderheads, beckoning him.

On the north side of Lawrence are dark bars, antiques and curio shops, a video store with window posters of lips and angels and guns. Sarah parallel-parks on Locust Street, at the bridge's junction. She pulls an umbrella from behind her seat and heads across the walkway. "C'mon."

Boris trails behind her, securing his hand first to the LAWRENCE RIVERFRONT PARK sign, then the edge rungs of the railing. He bends to tie his shoe; sees bits of glass, a discarded yellow parking ticket, a broken treble hook, and the grip from a pair of fishing pliers. At this hour the bridge seems spooky: no drivers, no cars trailing their bright whites or maraschino reds.

Sarah chooses a spot, brushes pebbles from the concrete, sits. They hug their arms to the gunmetal vertical rails, dangle their legs over the edge. Boris, both acro- and hydrophobic, grits his teeth and looks. The river has risen higher since Sarah last drove him here, three days ago. It sluices past open-faced Bowersock Dam, pounding the descending embankment of stones, the abutments of graffitied cement. During the day its color is creamed tea; now it's only black. It swells and foams and drinks the endless rain. Further down shore, illuminated by laddered highway light, a trio of fishermen cast catfish lines. They wade through the water, reel in, rear back, toss their hooks into the drizzle's curtain.

Decades ago, a movie called *Carnival of Souls* was filmed at this very location. Sarah has seen the film seven times, knows integral snippets of the heroine's dialogue. Once she even viewed it with Boris, at the farmhouse, while in the kitchen Harriet crushed herbs with a pestle and sprinkled them into Marshall's empty plastic pill capsules. Sarah mouthed the words, nearly all of them, as the alien television light made fireflies across her face. On screen, dour zombies rose from the brackish water, eyelids smeared with kohl, dark robes dripping. Boris will try to recount their creepy appearances in further descriptions of his novel's undead protagonists.

He wipes rain beads from his wristwatch: it's nearly three. If the supervisors catch him sneaking off again, it will mean two demerits, an extra night of dish duty. And sometimes, if a CINC turns up missing, he or she's considered a runaway. The supervisors rush for Sunflower's hall telephone, punch-punch-punch a furious 911. So far, the police haven't bothered Boris. He hopes to leave it this way.

A semi whizzes past in hot gasoline fumes. It rumbles the bridge beneath them, heading deeper into North Lawrence, the poorer side of town. "Where the sad people live," as Sarah has told him. Where she, too, lives. Boris follows her gaze out, out, to the weed bed spot where the little group casts for fish. She could be thinking about movie zombies, their sawteeth and their cutlass claws; more likely, she's thinking about the funeral. "I know nothing about fishing," Boris tells her, "but I've heard they bite in storms." His attempt at distraction sounds artificial, so he retries. "I'm adding lots to the Suffering Box."

A second too much time passes before she responds. "Marvelous. Maybe I'll have to build a bigger one."

Boris clenches his fist and holds it in front of Sarah's lips. They do this sometimes: the newsman conducting an "interview," using a "microphone" for the starlet's "speech." "So tell me, Miss Hart," Boris begins, "what exactly did you mean to say when you created your work of art?"

Sarah rests her head against the rail, then reaches to move his microphone closer. "It was supposed to represent how we treasure material items during life." Her voice lowers, serious, her face slack with a seen-it-all expression. "But after we die all becomes nothing, we're right in there with the bones and shit and feathers, people are buried in their jewels and nice clothes but then in only a matter of months . . . you know." Now Sarah's real voice has risen again, no more make-believe, and Boris takes his hand away from her mouth. "It's like Marshall," she says. "You know. The way he looked and all? Oh, I'm not sure what I'm saying really."

The breeze startles the distant branches, all the needlestick reeds that waltz the water's edge. It lifts Sarah's hair from her shoulders, shaking free the rain. "Well, the box is yours now. I bet you've been stuffing it full of . . . full of what? More this-and-that of Rex's, I hope?"

"I'll never get him," Boris says. "I have this huge fear I'll be forty years old and still in love with this perfect human being from high school, still, like, following him around in secret and jamming my pockets full of whatever he drops. He has no idea I'm alive, but, god, he's so perfect. If I were that beautiful I'd make certain I'd be famous."

Sarah stops sponging her brow and transfers the hand to Boris's head. "Stop. You are beautiful. You have the most amazing lips, and your hair's cool, and those cheekbones! I'm envious." Boris worries that Sarah's only saying this, adopting the obvious adult stance to offer support a mother might give. "Rex," she says, "is dumb for not realizing what's great about you. If I were him," she adds, *"I'd be deep in love with you."*

The rock embankment to their left is littered with snarls of flue, with the remains of two white trees, a giant ulna and radius coughed up from the water and left to dry. A bike trail slopes into blackness; the trees where, at certain times on uncertain years, bald eagles come to perch. Somewhere in that dark, too, the towering grain elevator near Sarah's home.

The fishermen slosh further downriver. Boris catches a hint of their ruckus, even over the rip-roar surge below. One of the men holds a flashlight, its beam striping the bulrushes, staining an egg-like stain on the water. Boris closes his eyes—Rex's face, so easily conjured, Rex's face—and he repeats out loud the words he wrote, weeks ago, on a page in his secret journal: "I want to put my tongue inside his mouth for so long I memorize every edge and texture and angle of every tooth. I want to taste his lunch, and beyond that even, his morning toothpaste." As he finishes the words, he sees Sarah trying to smile, yet still not masking, not quite, her leftover exhaustion and sorrow from the long day. Boris tastes the mistake, hot and dry in his mouth, and knows he should have thought of Marshall, should have refrained from spouting his own dark-red desires. "I'm sorry," he tells her.

"Don't be," Sarah says. "Never hold back what you're feeling. I want you to tell me everything, whenever you want."

Boris, after two breaths: "Okay. I will." A car rumbles past. "Then I want you to tell me everything too."

"I will."

In a film, one of them would blurt "I love you" here. In real life, Sarah sometimes says that, but for Boris it always seems inappropriate. He rechannels his thoughts by recalling afternoons at the beginning of summer, days without school, before Marshall's illness. The sun would blister, refusing to stop its burn, mocking soothsayers' predictions of its imminent deterioration. Sarah sported an early cocoa-butter tan. When she picked him up from Sunflower, Marshall sat in the passenger seat, and Boris would crowd into the back with Harriet. She would grip his fingers, the liver spots on her hand as delicate as the flecks on a moth. While Sarah chauffeured them through the heat-rippled streets, Harriet spoke of the demeanors of her cats and the afghan she was knitting for Marshall. She revealed surprises from her housedress pockets, things, she complained, "Marshall doesn't want anymore." An orange-yellow jawbreaker as big as an orange; a devil's claw she found at the exposed knuckle roots of a dying tree; a fortune-teller fish made of red rubber that, depending on how it curled or buckled within the bowl of Boris's hand, determined future days of success or sorrow or bliss.

Now, remembering this and wanting Sarah to remember too,

Boris opens his mouth to speak. But abruptly Sarah stands. He stops and follows the point of her finger. There: the river's frame, where waves crash and scrape the rock embankment. "Shhh," she says, though Boris hasn't uttered a word. She steps onto the first horizontal rail and leans her head over, jostling his queasy fear of heights. Only a single javelin of street light reaches for the murkiness, but Boris sees something nevertheless. At first he guesses a white trash bag, its form bobbing furiously at the water's edge. But no, this looks more solid.

Sarah steps around him, umbrella in hand, and gallops along the walkway between the street and bridge rail. "It's a body," she says, running. Boris pursues her, down the end of the bridge, to the declination of rocks. He aims his thoughts on the second missing girl. Her sorority has advertised a ten-thousand-dollar reward for information. Have he and Sarah found her, only hours after the discovery of the first body?

From the open-faced dam, the roar of water intensifies, its scent a wedlock of September's thundershowers and decaying fish. Hurry-hurry: Boris stumbles on the avalanche of rocks, his gaze pasted all the while on yes, what is certainly a body. It's the second girl. He knows it. She has been murdered and dumped like garbage. Mosquitoes pepper the air, and he shoos them. Fathoms away, the fishermen hunch pygmylike over their calling. A frantic thought zips through Boris's head—will they want to help, will they want to split the reward money?—but he stamps down faster on each rock, nearing the river's edge.

Sarah, thirty feet ahead, makes the shoreline first. She drops her umbrella, then bends to one knee to stretch an arm forward. A vision from *Carnival of Souls* flashes in Boris's head, and he bets she's displacing herself again, dreaming her actions are part of that movie. She yells, but instead of the pitch of terror, it's a disgusted "Oh." The water churns in rapid broil and Sarah reaches, grasps the body by the hair, and tugs, pulling it close. Its head makes an inhuman clunk on the rocks. Boris takes five, six more steps, rests his hand on Sarah's back, looks down at their discovery.

"Damnit," Sarah says, "damnit, damnit," her tone telling him that she, too, was dreaming of reward. The body—Boris kneels, seeing it—isn't a murder victim at all, but something artificial, a dummy made of hard plastic like those used in CPR classes. Boris saw one similar during a first-aid assembly at school. This model, a female, looks surprisingly real, even in its unbending chalky skin. Its hair is dark as coffee, moussed stiff with moss. Its three-quarter-closed eyes resemble bruises or Rorschach blots. The lips, painted unnaturally red, are parted almost seductively, and a crawdaddy clings there, bits of river foam and spinach-green algae sliming the cheek. Sarah brushes it all away. Its naked body isn't hollow, but filled inside and out, chilly plastic skin, plastic eyes, possibly plastic stomach and lungs and heart. Sarah and Boris examine closer, squinting in the absence of light. The dummy has been damaged, battered, chunks broken and chiseled in places. One of its breasts has been hammered away; the other wears a scarlet nipple, Magic-Markered by someone's unsteady hand. A finger missing here; another here, and here. Various stabs and lacerations tattoo its arms. Smaller gouges cover one plastic shoulder; when Boris fingers these, they seem the tracks of teeth, of bite marks.

Sarah huddles over the dummy and circles an index finger in its crotch. "It's a make-believe cunt," she says. "Feel."

Boris, fighting the burn of a blush, sticks three fingers in. A hole has been drilled between the legs, a cavity deeper than the length of his probing fingers. He remembers years ago when, on a fishing excursion with a foster father, he thrust his hand into a bucket of carp guts. Now the feeling is the same: Something spongy fills the dummy's hole, strands of wet-gristle flesh that Boris pulls free. The stuff almost pulses in his hand, like tendons of raw meat, and he draws his fingers to his face. "It isn't moss. It smells like liver."

Sarah notices something else. Someone has written letters on the doll's stomach, scribbled a word into its vanilla skin in the same color as the nipple. Boris reads the letters, but they don't make sense. Parts of the word have been chipped away, gouges or nibbles in the plastic confusing it. "O, S, T, I, T," Boris reads.

"Awful, it's awful," Sarah says. She wipes oatmeal sand, more ropy moss, from the dummy's leg. "Someone used this for fucking. Someone pretty messed up, judging by the look. He must have gotten tired of her, dumped her here." Sarah palms the outline of its facial features, dragging it further onto the silt. As she stands, Boris sees her fear and pain spelled simply on her face. He wants to turn away into the wind. "I feel sad," Sarah tells him. "I don't know why. I feel like I should rescue her. Put her in a blanket or something." She crosses her arms, hugging herself, then attempts lifting. "She's heavy. Help me carry her. I'll get the head, you take the feet."

Now an odor of spoiled meat and, heavier, of ancient miry earth. Boris hoists his end and breathes through his mouth. Sarah wedges the umbrella in an armpit and cradles the mannequin's head. They step slowly up the embankment, steadying their feet on rocks, as they carry the dummy to the car. Sarah whispers curses; Boris sees her clenched teeth and candle-flutter eyes. Below her face, sickening and pushing him closer to sickness, the ruined pagan face of the mannequin. When they stuff the body inside the snug trunk at the VW's front, Boris must push it further, harder, and as he does a single toe chips from the foot. He bends to get it; Sarah, not noticing, slams the trunk. Staring back at them, the graffiti: TRASH MOTHERFUCKERS.

Boris shuts his door behind him. His nailed-in-place expression fills the mirror square, and he looks away. The smell clings to his fingers, the smell of her feet, her stomach, her manufactured hole; breathing it coaxes a thick nausea inside him. He doesn't want the dummy in Sarah's car. Its slitted eyes, its artificial mouth drooling black bacterial water, its code word scrawled on its raped and butchered body.

Sarah gets in. Boris opens his mouth, but whatever speech he'd planned snags in his throat. She starts the car, pumps the brakes, and speeds off.

"Marsh and I took a CPR class once," Sarah says. "This was years ago. I had to take it for some reason. Maybe it was during my little stint at Sunflower. They probably thought it was good for us. Marshall just went along for the experience." Boris can smell the water on her too, the mossy plastic memory of the body. "Weird, but the dummy we used looked a hell of a lot like that one. Identical. Marshall did the CPR thing better than me. Always had the idea that someday he'd save somebody's life."

They pass gas stations, banks sentried by enormous flags, restaurants dark except for shining signs. Boris hadn't been queasy during Marshall's funeral. Now everything is different. He wants to rewind, whirlwind back to the bridge, and wrap his arms around Sarah's shoulders to hold close, hold dear. She will tell him she loves him, that everything will be fine. He will repeat her words: "It will be all right." And maybe someday Boris will find the courage to protect her from the world, from damage worse than the kind in *Carnival of Souls* or similar films. He will shield her eyes from horrors like the synthetic girl's rebirth on the shore.

The car veers toward the street dead-ended by the youth home. Sarah glances in the rearview, then across to Boris. "O, S, T, I, T? What is that? Something to do with the missing girls? What do you think?"

Boris doesn't answer. Everything feels slightly askew. His body slants forward, the world tilting further on its axis. The dummy's body lies before them, packed within the shadows of Sarah's trunk. In minutes Boris will ease back to sleep, snug inside his Sunflower bed. If he could he would program his dreams to forget everything. This day, the funeral, tonight's pair of hours. He wants sleep to obliterate the lost puzzled look on Harriet's face; the exhausted look on Sarah's. He wants sleep to make him forget the rain, the dummy, forget OSTIT. And yes, too, forget this poisonous unfathomable world, goodnight, goodnight, sleep tight.

3

Outside, in the deserted street, a radio voice crackles, "*Rise and shine.*" From the window Sarah watches the sun, hovering above asphalt gleaming with last night's downpour. Downed limbs decorate each shaggy lawn. There's a dead squirrel, an overturned tricycle. The radio announcer drones on, reporting high pollen and ragweed levels, his voice punctuated by the occasional cricket scree or sprinkler whir. Someone's garden releases scents of tomatoes left rotting on the vine, honeydew and cantaloupe made plump by the rains.

Sarah's street narrows north to south, each house more dilapidated than the last. Most neighbors have died or moved away. Others stay, hermits, peeking from black curtains when a child wanders past or the morning mail woman drops a bill into the box. Abandoning the north side of Lawrence for a better neighborhood seems the sanest option, but Sarah chooses not to. She loves it here. While some might consider her home an eyesore, Sarah calls it a forgotten piece of town history.

Years before, her square building and its backyard functioned as a miniature golf course. The place lies nestled at Cherry Street's dead end. From a distance, its chipping green paint and white shutters make it look like a prop. The house has one main room, its rounded cashier's cubicle still intact, its scarred wall rack once used for various sizes of putters. Farther back are her tiny bedroom, an even tinier bath. Sarah squeezes inside there now, bending to the sink to splash her face with cold water. Insomnia gnawed at her all night; she doesn't bother trying to sleep but shuffles, barefoot, to the derelict course. The miniature golf business went belly up long ago, yet all eighteen holes remain. The plot is shaded by oaks and sumacs and a single sugar maple rustling leaves the color of butterscotch. Hole 7 boasts a Dutch mill, plywood blades revolving lazily in the breeze, its blue-shuttered windows paned with real glass. At the end of the course, mist rises from a pool still stocked with red and apricot goldfish.

If Sarah had a better job than the convenience store, she'd spruce the place up. She'd transplant trees, peach and pear, maybe a weeping willow like the one outside Boris's window. She'd reconnect the yard's electrical supply to surge everything into motion. The course would mirror its appearance during its heyday: lampposts draping each space in yolky light, hurdy-gurdy music icing the air. Water would ripple the skin of the pond, trickling from the stones and clipper-ship statuettes covered with verdigris. The pirate's treasure chest at hole 16 would reopen its creaky lid to reveal doubloons, cobwebs, and strobe-eyed skull with a mechanized jawbone. "Beware Captain Belfegore's curse!" the skull used to cackle.

After she first moved in, Sarah utilized her offbeat home to lure men from bars. She'd stand proud, arm outstretched to display her yard. She remembers one man in particular: he'd marveled at the surroundings, stumbled O-mouthed around the course, demanded to fuck on the zigzagging AstroTurf. In the morning, her temples pulsed from the previous night's gin-and-tonics. Her ear was positioned two inches from the green's center, and even without a mirror she guessed the synthetic grass had nibbled freckles on her face. She unsnaked her arm from his bare chest. She'd passed out on the tenth hole, par three, the one where long-ago customers attempted to putt through a tiny gate carved into a volcano. The "volcano" would "erupt" blood-colored foam.

Marshall once scored a hole-in-one on No. 10. The memory survives in Sarah, from years before she'd made the course her home. Marshall had putted a 39, two under par; she managed a 50. The music, the rattlesnake wind in the leaves, the skull's voice. She even saved the scorecard: Boris has it now, in his bottom dresser drawer.

Sarah breathes a last breath of fresh air and, back inside, searches through a milk crate littered with the horror films she's videotaped over the years. Nearly all her favorites come from the early 1980s, movies that featured hapless girls, terrorized by disfigured madmen. As a teenager she watched, transfixed, Marshall protective beside her. These are the movies she returns to, and today she chooses a tape from the *Friday the Thirteenth* series. The flawed performances, the dialogue, the silly special effects. One actress's slit throat looks artificial; another's stab wound seems more strawberry-like than something to cease the pumping of a heart. Sarah fast-forwards to the film's grand finale; more than familiar, she screams three seconds before the actress.

The movie's final image—sobbing heroine sprawled amid a demolished barn's debris, superhuman shadow looming toward her—brands its details on her eyes. She remembers last night, the bridge, and thinks of Boris, his lowered eyes and shaky hands when she dropped him at Sunflower. She'll telephone him, Harriet too, at noon. But for now . . . Sarah rounds the cashier's cubicle, leaves the front door, checks for spying neighbors. Assured, she wriggles the key in her car trunk's lock.

Before the hood opens, she smells the water, the primordial mud and moss. The meat too, snug inside the crotch. Sunlight's crescent sweeps across the mannequin: hair twisted into tangles;

battered scars still glistening with river droplets. Sarah hoists the body into her arms and grunts her way back to the golf course.

The dummy crumples in the shadow of the Dutch mill. The head knocks to the ground, riffling the wig's strands. In daylight, she—it—appears less human, its lips raised scars, its eyes switch-bladed slits. Sarah twists the left arm, propping it beside one diminutive window, and spreads the legs as evidence of assault. She steps away, surveys her work, and races for the house. In a wooden crate is her collection of New Wave records from the 1980s, both her and Marshall's favorites, arranged alphabetically. She finds a compilation LP of horror-movie soundtracks and blares it from the stereo speakers; she straps Marshall's camera around her neck.

Butcher knife in one hand, oversized jam jar in the other, Sarah prepares the victim with the painstaking care of an autopsist. She dunks the knife, drawing out the stage blood concocted days ago—a mixture of corn syrup, just the right amount of food coloring, crushed raspberries—and lacquers gore across the dummy's throat. It dribbles, blots at the chest. She kneels to splash blood on the stomach and frowns at its counterfeit look.

From inside, the soundtrack song yields to an eerier one. Sarah drops the knife and lifts the camera to one eye. Click, click. She and Harriet have alternated turns with the camera. They've each snapped uncountable rolls of film, speeding the thumb-sized canisters to a one-hour developer, then filling their albums. Portraits of each other or Boris, close-up autumn scenes, objects intriguing at the moment but silly later. Also in the album are shots of her ruined car and a whole series of Marshall: Marshall in the hospital hallway, in his hospital bed, and—Harriet's idea—his body, at rest, in the funeral home.

Twenty-three, twenty-four: roll of film finished, Sarah deserts the camera. Performance time, and she becomes the heroine, disregarding the daylight and its marred ambience. As she tiptoes, low-hanging branches brush her shoulders, claw her hair like a villain's fingernails.

Sarah has rehearsed before, alone in her backyard, but today a prop, today an actual victim, will push forth her best performance. She stares, not blinking, until her eyes go shy and glassy as a calf's. She approaches the site where she *could have sworn* she heard her friend calling for help. Over the music, she asks, "Is something wrong?" Diminuendo: she breathes deep, whimpers, cocks her head toward the shadowy crumpled form. Silence: she pauses. The steely approach of crescendo: Sarah rushes forward, bends, finds blood splattering the mill's wooden slats. And below, the butchered corpse.

"Oh, god!" Sarah brings her hands to her face, gapes at the pasty blood, and sprints for the house, hurdling the course's feather-headed grasses and yucca plants. She's crying, eyes bulging in their sockets, mouth stammering prayers. The door slams, air whooshing as she runs for the phone. Sarah whimpers again, jabs the buttons. "Help me," she wails. "Someone's . . . trying to kill me!"

Sarah has devoted herself to her role as earnestly as any Hollywood horror queen. She's screaming now, her lips and tongue making a wet flower on the telephone mouthpiece. "There's a killer, he's murdered my friend! Oh, god, her body's right there . . . outside my house. Get help, please!" Sarah turns her head toward the door, certain she's heard footsteps rapidly approaching. Soon she'll see the sparkle of the hatchet, his maniac sneer. "He's trying to get in! Oh, god, please do something! He's going to kill me! My friend's dead, help me, oh, god, my best friend . . ."

She stops on the words. Looks back out to the course. The oat-colored plastic flesh, its drying jelly and maroon syrup, the letters of the disfigured word like a zipper on the stomach.

My best friend. She remembers the way his laugh carried across a room; the feel of her hands in his hair.

The bloodied whorls and ridges of fingerprints track the telephone's buttons and handset. Sarah's palms are smeared, as though they have squeezed the life from a bird. She feels the sinking shame

in her stomach, and knows these games are wrong for a woman—
yes, no longer a girl, but a woman—of her age. She hangs up and
looks away, pulse steadying, breath slowing. Dust motes dwindle in
the front doorway's swath of light. Outside are the syrupy puddles,
the crashed tricycle, the branches studded with mud and scraps of
schoolkids' papers. A still life of debris, a neighborhood poised and
silent. And then, suddenly, the neighbor's sprinkler revs into gear.
Sarah watches its oily arc of water, its orbit passing the border of
the neighbor's saturated lawn, nearing hers. The water stretches to
strike the back of her car, *thwack, thwack-thwack,* the syncopated
slap and thud against her bent rear fender. A sound the villain
would make, the whisper of the painted words on the car, the
words meant for her.

Boris gave Sarah an assignment: to write about something terrible, some black momentous sorrow from her past. "Tell me about
someone you want revenge on," he said, and for days Sarah has re-
created a story from years back. Flashback pieces from fifth grade, a
childhood punishment. Now, after sponging the fake blood from
the mannequin and returning it to the trunk, she finds paper and
pen. When she begins to write, she knows she cannot do exactly as
Boris asked. Some details slip by half-remembered, some truths are
uncertain, and the words get told the way she wants them told,
with exaggeration, deeper exaggeration.

When finished, she slides behind the wheel, her throat still sore
from screaming. She cranks the radio volume. The air inside the car
is hotter than the air outside, as though the afternoon is a kitchen,
her VW its blistering toaster. She hums the melody, glancing at the
twenty handwritten pages in her lap.

The Sunflower employees used to assign Sarah an upstairs room,
fearing nightly escapes. She was seventeen and wore her hair long,
knotted into a pigtail. Everyone knew how she'd sneak off with
the boy down the hall. She'd let him have what he wanted. In

reciprocation he'd shoplift beef jerky, grape soda, and candy bar gifts from the very convenience store where she now works. She'd pull them out at night, nibbling the circlets of puffed rice under the chocolate surface.

But better than the times with the boy were her nights with Marshall. He would come for her, waiting in the parking lot as she does, now, with Boris. Isn't that what she's doing, duplicating that history? Taking Boris away, saving him, as Marshall did with her? He would drive her to the farm, and they would ride Jellybean and a neighbor's horse, sometimes until dawn. Or he would chauffeur her through Lawrence: its campus, its cemetery, its bridge and choleric river. Once they saw a three-legged fox limping lonesome through the park. Once they found a paperback about the Boston Strangler and took turns reading aloud until the sun split the horizon. The supervisors caught Sarah sneaking out again and again. The day she turned eighteen, they baked a cake with the right amount of candles and wished her well. Elation shone on their faces; she was finally leaving.

Sarah despised it there. Marshall was her only indulgence, her grace. She wants to be that for Boris. To protect him, to act the savior.

The orangeade sun has shrunken in the west. She leaves the car idling and heads for the willow, the pages in her fist with edges shredded by the notebook's wire spirals. Sarah has inked the top page with an *S*, as per Boris's wishes. His window stands open a crack: She peeks, but no one's there. She inhales the lemony antiseptic, the restricted teenage sex, the sweat and tears drying on bed sheets. A phantom smell, a smell she would swallow her breath in order to avoid. Sarah rolls her twenty pages into a scroll, wedges it through the window, lets it drop.

Past the slides, swingsets, teeter-totters, past the crowd of perfumed rich girls w/their jump ropes & hopscotch grids, even past the soccer field, stood a scant row of birches w/more rows beyond growing thicker & crowding back to the small dank woods. It was there I made my lair, a bad little girl getting worse & worse. At noonday recess I let the boys have it, I'd learned what they wanted, had them all in my power, no stopping me. Climbing down from the jungle gym I saw them coming, heads swiveling on their shoulders to make certain teachers weren't watching, their hankering fist-sized hearts thudding thudding. On the day I remember best there were six of them, fourth graders, one year younger than me. They peered up the way bees must gawk at a flower at its sugariest. I leaned an elbow against the metal, shook my long blond braid in the breeze, stretched a graceful toe toward them like a ballerina. I opened my mouth to speak & made sure my tongue could be seen hot pink inside it. Well?

Their eyes burned copper brands up my shirt. The bravest stepped forward, We got the money just like you asked, his voice trembling & caught on spit like the sound of wet chalk on a blackboard. The candy? I asked. Who remembered that? Another boy pulled a bar from each pocket, Cherry Mash, Zagnut, my favorites.

The teachers considered the treeline a forbidden playground boundary, no student, not even us fifth graders, could cross. But I was wily & the boys were brave, I held my proud head high, moved my braid like a white sword slung on my back. Through the schoolhouse window I could hear Ms. St. Clair lecturing, scribbling state capitals or homonyms or long-division problems on the blackboard. She was the meanest of all teachers, Ms. Satan Clair some kids called her, I knew if she caught me she'd punish like I'd never been punished, in the back of my throat I knew it, she had it out for me, staring during lunch, her eyes squinting out that future day when she'd snare my badness & make me suffer.

But today she was off recess duty, I skipped fearless across the soccer field toward the trees, the boys traipsing behind like lemmings in a hut-two-three-four row. Assured of no Satan Clair I escaped, the woods swallowed me up. Poison oak & ivy, toadstools w/foamy skins like gray tongues licking my feet, mixtures of earthy & mapley smells like warm dessert simmering in a pot.

Playground chatter was just a memory, lost out to bird songs & cricket cheeps. I leaned against a birch w/dandelions at its base, looked behind me, saw a mere sliver of the boys' huddle, their windbreakers in blue & red, the school colors. Simpleton-silly, they'd mustered enough smarts to bring a soccer ball, giving it baby kicks & knee butts, the game their alibi in case a teacher squinted near our horizon. I thought of their pint-sized hairless cocks strained skyward, the elaborate exaggerated stories they'd tell about me after, I poked my index & thumb through my mouth's corners, whistled like my uncle had taught.

The bravest boy's turn first, Chuck Eidel today like most days, a boy w/black bangs past his eyebrows & watery umber eyes, full lips reddened w/lollipop drool. He marched into the trees, following my path, he turned to his friends once—Don't watch us, he whispered, if you watch you're a faggot—then headed after me. He cut through weeds & toadstools, didn't heed the patch of poison ivy, fifteen feet away he said Hi, w/out looking at my face started pinching pinching at my tits. Instead of closing my eyes or glancing at the moving silvery leaves or glowing birches I stared right at him, that was how I owned them, I kept looking until it was over & the next one's turn came.

Other kids avoided the woods, Pythons live in them trees they said, but I knew better. I felt the roughness of his knuckles as he lifted my blouse w/one hand, pushed his fist inside w/the other, I was what he'd paid for, Chuck had brought his candy bar & dollar, the lunch money from his mom. They all paid for it, going w/out meat loaf or hamburger casserole just to have Sarah, that fifth-grade whore in the woods w/the big-girl body, the mouth clamped hungry & tight.

After two, three minutes I bent & unzipped his jeans, went to my knees where he liked me. He didn't really care about feeling me up, what he wanted was my mouth on him. His cock was pink & lay pulsing easy on my tongue, in his breathlessness the balls swam shrunken inside him. I slipped my mouth up & down, blew him as good as I knew how, remembering my uncle's instructions, ready for the final throb when every ounce of energy made a pinnacle at his midsection & he came, dry & unmessy. I looked up, saw him bite his lip, shake the bangs from his eyes. Unlike most of the others Chuck would make me feel loved a little, he'd comb nail-bitten fingers through my hair or cup a palm under my chin. He even kissed me once, right on the lips, a slobbery hungry kiss that dripped from his mouth as if filled w/snow, but after the shudder & air-orgasm he was like all the rest, he galloped off criminal & defeated & never looking anywhere close to my face.

By the fourth or fifth boy I had the Zagnuts & Cherry Mashes ordered at my knees, I started drifting from the concentration on my hands & mouth, I thought about Ms. St. Clair's modes of punishment. Schoolkids had heightened her to a wild level of terror, up there w/werewolves or the brainwashers we'd heard were ambushing various Kansas schools & abducting children. Satan Clair wouldn't tolerate trouble, This unruliness has gotten out of hand, she'd say to other teachers, This utter lack of respect. At the beginning of the year she bought long coils of rope for the classroom closet, whenever bullies would attack she'd magically appear w/their remedy. When Johnny Morton slapped Maria Arce she tied his hands together, ordering him to keep still while she wrapped the rope tight around his wrists, doubling tripling the knot. Later another kid kicked someone, Satan Clair saw it, she was there wrapping rope for his ankles. The boy hobbled & tripped throughout that afternoon, moving skitter-skitter from class to class, the rope burning red bracelets on his skin.

Grades one through five had a full forty-five minutes for lunch recess, the freedom gave me time to do all six boys, on that day they made Todd Edmonds go last, unpopular Todd held back from fourth grade, whose roof got blown off by a tornado, who got picked last for soccer or kickball. When he saw boy #5 returning from the woods he checked both ways as if stuck in traffic, then skulked toward me rummaging through his pockets. The others had spurted bursts of dry heat into my mouth, they were off trying to eliminate the guilt by competing in that afternoon's game, now only Todd & I existed. I remember thinking how easy, soon the bell would ring again, we would hear its screech, zip up, wipe my chin, steady his breathing, end of recess.

Turtledoves mourned from high in the trees & kneeling before the school loser I remembered my mom warning how those birds could foretell rain. The doves called louder & louder, then stopped, I recognized the sudden cease of crickets, high cranky chatter of sparrows. Todd's cock stayed in my mouth but I felt him tense, I peered up at his face & he was spinning around to look behind us.

Before I saw her I realized I'd been in the woods too long. The recess bell had rung, but neither Todd nor I had heard a thing. Standing again I saw her storming at us w/her hand held out before her, palm shining white & fingers splayed like a traffic cop, I felt the way I'd feel between dropping the prize vase & the terrible blast when it hit the cement. Satan Clair pushed Todd out of the way to grab me, her clamp on my arm, her words Get out of here Todd lifting to the treetops & bouncing back as he pulled up his pants & ran. We retraced the path I'd taken, back through the woods, crisscrossing the soccer field & empty recess lot, nearing the back schoolhouse windows. My classmates were in there memorizing state capitals, I prayed they wouldn't peek out, Satan Clair's arm a tentacle pulling me, I braved a chance & looked up & sure enough my fears had come true, a row of shocked wide-mouthed but giggly faces staring, a teacher fluttering hummingbirdlike behind them scolding Get away from the window, get back to your seats. Satan Clair stopped at the far back northwest corner of the building, the red door w/the heavy gold lock that spiraled down to the basement & the sports equipment room. The phys ed coaches would tromp down here after classes to relax, it was forbidden to us kids, we'd only caught glimpses of the room during school tornado drills when we'd file into a line obeying every order, most of us whimpering or biting our nails fearing a real cyclone. I remembered seeing tablefuls of footballs, field hockey sticks, aluminum softball bats, best of all a gargantuan red medicine ball I'd only dreamed of touching.

I could still taste the raw taste of Todd Edmonds, the others before him. The nightmare teacher moved into the room w/out switching on lights & latched the door behind us, Sit there, she said, pointing to a wide wood table w/clipboards at one corner, Property of Lawrence Jr. High painted across it in white. Satan Clair went to one high window that looked out ground-level to clumps of weeds, she drew the black blind making the room fifty percent darker. She drew the other window blind & the whole room went near black, I could barely see her face, only her outline as she stepped toward me.

Lie down, she said. There on that table.

Ms. St. Clair, I'm sorry.

She said I've known a long time what you've been doing out there. I obeyed her & stretched against the table, banging my head, but I didn't dare complain, didn't make a run for it, couldn't look at her when she started searching through the coaches' cabinets. She came back to the table & in her fists were jump ropes, the kind kids use w/the candystripe & heavy red woodblock handles that clickety clack on the sidewalk when dropped. I thought of the bully boys & the way she'd tied their hands for hitting, their feet for kicking, I wondered how she'd punish me.

Satan Clair took her time, she hogtied my feet first, her hands expert & graceful on all the intricate knots. When finished she leaned to my hands, I offered them because I knew to struggle would make things worse. She tightened the knots around my wrists as if bundling wood for next winter's fires, I wanted to cry out but didn't. Three more knots & she'd finished, the handles clashing together as she dropped the jump rope.

Then she stepped away from me, the direction of the door, to survey her work. I squinted but couldn't see much through the darkness. The room's air smelled of leather & batter's box chalk & mowed grass, underneath that the hint of sweat from coaches' outfits no doubt hanging in some closet. I thought she was through but she didn't put the last jump rope away, she started stepping nearer, I could smell her rose perfume, could see her outline coming closer into focus, her hands held out, whistle dangling from her neck & glowing a tiny crescent w/in a needle of sun left in the room. This is what happens to little sluts, she said.

Then the tip of the jump-rope handle was on my lips, she was hovering above my face trying to force the red chunk of wood into my mouth. She centered her palm on the wood's end & jammed it down harder, mashing my closed lips against my front teeth, & in my pain I opened up. She shoved the handle in, pushing it back until it tested the limit of my throat, I started to gag, she was sliding it in, out, my spit a clear lather on the steely paint taste. Then my gag reflex eased & she stuffed it deeper, she said This is what a grown man's thing is like, you like putting them in your mouth so much.

A part of me wanted to tell I'd already had it, My uncle I wanted to say, but I knew I could never, I should obey & allow the discipline, if I struggled I'd face expulsion. She left the rope handle deep in my mouth & stepped away, the rest of the rope still in her hand as if she were going to pull me up from the table w/it. Instead she stopped at my feet, coiled the remainder of the rope around her knuckles like a lariat.

The rest she did w/out a sound, barely even a breath. I felt her unsnapping my dark blue painter's pants, unzipping, her hand yanking them down & the underwear w/them, I felt the air against the bottom of my stomach, my thighs. In her palm was the last of the rope, she grabbed my hands again, coiled the slack around my already-tied wrists, then took the opposite end of the rope & touched it to my cunt. I felt the rope tighten, the way the reel tightens when a big fish teases at the bait, I still held the wood scraping the teeth in my mouth. Satan Clair took care not to touch my body w/her fingers, merely smeared the end of the rope against my slit, teasing it. I thought of my uncle's way of one finger first before sliding the other in, before sliding the third. I closed my eyes & Satan Clair buried half the wooden rope handle into me, my body quivered, wiggling the table, knocking clipboards clatter clatter to the floor, after the sound ended she shoved in the rest.

Then she left, lights off & blinds drawn, I heard the door slam behind her. One end of the rope in my mouth, one in my cunt, the slack tied around my hands, my feet tied too, nowhere to run. Drool trickling down my lips & the sweat smell again, the sour smell of grown men not boys anymore, I thought of what she had said, I knew the smell of my future. I'd left the Cherry Mashes & Zagnuts in the woods, for one second I wondered if I'd return to retrieve them & the next second knew I would. There was no clock in the equipment room but somewhere I heard one ticking, I focused on the tick the tick the tick to forget the piercing wound of the rope handle tight inside my cunt, I swallowed back the drool & waited.

Then the voices began, the boys came one at a time, every three minutes, ordered there, I figured, by Satan Clair. The door would open a crack & I couldn't see any face peer in, I could just feel them standing there, she'd instructed them on the right words to say, must have somehow connived & invented a story or reason. The first boy said DIRTY GIRL, he said YOU'RE BAD, he said YOU'RE A WHORE. I lay back confused wondering who & why, wondering where was Satan Clair. After the first boy the voices were worse, they spoke in matter-of-fact tones, robotic, probably scared, probably curious about the shadowy space of the equipment room & the secret it held. HOOKER, a voice spat at me. NOTHING BUT A SLUT. I imagined her behind them, hand centered on their backs. Maybe she wasn't there at all, just as God wasn't there, it was all part of some dream or some horrible play where the children acted all the parts, no adults, no heaven, nothing beyond. NASTY WHORE, a boy said. PROSTITUTE, PROSTITUTE, PROSTITUTE.

Between two of the boys' visits I thought I heard a turtledove from far outside, I wondered was it raining yet, thought of my mother later asking how was school today, our house, my uncle's two streets over. NO ONE LIKES A WHORE. The wooden plug in my cunt had loosened to a feeble throb, I was accepting it now, I felt the contractions coming, drool from my mouth pooling in one ear, pasting my hair to the table. I couldn't move, SLUT, that's what I was, no changing, no going back. Sneaker-footed steps hurried out, the door clacked closed again. The door reopened its black V, the next boy said WHORE again & CUNT & I recognized the voice as Chuck Eidel's, imagined his stained lips mouthing the word. I shut my eyes & saw his lips in slow motion, no *he wasn't saying* WHORE *he was whispering* LOVE, LOVE, *Chuck, the boy who had kissed me once, he was stepping forward, I felt myself shudder at my center, his arms held out w/the nail-bitten fingers & those perfect full wet lollipop lips kissing me, Oh Sarah stunning princess, Oh Sarah the love of my life.*

4

*T*he carnival gilds the world; Boris shields his eyes as he ambles through the parked cars. Following him, Harriet. Following her, Sarah. From the house windows behind them, televisions glow identical green nimbuses: the outfield from tonight's Kansas City Royals game. A woodpecker hammers a maple branch; beyond that, the high, truncated notes of a teenager practicing "I Love You Truly" on a first trumpet.

The sky falls in their hair. It is dusk, clear at last of rain, and the horizon seeps a blood wound from the sun's scarlet bullet. Telephone-pole banners spill DOUGLAS COUNTY FAIR in candy-cane letters. As they approach, the crowd grows louder, yet above the noise a turtledove lulls five soft notes. Another repeats in hushed echolalia. Layered with the endless *too-wheee* of cicadas, that song seems ominous, but Boris can't feel even a fraction somber. All week he has anticipated the trip to the fair, although it was actually Harriet who suggested it: "It's what Marshall would want." And Boris's supervisors, agreeing the evening might be beneficial, gave him an allowance for recent shipshape behavior. They extended curfew until 11 P.M. Boris shrugged into his lucky black sweatshirt; wore the white gym socks he discovered on a bench in the school locker room, the ones he hopes belonged to Rex.

The carnival hit town five days ago, the same night as Marshall's funeral. It lies snuggled in the center of a vacant field somewhere between the city limit and the bosky riverbanks of the neighboring Wakarusa. At night the carnival lords over the horizon, a bright leviathan winking oranges yellows greens and spitting rockets at the stars. While the Douglas County Fair hasn't quite graduated to the expansive flashiness of the State Fair in Hutchinson—Boris visited the latter once, during a brief stint with a family from those parts—in his opinion, the Douglas Fair is better. Something wonderful resides in Lawrence's carnival. On its arrival the town seems snared in a time warp, all swarmy with smells of cotton candy and sawdust and diesel fuel, eerie with screams and mechanized laughter, marriages of accordion and fiddle.

Harriet has appliquéed little pink-petal flowers on a camera strap, and when Sarah gives her the camera, she hangs it from her shoulder. In her purse are extra film rolls, special onionskin tissue for dusting the lens. They pay admission at the gate, and Harriet freeze-frames the ticket taker: his oily palms, his glasses held together by a band of electrical tape. He presses his stamp on the back of her hand. "I've seen these before," she says. "The ink doesn't make a mark on you, but it glows in the dark. It's neat. Last year when Marshall and I were here, we left for a bit, and when we came back, they just shone a black light on our hands to prove we weren't swindling them. Sure enough, there was the stamp."

To their right, buildings advertise farm exhibits under squint-shine bulbs. To their left, inside a glass window, a local television station broadcasts live news, weatherman slapping his map pointer into the ridged corner of Kansas. Skip it, Boris wants to skip it all;

hurry, he wants to hurry ahead for the attractions of the midway. He knows Sarah has come for the rides, anything to make her scream, even the inane games (Skeeball, Deadbeat Dunk, Pop Bottle Rings) on which everyone spends pocketfuls of dollars but never wins. Carl told Boris to ride the Zipper, but Sarah wants the haunted house and tunnel-of-love. She wants the double Ferris wheel, a favorite of Marshall's, the tallest on the midway. Even from this far fairground end, they can see it cartwheel and churn, its citrusy lights flickering section by brilliant section. A girl screams from one of the revolving, delicately wobbling seats. And screams again, her melody more joy than terror.

Harriet blocks their gaze and says, "We'll ride that later." Tonight she wears her best dress, its sable fabric flecked with her housecats' hairs. She wears the wig, deep brown curls concealing her gray, that she uses only for special occasions. Rouge, lipstick, a perfume like violets. She is such a frail thing, Boris thinks. A tiny thing. "There's more to these fairs," Harriet says, "than rides to get sick on." As she speaks, she leads them to the building reserved for farm exhibits, horsefly-busy rooms with calf and pony pens, piglets and lambs. In the adjoining shed stand cages of rabbits and chickens. The air smells of manure, of brome and alfalfa. Harriet dawdles, checking cages for the ribbon winners, disregarding the signs by unlatching a cage to retrieve a New Zealand White. She nuzzles her cheek to the animal's fur and purrs, kittenlike, into its triton nose. "Your heartbeat's going wild," she says in a singsong voice, "but I'm harmless, I can't hurt you."

Boris edges a finger into chicken cages; touches the calves' barmy noses. *Maybe, just maybe, Rex will appear.* This afternoon, left alone by Carl at last, he wrote an autobiographical piece for inclusion in *March of the Zombies.* Then he scribbled his latest Rex feelings on a diary page. "I want to learn him the way I learn the pieces of a jigsaw puzzle," Boris wrote. "Ie, one teensy piece after another, zooming in close to examine each fraction until I've memorized EVERY INCH OF HIM." He sketched a close-up view of

Rex's eyebrows and eyes and then, at the page bottom, "REX JACKSON RULES FOREVER!!!"

Roosters stamp and scratch in the cages opposite an aisle of white chickens. They ruffle their feathers, scarlet combs poised curiously at Boris's gaze. "Rex's family owns a chicken farm," he tells Sarah.

"Is that so." She has dressed up as well, her hair secured with tortoiseshell combs, her lacy black dress too sheer for the cooling evening. In fact, they're all wearing black: one reason, Boris knows, why everyone stares so much. "Maybe some of these chickens are Rex's," Sarah says.

"No. He wouldn't show them here. He probably just feeds them, collects the eggs, whatever. I sort of know some people at school who sort of know him. I've never been to the farm, it's right outside town somewhere, but I know. Sometimes at school there's, like, chicken shit on his boots and on the hall floor."

Sarah looks at her own shoe soles. "We should sneak out to his farm," she says. Harriet approaches the last of the chicken cages, and Sarah steps beside her. "Some night when I'm not at work. I'll steal you away while everyone's asleep and we'll go."

Sprays of marigolds flank the doorway to a third building, where wind ripples a banner showing a misshapen shamrock. Four H's are stenciled on each green cloverleaf; four words below. "Head, Hands, Heart, Health," Sarah reads. Harriet steps ahead of them, feet tromping the flowers, one hand snagging at the air. The evening is full of fireflies, and Harriet has caught one. "A lightning bug," she calls it. When she shows Boris, it pulses its lemon-lime spine within her hand's cubbyhole. Harriet steps back to the walkway to set it free.

"She's like a kid," Sarah says. "Only smarter. She's been through so much now, she's much much smarter."

The building is the showplace for other 4-H categories. There are more cloverleaf banners and educational displays with slogans—RIVER POLLUTION DESTROYS WILDLIFE; TERRACING BENEFITS ALL!—

as well as exhibits by amateur photographers, entomologists, teenage chefs and bakers. Boris smells the displays before he sees them: deep-dish pies of gooseberry, rum-laced peach, strawberry-rhubarb; cityscapes sculpted with divinity; gingerbread men with red-hot buttons and raisin eyes. At the other side of the mammoth room, a security guard shouts, "Closing up in fifteen minutes," but Harriet heads for the glass cases of insects, camera in hand.

Boris recognizes a name on a butterfly display. "Hey," he says, pulling Sarah's arm, "this guy is a friend of Rex's." ELLIS DERMODY. DOUGLAS COUNTY ENTOMOLOGY. Below the sign, a blue ribbon, and a card with the word LEPIDOPERA. "That's misspelled," Boris says. "Should be 'Lepidop*tera*.' He left off the *T*." He examines the ink-scrawled labels: *red admiral, clouded sulfur, wood nymph*. "Wow. First place. Maybe it's not the same Ellis. I just can't imagine it." He swallows a laugh at the thought of white-blond Ellis Dermody, leaping across a woody knoll, butterfly net billowing in the summer air. Or Ellis arranging and labeling the insects with the same diligence Boris uses on the Suffering Box. This image doesn't gel: Ellis, usually stoned in the school halls, fits into the same mold as the rest of Rex's flunky friends, all incapable of anything remotely cerebral. If—when—Boris convinces Rex of his love, perhaps Rex will transcend those losers' perpetual curse.

"That one's lovely," Harriet says. "No insects like these on my land." She taps the glass that jails the pinned and alcoholed body of a zebra swallowtail. Boris quick-checks; sees that only three other butterfly collectors found this rarity. On snaring it, Ellis's arms must have brailled with goose bumps.

Sarah, mouth an open *O* of wonder, chooses the grape-leaf skeletonizer. "This here's my favorite." Skinny blue body, orange head, miniature antlers. "Looks like Ellis did some good work," she says. "He must think no one will see his little hobby." Sarah must remember stories Boris has told: Ellis's limp wrists when Boris passes in the hall; his words mock-lisped from the back of class. "You should find some way to use this against him."

More glass cases exhibit geology collections. Entrants have glued rocks to pieces of felt, lined them on burlap, labeled each with specimen name, description, and date and location of discovery. Purple grand champion ribbons; blue first places; garnet seconds. Boris finds a peanut-brittle–like rock called jasperoid, points it out to Harriet. "Just like your last name."

The security guard nears, bouncing a flashlight against his thigh as though preparing to club them. "Let's skedaddle," Harriet says. She tucks two curls of the wig behind her ears and lets Boris escort her. Outside, they make their way toward the small hill, past individual booths now closing shop for the night: merchants selling turquoise jewelry; ice-cream churns; personalized cowboy hats, belt buckles, and license plates. One man peddles a special serum to clean eyeglasses, brand-spanking new, for a mere two dollars. Another woman analyzes personalities through handwriting samples, her booth a discord of lights and mechanized bleeps.

Twilight has crept east to west, shadowing the sky, sealing it up. Boris can predict a storm by the sugary smell of the air, and he knows that soon, tonight, thunderheads will smooth across that blue-black. Yet for now the sky is clear, needle-pricked with stars. Crows perch on electric wires, while above them, the moon, waxing. Boris stops at the hill that leans into the midway. The landscape assembles its details. He and Sarah and Harriet, by standing there, are the last to be soothed by the horizon's glow. They are the blessed.

Their maiden walk on the midway keeps them sidestepping barkers and troubadours, men with painted faces and swindlers' hands who holler and croon in crackerjack pitch. Harriet smiles at everyone; outthrusts her arms as though all, for tonight, are hers to hold. Boris guesses the arrow of her stare: Under a scaffold of clammy light, children swoon to play games. They're wide-eyed, motionless, all haunted interchangeable faces. The next tent boasts a moat traveled by wobbling plastic ducks; the top-hatted barker instructs to "fetch you out a duck and win the prize" from a number scrawled on the bottom. Elsewhere, wives watch as drunken husbands select waterguns, then stumble into ripped stools leaking guts of foam. They will shoot streams into the mouths of plastic clowns, sending bowler hats rising toward a ceiling target. Up there, blue and salmon teddy bears hang from ropes, their flannel teardrop tongues whispering silent reward for the winner. The husbands will snag prizes for their wives, no doubt about it, time to get the show on the road. The barker yells READY AIM FIRE. All contestants take shuddering aim at the clowns' bullet-hole mouths.

They reach the Octopus first. A steel gate encircles the ride's boundaries, the sign flashing its silver flash. "Is three to a car okay?" Sarah asks the operator, and he nods. His skin is veneered with clipper-ship and mermaid tattoos; his lower lip protrudes as though it once held a hook. His eyes are ants swarming straight at Sarah's chest. Boris chooses a car in armored black metallic, a shiny pod that seems threatening. Still, he and Sarah sandwich Harriet between them. The tattooed carny pulls a lever, the Octopus lifts its eight-tentacled cars into the air, and the spinning starts.

From below float the scents of bierocks, funnel cakes, foamy sarsaparilla, and fried strip cheese. Down there, swirling, faces sip tomato juice beers through licorice straws; smear sugared lips on cotton candy. Giggles reel in the air, echoing. *Are they laughing,* Boris wonders, *at us?*

They ride the Tilt-A-Whirl, the click-clacking Matterhorn, the Rock 'em Boats that bungle and knock within a brackish pond. Harriet buys more tickets. The roller coaster reminds Boris of the spine and ribs of a brontosaurus he viewed at a museum; they step to its gate, but tonight it's closed for repairs. A group of staring kids stop in their tracks, and now two of the boys hoof after them, pointing *hey you,* laughing *yeah you.*

Sarah stuffs both hands in her pockets; grumbling, she's had enough. "These people are horrible. Just look how everyone gawks." Boris and Harriet wait as she pumps quarters into a slot in a waterless aquarium. Behind the glass lie decks of cards and tiny gumball machines, miniature robots and stuffed animals. Sarah turns a handle, and a crane attempts to munch up a prize. "Go, go, go," Harriet says. Finally, after six tries, Sarah's crane drops a plastic skull. It's an air freshener for the car, equipped with a string hooped through its forehead. Boris sniffs its piney smell and remembers Marshall's crystal. Sarah pockets the skull; it's off to somewhere else.

On a freakshow stage, the Fat Lady holds a head of lettuce, taking bites as they pass. There is a gallery of lurid-paint canvases and a calliope on which ride the sword swallower, the waving dwarf. Children cry for money and musclemen drop sledgehammers on silver weights. At last Boris spies Screamland, the haunted house, its barker dressed in mummy garb and urging customers with a megaphone. The nickelodeon tinkles; the cobwebs tangle an arbor above them. Only two per makeshift hearse. "I'll stay here," Boris says. He scans the crowd for any recognizable faces from school, hoping partly for Rex, partly for utter anonymity. He catches a snippet of a boy's dialogue with his girlfriend: something about "that faggot." *C'mon, Sarah, hurry.* . . . He hears her bloodchilling scream as, there, they emerge from the doors, a gargoyle's mechanized growl heralding their return.

The ticket booths are filled with women, but Sarah finds a single male carny behind one chicken-wire window. Leaning her head back, winking, she bargains until he doubles the amount of tickets for her money. "I'll wait for *you* later," Boris hears her lie.

At the fairgrounds' far east end stands the Zipper: an oblong regal throne of blazing, tumbling lights, a tuning fork sequined with gyrating cages. "That ride looks pretty," Harriet says.

Boris takes two steps forward. "It's the one everyone talks about."

Sarah: "It's perfect."

Legend claims the Zipper's a killer. This past week, Boris heard a classmate prattling about teenage lovebirds in Omaha who'd plunged to their deaths while spinning at the ride's pinnacle. They rocketed back to earth, skulls crushed, hands still clasped defiantly together. All Boris could think was, *I've got to ride it.* And now he lets the carny strap him next to Sarah. Harriet lingers behind the man's muscled, shirtless shoulder. Sarah puts her lips next to the gridded cage and shouts, "We won't be long. Say a prayer for us!" But Harriet isn't listening. She secures her camera at her side, then pushes a hand in the carny's face, her coil of tickets pinched between her fingers. The man leads her off and lifts her into a seat two cages away.

The carny hammers Harriet's pin in place. "She's actually riding it," Boris says. It shouldn't be happening; it isn't safe. But they can do nothing now. The pervasive smell of diesel in their cage: Boris holds his breath.

"She'll make it okay," Sarah says. "Maybe you can't tell, but she's thinking of him. I haven't seen her cry yet, but you know. Inside that haunted house she started blabbing about the funeral, saying how odd things were on the farm now, that she could have sworn she heard him breathing all night from his bedroom across the hall." Sarah grips her prize skull in one white-knuckled hand. "But she loves this carnival shit. Really. She used to bring Marsh and me to these fairs before we could drive ourselves. Tonight's like history repeating. She can't get enough." Below, the carny locks his hands on the levers, and looks away, oblivious. The ride lurches; Sarah whistles out a last breath. "She just wishes he was here."

The Zipper's cars rock topsy-turvy. Slow, fast, faster: swirls of screams and the yellow and the orange and again, deafening, the screams. Sarah grasps Boris's hand, leans to kiss his cheek. He watches for Harriet, but everything somersaults in shadow and light, and he closes his eyes. Images of those Nebraska lovebirds embroider the inside of his lids, their blood mingling on the pavement. The cage door rattles. They endure two minutes' spinning and backflipping. Then the ride quiets like a hurricane's eye and everything begins, backward, again.

A sudden focus to the world's gusty blur; brief scree of machinery. The ride has stopped. Boris feels battered and drilled, his heart pounding, his eardrums numbed with Sarah's yells. Below, the carny unpins cages. He withdraws people two at a time, and for the moment Boris and Sarah's car undulates at the Zipper's topmost precipice. They are seesawing, vexed with alternate glimpses of sky and earth. They are astronauts, drifting through space, their tethers cut.

Through the cage door Boris sees the crowd, slivered now and again like frames in a slide show. Harriet evacuates her car and shuffles to the midway, steady and nearly falling and steady again, her wig askew. He sees a tent that dwarfs its neighbors, its peaks speared with three lightning rods. Red, white, and blue pennants shiver in the breeze. Below, a hand-lettered sign reads AMAZING HEADLESS WOMAN. Next to that, another: HELP WANTED FEMALE 18 YEARS OLD. Boris's gaze wanders: a booth selling colored sand in bottles; another advertising wooden flutes, woodcarved and wood-burned signs. And there, huddling with a friend at the front of that display, is Rex Jackson.

At first his form barely registers. Boris waits for the carny to crank the lever, to extract another pair of riders. The Zipper repositions, and now their cage leans on its side, facing the woodcarving booth. Yes. There, the object of Boris's affection, T-shirt muddied, a tear in his jeans showing an oval of bony knee. Untrimmed windblown hair gone curly at the ends; red high-top sneakers. Perfect, Boris thinks. He'll have to remember this for his diary, this view of a god from a regular god's vantage point.

Rex stands close to Wayne Hinton. Boris has seen them together at school; assumes Wayne is Rex's most faithful crony. The flare from a lamp illuminates the two as they scrutinize something, a whittled flute perhaps, turning it over and over in their hands, as they negotiate with the girl behind the booth. Her hair spills across her face and she throws back her head, laughing. Boris can see her animal throat, her searing flirt. She takes the boys' money. She leaves her station and joins them, Wayne's hand resting on her arm.

"Jeez, Sarah, it's actually him, right there, look right there you can see him in actual perfecto flesh and bone and blood."

Sarah squints. "Where?" And then, as if loosed from the anchor of that word, Rex and Wayne move away from the display booth and march down the midway, ushering the carny girl between them.

Boris rattles the cage door, a beast wanting out. "I've got to follow them." The ride deposits another cage at the ground, another, but it takes two, two and a half, three minutes for Boris and Sarah's escape.

Harriet, survivor, claps twice when they step free. "Heavens to Betsy," she says.

"I'll be right back," Boris tells her. He repeats the sentence to Sarah, and he's off running. The crowd blooms around him, but he discovers the secrets of its maze, hidden cracks to slip through. Ahead somewhere are Rex and Wayne and the carnival worker. Boris must find them. Faster, sprinting, faster. The roar of laughter and tunnel-of-love terror; the intoxicant air swelling peppercorn mustard and tutti-frutti.

In seconds he's back where the night began. The green-siding buildings have been closed to the public, but one door to the 4-H house stands open. There, Rex and Wayne urge the girl inside, into the rooms with seamstress dresses and tiered chocolate cakes and the prizewinning butterfly collection. "C'mon," they say, "real quick, just for a minute." Boris crouches below the briary arms of a pine and, as they lead her in, creeps closer. He can hear the girl's laughter, her triggered breaths coming asthmatic, raspy. Behind him, the Matterhorn's siren lifts above its riders' screams. The freakshow barker delivers his drawl. Boris bites his lip and enters.

Only a scattering of lights have been left on. The place stands solemn, echoey as a ruined church's nave. Rex and Wayne lead their carnival-worker companion—clopping footsteps, copying along the hallway, clopping—into the bathroom marked MEN.

Wayne carries the wooden flute in his back pocket. He slaps the girl's ass; she offers another raindrop giggle; the door skids shut behind them. Boris crosses to it, checking all directions for security guards. He moves his face closer, eye level with the door's pair of BB bulletholes. He waits, waits. Then suction-cups his ear there.

Initially he hears the roughage of the carny girl's laugh. Then silence. Nearby, wind ripples the entryway's banner, and an uncertain Boris shifts his head, worrying he's been caught. When reassured, he replaces his ear and listens.

"I don't want no one watching me," Wayne says. "That means you, Rex. That's fucking sick, man."

The girl murmurs something indecipherable, and after a pause, Rex answers. "Well, what am I supposed to do? Hurry up before somebody comes." His baritone sounds slurred: maybe drunk, stoned, both. Boris has heard that voice on ultrarare occasions at school; it lilts in his discriminating ears like a lullaby.

Holding his breath, trying to imagine the scene, he cracks the bathroom door. "Knock out the lightbulbs," he hears Wayne say.

A clicking sound. Boris ventures a guess: the towel-dispenser machine, unlatching. Then a hollow shatter. Another. Boris envisions Rex, tall arms outstretched, smashing the bathroom's bulbs with a brown roll of paper towels. Wayne: "Stand guard." Perhaps Rex is only inches away, leaning on the other side of the closed door.

Silence reigns. Wayne must be kissing the girl, perhaps pressing matters deeper, but Boris can't conjure enough courage to peek. He squints into less shadowy corners of the building: the immobile bodies of mannequins; the glass cases with chunks of limestone and quartz, monarchs and swallowtails. Boris will have to leave soon, abandon this scene and his layers of gooseflesh to return to his friends. He will rattle the details to Sarah. And later he will scribble in his diary, imagining himself in the 4-H building's bathroom with Rex, no Wayne or anonymous girl, only the two of them, the dark-haired boy's fingers entwined with his, his lips kissing Boris's eyelids shut, Rex's glistening lungs pushing sweet breath back and forth to blend with his.

And there, now, Boris hears the sound of someone breathing. Wayne? The labored breaths wheeze unevenly, almost like snores. Then a choked "Okay, it's ready, okay." From the gush of the words, and the accompanying sound of the girl's wet mouth, Boris understands what's happening.

The stillness stretches out until it snaps. "Your turn," Wayne says.

Boris can't let this moment pass. He has to look; has to risk it. *Three, two, one.* He nudges the door a centimeter, pokes a fraction of his head into the slender wedge.

Too dark: at first, too dark. Without the glow of lightbulbs, the bathroom seems murky as a cave. Boris smells the mop-scrub pine of floor wax and, swirling within that, their bargain-store musk cologne. He is so close to Rex now. He cannot make a sound, cannot be seen.

Boris blinks as his eyes adjust. Two vague halos hover in the bathroom air, random ghosts amid coal-black, the twin glow-in-the-dark inkblots from the ticket-booth stamps. The elemental heat from Rex's and Wayne's hands cause the invisible ink to shine. Boris's eyes adjust further, and within the phantom gleam of those lights, the bodies emerge.

He stands, at least six feet two, at the front of a bathroom stall. The girl kneels before him. The sounds, full, feral: her lips, her tongue, the push-pull of her throat. Rex's jeans bunch at his knees, his cock buried unseen inside her head. He tangles fingers in her hair. He's chewing gum, matching the rhythm made by her mouth. His face looks almost serene, all blood leached from the high cheekbones, the ridge of nose, the square chin.

Boris feels the slow stiffening in his jeans. He sees the girl's bobbing head. He sees her reach up to hold Rex's hand, wanting that intimacy. But Rex pulls away, plunging both hands deeper into the girl's wavy hair, causing the phosphorescent stamp to disappear.

Please, god, don't let them see me. Boris inches closer to improve the view. In that singular moment, everything freezes, solidifies: the white *U*'s of urinals; Rex's erased expression of bliss; the girl's head, all fluttery concentration in Rex's lap. Boris presses his hand to the crotch of his jeans.

Footsteps. A walk, breaking into a run. The guard has seen him. Boris spins away, the bathroom's dark stereoscope fracturing into pieces.

As he runs, the night air shifts, blowing dust and chaff along sidewalks littered with sawdust, straws, tattered firecrackers. The wind soothes his skin, unguent against what he's seen. Curfew time nears and Boris wants to cry, wants to dash his head to the ground, but more than anything he needs to stretch back on his mattress and replay all he has witnessed, smelled, heard. He will replace the carny girl with himself, will bow in honor before the one he loves. No more fraudulent dreams of Rex, the fantasy Rex. Now he can substitute his audible escalating breath, the shadowy angles of his radiant face. Rex will rescue him, kiss his sleepy mouth, comb tanned valiant fingers through Boris's hair.

He doesn't search long for Sarah and Harriet. They stand under a sign blaring MONSTERS, browsing through fliers and souvenirs. Inside the booth are plaster casts of Sasquatch feet, photos of alleged beasts. "Marshall loved Bigfoot," he hears Harriet tell a woman at a cash register. Her wig has fallen off; she holds it in one hand, the camera in the other. He sees she is tired because when she is tired the wrinkles deepen around her eyes; too, the *V*-lines at her lips from years of gold-hearted smiles and smiles.

Boris would like to report something otherworldly, even super-human, to Sarah. Some sentence like "Rex's testicles were mammoth as coconuts" or "He bit her nipples and lapped up the blood." But thrust forth into the world again, Boris can't yet assimilate all he's seen. The words catch stony and jagged in his throat. Elsewhere in the Sasquatch booth, a woman is spanking a little boy, her hand curving through the air like a scythe ripping wheat. A girl switches price-tag labels on a pair of Bigfoot model kits.

He feels tears rising. No. Sarah holds his arm, motions to Harriet. She tells her, "Almost closing time, sweetie." Harriet snaps two photos of the monster's plaster footprint, a dehydrated mound of droppings under glass, and skips along.

Fireflies throb their lights, thick within the rows of trumpet creeper. Boris, Sarah, and Harriet head back to where they started. A janitor sweeps the sidewalk with a yard-long mop, leaving a foamy wave of bottle caps, shredded fliers from the 4-H and Bigfoot booths, countless corndog sticks like the remains of skeletons. Ahead, on one side of the field used for parking, mill crowds of people. "What's up there?" Harriet asks.

Boris doesn't care. He wants to isolate Sarah, to reveal this secret burning fever in his throat. But Harriet hurries closer, and Sarah jostles him along. Women and men, children and adults crowd around an animal pen, straining for a better view and yammering like a box of bees. An amateur obstacle course has been constructed inside the pen, low-standing boards and hoops and cement culverts placed here and there for the purpose of sport. Now, again, Boris hears the honk of ducks, the gurgle and grunt of pigs. Harriet gives him the camera—in two blinks she takes off and noses her way through the mass of bodies, pushing and pushing with the wig in her hand.

The emcee tells lame jokes. Florid clown makeup paints the hollows of her face, her mouth eggplant purple, her cheeks radish red. She calls the names of the pigs, spitting sunflower-seed shells between predictable titles: Petunia, Bertha, Bubba. Groans from the audience: everyone needs this, the evening's final entertainment, to consummate the head-woozy effects of the carnival. The announcer points her microphone at the pig in her assistant's arms. "And this one here's Cousin Elmer." Boris sees Harriet smile and applaud, ebullient, with the crowd. For the moment she has forgotten, she has floated away.

And watching her, Boris wonders if perhaps things will get better. Sarah watches too; perhaps she's thinking the same. They look ahead as Harriet shoulders closer in, attempting to reach the front. On her way, she accidentally pushes a man in a corduroy jacket and fishing cap. He glances at her, then back to Boris and Sarah.

Then it happens. The man returns her shove. Harriet is weak; she nearly falls. The man stares hard, his face twisting in recognition. "Crazy old bitch," the man says to Harriet. And to a woman beside him: "Crazy as a loon."

Boris swears they don't know the man, have never seen him prior to this night. Still, he turns toward them. Spangled points of light copy in his eyes, silver nailed inside circles of black. The man recognizes all three of them, knows their misfit enemy spirits. "Bitch," he says again, this time to Sarah. He scrutinizes her dress, glares at Boris; one side of his mouth crooks into a sneer. And then: "What happened to the other faggot?"

Harriet, close enough to hear, doesn't turn. Boris sees her face curdle. Her gaze falls to the feet of the surrounding crowd.

Sarah mouths something back at the man, but the speakers amplify the announcer's whoops, and her words are lost. The throng of people chuckle and applaud. The pig races are ready, ready to begin. "What we need right now is two or three volunteers," the woman barks into her microphone. Boris looks to his left, to his right. The man who insulted them eases away, wanting a better view of the sport. But Harriet heard. She has sneaked closer to the show, alone; Boris no longer sees her. Sarah grasps his hand, securing him to her side, but the rest of the crowd congeals around them. He stretches to tiptoes. Still no Harriet.

"Three volunteers from this audience." The speakers burble and buzz, the woman's voice at last spearing through to slam all eardrums in the crowd. "You there, come up here and get you a pair of pompoms." She is selecting cheerleaders from the audience, three bystanders to stand at the sides of the obstacle course and shake the bright paper chrysanthemums in the night air.

A brief moment of silence. "Oh, my god," Sarah says.

Boris peeks through a fissure in the onlookers, and he sees. The announcer has chosen Harriet. The assistant leads her, up around the fence's boundaries, to the announcer's cement plateau. Harriet smiles dumbly. Her eyes are glassy, mirrors of the eyes Boris has imagined on the missing girl, her body dumped in an abandoned field of thistle, all life stamped out of her like wine.

The announcer divvies up pompoms between the three chosen cheerleaders. Harriet holds one blue, one red. Their colors are the same garish shades from the diagram of arteries and veins Boris saw only days ago, before Marshall's death, behind a hospital desk. Harriet has dropped the wig and the wind blows her gray hair, hissing the pompoms in her hands. Her ears, ringing, must hear only one thing: *What happened to the other faggot.*

The assistant waves the edible trophy above his head. He moves to a handle that will lift the cage door: the race, now ready to start. "This isn't right," Sarah says. Harriet stands, directed in place by the announcer, looking to the podium for instructions. The announcer lifts her arms, miming a few shakes of invisible confetti. Everyone is watching. Harriet repeats the emcee's action, raising the pompoms in the air, eyes locked on something in the distance. Not on the announcer and her exaggerated clown face. Not on the pink-blushed shoats that stamp at their starting gate. Not on the hooligan crowd surging close and screaming "*Go! Go!*" Something else.

Two shots peal forth, echoing and reechoing in a faraway vacant litany. The assistant cranks the handle. The quartet of swine run loose to circle the cage, lusty and amuck, bumping heads and asses. Their hoofed feet scramble and scratch up a plywood ramp, then wriggle midair as they splash to a child-sized wading pool.

Harriet stands, her face gone blank, the mouth pried open. The other cheerleaders are jumping, hollering, kicking boots to the sky. And Harriet mimics them. Boris sees the movement of her lips. "Yay." She takes two hops into the air, punches the pompoms over her head.

Above the crowd, across the marzipan wash of stars, a blast of fireworks signals the carnival's close. Boris looks up, the sky gone spidery with chromes and greens and golds. It is late: he will miss his curfew, but now that worry seems trivial. He thinks of Rex and Wayne and the carny girl; of Marshall lying cold in the ground. He grips Sarah's hand tighter, and together they watch Marshall's mother cheer the pigs through the finish line.

Yaaaay. Harriet jumps and hoots and kicks her little foot. She twirls and shakes the pompoms, the bursts of blue and red, confetti shreds in her fists.

—B.

It's the basement I remember best. A row of ground-level windows looking out to pink and blue hydrangeas. Tiny American flags spiked into the lawn. A storage freezer, vinyl sofa, Ping-Pong table with a snagged net and chipped paddles. Steps with empty slats between them, making me worry that a monster's grizzled hands would clamp my ankles.

The foster father used to sleep down there. He worked graveyard shifts. Loved afternoon naps. Would stretch out on the sofa, its brown pattern with marbled black. The foster mother worked days, her two daughters together like gophers nosing to school. I was still too young. Coming up on five years old. Bone-thin and shy, my face thick with freckles. Skin swan white that bruised at no more than a touch. My hair redder then too. Not lightened and streaked blond like now.

The father was dark with darker eyes. Maybe the first evidence of the "type" I strive for? Maybe my first love? He had moles on both sides of his cheeks. A speech problem with his R's and L's that kept him silent and stern. Sometimes I'd watch him shaving in the mirror. Taking care around the edges of his mustache. More than sometimes I'd watch him sleep down there. He wore nothing but white underwear, white socks. Even when it got cold, there he was, half-naked. His left arm crooked above his head as a pillow. Hard chest furred with hair so black it looked blue in the somber basement light.

The girls had tacked posters to those clammy walls. They were twins and obsessed with pairs of anything. Pictures of twin albino baby tigers, two cartoon elephants uniting trunks into a valentine, double exposures of girl ballerinas. The girls and their mother didn't want me, I knew it. They were screens slipped between me and Mr. Mason. I longed for the afternoons. Just him and me. If I was good he might put me on his lap. Chocolate drops on my tongue. Wrap his arm and its soft black hair around my skinny boy body.

1983: Days frittered away. Late summer became autumn. Then winter. I was little and remember little things. My crowded back-porch room. Out its single window, the green lawn with midget purple heads of milkweed. Used tractor tires, their centers filled with soil sprouting cucumber vines. The girls and their secret language of smiles at the dinner table. Their calling me "Doris" and their "Don't touch that; it's ours." The sound of the father leaving for work at night. In bed I closed my eyes. Thought of the screen door slamming, its aluminum pattern framing the letter M of their last name. There would never be an A for my name. Not here, not anywhere.

But better I remember the father and the basement and the game we played. Just the two of us. Not Twister or Crazy Eights but something he invented. In my head I called it the dead game, and even today I can't forget it. Its details sewn blue in my brain.

Sometimes Mr. Mason couldn't sleep. There would be afternoon construction on the street. Or honking cars, police sirens. When he couldn't drift off he pretended anyway. He must have sensed me watching. I was never sure if he slept or if he just stretched there feigning it, all pasted-shut eyes and sluggish, even wheeze-breath. Sometimes his stillness got so genuine I thought he was dead.

I'd step toward him and stand there trembling, goose bumps rashing my skin. Twin cubs and princesses staring down and the only sound his breathing. I'd wait minutes, more minutes. Finally get the courage to ask, "Are you awake?"

I never knew what would happen next. My heart a baby snake in my chest, coiled. My feet ready to turn and run. Would he continue sleeping? Would he open one eye slowly as he'd done before, curling one side of his mouth into a smile? Or would he leap from the brown cushions and tackle me, his hands bent like scorpions, tickling and tickling?

That afternoon. Darkness already starting to settle against the house, a gravy-thick winter dark. Part of me wanted to rush through it. Mostly though I wanted to stay and play the game. He was there, unmoving on the sofa. I went to the lamp he'd left burning. Pulled the beaded chain. Outside was drizzle mixed with snow, and it moved reflected window boxes on the floor. I stood within one of those squares.

Three feet away from him. Part of me wishing like other days he was indeed asleep. Part of me secretly wanting him to pounce. That didn't happen often. Still I relished the memory. His ogre's roar. The scooping me into his steely grasp. The scrape of his naked arms and chest. What child doesn't want to be tortured a little, to feel the punishing strength of the tormentor, his warm, musky embrace?

Not a sound of snore or heartbeat. I could hear my own pulse, though, could see my breath but not his. Took a half-step closer. He was going to grab me, I knew it. I understood then it was him who'd been the monster all along, waiting between the slats of the basement steps. Waiting for this day. The wife and daughters away. Here to swallow me, to crunch me up and not tell a soul.

Still he didn't move. I imagined the real foster father dead, this monster in his place. Could see its jaws and fangs ripping through my muscle and bone. Its tongue lapping marrow for the last sweet drop of juice. I couldn't take another step. Asked, "Are you gonna get up?" in my softest voice.

This time seemed different. After a while I shuffled back upstairs to my room. Got out the box of sixty-four crayons. Tried to stay within the lines of pictures of gingerbread houses, happy brothers and sisters with real blood parents standing guard like scarecrows. I wondered would he march back upstairs and make things better. Would he get up at all?

I couldn't wait much longer and kept flubbing the colors from the lines' boundaries. Went back to the basement and leaned to look. He was still there, dead or asleep. "Hey," I said. Started stepping down, counting one two three after each. No monster's hand clenched my ankles, and soon I was on Mr. Mason's level. Lamp still off and the swirling window light lowering another layer of dark. Birds whirled just outside the glass, shadowing black flutters at my feet. Calling and chipping warnings in a stuttered language I couldn't understand.

In earlier bouts of the dead game, he'd faltered. Sometimes I'd hear him breathing and know he was alive. See his fingers move or one eye slit open. But not now. He hadn't moved at all. His lids were locked as if stitched with needles. I took another step. Another. A third and I was so close I could reach out and touch the hairs above his lip, the hairs on his chest. But I didn't dare. Not yet.

I waited what could have been a minute, thirty minutes, an hour. Lost track of the upstairs tick of the wall clock. The windows silvery now with crystal ice. "Don't be dead," I whispered.

I said it again and somehow tears had gotten into the words. I wasn't afraid of the monster anymore. Was afraid now of the dead body but knew I couldn't cry. Mrs. Mason and the girls could be home any time, they would see him there on the sofa and heap the blame on me.

He didn't move, didn't answer, didn't breathe. Counting to fifty then sixty I lay next to him. Could feel the heat of him on me. Even dead he kept that heat. I'd never been this close before, and something inside me rearranged. Teetering light and nervous. I put my hands against his arms. Moved my face to his chest. I breathed and brushed my cheeks, chin, eyes into his hair. Back and forth, its pattern changing, the coarse black like spider legs. A smell I wanted to swallow and hold inside me, earthy and dank like something lying warm and close and bleeding in the mud. I'd smell that smell years later, on a hunting trip with another foster family. A dead deer with the steam still rising from the bullet hole. And I'd think of my little-boy face pushing at Mr. Mason's body. Wanting something invisible and necessary like love.

If he was dead I didn't care anymore. The skin was warm, pliable, inviting. The glass inside me broke, and from the zillion pieces, a pain I couldn't understand. It wasn't sex but something before sex. Felt it swallowing me whole, mutating the way I blinked and breathed and licked my lips. Something like the first time you see a cut bleeding hard and realize it's your body.

I had to kiss him. I would start with his face. My lips on his cheek first. Then his eyebrow. My lips pressing together. Clapping the eye open/closed, and in that moment no sign of recognition or anger. Kissed the eye. Little-boy kisses, uncoordinated pecks without knowledge of open mouths or tongues. Kissed his nose, the squirrel hairs of his mustache. The mouth last. Behind his lips were more smells, his mouth a wet well lined with marshmallow and gingerbread.

He was so warm. I felt as though he were my gift, given now at the beginning of want. I could see chapped ridges on his hands. Up close they were lined like deserts cracked by drought. Freckles near his elbow. A scar so faint maybe only I'd seen it, a snail shell over his ribs. All those black hairs. I put my mouth there, rubbed them against my tongue tip. Ground some of the hairs between my teeth. Felt one catch. Tongued it out and swallowed.

I let my mouth travel down down. The hair disappeared into the white of his underwear. One blue pinstripe circling the waistband. I guessed more hair lurked there, wanted to see it. Stared at the rounded V pushing up from the cotton.

When I put my hand inside there was nothing but silence for two, then three seconds. Had his cock between my thumb and forefinger. Its flesh soft as angel food. It lying there in the gritty curls of his hair. I wanted to see it. Wanted to put my head down there. Get close up, kiss it too.

I heard the sound first. It was a breath but not mine. The third second became the fourth and I spun my head, the poster tigers and ballerinas and icicled windows blurring past. Mr. Mason wasn't dead. Had been playing all along. His arm poised in the air. Coming down. I heard something crack, again, this time earthquake-loud and the arm in the air still coming down.

Saw his body swerve upward from the sofa. Legs with the white-stockinged feet swinging to the floor. One knee pounded my chest. Then the words coming from his lips. He said, "What the holy hell were you doing?," blundering the L's. What the holy hell.

The hammering blows on my back. Their rhythm, dirty drums.

In my coloring book upstairs was a picture of Cherokees rowing their riverboat. I'd given them faces of burnt sienna. Warpaint in stripes of cornflower blue and carnation pink. Their oars struck the skin of water in great liquid heaves. The Masons let me take the box of crayons, and as I colored the world hurtled past. Cramped between the twins in the backseat with their secret smiles.

From that day on would be twelve more years of foster homes. The Crains, the Blevinses, the Deanoviches, who lasted a mere two weeks. The McLaughlins, the Keenans. The Nicholses, who lost me when they divorced. The families in between. I didn't know any of this yet. Just sat in the backseat as if stapled in. Thought of him lying still and dead on that basement couch. All that beautiful bone and muscle and skin stretched out just for me. The feeling that gave me. I'd always want it. Still want it.

The feeling I lost when the dead eyes opened. Eyes that looked away as he whispered goodbye.

5

*I*n the morning Harriet disregards the cats' hungry mewling and steps out the back door in her head scarf, nightgown, slippers. For September, the farm looks midsummer green. Before the storms, everything seemed draped in yellow. The milo fields to the east and west, leased to other farmers since her husband died over a decade ago, shimmered an endless gold. In the air were chummy bees and yellow-vested meadowlarks. Sunflowers thickened at fence boundaries and grass bleached in the sun's choler, overwarmed food for her grazing horse.

And then the rains. Marshall checked into the hospital and stayed. Everything changed.

Last month, her land was busy with combines, their paths determined by teenage boys hired to sweep through anonymous fields, of which Harriet's was just another. Mornings, before Sarah arrived to drive her into town, Harriet would rise and stand watching from the porch. As days passed she grew certain the custom-cutter boys felt her presence there, and she woke earlier each morning. She could still look pretty, her hair past her shoulders when freed from its pins. She began painting her eyes and lips; played Marshall's stereo at enough volume to push the sound past the house and porch and through the fields. Maybe they would hear, even want to dance. None of them knew her, could guess any detail of this wraithlike old woman's life. She had once won a dance marathon and a contest for homemade sandhill-plum jelly. She *always* hooked more channel catfish than Robert, and once, when he'd given her the chance, she'd used nothing but her bare hands to garrote and kill the neighbor's tom turkey for Thanksgiving dinner. This, and still Robert said she was glamorous. Her back, once candlepin-straight, now bent like a sickle, and as the custom-cutter boys chugged along the rows at the field's far west end, Harriet strained to conjure that poise and grace.

But now harvest has ceased; milo cut, sunflowers drowned. The almanac was right. Anvil-tower storm clouds cover the morning and the night and she endures them, waiting for something, yet not waiting at all.

Sarah didn't believe when she claimed she'd heard Marshall. She could tell by the way Sarah sucked her bottom lip and stared without blinking. But his bedroom across the hall still hints at his presence. Night breathing at first, once a faint *achoo*, and now, just before sunrise, Harriet heard him call for her. A frustrated request for assistance, a yell like he'd yelled sometimes, hesitant and stubborn, before the hospital.

The grasses whisper and clap, a song more welcome to Harriet's ears than any lawnmower. She avoids the barbed-wire fence; climbs the gate instead. It takes time, but she can still do it. She stands in loose sand, snug within a pair of her horse's hoofprints. She pays Mr. Evans, a neighbor down the road, to feed it with the hay bales stacked behind the house. They had bought the horse for Marshall when he was twelve. He called it Jellybean. Years and years have passed, the animal's age now written in hairless circles around its nostrils and eyes. Harriet notes the mud spattering its mane and coat, its tensed neck muscles as it bends to drink. She must remember to take photographs before it's gone.

Acres away are the semicircle copse of trees, the fish pond that marks her land's northern border. She walks with slippered feet, clover dew freckling her ankles with its chill. To her left, swallow-tails chase arcs in the catalpa Robert planted when he bought the land. Its mammoth leaves shudder and beat; a robin's nest has fallen and cracked, but no eggs were inside, nothing sacred was lost.

When Marshall was little, Harriet used the image of that tree as the basis for a fairy tale. A treasure was buried beneath, its enigma known only to a dwarf and his talking hound. Over many years, she wrote six, nearly seven different stories. She bound them herself and charcoaled pictures on each cover. The books line a top shelf in Marshall's bedroom; although they could use a good dusting, to reach them means climbing a footstool. She'll ask Boris, next time he visits, to help. For now Harriet walks: here, a thatch of shriveled sandhill plums; there, the hesitant mud tracks of a rabbit. Top-notch photo opportunities, Harriet thinks, and best of all the pond, now risen with the rains. Jellybean visits in the evenings, even the Evanses fish on its banks, but she hasn't ventured there in over a year.

Today, today, she will.

A memory: spring, 1980. The mulberry trees had taken bloom early. Robert had just been buried in the town cemetery, on the left side of a plot for a family of three. One seventy-degree afternoon she rearranged pictures in the family album and slid it beneath the couch and, at last, allowed the television's laugh track to lull her to sleep. She woke to the slam of the door and waited to welcome Marshall home from school. Her son stepped into the room, yes, but together with him, her hand in the crook of his arm, stood a thin, grinning girl wearing plum-wine lipstick, her hair in ponytails above her ears.

Sarah's mother had "given her up," as Marshall said, to a youth home called Sunflower. Various nights, after homework, Marshall began driving to town in Robert's car and returning, thirty-five minutes later, with Sarah. Harriet dallied at the door and turned on the porch light at their arrival. The whole process felt criminal, and weirdly, wildly, she loved it: loved that she formed the indirect link to her son's illegal night kidnappings, loved the bitter fruit-peel taste in her throat as they laughed, together, at the successful deceptions. She splurged on cartons of vanilla Sealtest, the box covers decorated with photographs of snow-starred ice cream. Harriet found her best bowls, blue glass wedding gifts, and took painstaking care with three sculpted mounds. She then anointed the scoops with liquid chocolate, Hershey's in the can with the yellow flaptop, sluggish and sweet. And she followed suit as Marshall and Sarah made "ice-cream stew." They waited for the melt, until the thin string of their patience snapped and they had to stir, stir, chocolate swirling in the vanilla, no flecks of brown remaining in the soup. Then, and then only, they ate.

One rainy late-May evening, Harriet had just fetched the Sealtest from the freezer when the television newscast interrupted Marshall's favorite show. Harriet hustled into the room and found a place beside the kids. She could smell their insect repellent from an earlier horseback ride. "Listen," she told them, while on screen came a tiny *Tornado Warning* funnel. Out the window, the squall of raindrops clustered with pebbles of hail. The newsman said that a cyclone had been sighted in Douglas County, and all affected should take cover immediately.

She pretended to be brave but wasn't. Fear took root on her spine as she opened every window, found the transistor radio Robert had used for nighttime baseball games, and led the children down the basement stairs. The space smelled of wet feathers, pickle brine, caulk. The dangling lightbulb didn't work, and the dank expanse only accentuated the storm's noise. Between wind gusts and hailstones, she heard a siren, somewhere, shrieking its red-armored throat. The fence slats from her backyard garden, toppling. Branches scraping the windows like the fingers of thieves. Jellybean whinnied; the neighbors' horse replied; something thudded a great dead weight against the house. Sarah's eyes quivered and widened and Harriet put her hand out, started to tell her, *Stay calm, everything will be fine.* But she couldn't muster the correct brave tone, and before she opened her mouth, it happened: Marshall put his face in his hands and wept, not Sarah but Marshall, deep racking sobs that surprised and scared her. More surprising, too, was the eagerness with which he leaned into his friend. Marshall went to Sarah, not his mother, and Sarah wrapped his shoulders with her arm and whispered in his ear.

"It's going to miss us, honey," Harriet said. "The funnel won't even touch down, and besides, it's in another part of the county." Neither of the kids seemed to listen. Marshall hid his face, deeper, into Sarah's breast; Harriet could see the bump of the girl's nipple, hard beneath the sheer blouse, so close to his mouth.

After ten minutes the storm passed, leaving the curves of a double rainbow over the neighbor's field. On tiptoes, Marshall and Sarah watched it from a basement window. "I feel like a big baby for crying," he announced, his face turned away. Harriet wanted to call him *Silly goose,* wanted to reassure with *There's nothing to be ashamed of, I was just as scared as you.* Yet she only jerked her thumb toward the basement ceiling, gave him a quick wink, and said, "Ice-cream stew."

As soon as they heard his feet above them, Sarah sat close beside her. "I'm not his girlfriend," she said. Her blouse wore a stain from Marshall's tears. Harriet could smell her wintergreen gum and the horsehide musk on her bareback-rider jeans. "Just so you know. He told me you know, oh, about him not liking girls, not in *that* way, right? I'm just his friend."

Harriet understood exactly what Sarah was saying. Although the voice was sweet and soft, the words stung like curses. Marshall had not told her; why hadn't her son revealed himself, before anyone else, to her? Harriet took a deep breath and nodded; started to reply but couldn't. In the ground-level window behind Sarah's back, splintered sticks, leaves, and underripe mulberries littered the lawn. At last Harriet said, "I already knew *that*." But her tone came out wrong, and she knew that Sarah knew.

Robert was dead. In four more years the doctors would find the cancer that waited, persistent, inside her own breast. Now, however, sheltered and cool against the basement wall with her son's best friend, she could not guess any of this. Marshall returned, clopping his mock horse-canter rhythm on the stairs. Although the ice cream was a liquid mush, they ate. Harriet watched her son's spoon and his full-lipped mouth moving over the spoon. She felt she knew him, somehow, less; she loved him the same, even more if that were possible, but she would never own him, never be able to keep him safe at her side. She waited for this jagged sadness to subside, but it did not. Many years later, she would feel this precise sadness again, on a starless rain-blown midnight when Marshall clicked off the television and sat her down, in the front room directly above that chilly space of the basement. "Mom," he would say, "do you know what AIDS is?" And as she listened to her son, she grew fiercely aware of the love that rippled and burned its blistering course through her body. She knew once again that her simple love couldn't own him. Her love couldn't save him, couldn't keep her only son forever sturdy, here, alive.

Morning glories crowd the field. There are lavender asters and prairie phlox and, everywhere, color. "I always think of this area as black and white," a distant relative had said at the funeral. "Like in that movie." Harriet knew he'd pictured a range of gray hues between the light of that farm girl's gingham dress and the dark of the whirling cyclone, swooped down to whisk her away. The last time the relative had visited, Marshall had been a little boy, and now the man was paying his respects in a gesture of sympathy, as representative for the extended family. He didn't know her son, not really. Harriet held tighter to Sarah and nodded, smiled, nodded.

Bluejays train their caviar eyes on Harriet and begin chirring in F sharp. The trees make their ghost rattle. Once lightning struck the oldest oak, but still it stands, a tire swing hanging from one branch's burled elbow. Over the years the swing's rubber has cracked, parts of rope have unraveled, the ground below it overgrown with weeds.

Harriet steps out of her slippers, fearless of sandburs or copperheads. She hurries now, nearing the pond's edge shaded with cattails and loblollies. When she bends toward the water, her face floats back: hair falling in strands from the scarf, wrinkles deep as knife grooves around her eyes. She is sixty-two, but if her back straightened and her hair was its original color, then maybe, maybe she could pass for much younger. Sarah says so. Her teeth are still good and she requires glasses only for the morning newspaper. Below her reflection, minnows hesitate before regrouping, made curious by her shadow. She dips in a hand to scatter them. She examines her grapestem bones and veins, displayed within the water like the rachis of a leaf.

Mom, the voice this morning said. That was all. Its murmurous tenor in the room, the shallow breath on her ear as she trembled from sleep.

There had been a day, less than a month ago, when Sarah couldn't change her shift at the convenience store. Harriet spent the day at the hospital, alone with Marshall. She sponge-bathed him with water as cold as the pond's. She served food she'd cooked that morning, but he couldn't finish it. "Help me out here," her son said. He was losing his hair, inch-long strands dropping from his scalp, and as Harriet ate with him, she noticed a single hair pasted to a spinach leaf. Making certain he didn't see it, Harriet speared the leaf with her fork and swallowed it.

Afterward she scratched her son's back. It was something she'd done years ago. The little-boy Marshall would stretch on her lap, keeping still while she lightly scrubbed her fingernails back and forth across his skin, drawing outlines of animals and houses, faces, entire towns. After a time, she would use the same fingers to tickle him.

But in the hospital Marshall couldn't lie on her lap. He leaned forward, his robe tied tight around his rib cage. He wouldn't show the body beneath it. Harriet hummed a half-remembered melody as she used her fingernails, just as before. After she had scratched his back for what seemed half an hour, Marshall cleared his throat. He told her, "You're going to be okay, Mom."

At first she thought it an odd slip of the tongue, that what he'd meant was "I'm going to be okay." Then she realized what Marshall was saying. Her hand ceased its crisscrossing motion. She held her son tighter, just a little. They stayed frozen in place like figureheads. Carefully, Harriet leaned to rest her head against his shoulder.

A violet tone in the sky looks like a bruise, like the marks on her body left by the rocking and twirling carnival ride. To the west, a green crescent of cloud signals hail; there, in sudden nebula, the burst of heat lightning. As a girl, she was told never to walk in open fields. One should wear a china cup on a string around the neck to avoid lightning. Cross your suspenders, hide beneath the feather bed, refrain from petting animals. Now those superstitions are gone. No one left to tell them; no one caring enough to hear.

Near the spot where the tree shelter thickens, ducks glide along the pond. A mallard unzippers the water. Nothing and no one is around; nothing and no one knows she is here. Harriet removes her scarf and brushes cat hair from her robe. She pulls the robe over her shoulders, lets it drop. The air is lace on her legs, her stomach, the scar where her breast used to be.

People call her crazy but phooey on them: her vision is still good, her hearing shipshape. Even here, beyond the pasture's towering grasses, beyond Jellybean, she can see the individual ridges on the farmhouse shutters. She could take off running, could leap the barbed wire and jog through the dark wood; she would be an animal, she would let the storm drench her.

Banked at the water's edge is an abandoned boat with a faded blue interior. It holds a tattered rope, an orange life vest. Does the boat belong to a neighbor? Surely it isn't hers or Marshall's. It would be easier if something here *were* his: a sapling he'd planted, a stranded fishing line with yellow-and-orange bobber scissored loose and floating after his unfortunate cast. She could anchor herself, then; could crouch at the tree, could cry, could rake her fingers through the nutmeggy earth. She could wade in, drag the line free. But there are none of these things. *As if he were never here.*

Yet there is something. Harriet goes to the tire swing and stands before it, running her hands along its squeaky circumference. She remembers the way Marshall fit snug into its center; how swinging high enough would take him spiraling over the water, a whoop and a jump slinging him out, a nimble satellite, to splash into the pond.

The tire proves difficult for Harriet. Its lower arc sags when she slides in. The tumescent rubber stains her skin, rubs it raw. She stabs a toe into the percolating mud and pushes herself in motion. Forward, returning, a pendulum, the rope straining, the branch protesting its ancient whine. Sarah will be calling any moment now, checking up on her. Harriet closes her eyes; arches her feet to swing higher. She visualizes the kitchen telephone, ringing. The teapot on the stove's front burner; the cabinet where the blue glass ice-cream bowls wait and wait for someone, anyone, to use them again; the battered refrigerator with its alphabet magnets. The green and pink and bright-lemon letters spell Sarah, spell Boris, spell Harriet and Marshall. He had run out of some letters—*Silly goose*, she had called him—and had inserted the final *R* into her name but omitted it from his.

Harriet navigates the swing, lifting over the pond. She leans her head back: the world dips, turns, whirlpools. There are shadows and light, but the shadows are more beautiful. The swing was meant for a child. Now Harriet and Harriet only; she is all that is left. She is small enough to squeeze here, to defy gravity's cradle and loft her body up, up. In her mind she can see it: Right now, the cats are hovering patient beside their feeding trays. The chairs wait empty at the table. The answering machine clicks to life on Sarah's call. The recorded voice, filling the kitchen air. "Hi, it's Marshall. Mom and I can't take your call right now, but if you leave a really quick message, we'll get back to you ASAP." *Beep.*

6

holding you, my duty assigned by the gods,
oh, allow my arms your blessed strain.

*B*oris, teeth gritted, finishes his latest poem with these lines. The paean to Rex is as yet untitled, three pages long, all letters written in lowercase. He has troubled over this one all day, furiously jotting stanzas between classes. Now he folds and pockets it. He sits outside, beneath the cafeteria windows, disconnected from his schoolmates' lunch-hour congregation. A tape blasts top volume from the machine in his belt loop. Guitar feedback distorts the music's voice beyond comprehension, so Boris invents his own lyrics: Rex this, Rex that.

Boris picks at his lunch, tasteless cafeteria fodder the state provides free for foster kids. He chucks his bruised apple at the street. With forefinger and thumb he bulldozes a path through the damp earth, chips of mortar and pebbles, ending where ivy starts its green creep against the school's bricks. Boris brushes off his hand and waits. Waits longer. Just as he prepares to give up, Carl finally shows.

They've agreed to meet here, a spot remote from the hazard of being seen. Carl's only a freshman; a chat with weirdo Boris, if someone caught him, would annihilate his burgeoning cool reputation. Boris can guess his reasoning: glimpsed together at Sunflower is one thing; at Lawrence West, out of the question. To Carl's eyes, Boris wears his hair too long; looks, talks, and acts a smithereen too feminine.

No matter. Last week, when Carl discovered Boris ordering his mementos of Rex, they struck a bargain. At Sunflower, the CINCs get daily "checkbooks," receiving "payments" for good behavior, yet fined demerits for missing curfews, fighting, swearing. Boris thinks all of it silly, but the supervisors believe it builds social skills. Since Carl's currently low on checks, Boris devised a scheme. "I'll repay you with my extras," he told him. "All you have to do is collect Rex stuff for me. Don't worry, you don't have to do anything weird, and you won't get caught. Besides, I'm going to use all of it, like, for my novel. You just gather everything together, and I'll get you the checks."

This afternoon, Carl wears his shirt buttoned low, a gold chain around his neck, a Royals baseball cap behind which curls a piggytail of blond hair. Under his arm, a textbook for remedial algebra and a notepad scrawled with more doodles and band logos than math notes. Backpack secured behind him. His slack face looks tired, stoned. He takes a furtive glance around his shoulder, miming a detective. Boris reads his lips—"I got things you'll want"—and removes the headphones.

Carl wriggles his body free from his backpack, drops it to Boris's level, kneels and unzips it. "First, I got to say how dumb I feel. Being your spy. But I'm doing it. Anybody could pick the locks on them hall lockers. At first this shit might not look like much, but I figure this should get me out of the hole, check and demerit speaking."

Laughter from inside the building, tens of throats vibrating harmonies: Is Rex's voice a part of that? Boris imagines Rex in the cafeteria, among his group. On the plate before him, a thick hunk of meat, a gluey lump of potatoes. Buttered roll, milk carton, gingersnap. As usual, Rex has pressed the gum wad to the plate for later chewing. He sips his gold Mountain Dew from a straw buoyed within the can, utterly oblivious of anyone, especially Boris, who might be watching.

Carl unsheathes a mess of papers. "Rex's homework or something." He hands sheet after sheet to Boris, who glosses over each: incipient sketches of a shop-class project; lyrics to a metal song; a paper, rife with spelling and grammatical errors, describing abolitionist John Brown's raids on nineteenth-century Kansas. Perhaps Rex needs these notes, but Boris's brain whizzes too fast with excitement to consider giving them back. He grabs the next thing from the backpack, a gray-speckled stone. "Who knows what that is?" Carl says. "A paperweight? It was just sitting there, top part of the locker, nada beneath it. I bet it's that fuckhead's pet rock."

Boris nearly barks, "Don't call him that"; decides against it. Carl never hides the loathing he carries for Rex and Rex's friends. The week school started, Carl was one of the gangly freshmen preyed upon by Wayne Hinton, Ellis Dermody, other seniors. The bullies chose a specific evening after final bell to attack; that night, Carl stumbled bloody-nosed into the Sunflower bedroom, his body drummed and walloped, a hanky of ice cubes pressed to his lip. "Look what I got from that guy you like and his friends." Although Rex had stood at the sidelines and had thrown no punches, Carl ultimately lumped those senior hoods together in his net of hate.

More trophies in the backpack. Carl draws out the suspense: "You probably know this, but that dude Ellis, he earns a half credit for working an hour for the vice principal, errands mostly, delivering interoffice mail and stuff. So earlier today I hid behind that weird bird statue, and I seen him give one of these to Rex"—Carl unveils a large manila envelope—"and I, like, got my hands on it." He gives the package to Boris. "Don't worry, I saved you the pleasure of opening it. Go ahead."

"I'd rather do it alone, later. That's all?"

"Well, the last is just information," Carl says. "First promise me again how many checks I'm getting."

Boris rolls his eyes. "You'll get the necessary amount." He turns the stone in his fingers, lifts it high, drops it to his other hand. "You can have ten of them, I don't care."

"Make it twelve. I'm practically risking my life here."

"Twelve then."

"Great." Carl begins by reminding him how Rex, Wayne, and Ellis are all enrolled in senior shop. "And you know that field trip your art class is taking? The one you told me you're planning to mysteriously get sick for?"

Yes: Boris's teacher has negotiated a tour, some Saturday in October, a three-hour bus ride to the Lucas, Kansas, home and gardens built and sculpted by a long-dead folk artist. She showed the students photos where a swami-faced Adam and Eve stood sentry before a grape arbor, a cement sign announcing GARDEN OF EDEN. Boris, inarticulate in class, thought the day sounded . . . *intriguing.* Yet he's so certain someone's going to laugh at him or thrust a fist against his face, he'll do anything to bow out. He'd rather spend the hours lying in the silk grass on Harriet's farm; moseying through town in Sarah's car.

"I found out the shop class is planning to go along," Carl says. Boris wants to question this, but Carl continues: "That shop-teacher dude is letting them take their own cars if they want. And all them fuckheads are planning on going. I bet money they'll get fucked up wasted and whatnot, and make a day of it. I also bet you wouldn't miss going along for the world now."

Carl has reached the end of his surprises. "Time to split." His eyes look bewitched, low-lidded and bloodshot. He shivers into his backpack, hustling off to copy a friend's math homework, to nose around various shady breaktime channels to see if anyone's selling weed.

Almost bell time, and Boris reexamines all that Carl's looted. He double-checks each direction as if for traffic, then unbends the envelope's silver clasp and tenderly slides a fingernail beneath the flap.

On first look at the contents, his emotions swirl and collide. Amazement, horror, a triple dose of confusion. There's a tattered map of Lawrence, some areas marked with small scarlet circles. And Polaroids: first, Wayne Hinton standing beside the girl from the carnival bathroom, her eyes lowered in embarrassment, his arm ringing her shoulders, fingers pinching her nipple. Second, a girl Boris hasn't seen before, sprawled on a bed, her denim shorts pushed to her knees, tank top hoisted to her neck. The girl's face is obliterated with slashes of ink. And layered beneath these are papers, pages torn from magazines. The pages show women, all naked, myriad sizes and skin tones. Curiously, bizarrely, all the women's heads are missing, severed from the magazine pages with single scissor swipes across their necks. A headless body spreads its legs, two fingers flaunting the startling carmine of sex. Another bends over backward before the camera, the cut V between her feet removing an upside-down head. A decapitated woman sandwiches a bodiless man's cock between her breasts.

Boris recalls the first time pornography slammed his senses. He discovered magazines buried under a foster father's bed. He listened hard as the house settled around him. No doors creaked open, no footsteps drummed on stairs. Boris turned the first page, and the room fell away. Adult bodies posed and lounged in hushed mummery, their faces like hornet stings. For years he's remembered that feeling: no lecture, no yardstick swatted across wrists can demolish it.

Pages, more cut pages of skin and makeup and secret smiles. Boris shuffles through them and, just as he's losing interest, comes to the photograph. He holds it tight, a simple three-by-five. A snapshot of Sarah.

She stands at the cash register in her burgundy convenience-store apron. Her face is unmarred, not Xed out like the other girl's. She wears the mute expression of boredom, her eyes glancing down and lost to the camera. On the nearby counter, behind their glass rotisserie, $1.95 sausages are stilled in their wheel and split.

What could the photograph mean? Boris stares at Sarah's face— *surely Rex isn't behind this, surely*—as an untranslatable knot of fear snags in his chest. He remembers Ellis Dermody's butterfly collection; imagines him assembling these pictures with that same persnickety detail. Boris reassures himself it was Ellis, perhaps Wayne, who took this photograph, who included it with the mutilated bodies.

He crams the contents back into the envelope; presses his nose to the flap's curve of glue; sniffs. A faint odor of mint, and maybe a hint of Rex's breath. He rewinds one integral line of Carl's: *Then he licked the letter closed.* Boris touches his tongue to the residue of glue, tickle-tasting the exact spot where Rex's lingered, earlier today. He's afraid to tell Sarah what he's seen. For now, he'll try to forget, to refocus his mind. His mouth sticks against the envelope. His imagination substitutes a film loop for the pictures inside. Within those magnified frames, two boys' eager lips pucker and meet, kapow, Boris's tongue connecting with Rex's in an immaculate kiss.

Boris loiters outside room 207, the door's polished BUSINESS AND ACCOUNTING plaque reflecting the worried slit of his mouth. He's late, no big surprise, for last-period typing class. The teacher's muted instructions float into the hall. "Eyes on copy. Ready, begin." Since his words per minute demolish the efforts of other class members anyway, Boris checks both directions for hall monitors, breathes deep, then speeds toward the bathroom.

Not a soul inside: only white walls, stall doors, urinals, five mirrored replicas of his apprehensive face. On the glass, graffiti is superimposed over his cheekbone in a color too tangerine to be blood. THEY'RE WATCHING YOU, it reads. Deeming that an omen, he ducks into the furthest stall, secures the latch, lowers the seat and sits.

According to his watch, Boris has forty minutes before last bell. He lifts his feet above the bottom level of the door. The bathroom air feels stifling, humid, like the air in a submarine. Still, it's a popular spot: final period usually grants misfits the opportunity to cloister in back corners of shop class, gym bleachers, parking lots, or bathrooms like this. Boris has skipped last hour before, but hasn't yet been caught. Here, he offers himself to daydreams, breathless on the toilet seat, legs cramped close to his body. He's memorized this stall, its predictable graffiti, its door's curlicuing knife scar like the trail of a desert snake. Sometimes he's spied Rex's buddies through the crack in the door, but You-know-who still hasn't appeared.

"To say John Brown was an angry Man would be telling an understatement. In this paper I will show Why he didn't want Kansas to go the way of Pro-slavery." So begins Rex's history paper. The teacher has calligraphied a small red D-plus in the margin, along with copious notes and suggestions for improvement, which Boris doesn't bother reading. Instead, he examines the signature at the page's upper corner. It's less cursive than child scrawl, the *J* of Jackson dangling an oversized fishhook into the text below. Boris loves the way that name sounds: the crash of it, the parallel fricatives of its two words. Yet if he and Rex were left alone, he'd call him lovey-dovey names like prune danish, cherub, little newt, petunia.

Boris reads the paper; pores over the notes, the heavy-metal lyrics. Ten minutes. Fifteen. No sound but the chittering drip of an unrepaired urinal, the wee vibrato from the typing teacher down the hall, and, for one moment, the noise of alley cats sparring outside the window. He turns another page, hears the bathroom door open, lifts his stealthy feet, and peeks.

Wayne Hinton appears first. Boris catches an unmistakable sliver: cowboy boots spit-shined, personalized belt buckle, curious brown birthmark smack dab between his eyes. Wayne stands with thumbs in belt loops. He chugs two throatfuls from a miniature bottle of whiskey, drops it into the trash bin, and disappears from view. Boris hears the faucet jetting water, the pump of the soap dispenser. In the following second of quiet, the door reopens. Drew, Bobby, Ellis—and finally R-E-X—straggle in.

Their bodies zip past. They crowd into an out-of-view corner, bragging about classes they've skipped, Wayne's voice dominating. The air clouds and thickens from their pot smoke, making Boris's head woozy. Although his back and ankles hurt, he crouches, face jammed close, pulse crashing against his temples. He remembers that night at the fair, his eyes squinting for details within that other bathroom's darkness.

One of the boys pisses, flushes, disregards washing. Their voices relay. "Five-thirty, right?" "I might be late." "Better fuckin' bring that ten bucks you owe me." Two forms flash past the door crack, then another. Ellis's hair—so blond it's almost white—and his near-albino face. Wayne: "Five-thirty." Ellis: "See you then." The bathroom door's creak. Its slam.

Boris waits, silently counting. Someone remains in the room with him, breaths steady, sustained. Fifteen, sixteen . . . Footsteps shuffle, skid, skid, stopping before the mirror. Twenty-one, twenty-two. Boris squints harder and sees: Today's inexplicable luck has doubled. Rex is there, alone, regarding his reflection by pushing forth chin and bottom lip as if mugging for paparazzi. Visible is a side of Rex's head, his mirror image, and the black sliver of the stall doorway. A ball of sweater fuzz sits caterpillarlike on Rex's shoulder. He keeps a wallet in his back left pocket, exhibiting top edges of bills, photos, cards, licenses. His licorice hair still needs trimming.

Right now Boris feels so smitten his thoughts are skewed, but later he won't believe the day's good fortune. Rex has never stood so near, now less than five feet away. Boris can smell him: Exquisite earthy odor of his sweat, and the heavy spice of his cologne, that muskiness from the pine-green bottle Rex dabs to his thumb between classes. Tomorrow, Boris will dawdle at the drugstore's health-and-beauty counter, sniffing a sample bottle of that cologne, like the integral clue to an unsolved murder. He will smear some on his wrist and drift off to sleep breathing it.

Rex takes the glasses from his shirt pocket: the chunky, black-framed spectacles he rarely wears. He positions them on his nose, close-inspecting a zit in the mirror. He moves nearer than a jeweler would for diamond dust. "His skin is holy, and my desire for salvation feeds from it," Boris once wrote in his journal. He believes its imperfections make Rex sublime; the higher the level of beauty, the more fascinating and profound the scar or blemish.

Zit eradicated, Rex removes the glasses and spins around, disappearing from vision. *I've been caught,* Boris thinks. His heart feels peppered and cooked, and he brings his fingers to his mouth. He bites, tasting the charcoal from that morning's art class. The neighboring stall door slams and locks, and then, then, the unmistakable sound of Rex's zipper unzipping.

Through the bottom of the door, Rex's red sneakers, facing the bowl. Rex is only pissing: *He could have used the urinal,* Boris thinks, *for that.* The piss hits the water, a frenzy of bubbles. Boris hears Rex briefly miss his aim, the stream a-wobble. He imagines the needlestick hole, opening for the release of pressure; imagines Rex's callused index and thumb, steadying himself toward his target. Boris feels the warm landslide of desire in his stomach's hungry center. His crotch swelling. Rex's flow weakens, trickles, stops, and then he stands still, the door crack filling with his frame.

Now the held breath, the sloppy heartbeat in his temples and wrists. Boris thinks of Sarah's face, amid the shrapnel of butchered pornography. It couldn't have been Rex, it couldn't. He imagines the halo encircling Rex's head, platinum light limning his face, wings sprouting from his back to uncrinkle into shape. Rex will scoop him in his arms. They will take flight above the high school, above Sunflower, above Lawrence and Kansas and the rest of this cankered world.

Rex leaves the bathroom at last. After a safe duration, Boris opens his stall. His mirrored face glistens, a mask of sweat and excited flush. From down the hall, the teacher's voice lifts its proclamation—"Forty-four words per minute with absolutely no mistakes!"—followed by a choir of cheers and applause. Boris takes three steps into the adjoining stall. Rex has forgotten to flush; the piss remains in the bowl, a bright marigold yellow. A jeweled bubble cluster floats at the surface. Bright drops fleck the rim like nectar bled from gold.

The rest Boris does without thinking, not caring if he's caught. He makes a beeline for the science lab. The room is empty. He hurries around a table, opening drawers. Scatters Bunsen burners, Klein bottles, blue-tinted pipettes. At last, a clattering drawer of glass test tubes. Boris selects one; finds a cork inked with "Senior '97," and sallies out.

The bathroom is still empty. Boris kneels before the toilet bowl, sniffs, then dunks the test tube. It makes a single comic *glug,* filling to the top. Boris lets some trickle out, stoppers its mouth with the cork, wipes his hand on his jeans.

The tears are rising but he blinks them back. At home waits another of Sarah's installments for his novel. He will read it; he will bend in diligence over the pages of his latest scene. But first, he will place the test tube at the top of the now-crowded Suffering Box, alongside OSTIT's toe; the plastic skull Sarah won at the fair; a rubber-banded group of Harriet's photographs. The urine will be the true treasure, the centerpiece. Boris grips the tube in his fist, relishing its warmth in his hand.

Outside the windows, school noise blankets the air: shuttle buses revving into gear; cheerleaders shrilling their two-four-six-eights. Near the football field, the marching band begins its after-hours practice, trombones and tubas and trumpets thundering the national anthem. As the final bell rings, Boris hums along with the band. He lifts the ultimate memento of Rex, star-spangled and gleaming, into the late-afternoon light.

—S.

At twelve I ached to be a gymnast, it was the only life I wanted more than movie star. My friend Suzanne & I stared transfixed at the Olympics on TV, we were going to become those girls, it didn't matter that french fries & egg sandwiches & malted-milk balls had made Suzanne dangerously overweight, that I'd already grown too top-heavy to accomplish the skill & grace of their flawless bodies. Late afternoons we'd huddle together beside the trio of evergreens near the junior high school, practicing practicing until the sky started to purple. The patch of browning grass became our mat for the floor exercise, a broomstick handle our balance beam, we'd prepare for our dismounts, jumping, landing on our toes w/arms out stiff, our flourish. We made cardboard cutouts w/various scores red-markered against the white squares: 9.75, 9.9, the exquisite 10.0 for those rare moments when we'd nail the landing, every elbow, hand & finger poised faultlessly toward a God we no longer believed in.

Jerry was Suzanne's older brother, sixteen, he used to tell me things like I know what you need & You're the school slut, made specifically for fucking & Won't you make somebody happy someday. He had shoulder-length curly hair the color of no one else's, a color straight off the honeycomb, he never washed but it still looked silky-pure. I can still hear him talking, every third or fourth word a cuss, he buzzed around town in a Ford pickup, back wheels jacked chest-high, him & his two drugged cronies dragging Main until wee hours trying to pick up chicks. Some nights I'd stay over at Suzanne's, we'd wake hearing them tear back into the house, slamming doors, devouring dead things her mom had thawed in the fridge, turkey legs, bologna, sausages in their pinkish casings. I was scared of Jerry & the other two, but I also felt something else, after Suzanne drifted off I'd push my hands against myself thinking of him, maybe the three of them, they were somewhere in the house, breathing, still eating, waiting for me.

One weekend when winter had only half arrived my parents left on one of their gambling trips, I stayed w/Suzanne, her mother so used to me by now she didn't bother saying Hi when I burst through the door. I remember Jerry was there & the way he gawked at me in my tight beaded sweater let me know he wanted to shove himself far inside me. I found Suzanne & locked her bedroom door behind us, the scent of those boys hot in the house, I wanted nothing but to hide awhile but Suzanne said What's wrong w/you scaredy, Jerry's taking us up to Pemberley's.

Suzanne didn't care much for her brother but like me couldn't pass the chance to be scared out of her gourd. The Pemberley place was legendary, an old mansion west of Lawrence, connected to a dark dirt road by an even darker stretch of driveway, someone had slaughtered someone else there, decades ago, leaving a rot of brown bloodstains & a moaning ghost tons of townspeople swore they'd heard. Cottonwood trees hemmed in the house, half destroyed by years of lightning blasts, animals creeping branch to branch w/eyes flashing flashing in the dark. In the surrounding pasture, clusters of birds & cows some caretaker fed now & then, when those animals cheeped or mooed they inevitably sounded human. High school kids drove to Pemberley's to fuck or scare each other shitless, us junior highers only dreamed about it, me dreaming the most, dreaming myself the star of some bloodchilling film where I ran room to room chased by packs of insane killers.

We scooted into the truck w/him, Suzanne in the middle since I felt goose bumpy, I could tell right away Jerry was shitfaced. I didn't protest & heard the engine thrum to life, then he looked over w/that same sick look & said Gotta get Paul & Bradford first, once again I didn't protest although Suzanne's pinch on my thigh let me know she wasn't enthused either.

When the other two got in, the booze on their breaths smelled the same as Jerry's, I knew they'd been drinking together earlier, all was part of a plan. I didn't remember which was Paul, which was Bradford, but one kept shivering, not a cold-weather shiver but the desperate kind from some feeling inside, that Oh-oh, I'm scared, I'm about to do something monumental feeling. Of course the girls got the boys' laps & Jerry was laughing, each haw-haw fat & wet w/whatever juice he'd been slugging.

The speedometer needle edged to the end of its arc, Jerry took the curves at 60 mph, houses & trees whizzing past the truck. Riding unsafeguarded w/a maniac driver, terrible but also thrilling, my throat & chest tightening ecstatic, we were outside town, moving further away toward something I knew I'd remember forever, no one spoke for a long time which meant they knew it too.

The boy in the middle shifted under Suzanne's weight, he fished out candy from one pocket, we took one each. They were Zotz, purple grape lozenges I loved because the middles fizzed, the boy laughed a little, he said The center is like cum, you know, not come but cum, the way they spell it in dirty magazines. I felt creepy & then he struggled to pull something from his other pocket, a bottle of Jack Daniel's & the black label looked scary, as if advertising poison, but when they passed it around I took two lame sips. I felt the burn & tensed up, the boy beneath me clasped his hand on my arm, the cold silver on his class ring pressed hard into my skin, hurting, the moonlight reflecting white & pregnant in its fake amethyst sparkles. If I'd been in love I would have found something romantic in that, but I was only twelve & couldn't even remember this boy's name & when I opened my mouth to say Ouch he just pinched harder.

Jerry cranked the radio, country-western, pedal steel guitar meowing loud, Oh darlin, the night is right for fallin in love. I stretched my leg, tensing the muscle, & thought of our heroes, those elegant skinny gymnast girls. Another round of Jack Daniel's & we were there, at Pemberley's driveway, the way Suzanne looked at me I knew she was scared too, Jerry started babbling, how years ago old man Pemberley had gone bonkers & hacked his family to bits w/a hatchet, then nibbled the tip of a shotgun, touched the trigger. Word has it you can still see flecks of blood on some walls, don't you girls want to see all that blood?

Recent tire tracks let us know others had been parking here, perhaps even that night, but for now we were alone, the five of us. I could feel the booze moving inside me like jittery hands, country-western clicked off, the silence made me hear my heartbeat. Follow us, Jerry said & we did. The boys held a flashlight each, three made of orange plastic, identical, as if they'd bought them specifically, we headed up a limestone path which I remember thinking perfect for gymnastics practice. The cones of white light passed across the rows of evergreens, two tree belts that shut out the wind & made things quiet, in one tree I saw spiderwebs, under another a child's toy truck crusted w/rust. Right then I got scared, the toy made it all real for me, a kid playing here in the path by the front porch as Pemberley came to get him w/the hatchet, chop chop, shut-eyed I heard Jerry yanking open the front door.

One of the boys said to drink more so we did, we each took another Zotz from the shorter boy, its sugar killing the bitter. Then the house was all around us, cold, floors carpeted w/dust & crumbs of fallen ceiling & concrete from the walls. The light beams bounced across graffiti in every color, I could see the names & graduation years & Suck My Dicks, we slinked to another room where a shattered window let in the chill. Here were shards of broken beer-bottle glass, more cobwebs, a fireplace stuffed w/the carcass of a raccoon, crumpled nudie magazines that Jerry's flashlight lingered over. In the corner a dirty mattress smelled of old rain, mice maybe, the steely stomach smell of someone's recent vomit.

Where'd it happen, Suzanne said, her words less than a whisper. Jerry clicked off his flashlight, now only two lights pointing to the floor like twin ghost skirts. Shut up about that, he told her, then I felt his hand on my wrist, Sarah you come here w/me.

Jerry eased me along & shoved me up against the windowpane. Another of the flashlights went out, now a single cone of light on one plaster-chipped wall, behind me Suzanne was saying words I couldn't understand but words I knew ended w/question marks, then I heard her take a deep breath & say That raccoon sure smells in here, c'mon guys let's leave. Suzanne, I said. Shut up a cottonpickin second, Jerry said, I got to show you something. Stop it, I heard Suzanne say.

Jerry put a fist on my shirt & yanked it up, then the hand undid my bra & pinched a nipple hard. He put his mouth on mine, right there the rough wintry chapped skin of his lips, his front teeth brushed my upper lip & I felt how one overlapped the other. The stubble on his chin &

cheek, whiskers soft as dandelion fuzz, I remembered Jerry rarely shaved in the winter, I liked the way that felt but was scared too. Then his tongue pushed in, for a second I let it lick there, then I licked back thinking this was all he wanted, he just wanted to kiss, that was okay, I could kiss back. Our tongue tips touched & he sucked at mine, trying to get at the back of it, drawing it into his mouth. The window felt cold on my shoulders & Jerry leaned against me, cock pressing at my stomach, he'd somehow gotten it free of his pants. I said Hmm which meant Wait but probably sounded like Yeah.

Stop it, Suzanne said again. Then she was quiet. I could hear the boys doing things to her, across the room. Jerry's head blocked most of my view but w/one eye I saw shadows, probably Suzanne's lying on her side on the mattress, another shadow on its knees behind her, one on its knees beside, its head thrown back looking at the ceiling, there were graffitied words behind them, gigantic, unreadable.

Jerry's fingers worked at my belt, unzipped my jeans, in two tugs they were at my knees. He reached down & curled the middle & index into my cunt, no touching or playing, just quickly painfully in. In one hurry-hurry motion he pulled his pants to his ankles, w/out thinking I reached for his cock, held on to it as if that would keep control over him, Jerry trying to kick out of his pants, I heard the clunk of the flashlight as it slipped from his back pocket onto the floor. He put his hand over my hand, guiding it up & down to stroke him, he made a motion w/his head to the floor like he wanted me there, that was where he wanted to do it. I knelt & pawed around until I found the flashlight.

I was on my knees, Jerry's hand moved from mine to clamp the back of my head, he pulled me toward his cock & I wrapped my mouth around it. I heard the watery squishy sounds the mattress made, sounds like boots tromping through leaves, I clicked the orange flashlight & w/Jerry deep in my mouth aimed the beam at Suzanne. There were three quick seconds before Jerry stepped back from the unfocused height he felt, three seconds between the light clicking on & Jerry smacking it hard from my hand, in those seconds I saw what was happening to Suzanne, what was happening to us. She lay on her back on the stained gray pinstriped mattress. One of the boys had hoisted her legs, the splay-out bent-kneed, the shocking white, I remembered how Suzanne could never do the splits. The boy gripped her feet, his pants were off, he was on his knees fucking her fast, six quick thrusts in the three illuminated seconds, his breath making cloud after cloud in the cold air. The other boy was stationed at Suzanne's head, his hands were on her mouth, I saw him pry it open, four fingers on one side, four fingers on the other, stretching her lips, exposing rows of teeth, pink gums framing them. The Zotz plopped purple from Suzanne's mouth, her stained tongue lolled as if it were a calf's the boy would drop medicine on, instead he centered his cock between the fingers, buried it in Suzanne's mouth like Jerry's was in mine. The cock fucked her mouth slowly, counterrhythm to the boy at the other side, I saw Suzanne's eyes clench closed.

All this happened fast fast fast & then Jerry's hand came down on the light. Turn that fucking thing off, he said, She's my sister for chrissakes, I don't wanna see that shit. One hand stayed at the side of my face, the other pulled at his balls, pasting them sticky & hard as plums against my chin. I smelled the dead raccoon again, Jerry withdrew from my mouth & lay beside me, fingers zooming back to my cunt & twirling to prepare it, I scooted to the wall, its cracked plaster, my legs bowing as he pressed beside me. Above was the window, the world beyond it, from the floor only a view of the treetops & higher higher the sky. An explosion of pain, pain a red pain, Jerry's cock inside me, now pain & again I felt his hands wedge between my back & the floor, clasping together as if praying, he pushed inside, pulled out & pushed inside again. I saw the sky, black w/holes punched here, here, & here. Jerry fucking me, I almost enjoyed it but knew I shouldn't, that wasn't right was it? Out the window were stars, everywhere, more clusters than I'd seen my whole life, as if I'd never really noticed them sparkle & hover & orbit. Jerry's fucking took on a weird rhythm I didn't feel part of, I remembered a school lesson about constellations & tried to remember their names.

Then one of the other boys scooted over, Jerry was standing but I wasn't, he was zipping & buttoning, I was still on my back w/my middle exposed, clothes bunched at my ankles & neck. The other boy stared at my tits & cunt but not my face & said Jerry is it my turn now, when Jerry didn't answer he leaped at me like a coyote. In my cunt his cock felt smaller than Jerry's & in my mouth his tongue wandered muscleless & lost. I didn't care anymore, I was there but I wasn't there, divided between stars that kept twirling beyond the window glass, odor of the fireplace's coon carcass, blurred motions & soft Suzanne whimpers at the opposite side of the room.

Then in the dead center of everything was the Bump bump. The noise came from above us, like a fist upon a back or a decapitated head striking floorboards. Bump. The boy stopped fucking, I felt him slide out of me like a knife exiting its wound, all the room's motion ceased. What's that, Jerry said, the boy wiggled away from me, their flashlights made two more beacons in the room, I let my eyes move over to Suzanne, naked but swiftly covering herself, face glistening.

It's Pemberley, I said, He's coming to get you. In the silence after my words faded a branch crick-cracked outside. No one breathed. Though I hurt all over, I smiled, baring as many teeth as I could, Pemberley Pemberley! He's coming for you!

The ghost, I felt them thinking, their terror whirlpooling amid the sudden smells of sweat & cum, smells more powerful than the dead animal because they glued to us, they were ours. The boys tucked & buttoned clothes, started stepping from the room w/out us, we paused, but w/nowhere else to go just followed, Suzanne staring at the floor but not seeing the piece of candy, her foot landed smack on it, I heard it crackle. I tried escorting Suzanne, I touched her arm, she drew away as if my fingers were ice picks.

When you're scared the faster you run the scareder you get, in no time the boys were back in the truck, Hurry the fuck up, I heard Jerry say. I tried to imagine myself one of two survivors at the heart-stopping close of a horror film I'd just seen, here I was w/my wounded compatriot leaving the terror lair of the psycho I'd just disemboweled in self-defense. But somehow the odd choking half-sobs Suzanne kept making as I led her through the front door killed the fantasy, I couldn't think

about it, I walked her back up the path w/the trees deep green-black &
whispering. Jerry's truck lights flared on, we flinched as if they'd just
tossed scalding water.

In the truck no one said a word, the kind of silence that stabs the
ears, I swallowed back the taste of Zotz & whiskey & over it all the
skin flavor of the two cocks, Suzanne seemed far away but strangely not
as far as the boys. If my gaze met any of theirs I knew some force would
send the truck out of control & we'd all wind up dead, I stared straight
down at my hand at the scratch of blood that wasn't there earlier. The
road zoomed under our bodies, it felt like it was moving instead of the
truck.

Later Jerry dropped us off on his and Suzanne's front lawn, then
sped away to take the boys home, he wouldn't come back, not tonight,
he couldn't look at us. Before we went inside we stretched out in the
grass, it was cold, we were still twelve years old, we lay & lay w/the
troubled unsinging birds high in the trees. Minutes passed, maybe hours,
then I got up & lifted my arms high above my head, palms out, fingers
stretched so tall the skin pinched. I took three steps, rush rush rush, then
leaned to plant my hands on the grass, in one fluid circular motion I
swung my body around, a flawless cartwheel, landing on both feet &
bringing my hands up to touch the lowest part of the sky.

I waited for Suzanne to judge me, our cardboard scores weren't there
but I knew what I'd received, knew I'd hit the perfect ten. She stayed
mum, didn't even glance up, & after I sat back down I pulled at the
grass which w/the oncoming cold had retreated into the earth, now dark
& withered & small as the curly hairs on a boy's bare leg. That was a
10, wasn't it? I asked Suzanne. Wasn't it? In the bruised silence I
could almost hear our hearts beating in synch. After a while I lay beside
her & stared where she was staring, beyond the overhang of trees, I
watched the stars disappear as pieces & pieces of sky took fire & burned
away.

7

*I*n the drugstore Harriet strolls down aisle seven, driven by habit. There are multivitamins and painkillers; bandages in neon, fleshtone, and tan. There are eyedrops and itch creams and glass thermometers magnifying filaments of mercury. Sapphire bath beads to soothe away the ache. "They know me by name here," Harriet tells Sarah. *Only now, there's no prescription left to fill.*

This is the sort of drugstore where an entire section has been devoted to soda fountains, desserts behind doored carousels, food that can be microwaved and served on chipped china plates. There is a Formica countertop and a part-time waitress carrying menus in an apron pocket. One can order rainbow sherbet; cheeseburgers layered with avocado or piccalilli; fish sticks shaped like the severed fingers of a winter glove. Once Harriet sat at the soda-fountain as she waited for her son's pills. She numbered four misspellings on the menu above the mirror. She thought and thought but only ordered ice water; plunked twenty-five cents into a midget jukebox. None of the tunes was familiar; she didn't touch a single button.

Behind the register, the saleslady watches a game show on a tiny TV screen. She idly clicks a ballpoint pen. Before her sits a coffee mug, in which rests a perfectly spherical scoop of pistachio ice cream, a chocolate cookie at its peak. She doesn't stir at their approaching footsteps. "Need help?"

Harriet looks to Sarah for assistance. "We're looking for wigs," Sarah says.

"We don't sell those no more." On the TV, a contestant punches a hole in a tissue-covered cylinder and pulls out a thousand-dollar check. The saleslady claps, then looks to Harriet with a gargoyle scowl. "We got hair *color,* if you want that. Back of aisle six. That's about as close as you're gonna get here."

"That's a great idea," Sarah says, and rounds to the correct aisle. "Shampoos, sprays, and oh, what are *these*?" She begins selecting boxes, holding the rectangular model photos to Harriet's head. "Now, hey, I need your attention. Which will it be?"

Mocha Creme and Roasted Chestnut seem too dark; Sunset and Claret, too brassy. Cinnabar most resembles the color Harriet used to have, before the gray began cresting her temples. "That one looks fine," Harriet says, "but this is something for youngsters. I'm afraid."

"Well, if it helps you decide, how about it's my treat?" They return to the counter. "I'll even do the dyeing for you." Sarah thumps down the box and reaches for money.

The hair dye bounces in the bag at Harriet's side. Thursday, and the stores stay open late; the sun shreds yellow through the trapeze arms of sumacs and maples. Years ago, parades would march here; Harriet remembers driving into town with the family. They unfolded lawn chairs at the sidewalk to watch the floats and high school bands pass. She saw a sunburned magician snag pigeons from midair; changeling children gussied up like sunflowers and shocks of wheat. Now, no more parades. Rushing rainwater has cracked the asphalt, crumbled the curb. Ahead are the flea market, the arts-and-crafts gallery, the candle store. Harriet will let Sarah shepherd her arm in arm, this shop, that. She will look for a sale on cat food, will spend her last dollars on rolls of film.

A group of boys congregate at the corner of Ninth. Every evening they risk police scolding, slashing the concrete with their skateboards, practicing new maneuvers and trick jumps in relayed bravado. Each is around Boris's age, their faces smooth and sheened with sweat. They are young enough to be Harriet's grandchildren. She would boil hot cocoa as was her habit long ago. She would recite fairy tales from memory as they drifted off, guarded close in sleep's warm carriage. She would tuck them in, would kiss their foreheads goodnight.

The pedestrian signal blinks *Don't Walk* to *Walk*. Sarah takes her hand, hurrying; as they pass, one boy stops mid-hotshot and stares. He has cotton balls stuffed in ears and a kneepatch giving warning: red exclamation point on gold pyramid. He laughs when he sees them, his sound a dart, striking bull's-eye. Harriet waves. "Greetings," she says.

The evening is deep blue and breezy, gloomy and subdued. Ivy cracks the seams of bricks. Pears rust on the branch. There are whippoorwills, mosquitoes, crickets wringing their serrated legs. And the cicadas, always the cicadas, groaning from elm bark and chimney-brick hideaways like martyrs, slowly burning.

Harriet crowds beside Sarah and lifts the bathroom window. Out there, wind whips the golf-course trees, moving shadows across the obstacles and lanes. The wind, its sound like butcher knives slicing the air. Too, Harriet hears voices from neighboring avenues; the grain elevator's trucks loading and unloading evening feed. Sarah wears a pair of plastic gloves and touches her, cautiously. "There's nothing to this," Sarah says. "Voilà! and you'll be beautiful. That is, even *more* beautiful." She prepares the mixture by jostling a tube of brown liquid, then tipping it into a bottle of white. There's a fizz like Coca-Cola, and a droplet plops to the floor.

Harriet grits her teeth and clamps her eyes shut. Curls the towel around her neck like a boxer. The serum drips onto her head, and Sarah massages her scalp. "You're better than a real beautician," Harriet says.

"I used to do it for Marshall." Sarah blunders a dye smear on the top arc of Harriet's ear, then smooths it away with her bare wrist. "And once for Boris. He wanted darker hair, but the second we finished, he hated it. He thought they'd kill him at school for getting a new color. I suspect he might have been right. We returned to the store and got the strawberry blond nearest to his natural."

"He mustn't've wanted his friends to see it."

"I guess not. I hate to tell you, though, but as for his friends, you're looking at them." Sarah gestures at the mirror, where Harriet's hair fans from her head. "It was more about that Rex character. The boy Boris likes. I saw him briefly from the Zipper that night at the fair. And I've seen him once before, part of the crowd when I've picked Boris up from school. He's okay I guess. Not really my idea of the utmost, though I'd never tell Boris that. I think Boris is better-looking myself. Marshall was more handsome too." At this, she pats Harriet's shoulder. "Rex is way tall, for one thing. Clumsy. And his nose is gigantic. Weird ears. Big big hands that practically hang down to his knees, big in the way of, you know, that one breed of puppy, when its feet are too big for its body. Oh, what are those things called?"

More voices in the street, laughing now. A moth stamps its talcum against the window screen. Harriet feels safe inside, soothed and warmed by the dye that will make her younger. Sarah's house settles and thumps: Marshall, dear one, insisted on calling it "the wacky shack." The paint is left over from the heyday of the golf course, the door frames cantaloupe yellow, the walls antacid pink. The sinks defy tradition, hot faucets on the right, cold on the left.

Checkerboard floors, slightly off kilter, clefted by the earth's restlessness.

Harriet feels the fingerbones scraping her scalp. "Doing that could send me to sleep," she says. "Off to Dreamland, you doing that. Even though it smells like the hospital."

After that they are quiet for a long time. The only sound the cold faucet's waterbead; the squeak of Sarah's fingers, spreading color.

All dye applied, Harriet waits at Sarah's front-room table. She wears a gabardine robe, wrapped up like a monk; she busies her hand in a bag of cheese puffs, making Styrofoam sounds as she crunches, the orange crumbs spackling her lips and chin. "I remember I used to buy you kids these things." Sarah would sleep over; Harriet would stay up with them, television blaring. Isn't that how it happened?

Sarah, cleaning the mess, answers "Yes" from the bathroom. She is older now, with her own house, own kitchen. She has arranged the gin, whiskey, and tequila bottles beside the cookie jar and sugar canister. A grape-blue bowl shows last night's corncobs and chicken bones. Thumbtacked to the wall above are her movie posters: blood-spattered devils cracking forth from bodies, men in masks raising relentless star-pricked knives. The pictures are make-believe; Harriet isn't afraid.

She checks her reflection in the side of the toaster and smiles. It isn't so hard. The dye looks more purple than cinnabar, almost resembling blood, her face ghost-floating below it. She listens to the sponge scratching on the bathroom porcelain; imagines the piston of the arm. "Boris is still working hard on that book of his," Sarah calls out. "He really wants to win that contest, just like I did, remember? I've been writing things for him, like he asked, though I'm afraid I treat the assignment differently than Boris. I don't quite—I get carried away. But you really should write him something, let him know what you're made of. Something like you used to write."

Before Harriet can answer, she hears the noise. It comes from the front yard, just outside the window. She pulls herself from the table, careful not to strain her back. She draws the curtain, breathes its stir of dust.

A car has parked in the street, behind Sarah's. Its high beams dazzle the VW, revealing its damage from behind. Harriet clears her throat—company, perhaps, dropping by for a visit—to alert Sarah. She ruffles a curtain corner, squints to examine, and in that moment something moves. An outline, a snowy, indistinct shape. Harriet draws back and focuses and now she sees the face, peering inside.

The face is a boy's, phantom-complected. There one second, gone the next. Within that moment its eyes shift focus: first a searching look for some possible excitement or mystery within Sarah's house; then the realization that Harriet stands there, a barrier. The boy seems to recognize her. His mouth opens like a tiny trap, and he sprints back to the passenger door. The car knocks bumpers with Sarah's and skids from the curb.

Harriet hollers. Sarah runs from the bathroom, the worry on her face. "Someone was here," Harriet says. "Some boy came peeking in your window." She feels her flustered heart, pumping. A prowler, someone undercover, the commotion! She clicks the screen door, her other hand scooping the air, beckoning Sarah outside.

The moon is a white rind; the stars, shaken out like sugar powder from some sifter in the sky. Pale brown sycamore nuts button the grass. Harriet smells the river, rushing, nearby, rushing. She sees the fiery glint from the car's taillights, there at the cul-de-sac's opposite end. Then the lights disappear. "Land sakes," she says. In her attempt to seem brave her voice goes soft. "Whoever it was, they took out of here in a hurry."

The wind bears the possibility of frost. Harriet feels its chill on her arms, on the bare ankles below the heavy robe, and, almost icy, the damp gluten in her hair. The fifteen-minute color has set; it is time to shampoo. She turns to say, "Let's get back inside," to link hands, but Sarah's expression halts her. Her mouth has widened and her skin has blanched and she stands, arms crossed in worry, staring toward her car. Harriet thinks of the day at the hospital, the identical position of Sarah's body when she saw the graffiti.

She looks at the car, Sarah, the car again. The night unwraps its noise: river frogs, crickets, grackles. The wind shifts shadows around them, disembodied velvets in blue and coal that conceal then reveal the painted words. Four seconds, five. And Harriet sees what has happened: more paint on the car now, additions so fresh the droplets still trickle wet trails, a sudden smell blending with the paint in Harriet's hair. She feels the fear, spreading cold through her body. They came back for them, they waited just beyond the wacky shack's windows and doors, trespassing on the place where she thought herself safe.

This time, the vandalism is simple. They have merely added to what was already there. A pedestrian black blot obliterates the S in FAGGOTS, converting the plural to singular. When Harriet shuffles closer to Sarah, she sees the same has been done to QUEERS. Finally, the people in the car have sprayed an X through AID'S VICTIM.

"They must have just heard," Sarah says. Her eyes are looking in instead of out. Her hands are fists, fingers tainted dark with dye.

In the street, the elevator's grain dust lowers its polleny luster. Harriet breathes it, motionless, husbanding her energy in case the car comes swerving back. Beside her, Sarah sits cross-legged in the grass; she finds a leaf, tears it, and tosses the scraps. Her eyes are closed and she has raised her knees to her chest, hugging herself.

The women wait beneath the chalk-shard stars. They wait and they wait, then turn and walk inside.

8

*B*oris and Sarah get lost, lost further, then suddenly aren't lost anymore. Out here, miles of land and nothing but. Acres gridded into plots that from the sky would look orderly and sensible but from the black roads seem an intricate maze. All is splashed with moonlight, guarded by planets and the seven sisters and the battering ram. One day Sarah will own land like this. She will have many people to love her and one person to truly, truly love. She will star in movies where everyone will suffer sobbing and she alone will survive for top billing in the sequels.

Sarah shuts off the ignition half a mile from the Jackson farm-house. They can't risk being seen, so she chooses a ditch thick with scrub and interweaving oak saplings. It is nearly four in the morning, two hours wasted from her wrong turn, but they have made it this far, they cannot go back. Earlier, before they left, Sarah parked below a streetlight; Boris translated Carl's sketchy directions and a county map. Left turn, right, pass a bridge, go five miles . . .

Meanwhile, she skimmed his school yearbook. On a glossy page, Rex's photo watched her with a face that would go slack with years of drink, would stare unblinking as girls stumbled, ruined, from his passenger-side door. Sarah prophesied this but didn't tell Boris. He tapped a green vein on the map and said, "Drive in this direction"; Sarah tore away, tires eddying rocks.

The emergency lights blink a crimson extraterrestrial glow over weeds and greenbriers, the lonely silt ribbon of road, the yellow warning sign with its silhouette of a leaping buck. Outside the splintered window, random night-bird songs trouble the air in low, clarinet-clear notes. Sarah slams the car door; Boris gently pushes his closed. In the emergency flare, his apprehensive face shines red. He wears a Band-Aid on his neck, disguising a pimple Sarah noticed yesterday. "Let's go," she insists, plodding forward, leaving the slanted shoulder for the open breadth of meadow.

First they cross to a broomweed field neighboring the Jackson land. Limestone posts stand guard at fence corners, antique mavericks shackled with ivy. Sarah trains her eye for puddles or cowpies; if she even thinks of snakes, she'll scream and spoil their mission. She asks, "What is his family like? Brothers and sisters? Their history?" But Boris only answers, "I don't know; have no idea; only what Carl's told me."

Carl has gleaned knowledge from one of Rex's previous girlfriends. Charlotte wears too much makeup, chews on straws and the skin around her fingernails, and speaks with both lisp and strangled voice. "Sounds like a replica of me at that age," Sarah says, then lets Boris continue. Charlotte told Carl that Rex's father works for the local rock quarry; of course, he farms, all chores assisted by Rex. Weekends, for supplementary cash, the mom delivers armfuls of egg cartons to a co-op; needlepoint pillowcases to a booth in Quantrill's flea market. Charlotte couldn't reveal much more. She dated Rex for three months last year, losing her interest when he began spending more time with his pals than her. Boris shrugs and finishes: "She told Carl that Rex was a lot stranger than you might think. She called him 'head-fucked.' Ellis and Wayne too: 'head-fucked.' Whatever that means."

They pass a shelterbelt of trees hunkering low in soot-shade robes and endless bonelike limbs. Their shadows tremble like fish in pool shallows. Bullfrogs burp, dreamy, slow. Further, further off, the whinny from a sleepy mare that senses their presence. Sarah thinks of Marshall, their teenage obsession with midnight horse-back riding. She thinks of his hair, streaming in the horse-drawn wind, yes, that silly bleached high school haircut she proudly gave him, all those years ago.

Risk rests everywhere: There are thatches of sandburs and this-tle; curls of poison ivy; ankle-twisting vines sprouting buffalo gourd. Brome dust sifts in histamine clouds; unseen wings flap low in the sky. "I'm remembering this," Boris says. "My mind is making zillions of notes. It will all fit into the novel. Somehow."

Sarah swerves a water-steeped trench in the soil. "Harriet and I are pulling for you. I can see her now, snapping pictures of you and your trophy."

Yonder is the barbed wire to separate the fields, towering rows of grasses, and, out of view, Rex's farm. Before they reach the bor-der, Sarah bends to the loose sand, the curious smolder of a spent fire. Someone has excavated a hole, made a pile, fanned the flame that still sifts gray smoke. Boris nudges his sneaker toe to the coals glowing an apricot brandy. Within the pyre are remnants of what has burned: edges of timeworn newspapers; warped vinyl arcs from records; the scorched, splintered corner of a Ouija board. Sarah fishes out the piece of board with forefinger and thumb: the somber face of the moon; the single word NO painted beside it.

"Maybe this means something," Sarah says. Once she might have saved the board; now she drops it back to the char and rubble. "I'm not taking chances after my little window peeker." When she told that story to Boris, he nibbled a fingernail and lifted his legs into her kitchen chair, hugging his knees. Later she retold the incident, downplaying, assuring him not to worry. She didn't want to fib to

Boris, not with everyday occurrences, not with the stories from her past. But it's easy to tell a lie, she knows, when nothing happens the way she wants it to happen.

Sarah helps Boris between two rows of fence, then stretches the wires for herself. The breeze shifts, scudding through the tall roland grass, the sway and the nod of its silver-tufted heads. She cautions him to ease through: the green leaves are ribboned with silver, stiff and razor-sharp enough to puncture skin. Beneath their feet are wingless insects and applesauce mud. One tromping step, another, each footprint filling with water.

Boris and Sarah emerge together, arms crashing from the reedy curtain. The noise awakens butterflies from slumber, an eruption above their heads like a tornado of blossoms. "It's beautiful," Sarah says. She means the swarm of insects; and too she means the farm.

The moon and stars illuminate a gambrel-roofed cottage, wood gone gray and splintery with age, its backyard flower garden now spread with manure and hay and mulch. There is a mammoth truck, presumedly driven by Rex's father—DOUGLAS COUNTY ROCK QUARRY, say the doors—and the bed brims with gravel. There are cantilevered livestock shacks, chickens and horses and perhaps a bacon-ready hog or two, all kept hushed behind weather-beaten doors. Beyond those, a plot of corn, now hacked and burned, the burnished quarter-stalks spearing from the sand. The whole farm resembles something from a book, perhaps a monochrome illustration to accompany stories of early homesteaders. Sarah watches it from the veil of butterflies. Their bodies meander and veer and lift from sight. Her hands grapple through their sky, and they ride the bridges of her fingers, colliding.

"This is where he lives," Boris says. "We're trespassing, right here where he lives."

She follows him to the ramshackle animal pens. At their left stands an ancient windmill, its slatted propeller wheel like a daisy of rusted tin petals, stirring in the predawn breeze. Horses, cattle, have patterned hoofprints in the earth around its circular trough. The windmill's pump is silver, heavy, knobbed like the excavated bone of some extinct beast; Sarah and Boris halt and clench their fists around its handle. They pull, cautious not to make a sound, and when it creaks they stop. In the hazy mantle of moonlight Sarah sees the shadows of her head, Boris's, the rotating windmill blades. The water shudders, platinum waves on onyx, and after a second of silence comes the feeble trickle, churning deep from the earth to pinprick the trough's level. Sarah lowers to it—once, in a movie, she saw a glamorous girl do this—and lets it drip into her mouth.

In the near distance, the horse neighs again. Another droplet strikes the water. "There is so much to learn here," Boris whispers, and Sarah knows he wants Rex to show him all, to instruct on the mechanics of the water pump, the chore routines, the ho-hums of his life. Sarah knows because she remembers that ache of unrequited teenage love, the sorrow every misfit and eyesore and loser feels. She understands why he loves Rex. Wrapped within that understanding is her own love for Boris.

A woodburned sign, wired to the screen door of one shed, reads CHICKENS. A neighboring door reads GEESE. Hanging from each sign's corner are respective pairs of birds' feet, the hard striated yellow of the chicken, the webbed tangerine of the goose, perhaps salvaged from holiday feasts. Animals: Sarah loves Marshall's horse, no doubting that; feels a galvanized charge when touching Harriet's purring cats. But chickens! Geese! They repulse and terrify her. "I'll watch from here."

Boris shushes her, grips the chicken door's hook, swings inside. He looks behind to assure security; disregards the chained bulb that dangles from the ceiling. One brave pullet struts closer. Its white sides flecked with jetsam; its generic head and wiggling crest; its demonic cranberry eye. Boris moves further into the chickenhouse, and Sarah hears the birds' low, somnolent clucks; their forked feet kicking wood chips and hay. She smells a woozy rush of tobacco and recalls one of Harriet's farmwife beliefs: tobacco leaves in hen nests to eradicate parasites.

Boris discovers a single egg; another; two within one roost. "One of my foster dads kept chickens," he whispers. "He had Rosecombs and a few prize Java blacks. He would smoosh his hand under, right as they were laying, pulling out eggs. But sometimes they pecked him." Sarah can barely discern his outline, exploring the shack. "Unbeknownst to him, I discovered this trick," he says. "It's amazing what they do. Sick too. Watch."

He shuffles into view and in his hands are the eggs; now he rares back and as she stares Boris hurls them, bam bam bam, into the base of a post. At the sound of the crunch, the birds spring forth from their thrones. They dip heads to the broken yolks, drugged, swirled silly with the smell, their beaks needling the oily yellow. Each fights, a cannibal, for the best throatful of egg. Boris stands back, and they devour the food in seconds.

Sated, the hens bicker and peck; scratch at each other with gold genie's feet. "That's repulsive," Sarah says. She can't watch anymore. "I'm going to check out the goose pen. Come on over when you want."

The geese live ten steps away, behind a screen door scarred with wire snags, sparrow droppings, two cicada shells like gold brooches. Inside, Sarah's eyes adjust to the half-darkness: rows of slatted pens, the miniature troughs filled with hills of sorghum and oats, watering jugs smeared with mud and meal and shit. Dust and tendrils of goose down float within the slurry window light. Hornets nanny the room from their pulpy ceiling nests. And, squinting harder, Sarah sees the geese. Their worrybead eyes regard her from a corner; some stand statue-still but others honk softly, saving their noise in the possibility she might roam closer.

Boris moves inside, door slamming behind him as he tap-taps her shoulder. "I stole us some eggs. Some for Harriet too. Breakfast. Some big, some small, brown and white and in between."

"Don't go near them," Sarah says. "All the ganders do is eat and shit and fuck. They'll kill you if you go near their women. Once I saw one attack a little boy." And she remembers that park, strolling beside the goldfish pond as she held her uncle's hand. She remembers the boy, the careful way he inched too close. The squeal of the goose, its churning wings against his back. The boy screaming, blood in speckles on his face. Her uncle gripping her hand tighter, hoisting her in his arms, in just the way he held her sometimes, not often but yes sometimes, in his giant bed with her eyes closed and her face pushed flat into the pillows smelling of trees.

"There, there in the corner." Sarah steps into the charnel shadows and brooding quiet. Now nearer, more terrified, her body coursing with the same apprehension she felt as a girl. She tries to count them, but their bodies seem a single blur of white feathers, spiriting and swaying within the dark.

Boris ambles toward her. "I can't believe I'm here." His eggs tickle and clack, cradled together inside the pouch he's made from his shirt. "This is the place," he says. His voice rises, thrilled and girlish. "This is where he comes every morning before school, he stands precisely where we're standing, I can picture his face, his hand filled with grain and scattering it at the birds." Boris has forgotten to whisper, his volume agitating the geese, and although Sarah says, "*Shhh,*" he doesn't listen. "Jeez, Sarah, I swear to god I would do anything for him, I know that sounds totally stupid but he's completely taken control—"

Closer, an arm's length closer. Now she has moved too close. Boris stops midsentence; says, "Oh no." Most of the geese remain huddled in the corner, but one begins strutting from the pack. It is huge, nearly as tall as her chest. Sarah jumps back, inhaling quickly, and spurred by that sharp whistle of breath, the bird comes trumpeting for her, bill pointed to the roof in fanfare. Sarah freezes, stunned. She hears Boris spin, his fist smacking the screen door.

And then it leaps. It honks, throat angling on the rigid diphthong. A single nauseating soar in the air: its flapping cymbal-crash wings, the bleached *W* of its feathered scut. Its mouth like two unsheathed pocketknife blades. Sarah screams and screams and she whirls, but the goose is upon her. Its webbed feet catch like orange forks in the small of her back. Its beak clamps the nape of her neck, piercing her flesh. The goose pounds its wings, great slaps of its angel arms, faster now, shuddery beats pummeling her back. The air heaves around her, smelling of sawdust, grain dust, the dead peppery feathers.

Sarah falls then, face first on the shack floor. The earth pushes into her mouth and nostrils, a residue of goose shit and mud. The bird falls with her, persistent as a lover. It continues voicing warning, the bill like thin scissors at her neck, slicing up, flicking at her earlobe. The bill finds the silver hoop of Sarah's earring, pulling, pushing-pulling, until the circle tears away. Sarah screams again, pilloried and struggling to free her arms. She tastes the floor's jellied recrement but still she fights the bird, her arms punching at her back.

The goose beak strikes her neck, brief and hot, cutting at her flesh in staccato, steel-brand slaps. Its shriek on her face: the neb clapping closed, clapping and breaking her hair. And then Boris is there. His face ashy, jaw clenched, his arm flung behind him in a pitcher's windup. Sarah feels the first egg explode on her shoulder. The next catches the bird mid-scream in the face. It flaps away, and when Boris hurls another egg, it scurries off.

Sarah stumbles, helped up by Boris. He jerks his head in the direction of the door. "They've heard us," he says—"Run"—and she bursts from the goose pen. She feels twin trickles of blood on her neck; wind whistling through the wound in her ear. The farmhouse porch light sends a blinding glare across the yard. *They have heard the noise, they're cocking their guns and coming to stop the prowler.* . . . Sarah must protect Boris; they cannot be caught. She grabs his hand, and together they fling themselves through the scratching jetty of juniper trees, hair tearing in branches, arms freeing grayblue berries that stain starbursts on their skin.

They gain momentum. Dew explodes against their faces, atomized from the predawn breeze. *The arrest, the mug shots, the headlines in the paper . . .* The road isn't far; if they rush they will reach the paddock fence, they will climb over. There. There. Boris still clutches the eggs, one hand pinching his shirt pouch, cautious to avoid breakage. "No one saw us," he says. "Please, please no one saw us."

The dawn's anticipatory light blushes everything, reminding them they haven't slept. Sarah thinks of blankets and aspirin, of warm tea, of lullabies oozing from the bedside radio, and as they get in the car she clicks off the emergency lights. "We made it," she says. Laughter surges a root-beer taste in her throat. She opens her mouth; the sound slips out.

Boris laughs too. He reaches out to brush egg smears, blood smears, from her neck. "It cut you," he says. He licks his fingers, swabs at her hairline. "It got your earring and, like, half your ear with it."

And now they laugh. No further sounds rise from the Jackson farmhouse; Sarah checks herself in the rearview, holds her breath, and starts the car. Around them, everything begins to pale, darkness lifting its socket. Harmless birds start to twitter and sing. Boris unwraps the thin adhesive strip of bandage from his neck, brings it to Sarah's ear, and folds it gingerly on her broken skin.

Sarah fries one egg side up for Boris, another over easy for Harriet, an adjacent sunrise and sunset in the silver pan. At the table, Harriet rubs her eyes, woken from a dream only minutes earlier by the tinny honk of Sarah's car in the drive. "Why so early?" she asks. "Trying to deprive an old woman of her sleep?"

"We're trying to get some protein in you," Sarah says. "Then I've got to hurry Boris back to Sunflower." She rattles the cactus pepper shaker like a maraca. She finds slices of bread and springs the toaster's lever.

Harriet slides her slippers across the floor. She has busied the kitchen walls with antique silverware and cooking implements, dried sprays of wildflowers hanging here, acrylics of bonneted children there. A calendar with a photo of a covered bridge, the page still folded to June. A weather barometer, a cuckoo clock she stopped winding months ago. Grinning, Harriet stretches to tip-toes, reaches high, tugs a cabinet handle. "I'll get the table ready." Boris goes to help, pulling Harriet's best silverware from a drawer.

When Sarah turns from the eggs, Harriet has set the table. There are four blue grosgrain place mats. Sitting atop are four plates, creamy blue rimmed with red roses, each centered before a chair. Boris hesitates, holding three sets of forks and knives; then he reopens the drawer, flanks the fourth plate with the final set. "Me and Boris will not enjoy a single mouthful," Harriet says, "until you cook one up for yourself."

The slices of toast leap free. Sarah arranges them with the eggs on Harriet's plate, then Boris's. Turning back to the stove, she sees the refrigerator magnets displaying their names: Sarah, Boris, Harriet, the misspelled Marshall.

"I'm scrambling mine," she says. "Chicken caviar." She cracks a large brown egg into a bowl. "Oh, nasty." A sludgy clump of red floats within the wedge between albumen and yolk. Harriet tells her to stay away from blood in the yellow: It's a terrible omen; a year of sadness, sheer sorrow concerning matters of love. Sarah should drop the egg into the sink and blast it with hot water until every molecule has disappeared. But Sarah refuses to believe such mumbo-jumbo. She cracks another, whisks the two together in the bowl. When the eggs are scrambled and fried, she heaps a fluffy lump on her plate, then one in front of the vacant seat, both lumps tarnished with scarlet.

Together they eat, soundless. Sarah reaches for the salt shaker, and as she does, Boris touches her face. "Look at this." He picks a single goose feather from her shirtsleeve. It is barbed and whorled, rounded at the end, a white quill that drifts in zigzags when he drops it. "I'll save it for the Suffering Box," Boris says.

He searches his pockets and pulls out the test tube, resplendent and precious with yellow. Sarah knows what is held inside but Harriet, unaware, only looks at him briefly before her gaze floats away to stop at the empty chair. Sarah continues to watch: Boris grins, lowers his head to his plate, fills his mouth with a forkful of egg. Then he tips the cylinder to his lips. He drinks half the amount of piss, swallowing one-two, washing down the buttery egg dropped from Rex's chicken.

Sarah goes on chewing. She finds his gesture beautiful, fused with love, nothing shocking or sensational. He must be thinking of Rex and the night's successful mission. He wipes with the back of his hand, as if drying his mouth from a slobbery kiss. "We did it," he says. Boris returns the test tube, half full, to his pocket. He stares at the sun's miraculous ingot, lifting red-gold and dripping wet, where the earth connects the sky.

"Yes, we did," Harriet answers. Sarah knows Harriet can't understand what Boris has meant. But it doesn't matter. "We did it together, didn't we?" Her voice sounds barnacled, messy with sleep. The left side of her hair is mussed. Harriet rises from the table and tugs at the kitchen curtains, moving them aside to allow the entrance of light.

Sarah stands. Boris stands. They surround Harriet, arms linking. Right now, none of them cares about another ill omen. The scraps of egg clot on the plates. The world corrodes and wanes. Together they wait at the window, faces glowing in utter awe, as the sun offers itself, hot and wobbly, to the blue blue morning.

Chapter 5

The trees slept standing up. When the Zombies lurched through them they woke, one by one, and began whispering secrets. They had witnessed the revenge upon the boy's foster father. Upon the girl's childhood teacher. They had heard the screams and smelled the blood. Through midnight fog they had watched the victims' shuddering bodies steaming red steam, lifting from where the claws had scratched, the teeth had bitten.

The man stood alone in the trees' solemn countryside. The boy saw him first. He motioned for the women to keep still. The Zombies slid behind two knotted oaks that the lightning had felled, the wind had tangled. The cold air had shrunk the moon small as aspirin, but even within this darkness the boy's eyes made out each detail of their victim. His hair and his skin, the bones and blood beneath. He seemed exhausted from woodcutting. Now he rested his ax blade on the earth and leaned on the handle. The boy remembered his friend's stories. How, long ago, this man had told her false promises, taken her far away to a dark abandoned house and done a terrible thing. A hand clamping the girl's mouth, the cold floor against her bare back.

And now, the revenge. Now he would pay.

The man's breaths clouded the air. They were among his last. They were hot and full, exhausted from chopping logs for the oncoming winter. As he raised the ax again he couldn't hear them, couldn't possibly hear the sticks snapping, the leaves crackling beneath dead feet.

The younger woman smiled; the older smiled back. They listened as the trees stirred the sticky wind. They walked on both sides of the boy, moving deep into darkness. Their clothes still fresh with their victims' blood.

She touched the man's back. It was the same that had bent over her, muscles tensing, all those years ago. From his throat came a strangled sound like a trapped animal, and he turned. Dropped the ax. From beyond the moonlit trees the boy saw the man's face change. Somewhere within his eyes and twisted mouth moved the electric current of recognition. His friend raised one hand. Landed it spiderlike on the man's face. Her jagged fingernails ripped across his temple, cheek, chin. Three lines of blood opened, spilled in hot parallels to the earth. The fingernails stopped at the neck, and after a moment's silent pause went digging for the throat.

The man's scream was cut short. He fell, and she fell with him. Now *she* was on top of *him,* as he had pushed himself against her, years back.

The remaining pair of Zombies rushed forward. The boy first. The old woman three steps behind. They leapt like dogs upon their victim, crowding in next to their friend. The man's fist pounded the earth, fingers opening and closing, desperately searching for the protective handle of his ax. They could see his stomach now, ripped in two long swaths of their friend's arm. They loved the way it felt, the easy cleft of flesh, hands tearing the body open, hot and seamless on their fingers like slitting fish down the middle. The boy tore through to the guts, blood splashing at first, then oozing out slowly. The old woman sat on the feet to prevent his kicking and bent down to sink her teeth into his leg.

The girl bit and lapped and licked at the wet exposed throat. Her victim made his final sound, a moan that wobbled with the roiling bubbles of blood. The Zombies ate, and when they were finished and full they stamped the man's remains into the earth, erasing all traces, and leaned together.

From a distance they looked like three animals, hunched in shadow beneath the trees for warmth or companionship or love. For a while there was only silence. And then the sound of laughter. It was human but not human, three voices sounding like two and then, at last, one. The sound lifted above the trees and carried on the wind and was gone.

On Fire

Part 2

9
October

*R*ain. On the fifth of the month, a pair of ten-year-old boys discovered the second missing girl. They were playing soldiers near an abandoned bicycle trail. They looked down from make-believe bazookas and grenades ("What the hell is that?" Boris imagines them asking, echoing Sarah's words when she spied the dummy) and there she was.

Unlike those of the first death, the particulars of the second death have leaked to the press. Boris and Sarah collect the daily newspaper clippings. She had blond hair, seafoam eyes, her sorority's Greek letters in diamonds on an ankle bracelet. Storms had decomposed her body, but couldn't obliterate the fact of murder. A dog leash twisted around her neck. She wore argyle socks, a single tennis shoe, a hooded sweatshirt. There were ocher carpet fibers in her fingernails; knife cuts upon ruined palms as pale as vellum. She had been stabbed fifteen times in the stomach and chest, but the river drained the blood, each wound now a shut mouth. Vanilla-scented candle wax plugged each ear. Her cheeks had withered to the bone, the lips below hardened dry as rubber bands. Inside their O was peach pulp, preserved in her molars, her final midday snack. Also river water, an elm leaf, and her wadded pink underwear. The sweatshirt's front pocket held the fortune from a Chinese cookie. The tiny slip of paper listed the girl's lucky numbers: 7, 23, 50, 99. The sentence, written in red, said: SOON YOU SEE REWARDING FOR ALL THE HARD WORK.

This morning's newspaper picture, an earlier shot than the one from the MISSING posters across town and campus, shows the girl in sorority dress and pearls. In the adjacent photo, weeds and snarls of shoreside branches obscure the twisted corpse. A small white circle delineates where the boys spotted her body. Three feet away, the Kansas River meanders, indifferent. It's all how Boris imagined it, just how he prophesied! He aims a borrowed magnifying glass, adjusting further, closer, trying to spot some microscopic clue. When nothing crystallizes, he tosses the paper three-quarters across his bedroom's length. He can't stop thinking of that night at the bridge: the mannequin; its hollowed-out sex.

Tree leaves drizzle rain against the window. Boris watches drops bead the glass, hold their trembling weight, then break in individual streams. Carl, snoozing, doesn't stir. The mobile above his bed drifts and spins, its stars and planets wobbling at wire ends. A long moment of quiet, eureka, but before Boris can enjoy it, the hall telephone cuts the silence. He half knows it's Sarah; waits for another CINC to answer. Knock, knock: "Phone. For Boris. Make it snappy, pretty please?"

Boris lifts the mouthpiece. "I can't leave. Saturday, and they've got me locked in. I'm on laundry duty too."

"But the afternoon horror series starts today," Sarah says. She's calling from work, but her shift "will be ending *pronto*. I want you to go with me. Now until Halloween, all month long. Double features." Boris hears her straw sucking the last dregs from a cup. "I'll see the first show by myself then."

Boris promises he'll try to break free, and Sarah lists the run-down of double features. But there's something even more excit-ing than horror films. "So, what about the newspaper today?" she says. "I'm sitting at the counter right now, reading and rereading. They told everything! What they found in her mouth! The under-wear! And wow, the fortune cookie!" On her end of the line, the cash register makes a quick series of blips.

Evening. Boris salves the floor with a soapy mop, pushing its white fibers one-two, one-two, matching the rhythm within his headphones' feedbacky blare. A supervisor yells from the laundry-room doorway; Boris's attempt at lipreading picks out the word "homework." Off to his room. He'd like to stomp there, but his movements are more like hobbles. Inside his left shoe, a fungus has been gnawing the gaps between his toes, no doubt from the show-ers after gym class. In fantasies, Rex's feet originally harbored the infection. His feet passed germs to Boris like a love token. Boris wants so desperately to believe that, he avoids the wealth of Sunflower's medicines and creams.

He tries his door; retries. Here, locking doors is forbidden. Boris assumes the rule was set after a past resident's suicide. On certain insomniac nights, he fabricates a scenario: a kid not unlike himself, splayed on the bed, with glassy rhinestone eyes and wrists gushing blood, as supervisors pound the door. Now he raps a knuckle once, twice. This isn't the first time his roommate has shut himself in. One month earlier Carl, on opening, grinned his snaggle-toothed grin and claimed the bolted door was "an accident." Boris smelled the musky animal scent of sex and smiled, but Carl knew he wouldn't tattle. They'd secured an agreement; Boris will never refer to the younger kid's shoplifting habits, his fascination with fire, or any other idiosyncrasy. Carl won't blab about Sarah's occa-sional night visits. He'll keep his nose out of Boris's bottom drawer.

According to the story, Carl's mom booted her son from the house after he poured kerosene on her kitchen floor, lit a match before her screaming face, let it drop. Carl prides himself: adolescent arsonist, thief, self-professed murderer ("more like *liar,*" Sarah said when Boris related these stories). Once Boris listed some of Carl's characteristics in his diary: (1) wolfs his food, (2) collects comic books, (3) enjoys watching things bleed, (4) longs to fuck every girl at school. Perhaps Sunflower's supervisors stuck Carl with Boris as punishment for both parties, but in the long run the setup's proved advantageous. Unlike most other CINCs, Carl doesn't wield the word "faggot" or tease Boris about his friendships with Sarah, Harriet, or, back then, Marshall. Lately, with Carl spying on Rex and Boris paying daily dues, they even consider each other friends.

Boris knocks a final time. He can't really call Carl "roommate," because that implies a home, an apartment, a dormitory even, something more stable than this. At Sunflower they've referred to each other as "cellmates" for so long even the administrators sometimes flub and mutter the term. And today his cellmate isn't answering. Asleep before midnight? Doubtful of that, Boris wedges his school-cafeteria ID into the door chink. The lock's simple mechanism gives, and *click-click.*

The smell in the room is unpinnable, not sex this time but something like cologne and, underneath, something heady and aerosol. The curtain is drawn, wimpling the room with periwinkle shadows, and dust swirls as Boris whisks it open. He sees the hedge apple in the corner of the room, a gift from Harriet to keep away miller moths, its rind lime-green and warty. Beside it, a torn poster of the missing, now proven dead, sorority victim. He sniffs the air again and turns toward his dresser drawer; in doing so, he spies the open closet door and, sprawled there, Carl.

Dead is Boris's first thought, but no, he hears Carl's breathing. His cellmate slumps on an avalanche of dirty laundry, pigtail flipping from behind his ear like a talking toy's windup cord. Drool glows against his bottom lip. He's shirtless, with—Boris takes three slack seconds to register this—his jeans and underwear bunched around his ankles. Carl's cock has softened, a raw reddish-pink. Lacy dribbles of sperm cover his abdomen and the chained silver dogtag on his chest, one puddle trailing an arc of smaller dots, a pattern resembling, to Boris, the Hawaiian islands. More come speckles Carl's laundry; clots in his pubic hair's blond tangles. His right hand grips a paper sack, its mouth cuffed and pinched shut in his fist. Between his head and a grimy sock, sparkling on the mound of clothes, lies an uncapped blue tartan can of Aqua Net hair spray.

One step forward, two back. Boris breathes the word "shit" so slowly its spelling would require at least ten *i*'s. He knows Carl's obsession with jerking off, and he's previously seen Carl inhaling paint fumes, hair spray, the glue from model cars. But he never guessed he might stumble upon *this*. Boris holds his breath, petrified the slightest noise will rouse Carl, and leans closer for inventory. In the dim light, Carl's eyelids look like violet petals, the eyes beneath them motionless. He has prepared himself as if for a date: wrists and neck daubed with cologne, hair slicked with the outdated brand of brilliantine from under the Sunflower bathroom sink. His nostrils are red-rimmed, dilated from the Aqua Net. The boy's lips have parted, whistling breath through a lima bean–sized hole, and Boris sees the jagged front tooth Carl claims was chipped during a convenience-store robbery. It's a mouth Boris might fantasize kissing if it weren't constantly sneering, if the breath behind it were less rancid. Carl's pug nose, his chin, his Adam's apple. Down to the hairless chest, the stomach, the white-lace dribbles . . .

The combination of the fumes, the half-naked boy, and the evening light that spools the room almost floors him. The sound from outside repeats and rerepeats before he actually hears it. Boris goes to the window: In the grass beside the weeping willow, a turtledove makes slow convulsions, its wing shattered and glossy with blood. Boris can't decide what happened—dog maul? car collision?—but the bird is undeniably in death's throes. Its drowsy *ohs*, its hiccups. And Boris is hard. He feels woozy, stoned. He moves a thumb along the stiff outline in his jeans, repositioning himself, then lies facedown on his bed. The bird fusses, throating its agonized noises. Then silence.

Above, in the top compartment of Carl's closet, is a row of bulky sweaters. Behind those, shoplifted goods Boris has sworn to keep secret. There are cassette tapes and batteries, model F-14s and Lamborghinis, six-packs of generic beer, dwarf chocolate logs pebbled with pecans. There are porn and karate magazines, condoms and glass tumblers displaying women whose inky bikinis evaporate with the miraculous chill of water. The closet is Carl's secret sanctuary, his palace. Prince Carl, blotto, on the floor beneath.

The boy's hand moves, spurred by a dream, his grip unfolding from the paper sack like an orchid Boris saw in a film, struck by light and s-l-o-o-o-w-l-y o-o-o-p-e-n-i-n-g. Boris bears witness to his whole body, a third of his face. The eerie blue of the spray can. One shoelace, untied. Carl's hipbones protrude in parallel knobs, and his cock looks fleshy, bigger than Boris would have guessed. He longs to hover there, to disregard the memory of the early foster father and that shadowy basement, that punishing hand coming down, coming down. Boris longs to rub his hand on the cock, to guide it into his mouth. He wants Carl to entwine his fingers in his hair and whisper, *Yes, Boris, this is what I've always needed.*

But no, that is not what Boris wants at all. What he wants is Rex. Carl's stupor conjures old fantasies: Rex, immobile, six feet two inches of unparalleled beauty stretched out, his only motion the slow rise of his hand, his index finger curling, curling in an unspoken *Come here, Boris.* Journal entries imagine Rex as "half hyena, half swan," and it's the swan part Boris wants to unearth. He'd swoon if Rex would lie this still. He wants to kiss Rex's mouth as though grazing there; to explore the hairs and pores and recesses of his pale and lanky body. To treat him like the sacred soul he truly is.

Boris tunnels his face into the sheet, breathing its detergent smell, but the hair-spray fumes have agitated his brain. Hammered by the head rush, his heart thrumming, he pushes his crotch against the mattress. Outside, the turtledove gurgles, snared within the last pains of its shuddering death. Boris presses harder, pulling back and pushing forward, fucking the bed through the barrier of his clothes.

Carl's breaths even out, liquidy with sleep. Boris, thinking of Rex, looks away. Slamming the bed, in and out, straining. Close, closer, so close. Rex is there in the hallway, in the school-bathroom mirror, in the stall with the girl at the Douglas County fair. He can see Rex, can smell him. Another aerosol cloud descends and splits open, the turtledove's voice stills, and Rex, and Rex, and within this high Boris comes.

Jumble of walls, ceiling, the lightbulb's globe. The twirling and drifting charms on the mobile. There are planets large and small, orbiting moons, comets, bright green asteroids. For one amphetamine second they seem to rise, piercing the ceiling. Piercing the sky. Beyond. They lift like the bird's lament, like wishes, like the final emerald bubbles from the dead girl's lips as she drifted, alone, to the river bottom.

—H.

The Magic Garden
BY HARRIET JASPER

There was once a widow who lived in a farmhouse shack with her son; and surrounding the farmhouse were trees of all kinds and gardens full with cabbages and potatoes. At night, into the gardens to eat, came rabbits and raccoons and skunks, but the widow did not tell the animals to shoo. Instead, she called,

"Welcome! Inside the garden wall,
Enjoy! There is enough for all."

And the animals, shy as they were, scampered under the fence after dark and ate to their hearts' content.

Now the widow's son was a lonely boy, for he was beautiful, and indeed, in those days as well as now, a thing of beauty is a thing of scorn. The children from the nearby town would not play with him; some mornings they would congregate at the garden wall and watch him playing alone, and in their spite and their jealousy would point and laugh. The sun himself, which had seen so much, would wait a little longer over the beautiful boy, and when the children saw the crystal crown of sunlight spires they would lift their voices and shout:

"Golden locks and golden crown,
But he is poorest in all the town."

And inside would run the beautiful boy, and the children's mothers and fathers would call them home, and the children would make haste away from the little farmhouse with its garden of cabbages and potatoes and carrots and beets.

It happened one day that the children brought a pet kitten. On see-

ing the animal's luxurious stretching under the summer sun, the boy felt
an ache in his heart, for he wanted one like it. The rabbits and raccoons
and skunks, after all, would not play with him, for they were shy, and
too, in their own animal way, envied the little boy's beauty.

The widow yearned for a kitten, but she had no magic lantern to
shine or wish-granting genie to consult. Her husband, the farmer, had
left her penniless, and all she owned was her son, her little hovel, and
the summer garden of vegetables. At night her son cried for a kitten like
the one he'd seen in the arms of the jealous children, but there was
nothing the poor widow could do.

When the wild animals heard the boy's cries and the widow's lamen-
tations, they thought and thought for some solution. After all, in such a
state, the widow might forget to weed and water her garden, and the
plants would stop producing. And indeed the widow and her son had
been so good to them.

So to the surrounding forest the rabbits and the raccoons and the
skunks journeyed, and there they found a special tree that leaked a special sap. The animals made merry by dipping their tiny paws into the
pools of this sap, and in the quiet of night found their way back to the
widow's garden. Under the light of the full moon, the animals rubbed
the sap over the leaves of the cabbages and potatoes and carrots and
beets and onions and peppers.

The next morning was the close of summer. The widow woke to find
a different garden, filled with plants that looked like her usual vegetables, but now bulging also with round, multicolored berries.

"Dear me," said the widow, "can it be that my good vegetables have
become poison overnight?" And to examine the plants she quickly bent,
but in her fear she could not touch them.

It so happened that, since the day was bright with sun, the town's
children went forth once again to play, and feeling full of mischief,
hurried down the path toward the farmhouse. They arrived at the
fence just as the boy, hearing his mother's dismay, had ventured into
the garden.

"Look!" cried the children. And the song began:

"Golden locks and golden crown . . ."

But on this day the children stopped. For they had seen the plants, now full with candy in a great many shapes and colors, pieces gleaming under the morning sun. Oh! how the children shouted! "Gumdrops!" screamed one girl. "Chocolates!" cried another. And they made a ladder with their bodies, and one after another the children climbed the fence and entered the shining garden.

The beautiful boy stepped back, astonished to see the town's children coming so close. But the widow held out her arms, welcoming them as she welcomed the rabbits and raccoons and skunks each night, and she opened her mouth and sang:

"Welcome! Inside the garden wall,
Enjoy! There is enough for all."

And the children bent to pick the magic candy, oblivious of the widow and the beautiful son, and they filled their mouths. In seconds, the gumdrops and chocolates and queer berries were gone from the plants. The children sat back, lazing in the rows of the widow's garden, their sticky hands rubbing their stomachs.

Then a miraculous thing happened. The sun dipped behind a cloud, and within the shadows the children began to change. Their faces sprouted whiskers. The fingers of their hands became rounded and furred and spiked with tiny curved claws. Their ears became pointed, and from their little bottoms grew long tails. Soon, the children were no longer children. They were splendid furry kittens with eyes that sparkled.

When the boy saw this, he ran to the garden and in his delight stood among them. At his feet the kittens circled, purring and nuzzling their whiskers against him. For now they saw how beautiful he was, and they were sorry for what they had done and all they had said.

That night the rabbits and raccoons and skunks came back to the garden, and the plants once again bore only cabbages and potatoes and carrots and beets and onions and peppers. The animals ate once again to their hearts' content. And for a great many suns and moons after, the animals would return to the garden, still a little shy, though now not because of the kind widow and her beautiful son, but because of the crowd of cats that lived there too. If you go to that place today, you will still find the widow, and her son, and their happy family of cats, all together in the magic garden.

10

$\mathcal{S}$ome nights, on the job, little things scare her: the time clock's unexpected semiquaver; the swing and bang of the neon sign as it sputters ambulance red into the storm. Sarah's nerves flare like sparks. Can she help it? After the words on her car, the face at her window, after the goose attack. And now, following a short hiatus, the rain again. Lightning reveals the black ribbon turnpike, its zipper of gold. The fences and empty fields beyond. On the store radio, a newscaster warns about dangerous water levels. The river ruins lawns and flowerbeds, its seam widening, taking more than it gives. Soon, Sarah knows, it will spit back more bodies. For barter it will swallow up trees, houses, whole families.

Traffic, busy earlier, has slackened with the after-midnight rains, and Sarah tidies up a second time. Lately she's been discovering things at the counter, nearly every shift a new memento, left like a gratuity. This week: a coverless mystery paperback, a foil-wrapped bouillon cube, a dollar bill. Sometimes men from the gas company leave oil-daubed gloves. Truckers forget their sunglasses. Dads, pre-occupied with squabbling children, misplace one credit card after another. Sarah will open a drawer; slide the item across the counter until it drops in. Someone has lost; she has found. She will wait two weeks, then keep anything unclaimed.

A radio voice, programmed by the clever deejay, croons about walking through the rain with a true love. Sarah wipes the floor with a mop, joining with the verse she recognizes: *I know you're waiting there for me . . . gently, gently. . . .* She wrings the mop in the bucket. Some girls might begin dancing with it, waltzing and dip-ping its skinny wood body as the damp gray strands of hair sway like water ferns. Sarah pirouettes, then moors the mop against a trash barrel at the back of the store.

The paper sack sits on the floor, beside the outdated pop machine with its fogged glass and empty dispenser holes socketed like a honeycomb. Perhaps it was strategically placed before the EMPLOYEES ONLY door, where Sarah was certain to eventually approach. It could have been dumped here earlier, when customers bustled in the aisles, faces wavering past her spot at the register. Hands have wadded the sack's mouth closed. Something bulges inside. Sarah thinks: Python? Tick-tocking pipe bomb? Abandoned baby?

She opens it, then withdraws her hands as though from fire. Someone has mutilated a doll, a pink plastic newborn as long as her forearm, stuffing its feet in a white Chinese takeout box. Artificial blood—Sarah recognizes the similarity in color and thickness to her own recipe—mats the blond curls, sprinkled with brown bits of fried rice. Soy and sweet-and-sour sauce anoint it with an orangy silt. Candle-wax drippings have seared the pink-shell ears. Jammed into the cunt, a broken-handled par-ing knife.

Sarah pinches the sack closed. She tries to remember any face among tonight's customers, but none solidifies. According to the clock, her replacement's due in half an hour. Thirty minutes. Eighteen hundred seconds. In that time, anything could happen: The door could tear open, the villain could tackle her. Should she call Boris? The police? No, and no. *Another omen,* she thinks.

Within the quiet Sarah hears the rain, snapping, at the windows. She runs for EMPLOYEES. She shuts the door behind her, drops the sack on her boss's desk, and waits for the shift to end.

During Sarah's days at Sunflower, a supervisor preached words she's never forgotten. "When you're upset, you should concentrate on something good. A happy memory." Sarah tries this now. She goes back to an evening last spring, when they all traveled to Kansas City for a baseball game. None of them had been before, not Boris, not Sarah, not even Marshall or Harriet, and if not for the convenience store and its abundant countertop, the night might never have happened.

A man had forgotten his wallet. Sarah can't recollect his features: glasses maybe, hair going gray at the temples and thinning on top, possibly the personalized belt with shiny palm-sized oval buckle that so many farmers and truckers wear. He had fumbled for bills, had paid for his unleaded fill-up, his beef jerky and sugarless gum. Sarah heard the tinkle of the bell as the door swung closed. She heard his pickup rev to life, shift into gear, and chug away. One minute, two. She continued to stare at the wallet's black leather square, half-expecting it to inch across the counter. When it didn't, she unfolded its contents.

Her conscience wouldn't let her take the forty-three dollars. But layered inside were four baseball tickets. The paper was striped sky-blue with gray, and the words heralded the upcoming weekend's game. The Kansas City Royals, hosting the Cleveland Indians.

She had to do it. They needed the time together. Four months had passed since they'd met Boris; more and more, Sarah felt the urge to swipe him away from Sunflower. And Marshall was home now, energized a little, released only the day before from Lawrence Memorial.

During the drive, they played scavenger-hunt road games: Spot an object beginning with the letter *A*, *B*, the letter *C*; catalog state license plates; find each misspelled billboard or highway sign. Marshall won again and again. He saw plates from West Virginia and Wyoming and Maine; pointed out three separate unnecessary apostrophes. Harriet and Boris, cramped in back, offered the occasional correct answer and giggled at the jokes from the front seat. The car passed oil fields ghosted by the machine whir of hammer pumps, churning and churning their hackles. A green house was neighbor to another painted blue. From an overpass they watched the meridian of a cemetery, where a solitary caretaker stepped between stone rows, bending slow and arthritic to touch the grooved letters on headstones. Sarah sensed Marshall preparing to tell a joke, some crack about his ill health or impending doom, and wanting to spare Harriet, she put a finger to his lips. "Quiet as a mouse," he said. As the car zoomed by, Sarah peered down on the caretaker's truck, its bed piled with artificial flower arrangements in pink orange red.

After locating a space in the parking lot, Sarah held Marshall's hand. She had chosen a black dress that evening, and as they walked he ran his fingers along it, rubbing the texture of the fabric. Past the barrier of ticket takers, up the incline, into the stadium loaded and cocked with fans. Sarah helped him find their aisle, just as Boris helped Harriet. The sun smeared and drifted from sight. The carousel air shook with pregame cheerleader hollers; organ solos of "Take Me Out to the Ballgame" and "Say Hey, Willie"; variable murmur and shriek of the crowd. Marshall looked around, a smiling scarecrow in his clothes. His skin was wafer-white, thin, needle bruises on the arms, the veins below filled with poison blood. On his forehead, a pair of childhood chickenpox scars, nearly eclipsed by a small purplish lesion. His turtleneck obscured other marks. His hands trembled. Over his right eye, an eyepatch, preventing further infection to last week's conjunctivitis that resulted from his retinitis operation.

Sarah figured the nine out of ten Kansas Cityites unfamiliar with AIDS symptoms would never decode Marshall. He stuck out, sure, but so did she, so did Boris and Harriet. Four sore thumbs in a stadium packed with orderly pinkies, rings, and indexes. "We may as well be the Great Flying Wallendas," Marshall said, "the way everyone's gawking." They took their seats: Sarah at the aisle; Marshall beside her; finally Harriet and Boris.

"When Marshall was little," Harriet said, "Robert and I would listen on the transistor. We'd go to the back porch and watch the sun set or maybe a storm brewing and then came the game, crystal clear. I had an old lawn chair and Robert had an old lawn chair and Marshall would run around the yard pretending he was one of the Royals. I can still hear the announcer's voice. Batter up, he'd say, and Here's the pitch." Harriet had tied her hair into a tight gray skein. Her face had pinked from the weekend sun, and she turned to Marshall, satisfied. "Do you remember, honey?"

"I haven't started forgetting," he said. "Not yet." And he was right, not yet. He still had three months, almost four. Back then, none of them could know. They still believed in miracle pills, in healing colors and love songs, in crystals held in the palm of the hand until remedy spiraled through tissue and muscle and bone.

Evening neared, the mercury lights buzzing. The outfield, green; the bleachers, busy with blue: deep blue seats, the deeper blues of the fans' windbreakers and baseball caps and zealous painted faces. Lean boys in identical Royals jerseys sold popcorn, peanuts, hot dogs, sunflower seeds, cotton candy, Cokes both sugar and saccharine. Marshall and Boris agreed the cotton-candy vendor was cutest; Sarah shook her head no, pointing across rows of fans to the hot-dog boy with the long blond hair and the retainer. Harriet couldn't follow her finger's invisible line. Where? Over there. That one? No, that one.

Oh, say can you see . . . Harriet sang along. They sat down, and the game started. People were watching them. Between batters, heads would turn. "Look," someone said, too loud. Boris was afraid that the game officials would catch them; surely the man who misplaced the tickets would magically appear to eject them from the stolen seats.

Innings passed, the score leapfrogging between teams. Two to zero, three to two, five to three. They whooped and hurrahed with the crowd; Sarah bought four hot dogs and ate what Marshall couldn't finish. When his attempts at squinting couldn't focus the electronic words on the centerfield scoreboard, she recited the glowing lineups and advertisements and player biographies into his ear.

Harriet struggled with sleepiness. Boris drew his knees into his seat, hugging them, then fiddling his fingers around a curl of hair. June bugs and moths twirled in the high-beam domes of grandstand poles, junkies for the light. The announcer: *As we enter the top of the ninth inning . . .* The Royals were four runs ahead, and Sarah suggested leaving early.

They collected the trash at their feet. Behind them, a boy began crying, and Harriet swiveled in her seat. "Look," she said. "The little dear lost his toy."

Four rows back, a boy had dropped his souvenir baseball. Sarah watched the boy's father: He was handsome as a movie hero, all pepper-salt hair and gold neck chains and the beginnings of a beard. The father apologized to the lovebirds in the row behind Sarah. "Excuse me, but could you look under your seat?" Other fans stood to assist, laying aside Royals seat cushions and pennants and peanut sacks. The boy pouted now—"*Shush,*" the father said— the sob held behind his swollen bottom lip.

An Indians pinch hitter cracked a single over the shortstop's head. The fans around them momentarily forgot the lost baseball, and the boy cried harder. And Marshall stood. He winced, displaying the dimple that appeared when he smiled. "Here, mister," he said. "Down here." He had found the ball, had wrenched it from beneath his seat. The boy spied Marshall, the autographed Royals baseball in the bony hand raised in the air. He hopped one step, two, until he stood at their row's edge.

The father shuffled down, embarrassment mapped on his brow, the hinge of his jaw. Sarah wanted to shake his hand, to find some way to touch him. She felt his eyes grazing them. The four of them, so out of place: an eccentric and wild-eyed old lady, a blushing boy with the long hair of a girl, a woman in a low-cut dress. An obviously sick man.

Marshall placed the baseball in the boy's miniature glove. "Son," the father said. The tune from the stadium organ rose an octave. "Can you say thank you?"

The boy stared openmouthed, then swaddled the baseball with his glove and hid it behind him. "Thank you," he said. He looked once at Harriet, once at Sarah, back to Marshall. Sarah knew the boy was zeroing in on the eyepatch. His face flickered with wonder at this pirate, this oddity.

Sarah wanted to talk to the father, but he clenched his son's ungloved hand and led him off, sideswiping the cotton-candy vendor in his rush. Before the man reached his row, the little boy turned again to look at Marshall. The crowd roared around them, a wave crashing with the swell of the organ and announcer, but Marshall stared back. A moment passed, frozen there amid the blue bleachers. Sarah saw Marshall unflap the eyepatch. She could smell him then, each clue and condition of his sickness: armpits, breath, hair, feet, and groin; fatigue and surrender and a thousand little fears.

Marshall bowed, straining, one pantomime arm flourishing, his hand a-flutter in whirlpool turns. And on the bow Marshall winked. Only once, yet Sarah witnessed it: a singular shut and open of his diseased eye.

Quickly the father tugged the boy into their seats, and their forms disappeared. Marshall hadn't meant for her to see. She looked up, feigning concentration on the upper stadium tiers, pretending not to know. Marshall sat with a pathetic grunt; leaned into his mother. Sarah felt the distance between them. And, for one breath-stealing second, a selfish anger too, almost a hatred. In the moment of the wink he'd returned to the old jokester Marshall, a side he once would only show to her. So little of that remained—she put her fist to her mouth, she felt the hate, she bit her thumbnail—and now he was squandering it on this anonymous child.

An umpire was booed. A player fumbled a pop fly; another hit a home run. Sarah never should have stolen the tickets, never suggested this night. She wanted to whisk Marshall away, to take him to the beach, an oasis. Just to be alone, to stop time somehow and hold him.

Hush now; the organ stopped mid-song. Sarah saw the right fielder, laughing, running to the fence. A fan had dropped a stuffed lion into the world of the game. She motioned for Boris and Harriet and Marshall, but they weren't watching, they were leaving the aisle. The player rescued the lion by its furred and brindled ear—Sarah saw its beetle-bead eyes flicker—then lifted it back to the fan.

Days, weeks, months. Whenever she remembered, she tried focusing on the boy's father. She would lie in bed and look away from her window and the dead golf course. She imagined the man lying beside her, his eyes flashing hot and carnivore, the lamplight on his grizzled graying beard, the down on his arms and chest and legs. She thought of him straddling her; nailed in, panting, harder than steel. His mouth was on her ear and on her mouth, he was saying wet, strangled words as he came. She wasn't supposed to think these things; she tried unladylike to go further, deeper, warmer; but always, when the fantasy ended, Sarah forgot the father. She kept returning to the moment, the thing Marshall had done, the gesture. The game was always ending. It was always the ninth inning. The applause was about to begin, the organ's song about to cease, the lion about to drop. Fans were jumping to their feet, cresting, the boy among them, watching Marshall. It was true, he had only winked at the boy. Harmless, she assured herself. Yet Marshall had exposed something, his eye a portent, connecting with the boy as, before, he'd only connected with her. A lean into the glass of a crystal ball: *Here's what I was, am. Here's what will happen to me.*

In those last days, when he was slick with sweat in the hospital bed, Sarah remembered her brief hate for him, the force and fire of it. How it was almost good, because to hate, maybe, meant she wouldn't miss him. She could continue sleeping and eating and cashing her convenience-store checks, and when Marshall died, life would continue winding down to whatever end it held for her. She couldn't know. Perhaps she didn't care. Bedlam; reincarnation; a powdery white nothing.

And this is only part of the mosaic, a single tile of memory now mixing with her fear, and Sarah knows where the whiskey bottle is, and when lazy-eyed high school dropout Austin Milhauser relieves her of the shift, she invents an excuse and leaves the employee room for her car and opens the front trunk. She pulls the booze out, nestles the baby doll beside the mannequin. Before she slams the trunk she smells it again: the spoiled smell, worse now. Sarah sees its battered eyes and nose and mouth, the sad, sleepy face like someone sunk in quicksand, its features adult versions of the baby in the sack. *Slam.*

Sarah drinks. She steers through country roads, twenty-five miles per hour, twenty, fifteen. Rain trickles paths through the cuts on her windshield, and she drinks more. Ten miles per hour and five and another drink and stop.

Canopy elms deepen all colors to black, and for thirty seconds after Sarah shuts off her lights she sees nothing. But the rods and cones work their magic, surfacing the particulars of Harriet's far-acred pasture. She pulls a currycomb and bridle from below the passenger seat, then leaves the car to stand between trees on the road's shoulder. The fields have filled with storm water, seeping muck into her shoes. Cattails rise like scabbards leaning west. Above her, cloistered within shadows, marginal noises: a swallow stirring troubled from its dream, a chestnut squirrel leaping branch to branch. But beyond, too, some hissing thing sounding immediately sinister, some postmidnight spirit that could surge one swoop of its wraith wings for her very soul.

Sarah steps to the fence and strains over. The air stinks of skunk musk. Autumns, reckless farm vehicles crush animals, clouding on the wind. Harriet boasts an immunity to the smell, breathing it in the morning garden, on the road during an evening stroll, through window screens at night. Sarah thinks of Harriet sleeping and looks to the house. It broods against the horizon, blue-jet, its lone kerosene lamp glowing from the kitchen window. The rain drips into Sarah's clothes but she moves farther through the field, uncaring.

Jellybean recognizes her form. Sarah hears him before she sees. The hooves thudding earth, the breath heaved stormy and missionary-tired. He leaves the space of grass where Harriet's neighbor feeds him, trotting the distance toward her. Sarah displays the currycomb and bridle and hugs the horse's neck, hands patting the shuddering muscle. She unbuckles Jellybean's martingale, slides off the worn halter. She pulls hair from the concentric circles of currycomb teeth and combs him. His forelock and mane smell of woodsmoke, rain, dried alfalfa and clover. His eyes glisten in the feeble starlight, lashes damp and silvery with age.

Sarah tugs a fist of grass from the earth, and when she offers it, Jellybean's lips clap at her palm. Deep within each movement lies his heavy, huddled loneliness. The trees draw crucifix shadows on his sorrel hide. Sarah slaps his neck once again, a slow, singular applause into the night, then raises the bridle. She fits the bit between his lips, secures the headstall, swings the reins to meet at his back.

She tosses the currycomb to the fence. Sarah always loved riding bareback: When she was younger, she took the tamer Jellybean, and Marshall, brave, borrowed the neighbors' feral palomino, the same that had kicked a moon crescent into his knee when he'd drained its thigh of pus. "Let's go bareback," Marshall would tell her. "It's better." They would sing, harmonizing to their favorite New Wave songs, and they would ride downroad, no saddle separating her legs from the horse's breath-swelling body. Bareback was more intimate, carnal. The wind in her hair, the shuddering whinny pushed deep into her crotch.

"Giddyup," she says, because that is what they always said. She kicks Jellybean's sides, again harder, shoe soles knocking ribs. He obeys, taxing his spavined hocks, galloping when Sarah yells gallop. The elements hurtle past. The fences and trees start to wobble and blur, the distance so dark she sees only her fingers in the mane, the worn white stitching on the reins, Jellybean's head and frilled red diamond ears. Sarah thinks of sex, the desperate clutch at the partner's bucking head. She thinks of herself as Paul Revere, Lady Godiva, Ichabod Crane. The final name seems most fitting. She remembers a drawing from a schoolbook: the spectacled misfit, alone, pulverized with fear as his foamy-lipped horse rears and the night wrinkles close around him.

Jellybean curvets and runs, pace quickening as Sarah nears the pond. Her face feels numb, as though from subzero winds or cocaine. The horse retaliates from the order of the reins. He slants his neck to drink, a mirrored edge of their form in the water dimpled here and there with rain. Sarah eases her leg over and hops to the earth.

Beyond the far fence are the trees. To a pair of dreamy teenagers, the place was a forest. They vowed to someday enter those trees and subsist for days. They'd tag each trunk with yarn, strings of scarlet filigreed with gold. How many could they count before patience ran thin? Seven hundred trees? Twelve thousand? More?

And before the trees begin, at the edge of the fence, their hiding place. Sarah finds it, a lair behind the prehistoric oak with the tire swing, the spot where she and Marshall would rein the horses and lie together in shaded grass. Sarah sits within this sudden shrouded universe. Their hideaway has grown thick with eldritch tanglevine and ivy. Still, she discovers the souvenirs, the mysterious little hallmarks. Here are shards of animal skeleton, probably skunk or raccoon, remains from the same scavenged bones Sarah once used for the Suffering Box. Here is a splintered paintbrush. Here is an old coal scuttle, its surface nail-scratched with their initials, filled with red dirt and corroded early-eighties nickels and pennies and scraps of plastic roses. Mudstained tatting from some long-ago pillow they shared with their soulmate dreamers' heads. Scattered under rocks and in the mud, too, evidence of games they played. Jack of diamonds and three of clubs; artificial fifty- and hundred-dollar bills in pastel blue and yellow; silver top hat, Scottie dog, wheelbarrow, and sports-car pieces from a discarded Monopoly set.

Back then, the mud made her squeamish and sad. Always she thought of wriggling worms, and, further below, the seepage dripping onto the dead and their slick oiled skulls. Marshall would take her hand so she wouldn't fear. She would ease back into dandelion clover and touch a finger to his neck, as she would do years later in the hospital. Touch the pulse behind his white tissue-skin, proof he was here, he was hers.

After he died she returned to the hospital room. There were things left behind, but she wouldn't dream of Harriet's going back. She filled a plastic bag with the vitamin bottles, the crossword-puzzle magazine she'd bought him weeks before. On the table was a single pear, now brown, a chain of bite marks linked into its flesh. Had Marshall eaten it? Maybe Harriet? A hungry nurse? She held it to the light: here, where the stem had been ripped from the branch; there, where it disappeared into fruit. Sarah tore chunks from it, saw the stem separating into individual strings, the strings ending in seeds, the seeds birthing creamy grit and pulp. Then she threw away the pieces of pear and left.

She knows with frantic certainty what Harriet hasn't yet comprehended. She knows that Marshall is never coming back; that, no matter how hard she clenches her teeth or fists, how stiff she mixes her drinks, he is gone and can't boot-kick the neighbors' horse to breakneck speed alongside her, can't lounge cross-legged in this mud playing board games and landing on her Boardwalk or Park Place to fork over the costly rent. He's gone, he's gone, he won't be back! Yet there are things that can't leave: the way he gripped her hand during horror films, his thumb curled safe within their palms' dark cup. Or the instant crinkle of his eyes, whether healthy and glittery-blue or bloodshot with disease, when he smiled.

The warmth of his body when he hugged. The sound of him. The smell.

Sarah fingernails the game pieces from the ground. She spits on her thumb and shines each on the knee of her jeans. Mindful of Boris and the Suffering Box, she pockets them. Then she returns to Jellybean, taking the reins to lift herself once again onto his back. The world seems three notches out of her drunken focus. Her tongue is thick and fuzzy, a mitten in her mouth.

Not long ago she had a gorgeous, epic dream about a field populated with horses: an entire congregation, with Jellybean among them. They spoke in secret nickers and moved in ballet. Upon waking she needed to call someone. But Marshall was very, very sick and Harriet busy, and when Boris answered his hall telephone he sounded too fogged and numbed from his own blanket and pillow to listen. The images from sleep didn't translate well to language, and after Sarah told him, the dream felt cheapened, as though she'd viewed it on TV.

The rain falls heavier. She nudges the horse's ribs. Winds spin her hair and sing in her ripped ear. She leaves the pond behind, something mammoth and slashed and incinerated black in the foggy distance. She thinks of the baseball now, the one lost by the boy, the relic Marshall should have hidden from sight and kept, lucky charm, at his hospital bedside. She thinks of the baby doll, stabbed and burned and bleeding, cuddled close beside OSTIT like a malformed parasite twin.

Ahead now is the house, a rectangle of shadows with its back porch and surrounding trees. Sarah rides faster. The horse rumbles beneath her, an engine. A felled oak looms in the grass. Jellybean snorts, heat vibrating from his nostrils: Once he could have cleared it, but now he is too old. Sarah kicks his flanks nonetheless, digging her soles deeper. "Giddyup." She is aware, dimly, of the game pieces in her pocket, silver edges like switchblade bits against her hipbone. No, she will not give them to Boris; they were meant only for her, for Marshall. She kicks, and Jellybean starts his thunderous approach for the tree. She sees its furzy carcass; its upturned roots. "Go," she says, "up," urging the horse with choppy hiccups of sound. "Hey. Up. Up!" Her face a flame. Her hand in her pocket. "Up," she yells a final time, and then the horse becomes the air, soaring, the colossal knucklebone of log far, far beneath. And Sarah hurls her souvenirs into the rain. She looks up. In the heavy shadow-caul she sees them dazzle, piece by piece, the tiny objects struck in one supernatural moment by lightning-white light, four silver fallen fragments of a star, indeed, a star just burst.

11

*L*ight," Harriet says. "That's what we need." She ties back the living-room curtain with ribbon, and the sun, now dimmed, siphons in. Out the window, the front yard tangles with dead branches, weeds, loose strands of hay. Once everything was tidy, and Boris remembers last spring's picnic, hosted and guested by the four of them. Now he watches the tree dropping its leaves. He counts each separate gopher hill, the mounds of earth burrowed and torn and foaming mud from the rains.

Inside Harriet's eyes are miniature sunflowers. There is the glassy blue iris, the pupil, but buoyed between the two is yellow, a circle of fiery petals. Boris can't recall standing this close to her. She concentrates on taking his picture. Yesterday, searching under Marshall's bed, she found special lens attachments for the camera. A wideangle, a zoom, and this, a lens that allows her to move nearer, to magnify.

Pictures from the Suffering Box find Boris at age six, age nine, fourteen: Whether with that family or this, his almost vaudeville expression remains the same. Chin held posed, tight queasy smile showing no teeth. "Say cheese," the foster families would say, but he never said it. Under Harriet's scrutiny, though, he feels less nervous. The shutter rattles and rattles, while on the television screen a girl in candy-striped tights spins a whirligig sphere of numbers. "The Kansas Lottery is now worth over four million to some lucky viewer," the girl says.

Harriet focuses and smiles; hums and blows on her hands to warm them. She wears a white housedress; her lipstick is smudged. During the night her hair, no thanks to the haywire dye, turned the color of raw ham. Carmine, salmon, carnation pink—some shade Boris recollects from the crayon box. She has tied it back, out of the way of her camera. "Four million," Harriet echoes, curving the gooseneck lamp toward his face. "Now what would someone like me or you buy with that?"

"Gifts," Boris says. "Clothes, maybe. Music. Better food to sneak into my room at night." What could he possibly have that Sunflower wouldn't take away? "But gifts, mostly. For you. Sarah. Carl, even."

The girl beams at her invisible television audience. She plucks each numbered ball, 47, 19, 31, from the spinner. But Harriet watches only Boris. "The taxes alone would kill you," she says. "But after paying those I could buy me a car. Or a house. A plot of land the size of Douglas County. What would that get me? Fiddlesticks. How much would I have to pay for time? I'd have to go to God. How much would he ask? To stop time, to put it in reverse?" Harriet hesitates and then she laughs, as if fearing the conversation that inches near gloom.

Boris fidgets, a beetle centered below the burning magnifying glass. If he had spent the day in his room, he'd be dreaming up zombie scenes right now. But he doesn't dare disappoint Harriet. As she leans closer, she stumbles on the culprit cats that patrol her feet. She nudges them with her foot; grunting, she bends to scratch the Manx's stubbed tail. "Little Mister Lucius wants his picture taken too. It's stopped raining, so maybe Boris will help me put you outside for a stretch."

They herd all eleven cats outside. Some scatter in the yard; others loiter at the front steps. Harriet stands there, face turned to the west, clouds in purple and red, now royal with sunset. Then she slams the screen door. Through the window glass Boris sees the lazy row of her pets' tails, bristled and taut as cacti.

Harriet motions for him to sit. "Marshall bought this camera, bought all these attachments and other contraptions too." She refocuses on Boris and releases the shutter. "I always wished we'd gone vacationing. But I'm so old now. It's a travesty! There are so many places I haven't seen. Don't be sixty like me, sixty-two actually, and suddenly think of this. Oh, no! There's Mexico City, there's Alaska, there's whole countries with pyramids and beggar children and kangaroos and those big blocks of ice just waiting to be seen. By me! But I won't see them. Too late. Don't be like me!"

Harriet is shouting. She is close to Boris's ear, but he doesn't grimace, doesn't move. "I won't," he says. "I promise."

He remembers one afternoon when Sarah and Harriet picked him up from school. The final bell had iced the hallway, and as the women waited he hurried, slamming books into his locker. Before he got to the lobby, Boris heard two girls whispering. They were speaking about Harriet: about her wild, unbrushed hair and flower-bright makeup; about the songs she hummed, fraily, to herself. The girls used words like *crazy* and *witch* with a certain familiarity, as though Harriet were a town landmark.

Since the funeral, Harriet has grown scatterbrained. Boris has witnessed the kitchen faucet left running; dishes returned to the cupboard unwashed; the casserole, a funeral gift from a relative, spoiling in the refrigerator. Harriet has stacked meticulous pyramids of soup cans, peeled of their labels, in the kitchen. "This way," she announced, "lunch is a complete surprise until I get out the can opener." On the coffee table lie unopened bills, two lasagna noodles, an ashtray placed facedown. Sarah has told him how Harriet has taken to letting the cats explore the basement, sometimes forgetting them for days at a time. They leave urine puddles beside the packed trunks of clothing, the waterstained novels and bushel baskets of rotting apples, the unplugged freezer where Sarah and Marshall once played Murder Victim.

Yet none of this proves Harriet's lunacy. Boris knows she's fine. Soon everything will be smooth, topnotch, magic, again.

As evening lowers, Harriet runs out of film. She steps to the refrigerator—"Film keeps better when it's cold"—but has overlooked buying more. She rests the camera on the table and returns with a magazine. A contest promises a jackpot for the entrant with the best drawing skills. There are sketched heads to copy and mail in: the Prospector, the Leprechaun, a deer named Winky. "Draw your favorite," Harriet reads. She chooses Lucky the duck, her pencil tracing its beak and pinstriped beanie.

"Listen." Harriet cocks her head. "The house is making noise again." Boris closes his eyes and trains his ear. "I know every sound this house makes," she says. He doesn't hear a thing; maybe, if he had a house to call his own . . . "And that bathroom, what a racket. The rattling pipes! I'd take a bath right now if it wouldn't make me so plumb tired. I'd fill that bath full of nine-tenths hot water and one-tenth cool and a whole mountain of bubbles, and I wouldn't get out till all those bubbles popped."

Boris changes TV channels. Static; an angler in a camouflage vest, gutting fish; a sitcom concerning a robot child. He mutes the volume and watches Harriet. Her drawing reminds him of art class, which reminds him of the trip at the month's end. "Sarah's going to take off work on the Lucas day," he says. "The class is going by bus, but it's okay to drive too. I want you to go with us. Please? The trip might be sort of silly, this folk-art house and garden, but there are other reasons. Rex and his friends are going, I'm pretty sure of it. You should think about coming with us. Please? Sarah will drive. It'll be nice, a day away from here, right?"

"I have relatives near there," Harriet says. "I haven't been to Lucas, specifically. Sitting cramped in a car all day, I don't know . . ." She stops. "Listen again. Someone's driving into the driveway. It's—it's Evans from down the road. It's him, I hear his hillbilly music." Boris goes to the window: In front of the house, a man slams a pickup's door. He marches forward, and before he knocks, Boris thinks for a shuddersome second of Sarah's trespasser, the face peeking into her kitchen.

Harriet invites Mr. Evans inside. He stands there, callused thumbs hooking belt loops. If anyone around Lawrence should be called crazy, Boris thinks, it's Mr. Evans and his wife. Sarah has told stories: She and Marshall, when younger, would uproot sandburs from the couple's flower garden; would borrow their firehearted horse. Mr. Evans would corner them and brag about the war, parading his scars. His wife was fat and saber-toothed and wore wooden clogs year-round. The couple kept, and still keeps, bees, stored around their yard within white-drawered hutches. Behind their house, a cityscape of pigeon dovecotes, standing askew and wobbling, in a storm, with the groggy sway of drunks.

Now Evans leans against the doorframe wearing white beekeeper gloves. Once, when Evans came to feed Jellybean, Boris even saw his frock and helmet, the face gray behind the doily screen. The man always smells of smoky bee fog, of honey and caramel-sweet wax. A smell like sex. Boris feels his heart pump like a pedal and looks back to the silent television, to Harriet's penciled duck.

"Just to let you know," Evans says, "your horse is nearly out of hay. Thought you might want to get someone out here to sell you some, before winter comes."

Harriet nods and reaches to pat her neighbor's shoulder. "Yes. Thank you. They're predicting a bad one, aren't they? Yes, I'll remember."

All is still after Evans leaves. His body flickers white past the window; out there, the cats no doubt crowd at his feet, interrupted in their games of crisscrossing territories and gnawing weeds. Boris hears the grunts as Evans scissors the hay twine and hefts one quarter-bale over the fence. Boris pictures his simpleton grin and the strong gloved beekeeper's hands, patting and patting the horse's long and muscled neck. He thinks of Rex, on his family's farm, running through a list of similar tasks, chores so ingrained in memory he scarcely thinks while doing them.

Harriet sits again. "That man. He's good to me, though. Oh, he left a draft. Brr! I remember once—"

She stops. Within the silence, the pickup's tires slide and cough in the gravel drive. And at the sound, the worry shows on Harriet's face, her cheeks and chin blushed with it. "Oh, no," she says.

Boris wants to soothe her. To ask what's wrong. Harriet's expression matches the one she wore at the funeral, now less blank but still as troubled, and he falls silent. She stands, pulls a scarf from the coatrack, opens the door.

Only a little light left, and Harriet, draped in white, seems to contain it. In the cool, variable winds, her scarf's twin ends flap like the wings of a stingray. She sidesteps puddles and hurries forth. Her old woman's careful clumsiness; the heartbreaking clutch at her chest. And Boris sees the thing she has already seen. Perhaps she saw it moments ago, in the house, through some clairvoyant force: there, in her driveway, the motionless form of a cat, one of her eleven, dead.

She hunches over the animal, shielding it with her body. Boris again remembers her in the hospital, as he saw her that first day, hunched over her son with motherly grace. Now she has fallen in the mud. Her knee makes a white planet against the comet tail of the tire track, the track from the pickup that killed her pet. There is the animal's mashed fur, the crushed velvet. Its eyes are blank and opaque as buttermilk, and a tear drifts from one, equal parts salt and water and blood. The exposed guts tremble, gelatin purple, shimmer-shining in the grass.

"Maurice," Harriet whispers, and Boris stops. Harriet says the name again, Maurice, but no, Boris knows her cats, knows she does not own a Maurice. Her voice catches, a sob rising watery and slow, and he hears now what she is saying, he hears the name. "Marshall." She presses her body into the cat's and clutches at the earth. And now—for the first time Boris can recall—Harriet's sob breaks and spreads, and she is crying.

The other cats graze past, and Boris thinks of Harriet's fairy tale, how he hasn't the heart to tell her it won't fit for *March of the Zombies*. "Their faces sprouted whiskers," she wrote. "Long tails grew from their little bottoms." Harriet continues to cry, soundlessly now, her only motion the horrifying twist of her back as she breathes each sob.

Boris steps back and away, down the drive, passing each cracked wooden fencepost. Nailed to one, a weathercock; to another, a tin rain gauge. He stands at the mailbox, the ditch, the opening of the road beyond. *I'm a coward for not helping. A true friend and a real man would be down in the dirt with her. I should put my arms around her and kiss the spot of rouge on her little cheek and say, Oh, Harriet, let it out, let it go, it will all get better now.*

The wind hollers, and in the distance the polished trees shimmer palely. Geese drift boomerangs in the sky. As the sun drops, the fenceposts throw their lengthening shadows against the dirt road, blue rows linked by barbed wire. Boris heads further away, out of earshot from Harriet's sobbing, a sound akin to the turtledove's throes beneath his bedroom window. Softer, softer. He looks up: Telephone poles stretch diagonals to the horizon, each smaller than the last, their wires flush with local gossip. There, swallows descend single file, and when Boris approaches, they scatter; after the sound of their wings dissipates, he can no longer hear Harriet, no longer hear a thing.

The road mud hardens into coils that break on each step. Should he walk back, should he help Harriet? *I'm a coward.* Boris watches the road at his feet, stops, begins walking again. He remembers this afternoon, when he had joined Sarah at the movies, hunkering in the balcony's front center seats, far from the other customers— Boris looked down, silently counting four, five, *six*. "Marsh and I used to come here once a week," Sarah had said. A soundtrack rumbled spooky cello notes; Sarah's hand crept into his seat to intertwine fingers.

Ahead, on the Evans farm, are the dovecotes, the boxes of bees, an oversized cistern surely brimming with rain. He turns, again facing Harriet's: Tiny within the deepening shadowland is her mailbox, its red signal flag lifted skyward. What letter could she be sending? What news, apart from the obvious, does she have to report?

He keeps walking. There are miller moths studding the ditch grass, cicadas chewing the air. *Coward,* say their tantruming voices. *Coward.*

On the theater screen the victim shrieked, eyes like asterisks, mouth an unbelievably wide red hole. As usual, her screams reme- died nothing; the murderer's hatchet still hacked. Sarah didn't flinch, but Boris, less interested, surveyed the surroundings. Over the years, the balcony's seats had been massacred by vandals, leak- ing blond foam like guts. What were once chandeliers of intricate pink glass now looked like debris salvaged from a car crash. Even the screen was acned here and there with dirt smudges, spitballs, bubble-gum wads. The theater was a disgrace; perhaps that's what Sarah meant when she referred to its "atmosphere." It smelled of mothballs and butter sludge and, like everything else in town, soured rainwater.

Coward. Boris has wandered a good ten minutes from the farm, but now he must go back. He turns and breaks into a run.

At first he can't see her. The charcoal dark smells of strewn hay, the spilled animal blood. "Harriet?" Boris will help her inside, will gather the surviving cats. He will run her a hot bath and open his diary and, under the page marked "B," will write. He will not be a coward. He will watch her sleep until Sarah arrives.

Three more steps and he sees Harriet has drifted to sleep. Tears have scratched dry lines on her cheeks. She has removed her scarf, the hair unraveling, screening her face, the ground, the damp dead animal she makes her pillow. She is curled so close it seems as though she is whispering some terrible, crippling secret or, worse yet, as though she is making love. The thin sleeve of her dress has opened to reveal her shoulder, a corner of her crescent scar. She is so delicate, almost gaunt, all brittle-bone and peach skin. She could be his grandmother. She can last days at a time eating only chocolates from a box and tablespoons of crystallized orange drink. She sings songs from the forties word for word and chills her camera film. At night, sheets pulled tight against her neck, she hears sounds from the empty room across the hall.

Leaning nearer, Boris charts her breaths, now even and heavy. There are white speckles in the pink of her hair, alive, a-flutter. Night moths have lit there, nesting in her hair's oily warmth, winking and unwinking in cipher.

Boris brushes her hair with his hand, and the moths spiral away. He bends to her ear and whispers, "*Abracadabra.*" But Harriet doesn't wake. Next he tries "*Open sesame.*" Her eyelids will not flutter. Boris takes a deep breath, two. Then he gives up; lets Harriet sleep. There's no such thing as magic, anyway.

—B.

We played hooky in the cornfield. Fuck school: All that mattered was the late autumn sun, singeing us. Him and me. We exhausted hours gobbling stolen candy and twisting hide-and-seek through the cornstalks. Burrowing foxholes for bucketloads of olive green army men. Bare feet crisscrossed prints in the loose sand. We found tumbleweeds and a purple-black caterpillar constructing its cocoon. Snared grasshoppers in mayonnaise and pickle jars. Ice pick holes in the screw-on tops. Stretched on the ground to watch them spit their sticky juice.

Evening neared. The Blevinses—permanent parents for Allen, only temporary for me—would never suspect a thing. And Allen, grinning blond Allen. He felled cornstalks with his dad's machete, borrowed from its nail on the chickenhouse wall. Chopped out a small clearing. His hard shining arms and upturned gentle face. We stayed here, near the west edge of the field. Waited for the school bus. We could see it now. Its yellow hulk rounding the curve, approaching. We would sprint in from the road. "We're home from school." Bright and breathless and deceptive. Breezes rattled the empty cornhusks. The noise like magic bones clicking in a bag.

The bus rumbled forward. We huddled close to the ground. Smelled the salty husks. Dead cornsilk, turned earth. For a single sterling moment I felt truly happy. Held my breath. I was with Allen, my Allen, temporary brother. We had fooled everyone, the day was perfect.

Suddenly a sound I hadn't anticipated. The screech of gears. Wet warning of tires against asphalt. Then silence. Allen and I left the corn maze clearing. Rushed to the barbed-wire fence that separated the field from the county highway. "Shit," Allen whispered. We sensed it. The electric danger.

The school bus had braked in the center of the road. Its position a curious angle from the broken yellow of the blacktop median. Schoolkids were standing inside the bus. Our classmates. Their faces pressed to the windows, mouths open. Some screaming inaudible sounds. Allen said, "We're in for it." Me, "They've found us out." But the kids weren't looking at us. I followed the arc of their panic, the direction of their frenzied gazes. There, at the roadside, near the ditch of gravel and sparse yellowing grasses. A dog.

It was a Doberman, black with brown nose. Hit head-on by the bus. It lay twitching in a reservoir of blood. Back legs bent behind it, the bones snapped. It tried to move and couldn't. Each attempt sent its head writhing toward the sky. It opened its mouth, bared its fangs. Twitched puppetlike and cried out, barking high octaves.

The bus started again, grinding into gear. Criminal tires swerving around the Doberman. From the windows our schoolmates still watched, mouths lingering open in protest. I saw the bus driver, Ms. Shirley, glance in her rearview. She hollered something. Steered the bus back onto the right lane. A tire rolled across a pasty edge of the blood puddle. The bus sped up, rumbling further down the blacktop. Ten minutes we stood watching the dog. Its herky-jerky motion slowed, and its yelps softened to whimpers. At last it stopped writhing and rested its head against the road. We stretched two rows of the barbed-wire fence and crawled through. Checked both ways for cars. Stepped onto the highway, sneakers close to the thickening blood.

The Doberman's eyes were glassy, but the level of its chest still rose and fell. Its eyes beautiful. Face beautiful. But its back legs angled behind it. Stiff like tines on a broken fork. One splintered leg bone protruded from the black hair. "They've nearly killed it," Allen said, lifting his foot to the dog's rib cage. He pushed. Kicked it a little. It grunted but didn't move. The wind gusted. Now stewed with the smell of cornhusk, the black and anxious blood odor.

"We've got to finish the job," Allen said. Nudged the dog again with his foot. Its unbroken front legs still moved in spasms, shiny toenails skittering asphalt. But its eyes stayed locked on me. Eyes rheumy now, half closed and crusted with dust.

I knelt and touched the face. I'd never owned a dog. Four different foster families—Allen's parents, the fourth—but none had allowed it. I didn't know where the Doberman had come from. Why it had crossed the highway in front of Allen's parents' farm. Perhaps it was coming to find us. Maybe it knew we lived there, knew we would want it. Maybe the parents would have let us keep it. Like brothers. "A Doberman," they would have said, "the perfect watchdog. For both of you."

Maybe together we could save it. Heal it. The dog could bring us together, and Allen, beautiful Allen, would love me. But from the corner of my eye I saw him raise his arm. Looked up and remembered the machete. Allen raised it even with his head. Paused for me to scurry away. Then raised his arm higher. Brought the blade down to strike the meat of the dog's neck. The first two blows just broke skin, sawed bloody lines. The third broke the bone. Fourth severed the head. The dog stayed silent, its eyes still on me.

At the road I watched it twitch. Allen nudged it deeper into the ditch, four kicks for the body and two for the head. Gravel pebbles studded the blood. "Hurry hurry run," Allen said. "My parents will be steamed." Not our parents but my parents. The dog stopped all twitching. Blood stopped seeping and I followed Allen back.

But late that night I snuck out. Left my bed and left the house. So late the whole world was black. No cars moving northward or south, but the dog was there. Centerpiece for ants and flies. And leaning close I could still see the eyes. In the cornfield the wind made a rustle like an angel or devil stomping through to get me. I put my foot against the head. Brushed it closer to the neck as if to make it whole again. Lay next to the dog, careful to avoid the blood.

Its eyes had milked over. Somehow consoling as if I were the one needing comfort. I'd never owned a dog. Thought of the way it could lope beside us with love in its eyes. Dog on one side and a father on the other and Allen and me, arm in arm, in the middle. But no. The parents didn't want and Allen didn't want. Here and now and outside but I knew if I stayed they would find me. The morning. The fights. If they found me, another orphanage, another family. And they would find me, they would send me off. Another, another.

Warrior ants in the sand heading fast and furious for the blood. Sandburs and cottonwood fluff and torn edible leaves of dandelions. Twenty feet away the cornfield made a hissing sound. The dog might *have made us a family but the dog was dead. Somewhere above a bird was fuming its high thin scree. In the quiet starless and motorless night I heard the wings clapping, an echoing pair of hands. It could see the blood below and it knew the foster father from my past, knew my love for Allen. Knew my misguided wasted future of Rex. The nightbird above, the wind from its momentum ruffling my hair. It swooping down close and away, until only me, alone, again.*

12

*D*ragonflies skid across the water, so drunk they sometimes drown. When Sarah waves her arms, the survivors veer off in pairs, their wings humming in green. In their wake are mosquitoes, swarming. No matter: a film of repellent smears her arms, neck, and face. She wears jeans to disguise the bruises from riding bareback. Right here, now, if she descended the rocks, she would stand near Bowersock Dam, where she and Boris found the artificial body. Somewhere, miles downstream, lies the spot where the real girl washed ashore. And somewhere else, hidden in this city or close beyond, the murderer waits. Sarah spins, but no one has followed. She can see the border of North Lawrence, a sliver of her golf-course gate. To the south, the bridge with its speeding cars and forever its river, pushing forward, silver and relentless.

Sarah has left the car in the drive to set out for Sunflower on foot. She will climb the hill at the town's nucleus, passing its beige university buildings and its bell tower. She will brave the football-game traffic, the squads of fraternity and dormitory fans, and cross Iowa Street to reach Boris's window just after dark. If he's there, she will sneak in. If not, she will drop more handwritten pages in the window. For his bottom drawer collection, she has brought reprints of favorite photographs: one, a ninth-grade five-by-seven class picture, her bored red-lipsticked face beside Marshall's in the front row; two, a shot of Harriet, sunbathing, from nearly a decade back; three, taken only days ago, where Boris shields his eyes from Harriet's camera.

Sarah has bitten three separate fingernails to bleeding. It's a habit she detests in Boris, but given the circumstances . . . Today she reexamined the words on her car. She tried imagining the handwriting of everyone she knows for possible similarities, then replayed the hours leading up to the mutilated doll. "If those guys come prowling back," she said into the phone, "if I find any other freaky thing, if anything, mark my words I'm calling the cops." On the other end, Boris assured her all would be fine.

Sunflower shines fewer than half its lights. Posted at the curb, beside the mailbox, a ghost sheet watches with scissored, blinded eyes. In the parking lot, the pair of company vans are missing. The only sound comes from a neighboring house, the ping and bang and yell, three brothers aiming basketballs at a garage-door hoop. Ahead is the damp earth beneath the weeping willow, littered with flecks of paint and excelsior, birdseed and dungy feathers. She slinks four secret-agent steps to the square of glass and taps twice.

When Carl sees her he shrinks comically, a vampire from sunshine. Then he jumps from bed and lifts the window further. "No Boris tonight," he says. Inside his mouth rests a gold cough drop. "At least not until late. He's doing dinner duty at the old folks' home. Part of the community-service thing. Me, I got to stay. 'Big algebra test tomorrow!' Good excuse, right? They fell for it. Like I'd study anyway."

Sarah leans head and shoulders inside, helped through by Carl.

"*Gracias*. I just need to leave something for him." The boy's hands fumble at her upper arms. When she looks in Carl's eyes, he smiles; when she stares longer, he looks away.

Surely the weekly maid has visited: The beds display new tartan blankets, their creases smoothed; swaths of vacuum marks cover the rug; the requisite wall crucifix, usually tacked wrong side up by Carl, has been righted. Everything shows the rigid spotless decor of submission. Only Carl's bed gives evidence of mess. Atop it, a J-K encyclopedia; a remedial algebra book, spine broken; a canister of barbecue potato chips; a wrapped and rubberbanded bag of grass. "Better put that away," Sarah whispers.

Carl bolts the door and sits on his bed. On his hand, he wears a skull-and-crossbones ring; his wrist sports a leather bracelet, studded with silver spikes. His rat-featured face shines as though polished, slicked hair raked through with a comb. Daubs of fleshtone makeup conceal the blemishes along his jawline. He's scratched ballpoint manifestos on his T-shirt, faded into obscurity by detergent. When Sarah attempts to break the silence—"That's a pretty smooth mustache you've got going there, Carl"—he looks to the ceiling, huffy.

"Why you got to treat me like I'm twelve?" he says. "I get that every day in this kiddie prison."

"I'm just joshing." She dimples Boris's pillow, centers the story and photographs there. "Actually, I think it looks pretty cool. Don't know about the piggly-wiggly at the back of your hair, though."

Carl swallows the cough drop. Sarah can feel his stare, warm and lingering. *I could so easily toy with him. I could smile and lift my blouse and open my legs and pull him close. He would be all fumbling hands and tense drooling mouth, he would tell everyone about me.* Then, daydream gone nightmare, Sarah imagines Carl as her stalker: sees his blond head at her window; his budding arsonist hands dismembering the doll. But no, and no, not possible. She's never found reason to disbelieve Boris's explanation, how Carl is "all talk, really. Wouldn't harm a fly."

"You used to live here, didn't you?" His voice, wet and oily, unnerves her. "Your family turn you over to the state like mine? One too many misdemeanors, and I was gone."

"Yes. I lived here. I hated it, really hated it, but then I had Harriet and Marshall, and after a while I was old enough to go, so I went."

Conversation seesaws. From Sunflower past and present, to her job, his grades, her best friend's recent death. "I wanted to tell you I was sorry and all," Carl says. Sarah can smell the aqua-blue bar of pumice soap, the same all foster and problem kids have used here, through the years. "For him dying and all."

Yet he wants to tell her something more. She detects it in the way his fingers claw the blanket, tap a rhythm on his hipbone. The way he opens his mouth only to snap it tightly shut. Sarah hears footsteps knocking the hall floor; a voice somewhere, requesting help. When Carl's mouth moves again soundlessly, she raises a finger. "Let me have it."

He starts. "You're going on that trip with Boris, aren't you? That art-class thing?" Sarah nods yes. "I should tell you—but I don't really know—I don't know how to tell it. Plus, it's something I don't want getting back to Boris. Might worry him or whatever. Because this is about you."

The Campanile bells begin ringing at the campus. Perhaps the Jayhawk football team has clinched victory. Perhaps today is a holiday, forgotten. The bell echoes settle in the room, and when they stop, the silence ripples in her ears. "Go ahead," she says.

"You might not believe me, but I think you're a great girl and all, and also Boris is pretty cool. He's done a lot of okay things for me." When Sarah nods, he continues: "Hmm. You want to hear what I think? I think Rex and his friends, they're fucked in the head. Don't think I'm saying this to get back at Boris or anything like that. He's been giving me stuff as payment for, you know this already probably, this spying trip I've been doing. Sneaking around all the right places, here, there, and everywhere, to snoop on those guys, especially Rex. I could get myself knifed. But I'm starting to figure out weird things about those dudes. Things I haven't told Boris."

Carl looks to the wall above his bed, where the green planet mobile swirls and drifts, where the gold crucifix hangs. "Maybe you could get him to change his mind," he says, "about going on that field trip. Rex and them, they'll all be there too and I don't think it's such a hot idea anymore. You know what I'm saying?"

Carl stands, bowlegged and bony-kneed. He waits for her to answer, and when no answer comes, he sneers. "I can't really tell Boris about the shit I've seen and heard them doing. And I can't persuade him not to ride with you out to that town, whatever the name of that town where that weirdo place—"

"Lucas."

"Lucas." Pause; pause; a breath, wheezing in, out, through his chipped front tooth. "It's not like I heard everything at once. But I kept up, into their classrooms, like, hallways and back corners where they get stoned, them blabbing on and on about bullshit I couldn't care less about. All of this for Boris. See, I'm a nice guy! Anyone else surely'd bitch about his obsessed fag shit or something. But I'm not doing that! No.

"At first I thought they were just weird, some of the things they were saying. But they kept talking about that murder, not the latest one, because the cops hadn't found her yet, but that first girl, the one that washed up. They knew a lot about her. More than anyone else, on TV or wherever. Pretty soon I started thinking sure they'd done it.

"And then later I knew they weren't the murderers that had killed them girls, but it was almost as bad, because they're like so into it. Obsessed. Like they wished they'd had the courage to do it. I can't believe they didn't know I was spying on them sometimes. Man, the stuff I heard them say. How they wished they'd known what a knife felt like going in, about whether it hurt your wrist when it hit the bone. About how much of the death she could feel, whether the guy tortured her long enough before he actually did her in. About how tight her pussy felt, about if it got all moist and tightened up when you was fucking her and she started in on the dying.

"Then they stopped talking so much about the dead girl. They talked more in whispers and I could only hear pieces. Turned out Ellis, he was in love with this one girl, the school slut. Sammi Snow. Funny name, huh? Ellis was like, how much she was going to scream for his prick, she wanted it for sure, she was just, you know, playing Little Miss Tease about it. Wayne and Rex, they're like, 'Yeah, we should tie her up and you could ram her with your big fucking prick and we'd kill her afterward.' They're laughing about it at first but then later I heard them talking again and that time they didn't laugh so much. Ellis drew pictures of her body and I tried to get hold of them, but not so much for Boris because I just wanted those things for myself. But I never got one. I figured by the things the guys said that the pictures'd be drawings of Sammi, tied up with knives and swords and bayonets in her body. One of the things Ellis drew, or so he told them, was a picture of her chopped-off head, two pricks stuffed in the ears and a third in the mouth. Another was a picture of her pussy after an M-80 blew it apart."

Carl is breathless now. A noise outside—he stops—and Sarah goes to the window. Just a car revving in the street, not the Sunflower van she'd feared. The basketball players have retired for the night, their ball abandoned at the front-porch steps.

Carl sits back. He motions for Sarah to take the other bed. "Don't stop," she says. Her voice scares her a little.

"Then one day I hear them talking about the things they'd actually done. They'd be in crowds of people, during assemblies or at their lockers or wherever, and I could just stand around and they wouldn't see. They'd talk in codes but I'm knowing what they're saying. I found out how Wayne and Rex had fucked this girl at the fair. Rex was like, 'She sucked on me like I was the best-ever candy cane.' On that night Ellis was grounded or something and he was pissed due to he wanted a piece of ass too but couldn't get it. And besides that I found out they'd been stalking this Sammi girl. Following her around and doing things to her locker and her front door at home. Writing things in paint like YOU'RE NEXT SLUT and stalking her. And they'd been stalking somebody else too. Somebody that wasn't a kid at school. Somebody that Wayne wanted to fuck. I didn't hear them say this girl's name, but I could tell Ellis wanted him a piece of Sammi, and Wayne wanted him a piece of this other girl, and they were going to keep torturing these two girls or whatever in the hopes that maybe they'll get away with rape or something or at least keep the fantasies going. I don't know why. And I don't know about Rex. Who he wanted and all. He mostly just laughed with the other two and talked about how slitting a throat would feel and how tight the pussy.

"One time, a few weeks back, I guess, I saw them out by the shop." Out the window, the tree leaves are green and wriggling and alive. The sun, gone; the sky, burned to a coal cinder. "There's this spot by the shop where the assholes park their cars, and in between classes they, like, go out to get high. They huddled over something, and I thought it looked weird and whatnot and, you know, could I report this back to Boris? So I keep watching. They got this big watermelon, something about the size you'd see in those prize-winner 4-H things at the fair. Ellis and Rex've got knives, they're stabbing it and stabbing it, one stab after another. In and out. *Chunk-shhloosh. Chunk-shhloosh.* And Wayne has himself a tape recorder. He was recording the sounds they made, I guess, when the knives went into the melon. I really didn't think much of it, I just left and didn't tell Boris. But then, a couple days later in the library, I overheard Sammi Snow, she was talking with her slutty friends. One of the things she said, wow. She said someone had sent her a tape. In a heart-shaped box. 'From Your Secret Admirer.' That when she played it, she could hear someone getting stabbed. Sammi said to her friend, maybe this has something to do with that girl being murdered. But I knew the truth. I couldn't tell her. Because she barely knows I'm alive, I'm just a fucking freshman, and if I said *anything* those guys would kill *me*."

Carl's face is small and fuzzed like an apricot. Sarah could take it in her hand, could bite its chin and lick its mouth. At last she says, "You're quite the little detective, aren't you?" She knows the direction he is leading, what words are coming next.

"Sure. Sure I am. It was sort of fun early on. But you know what I'm going to say, right? The girl Wayne wants is you. Because Boris said something to me about what him and you found by the river. And now you know who did that too. Because I heard them talking. I heard them saying how they'd stolen it from the First-Aid and Health closet one night. They got the auger from the shop and they made a hole and they took turns fucking her. Ellis thinking the first-aid girl was Sammi. Wayne thinking you. And they must have followed and planted it and watched as you took it out of the water. No, no, you got to see I can't tell Boris this. And then . . . then there were these."

Carl walks to Boris's bed, stops, crouches. Sarah leans over the edge, inspecting the dark world beneath, where his hand now rummages. Scattered below the mattress, sugared with dust, are three wadded notebook pages; a styptic pencil; a keychain without keys in which a four-leaf clover floats preserved, kelly green and deceitful. And Boris's required New Testament. "Don't tell him I'm doing this," Carl says, voice straining with clandestine purpose. "Just please don't tell him."

He moves with swift measured steps, finding the drawer key. Sarah hears the tiny lock capsizing. She remains splayed and ragdoll limber on the bed, head bowed to the floor. The Bible has fallen open to the inside front cover. A sticker bears the legend: *This Holy Word of God courtesy of your Pastor Raymond J. Carmichael of Lawrence Church of Christ. SEE YOU NEXT SUNDAY!* Below it, in red-lettered script: *Even beyond death we shall enjoy eternal life! Have faith! Believe!*

"And then there were these," Carl repeats. He draws close, sits beside her, one eye squinting as though through a loupe. *He thinks I am scared. He wants me now. He wants to hold and protect me but I won't let him have it. He is only a boy, I am almost his mother. They are all boys, all of them. I am not frightened by any of it.*

There is a manila envelope, pregnant with pornography: Tits and asses and cunts have been circled, the faces crossed out. Sarah watches Carl's fingers unravel it all like an intricate knot. She can feel the hummingbird fidget of his exuberance. He is sitting beside her in bed, he is showing the secret to her before anyone else, but she will not look at his eyes, nor his dull chapped mouth, scarred inside with terrible teeth. "I knew about this before I gave it to Boris," he says. "I thought maybe he would have shown it to you, and you would have guessed everything. And his thing for Rex would end."

Also inside is a city map, red-ink welts scarring random streets. One welt targets her house, there on the north part of town, beside the river *where the sad people live.*

And now, the final photograph; he hands it over. "Here," Carl says. "Now you know I'm not making this up." Sarah feels the way she felt in the hospital lot, the words on her car, the icicle shards dripping in her stomach. It is a picture of her. Its focus centers closer to the cash register than to its subject. The film's colors are blanched, almost rustic. Her hair was shorter, slightly, then; her jaw is clenched, as though chewing gum. Sarah cannot guess when the photo was taken. She raises her knee, kicking the envelope, the city map and baffling treasury of naked bodies, this bored face of the girl behind the counter snacks and cash register, to the floor.

"Aaaaah." Carl's mouth goes wide on the vowel, offering a flash of silver caps. And then, as though that flicker sends an arrow through her chest, she's suddenly no longer the adult, no longer Miss Devil-May-Care-and-Composure, and she comprehends what this boy, on this bed, has been telling her. Like in the movies, the pretty girl is targeted by the dunderhead boys. They want to watch her squirm, they want their pricks cannoned inside her. Only now the movie villains are Boris's classmates. The innocent victim is Sarah. "I should be frightened, shouldn't I?" she says. The X-faced photographs of harlot girls, the photograph of *her,* lie on the floor. A mirror leans above Boris's dresser and within its moony glass she sees the abridged face of Carl, nodding and nodding as he tidies the mess.

The smell of something baking. "Cookies," Carl says. His old voice is back, a voice trying to take power over her. "Kitchen staff bakes them as a kind of treat after they get back from catering to the oldsters. They used to make chocolate chip, but not no more. They always screwed them up, and the inmates' acne got too out-of-hand. But who cares."

Sarah must leave. She must run home, find a taxi perhaps, then drive away to Harriet's. Little time left; it seems that, soon, some apocalyptic thing will happen.

"Chocolate," Carl says. "Did you know I have allergies? It's true. I'm allergic to chocolate. And shellfish. I'm allergic to penicillin. They make me wear this." He lifts the lower part of his shirt, revealing a dogtag on a chain. Sarah sees the ribs in his flattened chest, his pair of droplet nipples, a rash of pimples and a few fledgling hairs. "But I'm not so stupid," he says. "I know stuff about cars. Karate and Bruce Lee and the martial arts. I could help you get them off your back. I could get me some numb-chucks, I know a place without those thief-door sensor thingies where I could steal me some. Let those guys just try and fuck with me then." He stops. "I want them dead," he says. "Not just hurt. I want to see them *dead.*"

Carl's words make bayonets of sound in the disinfectant air between them. He returns the envelope to Boris's drawer. "I know where they live. Rex on a farm. Wayne and Ellis in the exact same trailer park, south of town." Sarah wonders what else he knows. The words on the car, the night spying, the doll in the store aisle?

The first victim was buried in her sorority-letter sweater in

Lawrence Cemetery. Her parents live in Omaha but thought it fitting their daughter be laid to rest near the school she loved. Tonight the girl lies there, a thirty-second stroll from Marshall; tonight the rain will scatter on them both. Does Carl know this? Can he know the things important to Sarah, her genuine fears and hundreds of disappointments? Has he looked through the rest of the Suffering Box?

"The buses will be coming back soon," Sarah says. "Don't tell Boris about this. Please. Just don't, not yet. Just tell him I dropped off that stuff on the pillow." She begins to thank him; decides no.

The boy follows her to the window and helps her feet through. "I'll do whatever. I'll help you if you need it, whenever."

Sarah shakes her head, squeezes his hand, and steps out. She cannot go home, not just yet. Down the street are a record shop and a vacuum-cleaner repair and a Chinese restaurant famous for its Crab Rangoon. Just three streets beyond is the grade school she attended. In a second-floor window dangle tissue-paper phantoms, cornhusk witches riding hairbrush brooms. Above these, the yearly jack-o'-lanterns stare out, frantic for Halloween, crayoned and cut and strung in an arc by that classroom's students. In daylight Sarah, driving past, has seen their triangle eyes, their scatter-tooth grimaces and grins. At night, a burning hallway fluorescence casts their cardboard cutout silhouettes across the sidewalk below. She will pass them tonight on this, her jittery ramble home. She will remember the smells of glue and crayons, think of their waxy autumn-orange skins and burnt-sienna stems, but she won't glance up for fear someone will be standing there, the genuine villain face among the art-project pumpkins, watching each footstep she takes, sucking each breath she exhales. It could be Rex or Wayne or Ellis. Or it could be the real murderer, the nameless one who bides his time, now as in tonight, or then as in tomorrow, for her.

13

*M*usic rouses Harriet. On the blue-black skyline a planet twirls among dimmer stars, and although no longer night, it is not yet dawn. She was dreaming of winter. Two feet of snow fell in twenty-four hours. Faucet water froze to ice and the woodstove wouldn't flare, but the children made a midget snow fort, found a robin's egg preserved within a sleeted globe. Marshall and Sarah, thirteen again . . . but the dream had wavered and burst, and with the thin pipe of music she opened her eyes.

There, now: something making its sorrow song, a low whistle of melody that might be outside, might be in, perhaps floats on the air from Marshall's room and perhaps only sings its carousel music in Harriet's head. There is dust on her pillow and, in her mouth, a hint of gingersnap and sandhill-plum jam from her late-night snack. She stretches to the back window. The clockface reads 5:52 A.M., an abbreviated S-U-N. From the roof to the horse trough, swallows cross and recross, returning from trough to roof, their scissored feathers snapping and throats calling *no no no.* In the spectral half-light, Harriet can almost see their afterimages, etched in the sky like the red and gold sparkler trails the kids once drew in the Fourth of July air. Sarah still lies there, curled on the floor beside the bed. She arrived unexpectedly after midnight. "Don't ask why. I'm just a fraidy cat. Just being silly." She tucked Harriet in. They spoke in murmurs of the incessant heat lightning and the sores on Jellybean's legs; then they each swallowed a pretty pill and went to sleep.

Again, the soft whistle, the melody. This time Harriet unwraps the blanket. Odd, but the room is cold. Her feet, cold, as if the night has pickled them. Her slippers rest beside Sarah's head, beneath the chifforobe crowned with Harriet's collections. Her jewelry boxes, gifts from Robert's relatives, trundled back from distant states and foreign lands. Her display of Avon bottles, cobalt and emerald and milk-glass shapes filled with perfumes she never wore. Their exotic names: Desert Moon, Windshadow, Fleur-de-lis, Charisma.

Harriet knows what the chill means. She can smell him now. She whispers, vigilant over Sarah, her breath rising in the room. "It's okay, honey, if you want to let us know you're here. Give me a sign. Now's a good time. I'm here, Sarah's here, we love you, dear." She waits and waits; the clock's numbers flap. "It's okay."

And now she hears a boy, laughing. Of course she thinks *Marshall,* but the voice is lower. *Robert,* maybe, only younger. Harriet has heard from Mrs. Evans about a boy who died not far away, in Baldwin. On his farm now, a haunted silo. The idea is preposterous—not a house, but a silo!—yet Harriet believes. A decade ago, a boy had been playing with friends, hide-and-seek, scaramouch tag. They climbed the combine, the barn roof, at last the rickety side ladder to the silo, each rung a hazard with its grist-powder glaze. The boy scrambled all the way up. His friends followed, breathless. There were hands waving and windmilling, rushes of July wind. There was nowhere to escape. When his friends reached the ladder top, the boy hurled himself through the tiny empty window—heck, no, he wasn't pushed, they swore and swore—and plunged deep in the center of the silo. The grain sucked him under, an abyss, a quicksand of kernels. Later the farmhands drained it all like an enormous orange bath. The boy's mouth, throat, and lungs had packed with oats, eyes crusted with the chaff. Yet still he looked curious and amazed. His life swiped so swiftly and easily. Shattered bits of gold, swallowing him whole.

Out there the light has yet to take hold. Dangling from the gutters are Harriet's birdhouses and ding-dong bells, made entirely of seed. She can see her field, guarded by inkjet clouds; the mulberry tree below them; and, wrapped in stranglehold to the fence, a dying bladdernut vine. All beyond is without definition. Yet something is there, forms behind the space where Sarah has parked her car. A company of shadows: moving, mingling. Jigging around the driveway stones that knuckle from the soil. From the shadows comes the laughter, the sound. Sometimes she wakes to Evans down the road mooing his human moo, signaling his Simmentals it's time for morning feed. But this is too early, even for Evans. Harriet recognizes it now—the music—a melody from a wooden flute. The instrument flaunts no crescendo, no urgency, simply biding its time. Come out, come out, the song is calling. It could be the Pied Piper or the county confections truck. It could be the decade-dead boy from Baldwin, dribbles of grain still spangled in his hair. It could be Marshall.

Summer noons, with Marshall very young and very, very small, Robert would unsnake the garden hose from its anchorage at the house's foundation and fill the horse trough to spill level. The water, glacier cold, was frothed and baby-bubbled like spit. Harriet would ease Marshall in, toes to knees to belly, until only his head loomed above the edge. He gripped her fingertips as though they were jewels. When she said, "*Now drift,*" he drifted, bobbing away, his dark bowl-cut hair fanning about his forehead and neck like the pendant fringe on some panicked animal. His admiration for her was so limitless and uncomprehending, so puppydoglike. Robert believed with practice their son could learn to swim there, but instead all Marshall did was daydream. He shut his eyes and lurched to and fro and thrust his arms into spruce poses. He stared at the sun's smear on the water; tried pinching it in his hands. One cloudless afternoon Robert let a catfish loose, hooked from the far-pasture pond, trapped in brackish mire within the knotted sheath of a polka-dot bread sack. When it zoomed the boundaries of the trough and brushed its whiskers past one bare leg, Marshall made a series of *help, help* hyena whoops and thrashed his palms on the water. Harriet tugged him out and held him, his savior.

And now the shadows outside move nearer, striding forward as though they sense her in the bedroom, hesitant within her glass frame. Someone was out there only nights ago, riding Jellybean. While she presumed it Marshall then, she wonders now, was she wrong? Interlopers, foes. Fear spills through Harriet's chest, making her lonely the way fears do. She longs to bend to the floor, to wake Sarah.

She sits cross-legged in bed, shrouds her head with the blanket. The shadows amble toward her. "I don't know who you are," Harriet says. Three, definitely three. The taller two, dark-haired, the shorter blond. She sees one's motion of hand to mouth and once more hears the flute. The hundred veils of darkness begin to lift, one hundred, ninety-nine, each blue lighter than the last, ninety-eight, and then Harriet sees the blond's face: the same face she saw at Sarah's window. The flute summons and teases. A black mouth opens and a voice calls, "She's in there. In bed with the old bitch. Do the Chinese voice, do the fortune." As Harriet watches, one shadow presses its hand against the window. The fingers smudge their dark red. A handprint splays there, thick counterfeit blood, the one-two-three-four fingerbones and the thumb. There is no oat dust or milo in the nails; it cannot be the phantom child. The hand is not molded from her own; is not Marshall's. First a giggle and then the tomcat hiss of morning grasses and then, after a pause, comes moaning the spirit voice.

Harriet holds her breath until the shadows leave the single bloody handprint and run away. But still she hears the words. *Soon,* said the spirit voice. *Soon you see rewarding, for all the hard work.*

14

At school all the clocks run late. Amid smells of graphite and chalk are janitors with names like Edwin and Marge, student-council hall monitors wearing pastel felt badges and walkie-talkies looped to their belts. A glass case flaunts football, basketball, tennis trophies; adjoining shelves of the art class's papier-mâché watermelons and hamburgers. Signs on teachers' doors: OVERWORKED! and QUIET—TEST IN PROGRESS. The U.S. flag hangs star-top to stripe-bottom from lights in the gymnasium, its field larger than Harriet's front lawn. Sometimes, walking alone to class, Boris has tried running and leaping, fingertips upthrust, to touch its faded white edge. He hasn't yet succeeded.

After lunch, the library. Boris takes his notebook—chapter eight of *March,* now two-thirds finished—and a bruised banana he stole from under the cafeteria's glass sneeze guard. He has twenty-five minutes before next bell. He finds a seat in the back corner, an orange table tattooed with graffiti below rows of spine-snapped books ordered in obsolete Dewey Decimal. The librarian has vanished, on break until next hour begins, her only evidence the empty stool behind her desk. Her trademark wooden map pointer marks a place in the Bible left open to Revelation. Most of the regular library crowd still packs the cafeteria and hasn't yet shown.

At Lawrence West, students spend break times within their nicknamed factions. There is the football bunch, the band geeks, the stoners, and the math nerds. There are the pompom girls, death rockers, Young Dramatists. Boris belongs to none of these crowds. Others exist, detached pariahs who cower at lockers, arrive early to class, hunch over library books until the bell's high-C sanction. If Boris joined them, if they all pooled together, they might be called the wallflowers. But they don't: each is separate, quietly duped, a satellite pulling remote from orbit.

A podium supports an unabridged dictionary. There are atlases of the United States and Kansas and a reference book showcasing all kinds of lists, its fourteen-page chapter on sex efficiently excised. Above shorter shelves hangs an aerial photograph of Lawrence circa 1960 and, behind splintered glass, a Monet reproduction. Boris spreads his work before him: notebook, Harriet's folded fairy tale, guideline sheet for the arts competition.

From this vantage point, Boris can see all who enter. Most afternoons, not much to behold, he bides his time. . . . But today, Ellis Dermody storms through the door. A group of girls follow, chattering. Boris can't help gawking: a dark blue sling wraps Ellis's neck; in its nest balances a plaster cast, a shell covering Ellis's left arm. "A bad fracture," Ellis says. He tells the mob about an incident "down by the river"; says that it's only his wrist, "not the whole arm, not all of it."

Boris spies and spies, training ears and eyes on Ellis's glory. Maybe Wayne and Rex were there for the broken wrist. Or maybe Ellis was alone, hunting butterflies? The girls circle the injured boy, all the unpopular girls, the ones snubbed by football players, the ones who smoke in bathrooms and fabricate terrible lies about each other. They will waste their lives in Lawrence, they will have children before their twenty-first birthdays, in time their hearts will crush like ice. Boris foresees it all. For now, he watches Ellis sit at another table and offer his arm as if for inoculation. He notes the eyelashes fringed with white, the hair the color of butter brickle. Boris finds a blank sheet in his spiral book and writes. *Perhaps, if Rex's beauty weren't so amazing, Ellis might be the object of my affection.* He scribbles possible pet names: *White Dandelion. Baby Harp Seal. Little Butterfly Boy.*

One girl hunts through a gold scallop-shell purse to retrieve a Magic Marker. She wears a charm bracelet, a class ring in artificial ruby, too much eyeliner. A maroon hickey shines below her ear, no doubt a gift from someone's beery mouth after the last football game. "Let me be first," she says, each word summoning innuendo, as she bends to sign the cast. The others stand patiently, poised like ostriches. One is the girl whose sculpture snared last year's contest award; another, the girl who sits behind Boris in typing class, her walnut eyes searching the keys.

A second girl signs the plaster; tosses the Marker to a third. Above their heads, a handwritten poster lists the week's overdue books: Boris scans, finds that Carl Kavanaugh, Grade 9, owes twenty-eight cents for *101 Secrets of the Karate Masters.*

"My turn." It's the typing-class neighbor, bending to the space between Ellis's forefinger and thumb. Her sugar voice, singing: "I'm making a smiley face and my signature and a get well soon. And—"

The door swings open, interrupting her. A-B-C-D they file in: Wayne leading, Drew and Bobby, Rex the caboose. They trample the floor, pitching wars of laughter and slipstream clouds of smoke. Boris lifts the notebook and covers the bottom of his face as the boys make the table their own. Wayne lounges at the crowd's center; Rex kneels beside Ellis. Everyone surrounds the cast as though it were a prehistoric bone, just unearthed.

Only footsteps away now, Rex. Boris could stand, skip over, place his hand against that face, trace the outline of the ear, whisper and whistle there. Kiss and lick. He watches as Rex unpockets a pouch of sunflower seeds, rips a corner, offers them. The girls wait with cupped hands, and the boys take the leftovers, cheeks plumped, shells spat to the brown library carpet.

Rex knocks a vacant one-two on the cast and makes a low whistle through his teeth. "Don't let him fool you," he tells the girls. "This pussy whooped like a banshee when it broke." He takes the marker from a protesting Ellis. "Hey, you don't just want red on the thing. Let's get you some color." Rex crosses to the librarian's desk and hurdles the slatted partition: Boris hears the creak of the drawer, the scattering of pencils and pens. "A black one," Rex says. "Yellow and green and blue."

The boys fill the spaces on the cast. Wayne right-handed on one side; Rex, awkward lefty, on the other. Squires Bobby and Drew standing behind. Unexpectedly Boris remembers the pictures in the envelope. Heads scissored from bodies, mutilated skin and bone, and above it all Sarah, Sarah. At this moment, Sarah works on the other side of town, six hours shy of shift end. Once, when Boris visited, she showed him a trick. She drew the blue-paper blinds and shut off the lights, then wrenched the dainty silver key on the cash register to the right, forcing the numbers to become letters. When she tap-tapped, their green glow filled the store. TONIGHT! WORLD PREMIERE STARRING SARAH HART. He took his turn. BORIS APPLEBY LOVES REX JACKSON. No, no, try again. REX JACKSON LOVES BORIS APPLEBY.

Heartbeats flood in his ankles and wrists, blood rushing in both ears, breath heaves coming quicker and defensive like chops of a knife. Boris fixes his gaze on Rex and cannot blink. So close. If only he'd borrowed Harriet's camera, if only he could sneak behind the books, mute the shutter, aim, and shoot. So close! Rex's slouched posture and dingy, unclipped fingernails. His red sneakers baubled with farm mud; untucked T-shirt with off-kilter neck gap and front faded gray. His glasses, veiled within the pocket. His giant hands hanging inches past the hips. His nose, fuzzed chin, heavy charcoal hair. Compared to all this, how could Boris even consider loving Ellis? Loving anyone else?

Then Boris swims back. Blinks and swallows. Someone is speaking to him. For the first time he hears music, piped-in and snowing from the ceiling, a Brahms lullaby, he guesses, but granted, he wouldn't know Brahms from a dolphin's song. He was thinking of Rex, the places they could go, alone, the things they, alone, could do together. . . . There, the voice again, and Boris looks away from Rex to focus on the rest of the students.

"Did you hear me or what?" Wayne. It is Wayne speaking. "You see something you like over here?" In the moment's crackle, Boris notices the room as if from above: a crowd of ten kids at one side; himself, trapped behind his orange table, at the other. It is only natural they would spot him. Now, Boris understands; everything comes together. He knows that Wayne will smile. Yes, he knows Wayne's drumtapping marker on the desk. "What you looking at, faggot?"

All of them, watching. It is as though they have never seen him before, as though the girls haven't snickered into fists in the hallway, the boys haven't stared at his weekend arm-hooking-arm walks with Sarah and Harriet down Massachusetts Street. Ellis puts away his prize fracture, snuggling it back into its blue cloth holster. Bobby and Drew are looking, the girls are looking. And Rex. For the first time, Boris stares into Rex's face, and Rex stares back. There are the green eyes, the uneven black bangs draping to the space where the brows connect. *I would lick the sleep dust from his eyes,* Boris once wrote in his journal. *Would drink from his mouth. My face on fire from the friction of his stubble.*

Wayne heads over, cocks his head, and stands before Boris, blue Magic Marker in fist. "What's the matter?" he asks. "You jealous you don't have a broken arm too?" His smirk seems copied from the face he wore on the fairgrounds midway, that persuasive expression leading the girl into the bathroom. The WAYNE belt buckle glitters. His shirt is Granny Smith green with sweat stains under the arms, a grease dot at the collar.

Boris feels his shoulder blades falling, chest constricting with his tripled pulse. Clenched jaw and supplicant bowed head. The librarian has not returned from lunch break, and Boris wishes for her, back now, to save him. He grips the desk; one of the scars reads, ALL THE WAY SR.'96! Eraser residue lies snug inside its pocketknifed grooves like pink grated coconut. Once when Boris was little, he mistakenly chewed the eraser from a #2 pencil and swallowed, but he can't recall which father it was who punished him. *Everything will be fine. Wayne will walk away, he will leave me alone.* Yet even now, in synch with this thought, Boris knows he is wrong. He knows Wayne's unspoken words, and following, too, the inevitable frenzy.

"Or does this little faggot want some of my friend's dick?" The shell of a sunflower seed flutters from Wayne's mouth. He shakes his hand at Boris, taunting, then looks back to the crowd. Ellis laughs, Rex laughs. The boys, the girls. *They know.*

"I'm sorry," Boris says.

Wayne comes closer, his mouth chopping the words. "Come on, admit it. It's what you want. You and that bitch friend of yours. Hey, he's got a nice big one, all hot and big and ready." Ellis laughs still, slapping Rex's back with his unbroken arm. "But first you got to say it," Wayne says. "Tell all of us. Tell us you're a faggot."

Through the library isinglass the muted sun throws shadows to the bookcases; a trapezoid of white across the table. *The boy zombie is alone at last,* his latest line reads. Boris closes his eyes and opens them again and, glancing up, sees Wayne still there, nearer now, spotlit by the sun. He nods twice, as though answering Boris: Yes, I know you've followed us. Yes, I know your love for Rex.

And the fist is there. Even before he feels it, Boris smells its soap-pump suds and its dribbles of cologne. He almost tastes its warmth. Then the four ridged knuckles and the skin dry as jerky and the fake sapphire Lawrence West senior class ring come collid-

ing with his jaw, and Boris falls back. His chair spills; the rows of
tables and books turn a swift, spinning arc. His back hits the floor
in a snuffed thud. He crawls away from the chair and makes a soft,
quivering sob. Another brims close but he swallows it. He huddles
near the bottom bookcase row, drizzled by rushing dust. But
Wayne isn't finished. He crabwalks across the table and pounces,
eyes starred silver in his head, waiting and waiting for the flow of
blood. "Little fucking freak." Boris touches his lips but no blood
wipes away. Wayne, seeing this, rares back and makes a thin, falsetto
giggle and drives home another grand-slam punch.

Now they jump up, all of them running, Drew and Bobby and
Rex gathering above Wayne's shoulder blades as though for a
prizefighter. Hidden between them, Ellis, his cast poking through.
The girls are chanty-birds in the distance, their *oh my god*s and *stop
it Wayne*s and *we're gonna get caught*s. Boris feels a hand clamping his
mouth—Wayne's? Bobby's?—and the taste there goes dark gray
and metallic. The blood shuts his throat. He swallows, ears pop-
ping, and within the giggling of the girls worms Ellis's voice.
"Watch out for the blood, he probably got it from that other one,
it'll give you some disease."

Wayne rips at Boris's shirt buttons. He pulls the shirt free from
his jeans, raising it over his head. "Help me with this," he says, and
Drew shoves in front of Rex to pin the struggling arms, to unpeel
the shirt. Boris feels the stale, bookworm-dust air, chilling his bare
stomach and chest. Drew holds one wrist, Ellis the other, and in
that snippet of time Boris imagines the butterflies under glass,
Ellis's needles spearing them on the velvety black.

Wayne pinches the cap from the Magic Marker. The tip stabs
Boris in the belly. "F, A, G, G, O, T," each letter spelled on his ribs in
a diagonal banner.

Boris tries to move; again; no use. One girl's muffled protest:
"Stop, you're hurting him." But her sentence snaps into a laugh.
The others egg Wayne on, cheerleading, slapping his back and cir-
cuiting the room. The girl with the scallop-shell purse bends to

Wayne's ear. She yells, "More!" and clownishly hops once, twice, foot stomping Boris's hand. "Write more," she screams. "Think of synonyms! Write 'pansy'! Write 'candyass'!"

The boys must feel the girls' adulation, their gluttony, and bewitched by this encouragement Drew rolls up his sleeves, Ellis jams his knee into Boris's side, every grunt and act of force sending visible thrills through the admiring fans. Boris feels another word, this time spelled into his shoulder. The marker presses firm, seeping ink. His eyes dart there and here but see only the immediate faces in the rabble: Wayne, his forehead's birthmark and imperfect underbite and the drool on his lip; Drew; pale Ellis. And Rex, where is Rex? Fingers slide his pant cuff to his ankle, pull on the sock. Another Magic Marker pushes there, a finer point this time. The piercing dot makes letter, letter, letter. "Write 'queer,'" the girl screams. For a quarter-second Boris catches her, hovering over Wayne, her mouth wrung open in malice and glee. "Queer and queen, queen and queer! Cornholer, homo, swish!" Ellis rests his good arm on the bare chest, and Boris feels the blond fur tickling, scratching. Ellis trades his hold on the wrist to Bobby; slides his cast from the sling. Spits a sunflower shell. "Pansy! Fairy!" Boris feels the cast come down, drubbing his shoulder first. The plaster batters bone with the thunk of antlers clashing. "I'm sorry," Boris says, "I'm sorry," his voice thinned, not his. After a cutthroat second the cast rises again. Boris sees a girl's name written there, a GET WELL SOON, and, in blue marker, block letters R and E and X. The cast strikes, this time blasting into his face, splitting his lip. Something like a soul inside Boris breaks free, no longer part of this, drifting high to the shelves, lodging narrow between two unread books. He looks down on himself, on the knees in his ribs and the shoes grinding skin and the spreading delta of blood on his chin. The fists and the pens, the multicolored cast. Boris tries again to move, but Bobby and Drew are handcuffs, stifling his struggle.

Wayne points the marker at his bleeding mouth. Boris twists his head, neck muscles strained, slowing when Wayne mashes the ball of his hand against Boris's cheek. Another word: four letters, five, across the side of his face. The pen's muddy felt slides in the blood smear. Wayne yanks at his hair. "You can tell your friend how good I am," he says. His mouth stinks of pot and milk and pig grease. His voice yields to a murmur, words meant only for Boris. "You can let her know how strong I am, tell her I'll lay it in her pussy like a piece of steel and she'll beg for it forever after." Then Wayne's fist, once more, at the hollow of Boris's throat. "Tell her it'll feel," the fist, "like," the fist, "this."

At his right: Drew, closing a hand over the yellow marker. Atop his stomach: more markers, their ammunition, almost disembodied now, scribbling. Somewhere near his feet: his typing-class neighbor, loosing her linnet's voice, announcing the words she has written. "In red I put YOU ARE HERE." He tries to kick, and a fist slams his shin. "I made a teeny-weeny black dot," the girl says, "and in green I made an arrow."

Wayne stands, half-stepping a foot on his victim's abdomen. "Turn him over," he says, monarch over servants bidding sacrifice. "Hold him down. Get his pants down a little."

One last time, Boris tries to fight. But Drew catches his head, sandwiches it between the crook of his arm and chest—within a ribbon of light his biceps shows its sickle scar—and brings an already messy fist around to pound his face. "Hand me the marker," someone says. Boris feels more blood, a humid red spatter in his mouth and his nose and even, it seems, his eyes. He shuts his eyes and lets them move him. They are still laughing, twisting his body to kiss the floor as though he were made of foolscap or vanilla frosting or filled with goose down.

A figure steps out from behind. Without seeing, Boris knows it is Rex. Legs straddle his bare back, and Rex sits there, at the small—the fantastic weight and the texture of his skin, rough but somehow soft. Boris can't breathe. For the first time he feels the tears rising. From a corner of vision, Wayne hands Rex the marker.

"I can't think of any more words," the girl says. Her fingernails land, vulture-sharp, on the bare back. "But, oh, I know some from French class. Rex, French, write French." She stands and leaps in overexcitement, two times, three, clopping horseshoe clops on the carpet. "Write TANTE. Do it, do it! Write on his faggot ass! TANTE! Um, I can't think. TANTE, PEDE, CON, BATARD . . ."

"I can't spell it," Rex says. The marker tip touches like a god's wrathful finger. "I can't spell it." Below the marker, on the skin of his ass, Boris feels the tiny copper rivets from the pocket of Rex's jeans.

"*Enfoire,*" screams the girl, enunciating each syllable, then spelling—"*E, N, F*"—but Boris feels Wayne's foot, again, in the air-pocket space below his ribs, and he jerks. Rex teeters from his back, a defensive surfer. The glasses fall from his pocket. Boris sees them bounce once on the carpet to land beside his ear, facedown, the thick black arms folded. Suddenly his hand is free. Drew has dropped it, and Boris reaches, reaches for the glasses. He finds and lifts them, there within the shrill, violent sacrifice and the spellings of the words, the synonyms for Boris. He strains as far as this position allows his arm, delivering the secret glasses back to Rex.

"I'm sorry," Boris says. Lovingly, Rex's hand takes the glasses.

Then Drew's clamp is back. The wrist slams to the carpet, the pen point returns to skin. Boris feels it just above the crack of his ass, hears the girl giggling and her insistent "*enfoire, enfoire.*" Rex steadies himself with his right hand, writes the word with his left. The letters, like bottleflies skittering.

And then comes the bell: signaling the end of lunch, the commencement of fifth-hour classes. Everyone quiets, and within this stillness Boris coughs. The bell his bandage, his angel.

Drew and Bobby release the captive wrists and Boris sits up, a blood-dot dripping to his thumb. They file out, Drew and Bobby pursuing Rex, the girl still giggling and clutching the purse at her side. She offers a final unintelligible French word, an afterthought. Wayne turns, winks, holds a fist before his face. His footsteps join the crowd in the hall; the sound lifts and falls and only the echo is left. Then the echo dies, and Boris stands.

He pulls up his pants and finds his shirt, crumpled and tarnished crimson on the floor, like an after-prom corsage. His skinned knees and torn hair. The dusted blood coating the enamel of his teeth; its simmery taste in his carbonated head. But Rex has touched him. Rex stood above his body and looked down on him, and then Rex wrapped his legs around his body and their fleshes touched. Rex rubbed his fingers against Boris's hand; he accepted the gift and the apology and Rex, Boris is certain of this, did not want to hurt him.

He swipes the blood from his lips; rubs its claret stain into his knuckles. His stomach feels like an elevator cut from its cable. He breathes, holds it, breathes out. Above his head, the ceiling is more brown than its intended white. The pocked and dimpled surface resembles the peel of a decaying orange. Directly above it is the Learning Disabilities lounge; above that the roof; higher and higher, the sky. Thunderheads and bedlam downpours have been predicted for tomorrow, but for the weekend, for the day of the Lucas trip, they promise sunshine sweet as honey.

Boris abandons the room, through the empty hall, into the bathroom. Here, the same world where he spied on Rex; here, his lemon-pop piss exploded into the white bowl. Was that days ago? Weeks? Someone has overturned the rectangular gray trash bin. Spilling out are two cardboard toilet-paper tubes, wadded roses of tissue, a plastic foam cup with a bracelet of teeth marks at its rim. The ripped screen from a pot pipe, sifting its ash. Boris grows dimly aware of bulldozer noise in the street outside, and now the sound of footsteps in the hall.

The mirror is there, and after a pause he turns and looks. He tries to hold the sob but it breaks out, a thick seed split from its pod. His eyebrow looks bent, above an eye that will surely go black. Blood has dried crisp in one nostril. There is blood in his mouth, threaded beads of tartar and gum pulp like undissolved clumps of sugar in caramel. From the smudged edge of his lip to the height of his cheekbone, a single blue word: QUEER.

He removes his shirt. His wrists are abraded rare pink, and his muscles feel ironed, scraped out. On his neck and nipple and stomach are plaster and fingernail scratches. And the words, the words. Wayne's blue FAGGOT across his ribs and someone else's FUCKIN FAGGOT on his neck. HOMO under his chin. PANSY on his shoulder. His chest and arms show both completed products—CANDYASS, SHITEATER, DEEP THROAT, a green beside a black FAG—and unfinished–COCKSU, QU, FAIR. Around the axis of his navel, concentric blue letters like the numerals of a clock: twelve o'clock, *S*; one o'clock, *T*; then a *U* and a *P* and on and on until, gaping, Boris can make out STUPIDFAGGOT.

He lifts his pantlegs. On his right shin, a descending red series of QUEEN QUEER QUEEN QUEER; his left ankle, his classmate's YOU ARE HERE with the polka dot and arrow.

Boris stands tall at the basin, turns the hot-water dial, touches the skiff of soap. Only during the second washing of his stained face does he remember. He unbuttons, unzips, lowers his pants, and turns. He sees the blotches of pressed and knuckled skin, red now, gray-blue later. And below this, at the small of his back, the top of his skinny ass, lies Rex's word.

Enfoire, the girl said. But Rex misinterpreted her instruction. ONFIRE, he has written, the *F* in lowercase, the *E* hastily scribbled. Boris understands: it is Rex's sign, his confession. *On fire.*

QUEER, says Boris's face in the mirror. QUEER, said the side of Sarah's battered car. And FAGGOT on his ribs. And OSTIT on the dummy they found, one stormy month ago, on the riverbank. But now, overpowering it all, looms the perfect pair of words on his back. Rex's gift. Like the prelude to a psalm: ON FIRE . . . two words to reflect the burn and the yearning. *Oh, Rex, there is no need to fear any longer. Soon, soon. On fire.*

Outside the bulldozer stops. There are birds stamping the window with their wings, wanting in. Boris stops the water and tosses the soap to the sink. He wriggles into his shirt, turns, and leaves, walking back to the library. "*Enfoire,*" the girl said, again and again. Rex was uncertain; he hesitated. He was forced to make his choice, to spell what had to be spelled. Now the knowledge is unleashed. There is no turning back.

The librarian sits behind her partition, back from lunch, now replacing cards in a file box. A green artillery marker rests beside her elbow. Her eyes glance away from her work, peering over her spectacle rims. Her mouth goes slack and her face tilts forward, as though she is trying to smell something baking. "Are you okay?" she asks, but Boris cannot answer.

Here is where it happened. He is alive; he survived. He can smell, still, the marker inks and the boys' colognes. On the floor lies his pilfered cafeteria banana, a slit in its peel spilling white mash. Around its crescent moon, like hundreds of shrapnel stars, lie the shells of spat sunflower seeds.

Blood trickles from his nose to his chin. He tries to speak. Or rather he cannot speak, his tongue shriveled and swimming stone-hard through the blood in his mouth. He points to the librarian's table. He nods and taps the edge of her open Bible. The woman looks at Boris, furrows her brow, then looks down and gasps. There, across the pages of her heirloom, the dirty villain boys have scrawled twin red *X*'s, obliterating and annihilating these whatever words from her wherever god.

—S.

Marshall my soulmate, my sweetheart cupid, my dearest chum. We had everything in common, even fell in love w/the same boy, Howard Westenhoffer, a bookworm in thick-lensed spectacles w/a flawless square jaw & a smell like almonds. We'd pine over him during Marshall's visits to Sunflower or the forbidden nights I slept at the farm. We didn't fight over Howard because neither had a chance, it was hopeless, I was the school slut & Marshall was queer, a fact known only to me & Harriet but a scandalous supposition whispered by half the town. We were hated, misunderstood, called every possible name. Yet Howard never uttered a word to us, we translated his silence & indifference as admiration or kinship. He excelled at tennis, for hours after school we'd linger around the parking lot, in full view of the courts. We eyed his backhand, his bullet-thrust serve, wishing for binoculars, relishing the quick slick shriek of his sneakers burning arcs in the simmering concrete.

Sunflower required five hours of community service a week, some of us took an hour after school, some wasted weekends mowing church lawns or spooning food into hospital patients' mouths. A supervisor learned I could paint & set me to work on murals, Marshall snuck w/me through dirt-cheap scot-free stints at City Hall & the Arts Center, watching while I slapped the brush on the wall, endlessly endlessly discussing Howard.

Songs helped us through. We dove deep into New Wave music, every song speaking direct & immediate to us, we heard the sound humming somewhere inside our bodies long after the music had stopped. We also liked soul, hits from the 60s & early 70s, a divinity-voiced deejay on the Kansas City radio played all the songs you'll ever want to hear. *Big & willowy & sublime & sad on that oldies station was Roberta Flack, "The First Time Ever I Saw Your Face," Marshall & I would switch off all lights, stretch on the floor, my head on his stomach, to wail along w/her soothing voice.* I felt the earth move in my hands . . . like the trembling heart of a captive bird. *Our minds zeroed in on Howard Westenhoffer or whoever else we loved but couldn't have, oh god we wanted to be touched & held, to be told I love you like no other. Doesn't everyone need that?*

In my own way I struggled w/love, I can't forget the long long line of them, boys who did whatever I asked, boys who got what they wanted. There was Victor Earl who worked nights at the power plant beside the river, he'd take me there in the prize pickup he called The Hawg, some nights after we'd fucked he'd lure rats from under the lumber piles w/pellets of moldy raisin bread, then pull his shotgun from the back window rack & fire fire. There was Jan Skovgaard, the burnout Swedish exchange student flunking four of six classes, our hourlong rendezvous in the Sunflower parking lot the night before they shipped him home. There was Mickey Green w/the suedehead haircut who mailed boxes of chocolates to my Sunflower address, he stood drenched beneath my window one night in a late-autumn cloudburst, he cried on the telephone until I begged him Forget me. Even after him, after all these boys, I still shuffled through school in skimpy dresses w/my mouth kept pouty, forever half-open. The eighties were beginning, I was sixteen, every day both calamity & celebration. Guys not glued to sports or academics would see me coming, offer up a proposition or joke I'd always giggle at, they knew my parents had traded me to Sunflower, hoping to cure my petty shoplifting, my school truancy, the horde of other boys they'd caught w/me.

I wore my outcast status like a bright badge & soon Marshall grew vain too. Sometimes he'd join me at Friday Afternoon Frights, that was the year of Alien, Halloween, Phantasm, *on the days he wouldn't come I'd ask some boy from my recent past, Victor or some other name. The boy's eyes on the theater screen would go glassy, he'd put his hand inside my skirt or blouse & while heroines screamed on screen I imagined it was my real love loving me, Howard, oh Howard. I'd whisper to Marshall about it later, substituting Howard's name for the real boy's, then I'd yield five fantasy minutes to Marshall, he'd invent a Howard story too. Around this time he discovered the Campanile, driving the car Harriet & Robert had bought him, a 1972 bean-green Chevy Impala we nicknamed The Dragon. I egged him on, boosting his shyness, my* voice in his ear saying *Enjoy yourself, free yourself*, like some self-help tape. Zoom, Marshall would drive to campus, some nights after midnight, loving it. Oftentimes his sex became too important, I'd stay lost in my troubled-teen room or in the front balcony theater row, alone, envisioning him on the other side of town, his mouth on someone else's, only then would I get jealous.

But I knew Marshall thought of Howard too, obsessed like me, both of us inventing ways to catch a glimpse, maybe touch him. Sports was Lawrence West's #1 focus, all the coaches pampered their players, maybe we could join the pep club, use this avenue to snare him. Track or tennis, baseball or wrestling, all the boys got luxury locker-room herbal baths to soothe tired muscles, whether they were mighty basketball stars or mere podunks of junior varsity football. I've been in that locker room, Marshall joked, *A sign bars* GIRLS *from entering but nothing says* NO HOMOSEXUALS. He detailed the pair of elliptical steel tubs gleaming like giant spoons, regretting he'd only seen them empty, not filled to the brim w/hot steaming water & sloshing two noble soaped-up & massaged sixteen-year-old sports boys, preferably one of them Howard.

Then our luck struck target when one of Sunflower's wealthy sponsors needed a favor. Jack was his name, he'd visited Sunflower twice & I'd seen his eyes on me, he was landlord for homes on the north sides of Ohio Street, Kentucky, Tennessee, he wanted an expert to paint the shutters & door trims on his houses, burgundy & rose madder trim so potential renters could know which homes were his. Of course I volunteered, I would go from the Arts Center murals to Jack's north-side houses, by that time Marshall & I had figured where the Westenhoffers lived, I knew in time I'd paint there, of course I volunteered.

We waited four weekends for the Westenhoffers, painting different houses, my blouse & jeans stained w/burgundy. Marshall joined me each time, I remember him standing smoking below my ladder, prompting me lines from favorite film roles, reading aloud from romance novels. His sunglasses & heavy-bangs New Wave haircut, his stereo booming in the grass at his feet, alternating New Wave tapes, soul oldies. What I wouldn't give to go back there now, sometimes in the sleepy magnificence of dreams I can almost touch it, I reach out my hand but before my fingers find the ladder or the smudges of paint or the skin on my best friend's face it's gone, it's gone.

The night before Howard's house neither of us could sleep, we stayed up staring in the mirror wondering would Howard decide to help, would he sing along to the stereo & our absolute favorite tapes we'd brought for the day, would he deliver us lemonade in frosty glasses? We arrived at 7 A.M., a Saturday, his father met us at the door w/the armload of land-lord Jack's supplies, we set to work. 8 A.M., 9, 10, still no sign of Howard. We took our own sweet time, the sun aimed its steely needlepricks on our shoulders & we let it burn us, me applying the brush to the shutters w/the same care I'd use to touch Howard, if only he'd let me. Marshall below me, alternating Adam & the Ants w/Roberta Flack on his stereo, his usually bluejay voice gone soft & whispery & warped in anticipation.

Exactly why I stepped into the house I don't remember, maybe I got the nerve to ask for glasses of water, maybe I'd run out of some certain supply or maybe no reason at all, maybe I'd lost the coin toss & mustered all the nerve to volunteer, to take the chance to see him. Marshall stayed outside on the grass, humming to the music, there beneath the paint-chipped ladder where the bad luck swarmed.

No one answered my knock, I noticed their tiny orange-light doorbell didn't work, neither the Mr. nor the Mrs. nor flawless Howard heard me. I breathed deep, opened the door, stepped right in, thinking I'd beg to use their rest room if they asked. I couldn't find them anywhere, walked through two rooms but nothing, wound up standing over the sink washing my hands to kill time. I made mental notes for Marshall, the double bathroom doors leading to the parents' room on one side & Howard's on the other, the delicate shell-shaped soaps, the shower cur-tain patterned w/blue tropical fish & pairs of lovestruck seahorses. Attached to the inside of the toilet bowl was a warty blue disk, when I flushed the water bloomed a deeper blue, like water from some dreamy romantic Caribbean sea I'd forever wish to visit on honeymoon but knew I never would.

Then while noting the details I heard them speaking, Howard Westenhoffer & his father, there in the adjoining bedroom, thinly barriered from me by the pinstripe-papered wall. They were talking about us. I got on my knees & peeked through the skeleton keyhole, w/in that dusty droplet of air I could see part of the dad & a larger part of Howard. I'll never forget how he looked, he was shirtless, just out of the shower, only moments before he'd been here in the bathroom where I now knelt. His glasses off, tanned chest glistening like a water moccasin's skin, bathwater stars in his hair, his immaculate tennis-white shorts tightened w/an Indian beaded belt. PERFECT was the only word in my head, I could barely breathe & wished Marshall were here w/me. They were speaking, the father gave a funny splintered laugh, What a strange pair they've sent over to paint the shutters, he said. Howard was agreeing, up until now I never knew he even recognized our existence, now he was talking about us, my breath trapped a bubble in my lungs & my heart retangled its already complicated knot.

Oh, them, Howard said. He'd seen us from his bedroom window, w/out us even knowing he'd watched us in the backyard lawn, painting the screen door trim & thin strips of wood around the rain gutters. The male one of the pair, Howard said, If you can call him a male, he's, you know, he's one of those. There was a fat pause, in the silence I could see him there, beyond the bathroom door, the gesture he was making. The hand limp in midair, the pinky poised, the hand fluttering back & forth as the wristbone collapsed. Besides him, Howard said, the female, as for her, she's what you'd call loose, & that's, ha ha, putting it loosely.

I stood up from my aching knees, hurried out through the other bathroom door where they couldn't see me, they were continuing their conversation but I couldn't hear. I wanted to scream or ram the ladder through their windows or kill every flower in their garden w/the toxic burgundy paint. I wanted to do something unbelievably dramatic but couldn't. He knew who we were, Marshall & I, he hated & feared us just like everyone else. From that moment I tried to think differently of Howard Westenhoffer, tried to replace his body & gorgeous bookworm face w/all the victims from the films I loved. Him, buried neck-deep in *a hill of fire ants, those pests that stung a person's skin until red welts blistered bloody & the breathing slowed to a stop. Him, a human shish-kebab, a boiling human stew, cooked in those cannibal cauldrons that would remain over the licking flames until the flesh peeled off. Him, thrown hands-tied into the torture barrel studded here & there w/points-exposed nails, then rolled down a hill pierced & screaming through his painful wet bloody violent death.*

I tried to hate him but failed, I couldn't do it, couldn't switch the bull's-eye of my love to someone else. It was never that easy, it still isn't, only in movies or romance novels or bubblegum songs is it that easy, an uncontrollable love doesn't just erase or swiftly swiftly change. For days after I still let Marshall con me into watching tennis practices, smirking at the forty-loves, *for all I knew he still imagined it was Howard he was kissing & holding,* like the trembling heart of a captive bird, *those humid shadowy nights near the campus bell tower. I never told him, I kept my knowledge secret, thinking that moment in the Westenhoffers' bathroom was one of the little things I'd hold until we were old & it didn't matter anymore. Yes yes, later in our lives I could lean to his ear & whisper all the things I'd withheld, by that time we could both sit back, reminisce, laugh. But then, of course, I didn't know Marshall's future, what would happen. I couldn't guess that for my secret whisper, for our old-timer best friend's laugh, I would never get the chance.*

15

oris watches Carl sleep because he can't sleep himself. The clock shows 1:27, six hours shy of the morning's alarm and the trip to Lucas. The rain has stopped, now merely leaf drips on the glass, a ruined alto of crickets. He rises from bed, part by part and gingerly, a marionette. At midnight, Carl unveiled his half-empty Jack Daniel's bottle. Now Carl is oblivious, and Boris, eighty-six-proof smashed but awake. He wears Band-Aids on his neck, the torn cuticle of a thumb; on his lip, a glistening dab of salve. A bruise shows beneath one eye. He slips into jeans and sneakers and, after grabbing his portable stereo, a navy windbreaker. One last look at Carl—"Sleep tight," Boris whispers, sliding the sheet over his bottle—and he opens the window.

Lying to Sarah didn't feel so bad. "Some guy at school. I don't even know his name. I think he did it on a dare. He's a senior and ugly as sin and hangs out with the stoner crowd. He just punched me twice and walked away and I wasn't even looking at him, he just, *pow.*" By then he'd scrubbed clean the words on his face and neck. He didn't show her ONFIRE, still, and hopefully forever, remaining on his back.

Did Sarah believe him? She scrutinized a deep scratch, then puckered up and blew there, as though her breath could miraculously heal. "I should call your principal." She held the phone to her chest as Boris protested. He said *please* three times. On the fourth she gave in: After all, he told her, the effort would change nothing, and besides, weren't things, in general, going to get better?

Boris knows his destination and embarks. The storm has left a coppery smell in its wake, low clouds hovering in the obsidian sky. The tape playing in his stereo earpieces was Marshall's birthday gift to Sarah; after the funeral, she gave it to Boris. And tonight the music is loud. For the third time in his life, Boris is drunk. The world, astonishingly, appears not much different. If he stares too long—the attic window of that house; the airbrushed desert panorama on that Chevy van—the scene drifts a little, rocks from focus, then comes crashing back. He starts up the hill, wind funnels gusting leaves at his ankles and hair in his eyes. Stalks of shattered glass lie wedged into the sidewalk cracks; the gutters have overflowed; an upturned hubcap spills rain and sludge in a slow roulette. The corner streetlight casts a mammoth winged shadow, and for an instant Boris imagines a swooping bat. He looks up and sees his mistake. There, in the sycamore branches, spins someone's umbrella, a black steel-skeletoned ghost blown loose by the lunatic storm.

He reaches the lawn of the campus Catholic church. A violet bug lamp hangs before the doors; in the garden, ordered rocks form a cross in the dirt. There are trimmed hedges and two giant pre-Halloween pumpkins and a spotted mongrel dog trotting past. A water pump stands lonesome, a metal post with orange handle and spigot. Boris unclicks the handle, wrenches upward, and lowers to its whooshing sting on his wounded mouth. But the water only sends him deeper inside drunk. He dabs his jacket sleeve to his lip. It has stopped bleeding at last, yet in a way it still bleeds. In a way, he thinks, it will always bleed, tomorrow and three years from now and after.

Boris hums the tune from the tape that rattles his ears, volume upped to its limit. He passes an arc of dark houses, the last of which smells of sawdust and turpentine. A campus bookstore; an apartment parking lot; a sorority house with study lights dimly shining. Possibly the place where one, or both, of the victims lived? In one window, a woman strikes careful cameo poses while a flashbulb flashes. She lifts her arms to aim a make-believe gun; bucks her head for the camera. With each successive flash Boris realizes the woman is wearing nothing and, embarrassed, he moves along.

At the campus fountain, on the green-gray cement, someone has drawn a tic-tac-toe grid with calcite stone. In place of *X*'s and *O*'s are crescent moons and radiating suns. The moons have won: top to bottom, left to right, a lipstick victory slash. He steps across the game and shoos mosquitoes from the air, then descends to pause in the grass beside the sign for the Campanile.

Watching Carl's sleep in the closet; witnessing Rex and Wayne and the blowjob girl in the fairgrounds bathroom: lately Boris wonders if he'll ever be participant instead of observer. And tonight, his body still messy with the bruises and the pain, head yoked by booze, he decides to remedy his problem. All night he has replayed pieces of stories Marshall told, the shadows dancing among the trees . . . hands that pulled him deeper into shadows . . . mouths on his mouth and all those hands, as the campus ink-shade hills burned darker and the whippoorwills lifted into romantic song . . .

The occasional car eases through the winding drive, past the parking spaces. Here someone's silhouette, moving down the hill beyond the bell tower; there another man, smoking near a grove of mulberry trees. If Boris were holding the bottle, he'd take another drink to erase any and all apprehension. But the bottle is back at Sunflower, and he has come this far, all or nothing, now.

"Okay," he tells himself, "okay." He moves along the hillside, past Snow Hall, past the parking garage for the research library. He hurries across the curve in the road, caught for a moment in headlight glare. He thinks of that famous Bigfoot film—the hunter on horseback, surprised in a forest clearing, frantically reaching for his movie camera—and, savoring the moment, takes especially long, arm-swinging strides. He hurdles the curb and sidewalk, the bushes envelop him, and then the bushes darken and only shadow remains.

The guitars and drums sizzle through the stereo wire, Boris lip-synching words he knows. *My eyes have seen the glory that leaves me blind. . . .* He could sit on the chiseled stone benches near the bell tower, the same that overlook the valley and its football stadium. He could watch the jeweled nightscape of Douglas County lights and wait for someone to approach. Instead he turns left, the movement keeping his nervousness at bay, and begins cautiously downhill to Potter's Lake. "The ghost will get you if you come here alone," Marshall once said. "Never cruise too close to the water!" Sarah, smirking, shook her head; Boris knew they were teasing him, but for the first time in his life he could laugh together with those doing the teasing.

A lamppost near the bridge flutters off and on again, off, on, as if transmitting some furtive message. Within its lightning flashes, the pond: its scarf of cattails and reeds; its onyx surface, streaked by wind or the tails of fish. And someone stands there too, a man in a baggy sweatshirt who lingers at the bridge, elbows resting on its wooden handrail. Boris swallows hard, whiskey's memory nibbling the pit of his throat. *So dark down there,* Marshall once said, *you'd only know they're handsome if your hands were flashlights.* The lamp flickers one last time and comes flaring, brighter, back.

Down the hill, the grass thickens at his feet, frizzly and bright green like the kind lining Easter baskets. He leans against the knobby bark of a tree, but its plasma smudges his shoulders and back and gels in his uncombed hair. Nowhere to go but forward;

the man glances over and mutters something. Boris thumbs the stop button on his stereo and slides the headphones to his neck. He looks at the man, his narrow pinched face. There are two identical tufts of hair above his ears, a triangle of fuzz at his forehead. He could be a teacher at school, someone's foster father, the slaughterer of the two dead girls. Boris's voice bubbles up like root beer: "What'd you say?"

"Here's what I said. I said, 'Did you see what that lamp was doing?' That's what." The man turns to face him. He is eating an ice-cream sandwich: three bites left, now two. "Weird, hmm? Must've been the Potters' ghost."

The man finishes his ice cream and jams his hand in a pocket. His pants are maroon corduroy, the tiny ribbing over his thighs like dinner-fork patterns on slabs of meat. Slowly, the hand rubs at the thigh and the space beside the thigh. The man is holding his cock, hidden, gripping it within his pocket like a surprise gift. "You sure you're supposed to be out here?" he asks. "It's pretty late. How old are you anyway?"

The man comes closer, withdraws his hand, and rests it on his crotch to rub once again. Boris worries, suddenly, that the man sees the cuts and bandages and bruises, that he is teasing him. *He thinks I'm sick or suicidal.* Or worse, *thinks I'm too skinny, thinks I look like a girl.* Once, when he was very small, a substitute teacher had asked, "Are you a boy or a girl?" and Boris had coiled within himself somewhere, a warm blue room filled with music, away from the students' laughter.

Yet the way the man stares makes Boris feel shackled to him, and bang, there is no turning back. What follows, follows: one and two and three hesitant steps, sneakers throbbing on the boards of the bridge. Up close he can see the pores on the man's face, enlarged like poppyseeds; can smell the sweat and the civet-musk cologne's foolhardy attempt to conceal it. After a breath and one more calculated step, Boris answers, finally, his lie: "I'm nineteen."

The lamplight casts pinpoints on the man's pupils. "Howsabout all this rain we've been getting." His eyes clamp shut and he leans forward. To Boris it seems he is falling, accidentally, into him. He kisses Boris, first using only lips, delivering tight snaps of waxy lip balm. Then his tongue spills out, sloppy. Boris gags slightly; closes his eyes and lets the tongue wander between his teeth. The tongue tastes sweet, still thick with chocolate. Boris frets about his split lip, about Marshall and blood, and he jerks free. A gorilla hand moves into his shirt and down the stomach to unbutton his jeans. Boris tries to think of Rex but misses his target: in a startle-second he sees Wayne, hunched over him with fist poised, his eyes like puddles showing deep-down flecks of debris. When Boris looks again there is no more imagining: still the same man. One, the hand slipping into his boxers, two, the mouth stretched wide, and three, the tongue lapping at his smudged Jack Daniel's throat.

The man pulls back to usher Boris into a nook of grass beside the bridge. "You're really, really cute," he says. He flashes his teeth as if waiting for reciprocal praise; his spit turns to candle wax in Boris's mouth. From across campus a dog is barking, faintly, but the barking stops and a screen door slams and then the world is noiseless.

Panic clots in Boris's chest but he can't protest, can't stop the man from tugging at his jeans. They fall to his ankles and Boris remembers his exposed ass, only yesterday, as he lay pinned on the library floor. He feels the damp air, its shocking splash. *Someone will see. Police. Arrested, in jail before my seventeenth birthday.* Over there, fifty feet away in a tangle of juniper scrub—the top of someone's face? Glittery eyes? Now the man has lowered his own pants to his ankles, the corduroy seeping a mothball smell.

He wants to turn and run but the man is jerking him; in seconds the orgasm rises tight and ready and hot. The yo-yo arm, pushing and pulling, the vanilla from the ice cream glued within its thick hairs. "Let me suck you," the man says. "Lie down." Boris checks the hillside for spies and obeys the order. The man removes his sweatshirt. Boris sees him pumping one cock in left hand, one in right, and when the hands stop pumping the man lies beside him and the head drifts down.

Stretched against the grass, jeans at his knees, shirt bunched like snakeskin at his neck, Boris leans his head to the left. Again, the image of his body sprawled on the library floor; then another of Sarah, years ago, beneath the window in that haunted house. Twirling over the muddy earth beside the bridge are hundreds of mosquitoes, a cloud of them, a congregation. They glide for his skin, the man's skin, yet Boris cannot move his hands to swat. The insects make a rankling fog over the mud, over a yellow leaf fallen there, facedown, its stem torn ragged from the stipule. Both insects and leaf ripple in his alcohol vision as the man's mouth softens like the inside of an overripe tomato and his tongue laps and laps the tip of Boris's cock. Now would be the time to moan, to palm the side of his head and guide it back, forth, back. But Boris lies unmoving, the mosquitoes landing on his face in pacific magnification, as the man plunges deeper. Boris feels his cock press tighter against the base of the throat. The man chokes, a wet burble, choking on it. He pulls away, smacks his lips and swallows, plunges back. Twelve feet from his thumb's bandage, ten from the yellow leaf, mere inches from the edge of the bridge, lies the water, its ebony surface spinning with dace and chartered by more mosquitoes. A hand—the man's? Boris's?—knocks the tape player. The music from Marshall's tape unwinds, the singer untouchable and imprisoned and wee: *Beyond the comfort of loneliness, we follow our footsteps. . . . Dancing, dancing . . .* The man's hand drifts from his own cock to Boris's ass. It fumbles with the crack, separating it. The index scuffs at the hole for five, six, seven seconds and then the finger wiggles inside. A single exquisite target of pain. The pressure drives a soft, closed-mouth grunt from Boris's mouth. "No," Boris says, or maybe wants to say, but the man pushes the finger deeper, in past the knuckle.

Wind tosses the trees in a tambourine shimmer and Boris lies still, allowing the man to dictate his body's motion. One hand resumes the pistoning jerk on his cock, the balding head dipping now and then, like a bird to water, to suck. The other hand becomes the machine, driving home the finger, two fingers. What Boris feels is a kinetic green with winking yellow starlights; clamping his eyes tighter makes the yellow expand and his body goes warmer, warmer, hot, as the two fingers drive deeper. Something moves in the scrub, chopping sounds in the branches like a blade through muscle. And noise in the water too, perhaps the ghost that haunts the pond . . . Boris sees the drowned man lifting from his oil depths . . . like the zombies that populate his own novel, marching and marching . . . rotten viperous body with arms outstretched, eyes opalescent as pearls . . . the water. . . . Boris teeters there. The ghost is reaching for him. Boris hears the insects on the water, parting a welcome carpet, and then the fantasy splits and he feels the fingerfuck and mouth still sucking his cock and feels himself exploding into the mouth, a red wet fulcrum drawing the life from him.

The man hunches, vulturous. His arched back, his stunned face. He makes a little surprised cry and then his come spatters Boris's chest, an instant bleachy smell, like egg white in his navel, below both nipples, the foamy earpiece of one headphone.

The come dries in paisley crusts on his skin. Almost seventeen years, he thinks, spent waiting, waiting. Only an hour ago he was Boris Appleby, in his bed at Sunflower. When he shut his eyes his pillow became Rex's cheek. His own fingers could so easily be Rex's, caressing, trailing through his hair. To go back, to rewind and restart. All the particulars from the dreams, all hands and everywhere-kisses and sighs-in-ears burned to ash, now that Boris knows the truth.

The man's voice: "By the way, I'm William." He zips up, retucks his sweatshirt, and wipes his mouth.

"Oh. Hi," Boris says. The new Boris, saying his first words. "Um, mine's Wayne." The man pats his back pockets, undoubtedly searching for a ballpoint or a pencil stub to scribble phone numbers. "Wayne," Boris repeats; he finds his windbreaker, brushes it off, and buttons up. He steps to the cambered walk of the bridge, then decides against it. "I can't—" But there is nothing left to say.

He aims his feet away from campus, walking, then hurrying faster. No longer the dizzy head rush, no longer the jostling swirl of drunk. Behind him the man clears his throat, the spent "such a cute boy" seed falling through his body. Boris skirts the weedy grasses, reaching a telephone pole bearing hundreds of staples from outdated notices and, still, the red edge of another REWARD sign. Within the shadow, a fraction of the dead girl's face. As he sprints past, he sees it looks like Sarah's. Boris runs and runs, then stops. He huddles beside a tree and spits. Gone is the man's taste, his saccharine caffeine fluoride mucus. Boris spits on his hands, wipes them on the thighs of his jeans, spits again. He flattens his palms in his hair and shakes his fingers and lets loose a deep sigh, unfamiliar, like something from the lungs of a tortured animal. Over time Marshall's stories changed, smooth romance becoming softer and sweeter, and only now does Boris see how misguided he was, how wrong, to believe them. *I'm going to forget this,* he thinks. Perhaps he has revised Marshall's tales, the way he wonders if Sarah has revised hers—her Satan Clair, her Pemberley Haunted Mansion—and Boris feels his mistake in the clutch of his throat, a backwash of bitter like the library blood. He spits a final time. The clouds part into two woolen curtains and the stars between are off-color, pale pink, like the marshmallow stars in a bowl of children's cereal. In the moonlit distance is the entrance to the football stadium, two flagstaffs lined with handmade banners picturing the mascot Jayhawk. Up, up: on the left slaps the American flag; on the right, the blue Kansas rectangle. "*AD ASTRA PER ASPERA,*" Boris whispers, remembering the flag's state motto, a lesson from grade school. "To the stars, through difficulties."

He stands not moving with the mystery and meaning of that sentence flaring up in him. Within the silence, only the taut applause from the flags. Boris knows he should feel pride or allegiance but instead what he feels is Ellis's cast, once again, slamming against his cheek and chin. His bug bites itch and his body seems foreign, throbbing as though squeezed and gouged, not in specific places but all over. Beacon light, flag slap, wet wind shear teasing at his neck . . . He hears his heart as though it approaches from the dark distance, and when he puts his hand to his chest to test it, the come, not yet crusted, shocks him. No, no, the come is not Rex's.

On fire: Boris knows tonight's mistake, but perhaps—he tries to smile, crookedly, at this—perhaps it has prepared him, seasoned him, for Rex. Oh, Rex, who could do anything now, could bash both fists again and again into Boris, into his eyes, nose, mouth. It would feel like flowers falling. Rex could go much, much further than this man, this "William," has done. The force of his love would obliterate any evidence or memory of tonight. On fire. He could worm fingers between the rows of Boris's teeth and into his unopened ass, three fingers then four, he could slide his whole hands inside, one hand punching the inside of his body. *And this is what I deserve,* Boris thinks. On fire: Rex could fuck him, he could push inside deeper and deeper until the two bodies fused with the hot, soldered blend of sweat and blood and jism and tears, and Boris, soul lifting free, would be left feeling nothing but numb, numb and wonder and acceptance and always, on fire, love.

16

*T*ell me everything," Sarah says, and Boris does. It went like this. He got drunk. Couldn't sleep. Walked up to campus; nervously listened as a man spoke to him. Greetings, innuendos, propositions. He lay down in the grass. . . .

Now Boris is crying. She can smell the night on him, the alcohol and smell of sex. He sprawls on the dark floor like someone coughed ashore, his hair pulled back, the streetlamp glinting on his tears in horizontal trails. Sarah runs an oven mitt, still warm, down his shoulder and arm.

Fifteen minutes earlier, she stood in the bathroom preparing for bed. She finished plastering her face with the cucumber mud mask when she heard the timid knock at her door. She answered, fearless, not bothering to wash away the mask. By the force of his hug she knew that something was wrong. While Boris talked she mixed a box of brownies, adding cinnamon and a dash of rum, for tomorrow morning's trip to Lucas.

"In a way I didn't want to," Boris says, "but it was like something controlled me. I was drunk. I just, like, dropped there and let everything happen. Will I get something from the cut on my lip? Or his spit? Oh, god, I was only thinking about stuff Marshall said, all the fun things and how he loved going there."

Sarah almost laughs at this but instead grips his hand with the mitt—it is quilted with a cartoon cow—and sweet-talks in his ear. "You'll be okay. You won't get sick. And you and Marshall are very different people. *Were* different people." The hand inside her hand feels soft and boneless, like a newborn bird. "You've had a terrible week. No use beating yourself up over this. Tonight was your experiment. There's nothing to be ashamed of." A back window stands open, and June bugs from the golf course patter the screen. Checkered shadows drift across the floor, and Sarah listens: a cricket, another chiming in; the spinning chain and one-gear grind of a bicycle, speeding past the trail. Beyond that, forever and always, the river.

"But there is something to be ashamed of," Boris says. His lower lip trembles, his face hammered into shame. "That's not the whole story. Tonight's not the worst of it. I lied to you." With a hollow sound he loosens a cry from deep within his throat. The sound is heartbreaking, heralding another bout of tears, and now Sarah cannot lean close enough; she makes a clumsy gesture with her arms as if to shield every inch of his body and then gives up and merely raises his head to rest on her thigh. A clear thread of mucus trails over the sore on his lip; a tear breaks and spreads on her night-gown's white percale trim.

"About the library," Boris says, "I lied. It was Wayne. It was Ellis and Drew and Bobby and a bunch of girls, that's who beat me up, and it was Rex, sort of and accidental too. Wayne was punching me and they were writing things on my face and body. Wayne told me to remind you how 'good' he is. He said I should tell you how strong he is, how he wants to lay it in you like steel and make you beg for it. Then he punched me and said it would feel like that, like his fist smacking against me. Oh, I lied to you, I should have told you everything right away."

I lied to you, he says. Sarah thinks of her story of punishment, her story of rape, how she couldn't remember, not really, where truth ended and exaggeration began. But with her story of Howard Westenhoffer, her story of Marshall and their survival of the 1980s, she told the truth. Sarah knows she should reveal this to Boris, but before she can speak he starts again.

"They were the ones who wrote on the car," he says. "They have a photograph of you, I have no idea how. It's you at the store, behind the counter. They have it in a folder that Carl stole for me, along with pictures of other girls. I can prove it, everything's there in the Suffering Box. And I'm scared now. I don't know what they're going to do. It's like they're playing a game. I want to think Rex isn't part of it, he doesn't want to hurt you or hurt us. It's Wayne and maybe Ellis but really it isn't Rex." A long pause; Sarah pets his hair and face. The crickets stop singing and start again. "But maybe in a way I know Rex is part of it. I want him to love me too, god, I'll settle just for him to talk to me or something, I just don't want him to hate me and think I'm those names written on the car."

Sniffling, Boris wriggles his hand from Sarah's oven mitt and scratches his elbow, his neck. "I got bitten by seventeen thousand mosquitoes. Chiggers and mosquitoes." Every few words, his hand scrubs at another bite. "They ate me alive, why was I out there in that grass?"

Sarah stands. There, he has told her. On one wall, a rectangle of pink shows darker from the paint around it. Once, a glass case held position there, housing trophies on shelves, color-faded photographs of the course's grand opening jubilee. There are nailholes and hook marks, from which hung clubs used by the minorly famous. Television actors stopping through town; political native sons; even, one illustrious evening, a noted motorcycle daredevil. All had golfed here, and now it is hers. A little warren; home.

"Honey, I'm so sorry," Sarah says. "But truth be told, I know all this. I know they painted the words on the car and came looking in my window. A hundred times I've picked up the phone to call the police and then put it back down. What could I say? What can we prove?" She steps to the oven and twists the knob to kill the heat, leaving the brownies inside. "Now shhh." On the table is a dish containing the amber bottle of Harriet's hair dye. Also there are an apple and two oranges, but the apple has softened to mush and the oranges are stabbed with toothpicks and cloves, evidence of Sarah's tireless worried hands. She could have dunked the clove oranges into a mulled cider, the sort of drink served at parties, but her home is too small for a party, and besides, what's left to celebrate?

She sits down again, bends to his face, kisses it. "We've let this go too far," she says. Stamped on his cheek now, her cucumber smudge, a green frosting brightened by the streetlight. "We're going to let them know we aren't scared anymore. We're better than that! They can imitate the murderer but they aren't the murderer. They can write on our car but they can't keep us from driving it tomorrow and standing right beside them. Oh, they're tough all right, but we'll show them tougher. They can get us scared and moan words in Harriet's window and they can pin you to the floor and knock you around, but then what's left? We're still standing.

"Starting today is our revenge, a revenge like you're going to have in your book. We'll use the trip to Lucas as a new beginning." The words are like platitudes, mostly made for Boris's benefit, yet she keeps going. "From now on we'll be after *them*. *Their* terror will be *ours*." She recalls the opening to the section of his novel, the only part he has shown her thus far. "*After midnight the undead rose from the earth.*"

For the first time tonight, Boris smiles. "Come with me," Sarah says. Five long strides to the bathroom door. She coaches Boris toward the mirror and puts one finger to his lips. Enough moonlight falls through the eroded window to illuminate the room; she doesn't bother with the switch. The bar of pumice soap has smeared to a loamy lump in the sink. The window has recently cracked, as though from a hurled rock, but Sarah can't recall that happening. On the sill is a wadded dust rag, clumps of soil and marl, the chipped clay crockery from a flowerpot. She remembers a warm spring evening—was it only last year?—when Marshall felt ill and she had given him an Epsom salt bath. Just outside they heard an eerie snuffle and scratch, and they peeked out this same window to spy a family of possums on the backyard green, near the third hole. The mother's eye flickered in the night. Pink babies dangled, raw, weazened salamis, from her stomach.

Carefully Sarah touches the bruise under Boris's eye, the wounds on his face and neck, and once again remembers Marshall. For months he had accepted the three separate lesions—one on his arm, two on his thigh—but when the violet dot appeared on his face, he came to her, panicked. And, in her own way, she had cheered his spirits.

In the cabinet beneath the sink lies a blue pouch that contains mascara, lipstick, eyeliner. Also there are amber prescription bottles of unfinished painkillers, hexagon disks of birth-control pills; she fishes out only what she needs. She will do for Boris what she did for Marshall. "You're a gorgeous boy," Sarah tells him. "Don't forget that." She takes a votive holder from the cabinet and lights a candle. She twists the hot-water faucet, wets her fingers, blurs the smudge from his face. "Around here they all think boys your age are only good-looking with the short-cut hair and whatever kind of jeans and jackets and tennis shoes are in style. The tan leftover from summer farm work and the Royals baseball cap." She unsnaps a plastic box, wipes three fingers over its mound of foundation, and rubs the color over Boris's cheeks. "But they're wrong. I know that—Marshall knew that and maybe a couple of other bizarros around here did too—but sadly for us no one else knows that. Not the people on my street or the people at Sunflower. Not those kids in the library, not Rex and his psycho friends. Well, I say that Boris should do what he wants, Boris should stay long-haired and smart and skinny skinny."

In the mirror Boris observes the transformation of his face with dulled fascination and horror, the way he might watch a needle pulling blood from his arm. Yet he doesn't flinch. Sarah finds a candy-cane barrette and secures his bangs. She chooses her favorite lipstick; tickles his mouth's edges with a tiny ciliate brush; lines his eyes with black like the zombies from *Carnival of Souls,* and follows up with mascara. "No white-trash blue eyeshadow for my stunning boy," she says. "Maybe a little reddish brown, though, to accentuate your hair."

Sarah takes her time with him. She applies coverstick to the scratch on his neck; nurses his bruise until it disappears. A breeze flickers the candle flame like a moth's white wing. Again, on the river trail, the slow grind of the unseen chain, the bicycle returning from its destination.

You belong to me, Sarah wants to say. And within the lingering silence she remembers a night, back while winter was turning spring, when Marshall wasn't all that sick. She had allowed Boris to drive her car, and the three of them journeyed south to Wells Overlook park. They trespassed and climbed the fence, and she tore her antique brown dress. The park, Marshall said, was another place to meet men. Park Commission officers closed it up at night, but Sarah and Boris and Marshall went anyway, hiking the road that wound through the trees until they arrived at the tall wooden Overlook. A hoot owl flapped somewhere above, and they stared out over the whole county. Marshall put an arm around one of Boris's shoulders, and Sarah wrapped her arm around the other. They found part of someone's forgotten picnic: bread crusts and lemon rinds, artichoke leaves scarred with both child and adult teethmarks. They found an unopened bag of caramel popcorn, and while they ate they tried guessing which domelight came from Marshall and Harriet's farm. Thousands of white dots, like spotlights below them, shining.

That was the first night, Boris told her later, that he felt as though he "belonged." Now he presses his lips together, following Sarah's mimed instructions, to blot them. "Tastes like that guy's mouth. All this lip balm, like a wax dummy." This makes Boris laugh, the sound stirring a billowy feeling inside Sarah. She wants to say something people rarely say, words relegated only to love songs or holiday cards. She wants to take all the remaining swirling love from the wake of Marshall and transfer it; she wants Boris to stay forever.

The mirror gives back her green-masked reflection, monstrous, buoyed behind him. "I think you're all done," she says. She takes the barrette from his hair, pats gel in her hands, parts his unkempt hair down the middle. "You're all done, you're beautiful, and I'm completely speechless."

Sarah longs to tell him more: how soon the snow will be falling and she will buy him a new coat, something warmer and sturdier than the secondhand rags Sunflower provides. Soon she will get a better job, she's certain of it; soon Harriet will host parties like she always wanted to do and she will smile, always, again. And soon Boris, oh, she wants to be certain, will be whispered about through the school halls for winning the arts contest with his blockbuster best-seller. How she wishes. Happily ever after. The words are in Sarah's mouth but it is true what she said. She is speechless. She simply stares at Boris, staring at himself, in the mirror.

He blows them both a firecracker kiss. "Beautiful," he says.

The morningrise colors the sky a dull scrubbed silver like the backside of a spoon. Sarah leaves Boris in the parking lot; he gallops to the willow, looks back with a grinning face still glazed with rouge and mascara, and lifts the window frame.

As she reaches the end of Cherry Street the sun comes soaring above the bridge and the water. Inside the house she drops the keys on the table and wants only to collapse, but shuffling to bed she sees a shadow fluttering on the floor: a-skitter, now to the right, now to the left. She flicks the light and stares up, and flapping there, stunned by the glare, is a panicked onyx bird. Too big for a grackle; more like a raven, but sleekly oiled. Its eyes, burning, regard her with malice. Its wings buckle and it nearly plummets into her, then soars again to the ceiling. Sarah can't fathom how it got inside. She remembers something Harriet told them, long ago, years and years it seems now. *A bird in the house signals the devil, nothing for days but bad luck and no escape.*

Stepping closer she witnesses its plight: A strand of yellow baling twine has been knotted around its neck. The bird struggles to breathe, the noose nearly choking it. One wing's feathers have been pulled bare from the bone, the slick look due to the blood that still flows. Wayne. Ellis. Rex. In the time it took to drive Boris home, they came for her. They left the bird as another omen, a portent. Yesterday the trip to Lucas was only tomorrow away but now it is today; after a brief bleary nap she will drive back to Sunflower, then head to Harriet's farm, and they will be off. Wayne and Ellis and Rex too, traveling the same highway, demolishing the fifty-five speed limit with their car. She can picture them now, cozy in their black wax-scrubbed El Camino. The same that idled in Marshall's hospital parking lot as the words sprayed out in jumbles and misspellings; the same that sped away after their terrorist faces discovered the secrets of Sarah's house; the same that dumped the mannequin's body on the shore.

Sarah sees two perfect circles of blood on her floor, beside the telephone, another closer to the stove. The bleeding bird tumbles in the air and collides with a movie poster on the wall. Sarah tries drowsily to shoo it, but the bird only dives into the adjoining bedroom. She follows—flap, it swoops past—while in her head she pairs the black-wing bird with the white goose on Rex's farm. Devils and angels, attackers alike, both her enemies. She makes certain the window stands open. Out there, in a neighboring backyard, some child or daydreaming simpleton is playing a music box;

the melody stops and then returns upon itself. The box locks closed with a magnified snap, and the morning goes ice-quiet and sparkling and once again the bird dives for her. Sarah feels the soft *pap* of blood on her face. She lifts both arms in surrender, but the bleeding black thing disappears, vacuumed through the open window, a single swift bolt, as though it never existed at all.

Chapter 10

Slowly the crowd advanced. Twenty, even thirty of them, armed with their guns, their knives, their hammers and nightsticks and chains. All feet marched together in angry parade. Within the crowd were the students who had teased and fought with the boy, the husbands and wives and children who had whispered and gossiped about the women. Now they were here, joining together in vigilante terror. It was a showdown.

They cornered the Zombies at the alley's end, the city limits at the north side of Lawrence, where the sad people lived. Now the Zombies could make out faces, familiar faces, among the crowd. The town policemen, the priests, even the mayor. The old woman's neighbors, the young woman's boss. The teachers and supervisors who had hated the boy while he was alive.

The marching got louder, the moon and stars glinting white off the array of weapons. But the Zombies remained together, hands clasped, and did not fear. They knew the fight was hopeless. No one could match the power of their claws and teeth, no one could outdo the force of their revenge. By the end of the day, they knew, the townspeople would flee, screaming, back to their safe homes and churches and shops. And some, perhaps, would lie dying, their harmonic moans lifting as they lay in pools of blood.

For now the Zombies waited as the crowd of townspeople advanced. Around them, the darkness lowered. Soft gray, a deeper gray, then black.

March of the Zombies

Part 3

17

Kansas highways, seen through the cramped backseat: fields on both sides, green-yellow and yellow-green, back behind and up ahead. Rusted fences twist like hedge thorn. Their post rocks stand in wind-licked limestone the color of almonds, the color of cream. The barbed wire bears faded bloodstains from Guernseys, Holsteins, truck-stunned deer; too, from the men who fix and twist them into shape. Decades, even centuries. The years have drifted past, some straight-lined and some dotted, like the yellow slashes dividing the road below the wheels. The world whips by; as Boris watches he feels, instead, that he's the one being watched. There are grain elevators painted with crisscrossing shocks of wheat. Burnt-apple barns with block-letter verses from Matthew, Mark, and John. In fields the corn has just been cut; the hay balers have chewed and spat each wrapped gold circle. Whirling above are the ceaseless, senseless birds; in brittle ditches the camouflaged pheasants preen and stomp and flare their pirate eyepatches. Hey there—the red fringe-feather triangle—and now it's gone.

Sarah drives as though pursued by tornadoes, but still, Boris thinks, she is a good driver. The Volkswagen moves along I-70, Topeka/Junction City/Abilene/Salina, ever nearing Exit 206 and Route 232. Soon they will pass Fort Riley army base with its lobes of clover meadows and Flint Hill shadows and CAUTION WIND CURRENT signs. The sun is a burning wheel spinning lemon columns of heat. Window rolled down, the air smells of cheddar sometimes, vinegar others, but always the air is clean, clean. Boris's arm, thrust out, will surely garner a warning—"Put it back in or I'll break it," said a foster parent once; "You'll lose it doing that," says Harriet now—but the wind thrills him, rushing, pulling sleeves, and drying sweat from finger webs.

From the passenger seat Harriet smiles and sighs, seemingly in love with everything. A farmer waves from another baler, and Harriet waves back. "When you see a load of hay, make a wish and turn away." She wears a simple housedress and a brown cardigan of nubbled wool. And jewelry: rhinestone earrings, a tiger-beetle brooch with ruby-plated armor and one missing antenna. Her hair retains its boxed artificial color, but gray is peeking through the pink again, like filaments of fuse wire. Inside the car, Boris knows, float words unspoken because of Harriet. He and Sarah remain mute about their terrorists and the imminent standoff; they refuse to frighten or worry her. For now, everything is safe and good.

His pockets crowd with an extra roll of film for Harriet's camera; excess change for possible emergencies; a handwritten note, addressed "To: Sunflower" from his art teacher, okaying the trip. Boris forgot to deliver it to his supervisors. The rearview shows the remaining prissy gray on his lids: No slathering of soap would wash off the hint of eyeliner, the crimson smudge from his mouth, the counterfeit beauty mark Sarah made on his cheek. "You still look pretty," Sarah said when she picked him up.

Now she hums with the tiny singers that serenade inside the

radio. She claims it is one of the stations she and Marshall used to listen to, one half her life—Boris notes she almost said *their lives*—ago. The station plays Junior Walker and the All-Stars. It plays The Stylistics and Marvin Gaye. When Herb Alpert's "This Guy's in Love with You" rolls softly in, Sarah ups the volume and sings along, substituting her gender in the lyrics. "You had this forty-five in your collection," she tells Harriet, patting her knee. "The label was a light tan color with an orange symbol saying A&M Records, and there were plips and plops at the end of the song from one time when Marshall spilled strawberry jam and had to scratch it off." The sun is fixed on Harriet's face; she nods and smiles, nods and smiles.

Boris has brought this morning's *Journal-World* and a notebook with in-progress scenes from *Zombies.* On the newspaper's editorial page, a special report focuses on violence in the local school system. A color photograph, Lifestyles section, shows a woman reviving her great-great-grandmother's art of quilting. There are football scores, a comics section, crosswords and logic problems above a quarter-page ad for a pick-your-own pumpkin patch. After searching two minutes, Boris finds an article on the ongoing investigation of the murders. He translates for Sarah: "The cops have narrowed down the store where the murderer might have bought the carpet, you know, from the fibers in her fingernails. And the candle wax in her ears—obviously from Waxman Candles. Duh. They discovered that vanilla's one of their most popular scents. So that makes it harder to catch the killer. The owner told the cops how all the frat boys buy vanilla. Some magazine article recently claimed it's the best scent to seduce a girl."

They reach the turnoff for Route 232, Lucas now only sixteen miles further. Boris sees Sarah unfix her gaze from the road to find him in the rearview. "Let me guess what's next. Vanilla sealing up my windows and doors? Puddles of it making little trails through the golf course? No sirree. Today, today we'll put a stop to that."

Harriet doesn't question Sarah's words. The floor at her feet is still decorated with bits of broken glass. The brownies, wrapped in foil, rest on Harriet's lap, along with a box of chocolates she brought for the ride. Scattered throughout are candies she's sampled, their corners whittled with teeth marks. Her hands alternate between the chocolate box and her tattered road map, cradled on one knee to track their destination. "We won't be far from LaCrosse," she says. "Barbed-wire capital of the world, the same town where Robert was born." They spot the first sign advertising the Garden of Eden, and Boris watches it pass. "These round ones are coconut," Harriet says. "The rectangles, caramel. The ovals are just plain hideous and you ought not eat those." Later, again and softly, while chewing: "LaCrosse, barbed-wire capital of the world."

On the left runs a milo field with a hogback ridge. On the right, a stretch of trees caught and stunned by autumn. Their green changes color as the trees reach the sky, all the uppermost leaves dark orange, orange-red, then reds of numberless shades, as though birds have bled there. Boris centers his chin on Harriet's shoulder and follows her finger, tracing veins on the map. "Wilson Lake is up and coming next," she says, and when he looks to the road, he sees it looming.

They cross the junction for the lake, and after the junction, a filling station. Sarah brakes, pumps five gallons of gas, wipes a sponge across the cracked windshield. An attendant raises one bushy brow at the eyesore VW and offers help, but no, no, Sarah knows what she's doing. Beside the station's entrance stands a sandwich board advertising arrowhead necklaces, kimberlite, and fool's gold: FOR SALE! FOR SALE! Another plugs LIVE BAIT, the *I*'s drawn to resemble pink worms with grinning mouths and curled eyelashes. The signs prop beside a pop machine, outdated like the one in Sarah's store. Boris crawls from the backseat, digs quarters from his pocket, and extracts three Mountain Dews. "Rex's favorite," he tells Harriet.

On the air is the smell of skunk and, sweeter, of fire from wheat or milo fields. Sarah starts the car, and now there is no turning back. One final sign for Lucas and they exit, at last, onto 176.

Sunstream glistens on the emerald glass of their bottles. The sun is molten and whittles the everywhere elms; finds gaps left by the leaves; rests its light on the road like craters. Blacktop yields to dirt, and after five miles, six, becomes blacktop again. Boris can see enough of Harriet's face to tell she is yawning. Although he battles against it, his echo-yawn comes three seconds later. He drinks and thinks of Rex drinking and then the bottle is empty.

"Let's stop a second," Sarah says. She slows and swerves into a gravel ditch. Directly ahead is a bridge, the supports flecked with red rust spots and gleaming nickel-colored rivets. "Follow me," Sarah orders. "Bring your bottles." Boris exits from the driver's side to help Harriet from her seat. As they leave the car a pickup totters past; the farmer inside waves with one finger. Then the road lies empty. Lucas is five minutes away; in moments they will wait with a group of students and tourists, Wayne and Ellis and Rex among them. Boris feels his pulse thin and quicken. He remembers their hands on his body, their words shattering in his ears.

But now I'm ready for anything, Boris thinks. He has worn makeup and he has allowed a mysterious man to swallow his sperm. He has signed on for this trip, has made it this far. The sky's stubborn blue recharges him, almost religious in its intensity. The sun floats heavy in the east southeast. Higher, higher up, the moon, barely visible but swimming still its vigilant unsocketed eye. Some sorcery, some miracle: Boris feels, if he watches long enough, the sky will cause the car to drive itself; Lucas will magically appear; Rex will stand, arms out and begging atonement, at the Garden of Eden gates.

Sarah retrieves a miniature notepad from the glove box, tears off three sheets, and doles them out. They head toward the bridge rails, shoes suctioning deep in the sludge. Boris pictures that night on Rex's farm: his feet, Sarah's feet, sloshing among the damp reeds. "You'll muddy up your britches," Harriet tells him.

Sarah finishes her Mountain Dew and gives Boris and Harriet instructions, her voice demanding attention. She has only one ballpoint, so each will take a turn. "Write it down, one wish each, then roll it like a scroll and stick it inside." She scribbles on her square white sheet: her greatest craving, her greatest desire. Boris and Harriet stop close by, at the bridge's edge, the creek below them creamy as honey and winding its way through snapped cattails leaking airloft fur. The creek—"crick," as Harriet pronounces it— is so small it has no name. Beside the rail supports, rainwater has washed away the chalk and the shale, exposing limestone disks like flapjacks in the sugar sand. Unbucketed fishguts and fishheads. A knot of ripped reel. Centered within the redroot pigweed is a puddle of black mud, and centered within the mud, an upended bottle cap reading in failed-contest letters, TRY AGAIN LATER.

Boris wants to ask what Sarah has written but doesn't; wants to lean over her shoulder but won't. He takes the pen from her hand, levels the paper on his left palm, and scrawls in slanted letters:

1ST, FOR MY NOVEL TO WIN THAT PRIZE,
2ND, FOR REX TO READ IT *and like it*,
AND 3RD—IF POSSIBLE!—FOR REX TO LOVE ME BACK.

He hands the pen to Harriet. He rolls the paper as Sarah advised and holds his bottle ready to drop.

Below, the water meanders, no idle stillness like Potter's Lake or peaked speed-jet roar like the Kansas River over Bowersock Dam. Nests of absent swallows are cornered in the abutments, visited by spectrum-wing mud daubers. Boris can smell the summer, faded. He can smell the bandage on his neck and the residue of lipstick, and he can taste tears, bubbling somewhere inside his head, rising. But he leans close to Sarah and Harriet and smiles. They are all smiling now, one two three. Together they whisper, "*Three, two, one,*" and let loose their bottled wishes. The green glass flashes thunderbolt-swift in the sun, yet when the bottles hit the water they make a single splash. The sound floats wayward on the air, drifts, disappears.

18

*A*t last, Lucas. Twin sounds of lawnmower and cicada whir through the windshield cracks, and the sun, lifted to full height, slices to burning bits in the rearview crystal. A grocery store, a Methodist church, the Christopher Manor old folks' home, with its door wreath of faded roses. The radio's love song begins to *baby baby,* and before the chorus, Sarah sees, at Second and Kansas Streets, the Garden of Eden. It is a small cinnamon house with green-shingled roof, surrounded by cement statues and totems, eagles and foxes and dragon dogs, fake skeletal trees with crisscrossing arms. A concrete flag prides its red, white, and blue in frozen flutter. Every road in the town leads to the site, graveled fingers forever pointing at this pariah, this misfit.

Harriet's eyes have lost their heavy sleepiness, and now she stares, grinning, at the house. "It's marvelous." She puts a chocolate in her mouth and her teeth move gently over it. "A place where magicians would live," she says. "Someone religious maybe or very

very smart." She is shivering and Sarah wants to hold her hand; instead she hesitates as Harriet pulls a head scarf from her purse and ties it at the chin.

Sarah maneuvers into the ditch and parks behind the school bus, already there. And, across the gravel road, in the opposite ditch, the black El Camino. Wayne's outdated eyesore, part pickup, part car, curious model made with a single three-capacity front seat and a cab behind it. The same villainous getaway that Harriet saw tearing from Cherry Street, the same that surely idled beside the VW as the words were written, in black and blue and white, that August afternoon.

In the rearview Boris's eyes meet Sarah's. "Don't be scared," she says. "Leave it all to me." Yet hers are the fingers fidgeting in her pocket, rubbing and rubbing the serrated edge of her last quarter. They walk below the 1907 CABIN HOME banner, between a head-dressed brave stretching bow with arrow on the left and a frontiersman with a shotgun on the right. Sarah directs a path to the porch, where a makeshift clock stands on a cardboard tripod. Under the words NEXT TOUR, the clock points to straight-up noon. Smudged on the red minute hand, a single fingerprint. Sarah swings the screen door open, waits for Boris and Harriet, and enters the little house.

Standing in the hallway are the noontime tourists and the tour guide, a thin woman wearing overalls with a broken shoulder strap. A red reminder string is wrapped around her wrist; her tanned face surveys the crowd with an intense but slightly confused expression, like someone needing glasses. *Sixteen,* Sarah sees her lips count out, *seventeen, eighteen.* Sarah guesses identities from those among the group: the art teacher and her herd of six students; other random guests; and, in a separate corner, Wayne and Rex and Ellis.

They are watching her, watching Harriet and Boris. Wayne smirks but Rex and Ellis seem vaguely shocked, as though hot spotlights have been aimed at them. *Maybe, just maybe, this will hap-*

pen exactly how it should happen. They look familiar to Sarah; indeed, she has seen their faces in town, perhaps noticed them, unaware of their intentions, as they loitered in the store. And now, from their slouched sleepiness and goofy crook-grin expressions, she can tell they are stoned, mutinous, relishing this day away from duties and parents and rules. Rex seems taller, and admittedly more oddball handsome, than she recalled; on acknowledging her stare, he turns to a glass case of Garden of Eden T-shirts and mugs and fiddles its lock with his southpaw hand.

"Hello there," Sarah announces. She doesn't flinch or blink. Ellis looks away but Wayne locks eyes with her; lowers his chin in a nod.

The tour guide turns. "Oh, hello. You made it just in time. I was about to start another'n but as soon as I get the admission from you—what are you, one, two, three?—we'll get going."

Admission is four dollars, but the guide, so practiced her sentence flows in a single breath, informs that "The price would be three if you were Triple-A Auto Club members." Sarah lies and says, "Of course, of course I belong to the club," and she uncovers a pocket card as proof, something someone, months back, left at the counter. "That's nine including tax," the tour guide says. "Out of ten. Making your change at one dollar."

The cash register, Sarah notes, is the same make as her highway store's. Half-hidden behind it, perched on a stool beside the guide's hip, sits a little girl wearing a blue sweatband and bracelets, a mauve lipstick print on her cheek. The girl is eating her lunch. Featured on the plastic compartmented plate is Salisbury steak, surrounded by wax beans, pink applesauce, a cube of angel food cake topped with silver candy buckshot. It is the sort of cake Harriet would have decorated for Sarah and Marshall, whatever occasion.

A man in a John Deere cap stares them down, his mammoth thickset belly like an overturned wheelbarrow. Boris shuffles behind Harriet's shoulder and appears, in the talcumy cabin light, to shrink into her shadow. Sarah grips hands with his teacher; says, "I took art classes at your school, years ago." She catches a wheezy laugh from the boys and spins on them. They have leveled her car and mutilated the artificial girl and they have attacked her friend, but today will be different. *We'll be after them,* she told Boris last night. *Now it is our turn.*

The guide begins to speak as though for children, her mouth moving slowly. "Pretty please follow me into the front room, we'll begin the tour." The cabin home and gardens were built nearly ninety years back by the eccentric Civil War veteran Mr. S. P. Dinsmoor . . . floors and gables and baseboards are made with cement, the moldings and windows and doors with California redwood . . . the site is among the National Register of Historic Places. The guests listen and nod, all cricked necks and cheapskate pointing fingers. While Harriet joins in the swirl of fascination and Boris exhibits his jittery unrest, Sarah clenches her fists and keeps her composure. She pins her attention on them. Spies, knaves, tormentors. Wayne's eyes remain half closed, now and again his tongue darting from the corner of his lips, dark pink, lewd, and drugged. Rex jams hands in his jean pockets and shifts his weight. With his good arm, Ellis produces a pencil from behind one pale ear and scratches an itch inside his cast. The three are only boys, mere simpletons. She could easily outwit and conquer them.

Everyone wanders, floorboards creaking, into another room. The art teacher asks elementary questions and jots notes on a legal pad. Grainy photographs line the walls, group shots from the war, portraits of Dinsmoor's wives and family. None of the doors or windows match—one room even has six door frames, each a different size—and Sarah, pirouetting, realizes the whole place smells like the funeral home. Nearby is a spacious cowhide chair with bullhorns at the head and arms. "I'd give my eyeteeth for that," Harriet says aloud. Ellis disguises his sneer with his cast; Sarah imagines first his arm without the plaster, and second, his paint-frosted hand spelling FOSSLE on the car.

Part two of the tour will resume in the outside gardens. The guide allows them ten minutes to explore the cabin further. Stepping downstairs, they find an arched, cavelike chamber, used, according to a sign, partly as storage for canned food and cured meat, partly as a cyclone shelter. Upstairs are two bedrooms, the floors decorated with painted roses and filigree leaves. Here, Sarah waits at the staircase, peeking below at the three boys, now huddled and waylaid with secretive murmurings. Harriet calls to her, calls again, and she sneaks to the master bedroom to follow the photographer's directions: close together, on the antique bed, Boris one side, Sarah the other, poses held, as the flash from Marshall's camera bursts lightbolt novas in their eyes.

They regroup at the cabin's backdoor. Here the air is warmer, and Sarah helps Harriet remove her sweater. The boys regard them still, three soused mouths chewing visible blue gum, so close behind her back that for an instant Sarah fears a foot will kick out, an arm will tear away Harriet's scarf, rip her worn cotton housedress, or knock her camera to the porch floor. "Mr. and Mrs. Evans should visit this place," Harriet says, and again the boys smirk. "It looks crazier than I imagined. Doesn't it just look loony? I know a Mr. Somebody who'd love to be here. Let me take another picture. Oh, look now, here comes the lady!"

They step down to the flagstone path. Wayne begins to remove his shirt, stretching high for tiptop flex of his muscles. Sarah watches the tour guide grimace and, briefly, sees Wayne looking toward her for a sign of approval. His chest is smooth and he folds his arms, a cradle to parade his tanned biceps. He snaps his gum and then winks—he is winking at her!—but Sarah tears her face away, displaying her power, signaling she loathes him, she loathes but does not fear.

On the garden's southernmost side, an arbor unfurls to a yard of tangled ivy, weather-ripped trees, more sculpted figures and totems. There is a fishpool larger than the one on the golf course; a concrete pyramid for strawberry beds and autumn flowers. A single orange marigold towers above a galaxy of yellows. Ants have discovered a white nugget of cake—the same, Sarah bets, eaten by the guide's little girl—and they promenade away with the crumbs. Above, on the effigies and trees, loops Virginia creeper vine. The guide leaves nothing unnoticed, naming this plant, others, her arms gesturing as she lists what the folk artist kept in his backyard animal pens: homing pigeons, coyotes, owls, an injured American eagle. Her voice shrills a quarter-octave higher and she slows her words, as if trying to conceal her excitement. "Now the next part of the tour. What some people see as the best part, and others the worst."

At garden's end looms the mausoleum, buttressed with flagstaffs and shaped like a beehive. A sentinel angel soars high above. While the guide explains, Sarah feels Boris sally next to her, plainly engrossed in the lesson but still, as before, longing to steer clear of the bullies' scrutiny. When Dinsmoor was alive, says the guide, he built a cement casket with a square of glass in its lid; he'd lounge inside when someone offered him money. Now, his mummified remains can be viewed in the same glass-partitioned casket, here in the mausoleum he created especially for this purpose. "Remember all this," Sarah tells Boris. "May be something good for your novel."

Cameras aren't allowed in the mausoleum, and as Sarah steps inside she hooks arms with Harriet. A dead body. Yet Harriet stands fascinated and unfazed, one hand on the small of her own rickety back as she leans peering through the plate glass. Boris looks, a group of his classmates look, and finally Sarah looks too: Dinsmoor, at peace, embalmed palms crossing his skeleton chest. The fruit-peel skin stretches over a face as clenched and grooved as a locust's. Calcite bone, crumbled teeth, matted straw beard. A female student gasps and, turning to leave, blows a raspberry into her fist. But Sarah and Boris and Harriet pause longer, crowd closer to center front. Inside the glass, the old man's skull rests on snow-cream satin, eyes sunk to stones in their sockets, his visible jaw chipped and sharded like chitin.

Dimly Sarah hears the guide, in the mausoleum entryway, hastening the crowd along. "That's the close of today's tour." Again Sarah joins arms with her cohorts, and they move through the garden, from the mausoleum to the cabin's back porch.

The guests nod, satisfied, shading their brows and looking heavenward for last glimpses of the Bible figures. The guide thanks them, thanks them, for coming. Sarah sees the beer-bellied farmer slide gracelessly into a station wagon; the students, moving single file for the bus. And behind them, turning in secret shuffle around the side of the Eden cabin, the three stoned boys. Harriet grips the camera to her chest; complains she can't leave until she finds a decent rest room. Sarah: "There's one inside, I'll meet you beside the car." Harriet hurries off, but Sarah can't, won't, look away. As though he senses the curse of her eyes, Wayne stops, lets his companions forge ahead, and turns.

Sarah backs up three steps, four, brushing Boris's shoulder. "Go to the car," she tells him.

Wayne's eyes are seeds planted shallow in his brow, and now his mouth seems swollen, pushed-pout lips and pronounced underbite. In the sunlight his bare chest flashes, diamondback armor. Sarah could scream at him, could lope over the flowerbeds to wallop his face and scratch his skin. Instead she stares across the cement-barred lawn, stares him full-on, and in a second of surprise her eyes fall to the bulge in his jeans. His erection, straining a hard curve to the right of his fly, meant for her and her only. Sarah remembers his whisper in Boris's ear—*lay it in her like steel, make her beg for it*—and, unexpectedly as she looks back to Wayne's face, thinks of that long-ago haunted house, the older brother Jerry, the exaggerated story she wrote to assist Boris's book. No, that boy hadn't really raped her. The girls were there, stuck with the boys in that dark haunted house, and the boys made bashful attempts but the girls said no, no, and then the night was over. *Oh, Boris, that is how it really happened, I only colored it wild and dramatic because I wanted to please you, wanted to seem the star of the terrible suspense-drawn movie.*

For the first time, Wayne bears resemblance to all those faces, the dropout jughead boys from her past. Victor Earl pegging rats with his scattergun. Mickey Green dreaming silent serenades at her window. Everything she wrote about those suitors was true, undoctored. She exaggerated, yes, even blatantly fibbed to Boris about the rape, about the grade-school recess boys and their lewd adoration, about Satan Clair's brutalizing rope, but her story of Marshall and their desperate endeavors at sixteen-year-old love were all crystal, all truth. And she knows if she were there again, if she switched places and ages with Boris and felt the hammerhead burn of Wayne's desire, she would surrender. She would flit her tongue between his lips and trace the outline of Wayne's underbite and feel his ravenous breath go fleet and skittish in his chest. She would stare deep inside his eyes as though something wavered there only she, sweet Sarah, could see.

Wayne offers a drugged *come here* gesture: thrust of his bottom lip, quick back-jerk of his head. She nods and lifts one finger and hustles inside the cabin for Harriet.

One empty room, two. The bathroom door stands open, no one inside, and as Sarah enters a third doorway, she sees her friend standing in the front lobby, in the room's dust-drizzle corner. She begins to speak, to reach out and help Harriet forward. Noticing her pinched concentration, she stops and looks to the floor, to the space where Harriet stares. There, fuzzed within the shaft of light, the guide sits cross-legged on the braided rug below the register. She seems unaware of anyone in the room but herself and her little girl, whom she admires with glassy, exultant eyes. The girl has stretched out, lazily kicking both frilled-stocking legs in the air, busying her grimy but prudent hands at a coloring book. Sarah can see, on the page, an illustration of "Rumpelstiltskin"; the girl has colored the donkey green, and she selects a lemony yellow for the trickster dwarf's beard. "That's so pretty," the guide tells her daughter. The girl presses the crayon hard to the paper. "Oh, you're so good, a born artist! I love you, sweetie, my sweet sugar gumdrop."

The girl colors and kicks her tiny feet. Sarah moves her gaze from their spot at the floor, up and up to Harriet, but she already knows what she will see. Harriet, her smile close-mouthed with a barely discernible tremble, crescent edges of tears in her eyes. But Sarah notices something else. On the back of Harriet's housedress: the boys' obnoxious prank, their mess and their joke. Stuck to the blue gingham, there and there and there, are three separate wads of darker gum. Wayne and Rex and Ellis have balled them into blue-glue bullets and have stealthily bunched the back of her dress, securing three spots to hold the fabric in place, to reveal the old woman's purplish outbranching of veins, the underwear, beneath. Harriet stands absorbed, watching the mother and child, unaware of what the villains have done.

My baby, Harriet used to call her, as if Sarah were her very own daughter. Sarah came to her just as Marshall did, whenever anything went wrong. She was a loose, helpless, scared teenage girl. Harriet would comfort her, opening her warm arms that smelled of baking bread. *My baby.*

Without a word Sarah steps from the doorway and takes Harriet's hand. Surprised, the guide lifts from the floor and apologizes: "Oh, I thought the guests had already left." Sarah thanks her and rushes past the display of Garden of Eden postcards, mugs, and guidebooks, powder-blue or white T-shirts available in X or Double-X Large. They brush the makeshift clock and abandon the sculpted cowboy and Indian. Sarah herds her, pulling perhaps a bit too swiftly, to the VW, and swings open the door. Boris looks out, his eyes panicked and pleading. She almost wants to slap the fear from him but doesn't. She tells them only, "I'll be back, one second"; waits for Harriet's feeble knee to find its place in the seat, and closes the battered door. Back to the lawn, her heart in a trampoline beat, words prepared in her throat. Only her, here and now. Ready.

From down Kansas Street drifts a late-breakfast bacon smell, grease aloft on the breeze. Sarah walks so fast she nearly runs, the anger inside her crackling. The boys loiter at the west face of the cabin, below statues of Adam and Eve and the entangled slithering serpent, where the GARDEN OF EDEN sign meets the road. They brag about girls they've fucked, each striving to outdo the other two. "She kept on trying to take her mouth away," Ellis says, "but I told her, *Bitch*—" and then he stops, seeing Sarah.

She views them now as never before, claustrophobic close, the smoke cloud from their joint spooking the air around their heads. She can smell them, their breath and sweat, over the frying bacon and the pungent grass. Ellis sports a rip in the knee of his jeans; for a patch, he has substituted a bridge of safety pins to graft the snarls together. There are names and numbers on his plaster cast and, seeing her, he returns it to the sling. Rex places thumbs in pockets, makes a feeble cough, looks at Wayne. Easily Sarah decodes the ringleader, the mastermind lord over his minions: Wayne, greasy crooked part in his hair, mud-brown swells of it trailing behind his ears, one lobe glinting a gold hoop she hadn't noticed before. He stares flushed and shirtless and slick, with an upturned fierce face, as though his scowl could shut off the sun. He takes a long lungful of smoke. Sarah inches up a single step. She knows the smell is from him, Wayne more than Rex and Ellis, the same smell, she imagines, as a snake. All that dank, brooding evil, snarled like swampweed inside him, squeezing forth his sneer and sweat.

Wayne glances to her car, to where Boris and Harriet wait. "Yes," Sarah tells him, "it's all still there. All the words you wrote, your little work of art."

In the mud at her feet is the white-foam dribble where one of them hawked and spat. She buries it with her shoe. Sarah feels dizzy, vaguely sick, on the verge of making a drastic mistake, but she wants to move in close for it, wants to see the looks on their faces when she says the words she has half-rehearsed all day: in this morning's shower, on the drive to pick up Boris and Harriet, during the garden tour. "This is the day and the time and the place where everything ends," she says. "From now on, you leave us alone."

She can sense the agitation in Ellis, but Rex remains motionless and Wayne, as expected, breaks his smile only to spiral smoke from his lip like a shaman. "I know where you live," Sarah says. "Not just you, but you and you. Wayne Hinton and Ellis Dermody, way out on Thirty-third and Iowa in the trailer court, the one the tornado demolished a few years back that's notorious for all the wifebeaters and plain white trash. I know you, Wayne, have a trailer with brown trim, and Ellis, yours is faded green, and both homes are in sorry states. Rex Jackson, your farm lies way out southeast of town. Chicken feet on the chickenhouse door and goose feet on the goose door, and your mixed-up parents burned your metal records, didn't they, and your Ouija board too? You must have been steamed." At this she expects to see Rex wince, recoil, but still he only stares as Wayne, laughing, pats him on the back.

Behind them, darting past the rock path, a gray-green lizard. It would shed its tail at the slightest touch, but as a girl she could never catch one, and Marshall was afraid to try. Temerity overtakes her fear and Sarah understands, now, that Marshall would be proud of her. "You've been watching us and messing with us," Sarah tells the boys, "but you know what's really happening? We've been watching *you*. We're watching *you*."

Wayne smiles the smile of a prisoner or a bad baby and then he laughs again. "We're staying at the Atlasta Motel," he says. "Cool name, huh? Seen it on the highway on the way here, right before the turnoff. It's real small and rundown, like that motel in that murder movie with the killer faggot. You know the one."

He is teasing her; she can feel his confusion and surprise at all she discloses, but still he is teasing her. She wants to step closer, even closer, but the air shimmers with a restless tension and Sarah fears one of them might push her, strike out. "Did you hear what I said? You didn't expect us to be here, did you? You can do your jobs on us when you've been sitting around thinking about it for a while, but you didn't have anything smart to do today, did you? We caught you off guard. Nothing smart you could do to scare us, just a stupid lame attempt with your gum stuck on my friend's dress. Big deal."

A pause to let the wind move the trees. One of them is wearing Old Spice deodorant; she *knows* that smell. Sarah stares at Ellis only and waits until he looks up. "I know all about your collection," she says, now remembering more possible routes to hurt them, to keep them away. "Butterflies. Just like a little girl, in frills probably, out there with her pretty net, trapping the swallowtails and the grape-leaf skeletonizer. That one's my favorite. First place. Congratulations. Is that how you broke your arm? Goldilocks? Maybe I can sign your cast." She notes the skin on Ellis's face, milk white gone milkier, like the smooth exposed interior of a shell.

Ellis shakes his head no but Wayne shoves him forward, says, "Yeah, come on, you want her to sign it, right?" Ellis has a face like a god's experiment: bloodless, one eye's lashes yellow-blond, the other's a ghostly bleach. For a moment she feels guilty for her insults. He is Wayne's lackey and he obeys, taking the itch-scratcher pencil from behind his ear and offering it to Sarah.

But she doesn't budge. "You think you're going to get me. You think I'm going to give in like you thought Sammi Snow was going to give in. I know you better than you think, don't I? I'm scaring you now, *I'm* scaring *you*, right? But you won't get me because I don't waste my time with trash like you." And as she says this she knows she is wrong. *Wrong,* she hears those gone-by teenage trash boys saying; Victor Earl, w*rong,* Mickey Green, w*rong.*

Rex speaks; for the first time she hears his slow-motion bass. Immediately she recalls Boris telling her, droning dreamily on and on, about this voice. "We didn't do nothing to you," Rex says. She's had enough experience to guess that, behind the blue of his jeans, his knees are bruised and spindly. He has a triangle of dark hairs between his nipples and a cluster of zits on his back. "I burned those records myself, it wasn't my goddamn parents. We didn't do nothing and we don't know what you're talking about."

"Oh, fuck that," Wayne says. "She knows what's going on. She

knows everything." To Sarah: "I've got the dibs on you but we figured you'll want the three of us together. We've heard stories. What
you do and how you do it. You can't get enough. We're staying the
night at the Atlasta Motel because tonight's not a school night and
we got a ton of potent Mexican shit and some booze and we're
using it all up. If you're smart you'll be there too, you'll be there
with one in your ass and one down your throat and this one"—he
pats three fingers once, twice, over his crotch, and yes, the cock
inside the jeans is still hard—"right up tight inside your pussy."

This morning, mapping her scheme, she had sworn she would
laugh in his face; she would tell him, *You want to nail it in me like
steel but I bet I wouldn't feel it at all.* Only now she cannot say the
words. She watches Wayne in the center and Ellis and Rex on
either side and knows she must take them farther. She, only she,
has the power to defeat them. She can lead them with painstaking
shepherd's patience to the threshold, teasing them with sex like
some rich redemption, and they will believe they have won, they
will think themselves blessed with the kind of control and delight
the murderer must possess, a knowledge embedded deeper and
deeper with each victim. The threshold: it will be the same she
moved toward, again and again, all those years ago, with the suck-
erwit boys from school. That power was almost tangible. She knew
it so well she could taste its pulpy blood-orange taste inside her.
But tonight she will not give in. She will not let them have it! She
will lead them, Wayne and Rex and Ellis, drugged delirious and
stunned stupid all, and she will make them topple. She will ruin
them, and in doing so, save herself, save Harriet and Boris.

"We can all three take turns on you." She half hears Wayne's
exaggerated drawl, swearing words she has heard, sometime,
before. "Sorry," he says, "but your friends can't come. We don't
need no old wrinkly fossil pussy or AIDS-infected asshole."

Within his hatred for her friends, Sarah remembers the boys
from high school, how they hated Marshall, teased with *why you
got to hang out with that queer all the time.* Still she let them have what

they wanted. Her faithfulness stumbled and went astray, but tonight she will hurt them. She will flaunt her power, force them to retreat like the children they are, and in doing so, save Marshall too.

Sarah smiles a little, nods slightly, so lost in what she once did, what she could do now, that she hardly feels her own movement. Smiling, nodding, smiling . . . Now Rex finds the nerve to stare her face-on, Ellis replaces the pencil behind his ear, and Wayne offers a soft hoot and changes his grin from big to bigger. He shows the same teeth that left their mark on the dummy, on OSTIT's shoulders and breasts. "You like to bite, don't you?" Sarah says.

Along the streets stretch the telephone wires, full of stoop-shouldered birds Sarah first believes are sculpted, beaks and feathers and all, with cement. Then a quarry truck knocks past and each bird scatters, save one outsized brave soul, its glitter-eye hubbed on her. She turns back to the car: Harriet's shadow, front seat, and the pallid corner of Boris's backseat face, his hair mussed, watching and waiting.

Wayne finishes his weed in a gray fog and reaches out in mock handshake. His thumbnail seems made of tortoiseshell, the scarred skin puffed around it like wattles. She shoos the hand away. "I hope you're enough to handle me," she tells him, tells all of them. "I'm the best at what I do and it only takes the best to please me." Wayne's earring sparkles and he opens his mouth but, before he can speak, Sarah continues. "But if you think you can do it, all three of you, I'll be there." She knows the hearts beneath their chests beat black and unbreakable. But she will try to break them, tonight. *The time had arrived,* Boris wrote in his novel, *time to repay the years of torment, the sorrow and suffering.*

"Tonight," she says. "Now give me the directions."

19

*I*n the motel lot Boris waits, waits longer; silently reads the neon VACANCY and, out loud, the hand-lettered sign below. "Heated swim pool. Cable TV, air condition, low low rates." He reaches to the front seat for Harriet's hand, his chest clutching and unclutching in his worry about Sunflower. Demerits, detention, meetings with social workers. Sarah promised to call his supervisors from the motel room, to fabricate a "severe car trouble" story, but for now she negotiates, hidden beyond the office's glass doors, with the manager. The Atlasta houses only one other guest, someone with a white Ford pickup, and the El Camino hasn't yet arrived.

Sarah returns, jingling the quadrangular plastic keychain. "They say there's a pool," she says as Boris helps Harriet from the car, "but do you see a pool anywhere? Maybe I'm blind, but there's no pool here." A storm is coming but Boris senses it will wait, taunting, until nightfall. The sun suspends, deeper, in the west; its roiling amber fire dissolves a cloud, and when he shuts his eyes it pulses in his fret-fume head.

To the south side of the office stretch two one-story bungalows of interconnected suites, each with an orange door, a darker orange pair of window shutters. The first building consists of rooms 1 through 7. The second, 8 through 14. After 14 ends, a field begins: here, its silver propane tank like an enemy bomb, its clustered purplish weeds; further back, a deepening wood of bird and cricket pandemonium. Stacked strategically before the line of trees are dampened, mold-starred bales of sweet gold hay. Someone has pinned archery targets to their sides. Radiating circles of blue, inward to white, yellow, until the bull's-eye red. A solitary arrow pierces one of these reds, and as Boris stares he can almost hear the smooth separation of air, the thick *shlud* of the weapon as it hits. Once he asked foster parents for a bow and arrow—was it his ninth birthday? his tenth?—but he hadn't gotten his wish.

The key clasp, wrapped with masking tape, reports their bungalow as 12A, but Boris, sidestepping the sidewalk cracks, sees the mistake. "Nine," he says, "ten, and eleven." He points to the left— "that one's number twelve"—and to the right—"and that's fourteen. They gave us 12A but we're sunk, aren't we? We're really number thirteen."

"Shush," Sarah says. "I got us two beds at a single-bed rate. I persuaded the guy to give us the room next to the You-Know-Whos." She twists the key in the lock. "I paid cash and gave a fake name. Told him we were throwing a surprise party but promised we'd be quiet."

The door swings open, raising an ellipsis of dust. Inside, the mattresses wear mismatched spreads (pink begonias on one; repeating donkey, cart, and stick-figure farmer on the other); between them, atop a three-drawer nightstand, sits a rotary telephone with the receiver off the hook. "I feel like I should have a bunch of luggage to unpack," Sarah says. She sprawls across the bed, replaces the receiver, then picks it up and listens. "It works fine." Above her head, an unframed poster: leaf-littered trail, winding from a forest clearing toward a distant sunset. She tosses the car keys to the table beneath the picture window, but they slip from the edge to land on the single chair's cushion.

Boris rushes to the bathroom and unzips but, embarrassed for the possible noise, decides to sit. The toilet seat is cracked and pinches his thigh. On the linoleum floor are stray hairs and the edge of some past visitor's clipped toenail. As his bladder empties, Boris unwraps the trio of motel tumblers from their paper turbans. Perhaps later he will suggest a drive to the nearest town. They will buy a bottle of wine and fill the glasses. Try, on this special night he will try, to disregard the imminent Sunflower troubles, and they can celebrate.

The water gleams yellow and he remembers the Mountain Dew. His wishes, imprisoned within the bottle, drift downstream. And thinking of this Boris senses Rex's urine, its memory, still inside his body. Before he leaves the bathroom, he unpeels the bandage from his neck and drops it to the flushing water.

They inspect the frowzy room like detectives. Harriet, excited as though this is all part of some adventure, brushes dust from everything. A television, a ceramic sundial ashtray, a Sirocco box with a quarter slot for the bed's vibrating mechanism. And, surprisingly, there is a miniature refrigerator, a one-burner gas stove. Boris feels that every object—the telephone, the toilet seat, the stove, and the table and chair—must contain its own little story. Beside the telephone rests a votive glass clogged with the charred wax dregs of a candle. He bends to sniff: "It isn't vanilla."

Harriet spies his exposed cut, licks her thumb, touches it. "Ow," she says. "When we get back home, I'll put on some bag balm, heal that right up." With two light tug-and-pulls, she unsticks the top nightstand drawer. "A Gideon Bible." She lies back on the flowered blanket. "But no phone book. We don't even know where we are."

Sarah crooks the picture and runs her fingers over the wall

beneath, searching, Boris sees, for a peekhole. Some trick from a movie, some route from which to spy on the boys. She is pretending to be brave, faking a patient remoteness, but Boris feels his prickly inner dread and knows she feels it too. "All we do now is wait," Sarah says. "They want to be the murderer, they want to scare us to death. But they're just stupid drugfiend boys! Boris, you can do better than them. I'm sorry but it's true. They're stupid, they think I'm going to give in to what they want." She falters, looks at Harriet, back to Boris. "Turn on the TV, why don't you?"

The television has no remote, so Boris spins the dial. News on channel 12, channel 10; channel 3 gives back a streak of comedy dialogue, but the reception hovers and sizzles and transmits a formless fuzz. "Leave it there," Harriet says. Boris stretches beside her on the bed and flips pages in the notebook. Only three scenes remain before the *March of the Zombies* finale, every enemy moving closer to his eventual comeuppance. He finds, scattered through the pages, sections of unfinished poems and odes to Rex. *Inside I feel the hurting when he hurts,* Boris wrote in red art-class pencil, *the fire when he's angry. His heart lies inside my heart, snug and thumping, just where I want it.* Sarah maintained, just now, he could do better than Rex, but Boris knows he can never detail all the hours he's spent daydreaming, the nights spent focusing on images like Rex's slant-smirk grin; the half-button of an earlobe beneath messy black hair; or Rex's hand in his, delicately clasping. He can never adequately explain.

Distant thunder; at first Boris hears it as a noise from the screen but no, it is thunder, from the southwest. Sarah fluffs her hair before the mirror and opens and shuts the refrigerator door. From the highway, a semi peals its laughingstock horn. The hour passes, and after an array of commercials, another comedy begins. Harriet snuggles closer to Boris; he leans against the wall, allowing her head to fit on his shoulder. For the moment he feels older, somehow responsible for Harriet and Sarah and for this entire day. But then he looks down at the woman's body and sees, below two unbuttoned slots in her dress, the smooth salmon-toned scar where her breast used to be. Boris lowers his head to Harriet's, leveling his face on the pillow with hers.

When they hear the car, Sarah cants her head as though, merely from its idle that night at her Cherry Street home, she recognizes its racket. She steps to the window, peels back a corner of curtain, peers out. Through the crook between her stomach and arm, Boris watches the boys leave the vehicle doors: from the driver's seat Wayne; from the passenger's Rex, finishing what looks like an apple; finally Ellis. They, unlike Boris and Harriet and Sarah, have prepared for the stay, and they withdraw backpacks and liquor bottles from the car seat. "Storm's coming," Wayne says, his words entering clear into the quiet room. In the fields behind the parking lot, rainclouds sweep across the sycamore boughs, their attendant storm squalls whistling, warning.

"They know we're here," Sarah says. "They're laughing. They're staring at our car and laughing." She backs away from the curtain; after two, three seconds, Boris hears the lock on the neighboring room's door give, the low drone of their voices, words indecipherable, and the push-squeak of bedsprings.

Boris wants a breach to open in his bed and he wants to sink into it. "What are you going to do?" The room is No. 13 and Sarah hasn't yet called his supervisors, and now the boys have arrived. Sarah grits her teeth but her mouth's angle is distinctly a smile. "They're not kidding around," he tells her. "This isn't funny anymore."

"I know," Sarah says, near anger. "And I'm in control. For the first time in my life, let me be in control."

Wayne's voice again, from outside. This time Boris bolts to the window; he brushes a rime of dead flies from the sill and posts his elbow. They stand grouped, all three, beside their car, at the margin of the motel sidewalk. They are playing mumblety-peg with the archery target, alternating turns, whipping Wayne's pocketknife through the air. "They've got a knife," Boris whispers, and Sarah rises from the bed to join him. "They'll cut our tires or something.

Please don't go out there. Don't say or do anything. Oh, god, why are we here? They'll come after us with that knife; who knows what they'll do?"

With his good arm, Ellis slugs a beer. Wayne, glowering, grabs the can; he pulls a bottle—gin? vodka?—from his back pocket and tips its mouth to the beer, spiking his crony's drink. An edge of boxer shorts, red pimiento polka dots, pokes above Wayne's jeans. He tosses the knife one final time and leans back on his car, nursing his bottle alone. Cracks his knuckles, puts a thumb in one belt loop, takes another drink and whistle-breathes through his teeth: cool cockiness. Boris notices a sunburn, slight, spreading across the tops of Wayne's bare shoulders. His car's windshield is speckled with bird spatter and crushed June bugs. The bumper wears a faded sticker. Tied trophylike to the grille, just to the side of Wayne's elbow, are two squirrel tails, nearly the shade of his sunburn.

Rex appears beside the car and starts to speak, his words heavy with slur. Boris can't hear what he says. When Wayne turns his face to the windows, dead center to the spy spot, Boris drops his hold on the curtain and skitters back to the bed. "They've seen me." But soon he hears them running, running away, and when he looks to the window again the boys are sprinting from view, past the bales of hay, into the woods and the green clammy darkness.

Waits, Boris waits. A stillness covers the air outside, the ebbed quiet before a storm, sad and dangerous. He raises the window; hears wind chimes, sullenly mourning, from another bungalow. No boys' voices. A part of Boris still wants to leave, yet another part wants to explore the trees, to attempt eavesdropping on Rex and the others. Thinking of them there resurfaces the memory of Sarah's story, the first piece she wrote as assistance for his novel. The deep woods of her grade school, the shebang of chattering birds, the wind ripping leaves like rimshots as the boys came to her, wanting and needing. Once again Boris lies close to Harriet, and Sarah, curled in the opposite bed, smiles.

"They think I'm going to give them what they want," she says.

"But I'm thinking up something to trick them! I'm in control and I know what I'm doing." Still, to Boris, Sarah seems unsteady, unsure. She continues: "Midnight, I told them. They'll never never bother us again, not after tonight."

Channel 3 runs a third comedy; a fourth. Lines of dialogue float from the television through the room. "One of my favorites," Harriet says, "but I can't recall the name." Lightning smacks nearby and the screen blanks, leaving a silver cathode pinpoint diminishing, disappearing. With the thunder crash the television screen flares back, the program again visible. "Well!" Harriet says, stunned.

By eight o'clock there is still no sign of Wayne or Ellis or Rex. Boris imagines them setting fire to the underbrush, the rattle-husk cornfields. He imagines them thinking of ways to further terrorize. When he turns his worry toward Sarah, she jokingly offers her guess. "Maybe they got lost, got drunk, and passed out." More commercials, another television show . . . Harriet cozies her hands in the pillow as if praying, and when Boris turns, she has fallen asleep.

The fields past the window are flat as cookie sheets, and the prestorm sundown scours them. In minutes, little exists beyond the abandoned El Camino, the VW, the motel lot, and those fields: darkness, and darkness only. Boris pulls the curtain sides together, sleepily pinches them shut. "Please turn the volume down," Sarah says, her voice gone soft. "Let's just sit and listen. It's starting to rain. Sooner or later they'll be back." Boris adjusts the television dial and joins Harriet, crowding on the begonia bed, his ear trained on the adjoining wall. Silence drops like a great downy bird, silence wrapping his body, yet he tries to fight the nap and its heavy wings. Boris watches the staticky light, blue and silver, grainy gray and blue, from the television. Sleep, he feels it now, sleep. His eyes flutter shut, and after a time (seconds? minutes? many?) he hears a quarter, fitting slippery into the massager's slot. It is Sarah, he knows, sending the beds into toasty motion, coercing him and Harriet deeper. He can't fall asleep, he won't; gracefully though, with snail-trail slowness, he leans closer in to Harriet and feels a dream coming, pulsing, an impatient skewed storyline taking shape just outside his head, now entering his ear, overtaking. . . . The bed hums and hums and kneads its warm fingers along his spine. Outside, the world succumbs to shadow. As Boris escapes into the dream, each individual cicada, startled by the dusk, begins to pule shrilly from its isolated hideaway: the noise, altogether, like saws playing harmony in the sky.

Creak and slam of the motel-room door. Sarah enters, a dark silhouette—"Wake up," she says, "time to get out of bed"—and grapples for the lamp switch. When she finds it the room goes an eerie amber, the color of the yield bulb in the center of streetlights. Boris squints and considers the surroundings and shakes himself from his drowsy dream. They are away from home, yes, they are staying in a motel; Sarah is here and Harriet as well, and it is still nighttime, and Wayne and Ellis and Rex are there, he senses them, on the other side of the wall.

Rain soaks her clothes and drips, not in beads but in long glimmery streams, from her hair. "One hell of a storm," Sarah says. In her fist are two damp brown paper sacks; she tosses them to the bed, spilling their contents. "The roads are slick and finding a grocery took forever. We're smack dab in the middle of nowhere. Were you two sleeping the whole time? Some things for the bathroom, since we aren't prepared. Toothbrushes, a tube of my cucumber mask, some female stuff. And fried-chicken TV dinners and popcorn and ice cream and pop." She walks to the stove and fires it up, opening its squeaky maw to make certain it works.

Sarah positions the kitchen items atop the refrigerator and stove and orders the rest beside the bathroom sink. Boris, snoopy, dumps the paper sack. She has bought vanilla ice cream, chocolate syrup, and plastic spoons; curiously, a ribboned birthday bow, one black Magic Marker, a bottle of corn syrup, raspberry jam, and a box of

food-coloring vials in blue, yellow, red, green. Too, she has surprised Harriet with a magazine of crossword puzzles; a women's
novel, on the cover of which a swashbuckling man woos a scant-
dressed princess. "You were asleep nearly two hours," Sarah tells
them. Harriet, waking, thumbs the corners of her eyes.

Thunder joggles the picture window in its frame. The odor of
the room surfaces, resurrected by the nuisance swell and pound of
the storm. A mildewy smell, reminding Boris of the varicolored
clay modeling dough he used as a boy. He remembers playing
somewhere, in a bedroom—the McLaughlins? the Blevinses? He
reaches for his notebook and discovers he has slept on it, the spiral
wire binding pressing a ruby helix into his forearm.

Thrilled, Harriet gathers the ice-cream carton, the box of
spoons, and can of chocolate syrup into her arms. "Ice-cream
stew," she says. "Let's eat this first. And the Jiffy Pop." While Sarah
prepares the TV dinners, Harriet tries a burner on the stove: a blue
blossom of gas, a hotseat for the aluminum pan of kernels. She
regards the popcorn with one eye closed, as though through a
pince-nez, as it gradually expands its mercury cloud.

They tear through the popcorn tinfoil. Sarah spoons two bites
from the chocolate-drenched vanilla and carries the syrup, jam,
and food coloring to the sink. "Those chicken dinners take fifty
minutes to cook," she says. "It'll be near midnight before they're
done, so I'll finish this early." She selects a glass Atlasta tumbler and
mixes, pours, stirs. Raspberry syrup, Boris supposes, for the dessert.
He sits on the TV-lit bed with Harriet as, between popcorn and
ice cream, she retrieves her pills from a partition of her purse. She
takes them, one at a time, little sky-blue zeppelins. And Sarah, as
though preparing herself for a date or pageant, begins lathering her
face and neck with the curded diskette of motel soap. She washes
and follows up with the cucumber mud mask; when she catches
Harriet and Boris staring, she points to the reflection of their faces,
touching the mirror with two gray-green fingerprints.

"I've decided what they deserve," Sarah says.

Now, from room 14, the noise: a knocking: three sharp raps and a pause and then another three. The breath stops in Boris's chest. "It's them," Sarah says. "It's almost midnight and they're ready."

Harriet moves away from the wall, drawing her knees and stockinged feet close to her body. *She is scared,* Boris thinks. The rain thumps louder on the roof, and suddenly the drops blend with hail, bits crackling on the door, ricocheting into the window crack. Through the din, Wayne's voice, beyond the wall, drunkenly laughing.

The telephone rings. Sarah runs and puts it to her ear, and Boris hears the boy's laughter in duplicate, from both the room next door and their own room now, tinny and thin, inside the phone. "Give me ten minutes," Sarah says, and Boris sees she isn't scared, she isn't! "You're ready, all of you, you're good enough, right? Wait there. I'll knock."

She hangs up, the mouthpiece pasted with a dollop of the mud mask, and takes the glass of raspberry syrup from the sink. "Sarah," Boris says, and the sound of the word—upswung and girlish, cracking on the vowel—makes things dizzier, more frightening, worse. She shuffles to the door, pushing her hand at them in a flurry. *Remain,* she coaches, *stay there on the bed.* "What are you going to do?" Boris asks, but she doesn't answer. She opens the door carefully, attempting to make no sound, but no matter: the snaredrum downpour on the sidewalk, the thunder and pearls of hail. The storm seems to vacuum her away. Wind sloshes liquid from the glass in her hand, pitching a scarlet clump to the rug. As he watches it splash Boris thinks of the blood on Sarah's ear and neck, the wound from Rex's maniac goose.

"Stay away from them," Harriet whispers, too late, and Boris massages her shoulder. But he fidgets, he cannot sit and wait; two fast bounds and he stands, once again, at the picture window. The parking lot has transformed, a maelstrom of zigzagging gray like the damaged Channel 3 screen. Rain in black layers, rain in diagonal spears, rain. Sarah moves there, within his vision but somehow beyond it, like a dream, like something half remembered. She stands hunched over the front of the VW, the trunk open before her. Boris sees her slamming the trunk; hears the crisp bang and then, like an echo, another thunder peal. Before she can turn, before she can observe him spying from the window, he scurries back to Harriet's side.

Chocolate daubs the bedspread flowers. Harriet's spoon has toppled from the box. She has spilled popcorn hulls and now she bites her lip in the same manner as that evening, on her farm, when she found the cat. "I don't like those boys," she says. Boris hears, but the words hardly register. He hones his ears for any undersound from the neighboring room. The television light moves across Harriet's face, and when he looks to the silent screen, a banner of words swifts past, giving flash-flood warning for Russell County.

Boris touches her hair; he can smell her violet perfume. "Don't be afraid," he says. And, wavering: "I love you."

The storm stuns and screeches like a locomotive. When Sarah comes lunging in the door, the water spray grazes the table, the chairs, both mattresses. Briefly Boris doesn't recognize her, confused by her saturated hair and clothes, the gray flaking pumice of her mask cream, her wild eyes like buffed metal. "I did it!" she screams. She lifts her voice, outdoing the storm, a clangor that makes Harriet gasp and tug at Boris's arm. Raspberry dregs cling to the knuckles of Sarah's right hand, to her shirt, to the back side of her wrist like a corsage. Water streams from the sidewalk, seeping the edge of the rug. Sarah slams the door behind her, laughing. "I did it," she says again, and though her eyes show triumph they seem the eyes of someone else, some demon or enemy. She shakes the rain rills from her hair. She falls with a splash, facedown, on her bed.

Boris smells the chicken scorching in the stove; the thick marmalade of the red syrup. Sarah murmurs the three words, one final time, into the bedspread. He grits his teeth, and this time asks: "Did what? Tell me, right now, what's happening?"

Lightning strikes so close that Boris feels it numb his bones. Sarah doesn't answer, doesn't answer, doesn't make a move at all, and Boris's throat clogs with a terrified sob. He gives Harriet's hand one last squeeze. With the tears burning nearer and lonesome, he stands. Whispers, "Sarah."

Through the thunder he hears a door, somewhere, crashing open. Boris looks to the window. And then it happens. Just outside, in the lot, the slap of their sneaker steps. Running, fast, from their door—he hears No. 14 slam shut—and into the parking lot and then, horribly, faster and faster, for No. 12A. For one quarter split second Boris believes they will break down the door. But at the last flash they stop and, coiled within that gushing silent second, Boris realizes what Sarah has done. What she has left on their doorstep. But his realization comes too late. He sees their blurred bodies, in triple teamwork exertion, as they heft the naked battered body in the air.

The window explodes as if in slow motion. Both frame and pane capsize, a silver-mirror spray slicing the table and chairs. An eternity of glass, an avalanche: like bullets, like diamonds, with a noise of kettledrums and cymbals. The curtains soar like great dark wings; from between their open *V* falls the mannequin. Sarah jolts from bed and screams, Boris and Harriet scream. The rain is gushing and the glass is gushing. Boris recognizes the body: first her chordate back, the side of her head with its ratted mange. Then the mannequin twists and stills, facing its face toward the ceiling. The knife marks, the stabs and gouges and the plastic scar of mouth, at last her unblinking all-aware eyes. Stalks and blades of glass. Outside the boys are whooping and slapping hands; Sarah moves from the first bed to the second and shelters Harriet with one wet arm. But Boris stays standing, eyes locked on the dummy at his feet. Jelly and corn syrup and gore dye trail down the bare legs, smear the stomach. The birthday bow wraps in flawless charm around the neck. Across the store-bought ribbon, a repeating salute: Surprise! Surprise! The pretend murderers' teeth marks still riddle the unbending skin like the tracks of tiny animals, the indentations sopped with sham blood drops. Oozing from the dummy's cunt are scraps of muscle, the rank rotten sludge. The liver has spoiled and attracted a clot of maggots, which writhe in the meat and glass like fibers of electricity. And, oh, the word OSTIT. But Sarah has changed it forever, using the marker, replacing the gnawed and hammered letters. PROSTI-TUTE, it says now.

It is midnight—*the undead rose from the earth*—and Boris knows if he could see the sky it would glow purple-black, like carbon paper. Outside, the boys' celebration stops, and in its place comes the sound of the motel manager, barking a warning. *Police,* Boris hears him scream. And the boys, terrified at being caught but laughing still, run for their car. The El Camino surges into gear, revving and revving until the tires squeal away. "The manager's coming," Sarah says. "They're escaping but this isn't over. All of us, into the car. Now." Her words seem aped from a movie but Boris doesn't argue. He shuts off the stove and finds Harriet's shoes and shies her away from the ruin of glass, not looking once into Sarah's face.

They run into the tempest. To Boris the rain and nuggets of hail seem cold as snow; he helps Harriet into the back. Sarah's fingers fumble as she starts the car but on the second try she succeeds. The engine coughs in clogged scherzo. "Don't go after them," Harriet says, her voice an onionskin whisper. "The roads are bad and they've been drinking something terrible." Boris sees the manager running through the lot, but Sarah leaves and swerves, dangerously fast, onto the highway. Ahead shine the pair of rose-red taillights, and she follows, speeding.

Everywhere and everything is water. Boris rakes his fingers through his hair, bangs draping his eyes. He turns; Harriet, eyes closed, has snuggled in a backseat corner, hugging her knees, her head against the window. Sarah won't listen, so now Harriet shuts her mouth, lips a tight crease that resembles her son's. Her pink hair looks purple and both shoelaces dangle, untied, from her sneakers. She pulls at her pigeonblood ring, but Boris sees that her fingers have swollen with the rains.

Four miles, five; the yellow slashes in the median shoot past into a single hypnotizing line. A road marker says Highway 4 but Boris can't tell west from east and he worries about getting lost. Wayne's taillights jet deeper into the inky distance. Then, with a sudden turn, they veer from sight. "They took a side road," Sarah says. "They're speeding, they think we're the manager. They don't think we'd come after them, do they? I can barely see through this but they—we're going to catch them." She taps the brakes at the exit. When she turns, Boris feels the wheels glide and slide. Here the road becomes gravel, rocks crackling just below the floorboard. Sarah helms with her hands tensed tight, chasing faster as the fugitive car reappears: thirty-five miles per hour, forty, the wipers slapping the windshield.

She lowers the volume on the radio and towels her palms on her knees. "They'd better slow down." Boris sees Wayne's car whipsawing. It moves further away and then looms closer and then, taunting, away. Sarah passes a mailbox and a bus-stop shack for schoolkids, but beyond the driveway's curve is nothing but foaming, lashing water. The road narrows. It breaks a swath into a field of interconnected trees that paddle and beat and bleed their leaves. "I can't see," Sarah says. It is as though they are traveling the uncharted recesses of a body and are now, just now, entering the dark, mysterious core.

"We're scared," Boris says. "Me and Harriet." His pulse beat has risen, thrumming into his throat. If she turned the car around, maybe he could help her decode the long route home. "There's nothing we can do now, let's let them go. They're going to do something bad. Let's hurry back to the Atlasta Motel and tell the manager it was them that broke the window and let's just let them go."

"We gave her back to them." Sarah sounds like Sarah again, but the face behind the steering wheel, still smudged with the clay, isn't quite hers. "They were so ready for me when I knocked on their door. They were burning their vanilla candles for me! But they didn't know what we were going to do, did they? We gave her back to them. But this isn't over! They might get away from what they did to our room, but they don't know what else I've got planned. We aren't finished yet. We're—"

Sarah stops speaking. Once again she taps the brakes, easing into fifteen miles per hour, lower. "Where'd they go? It's too dark. Where'd they go?" Even with his face against the windshield, eyes squinted, Boris no longer sees the car's red lights. He hears Harriet shift and sigh from behind them; Sarah continues, slower, into the thundering rain, her high beam a spotlight in the storm.

The gravel gives way to asphalt, a yellow diamond sign warning NARROW BRIDGE. At the end of its wet, wobbling pool the road shears off, a curve vanishing into steepled saplings and the blue field of trees. Boris imagines Wayne and Rex and Ellis just ahead, idling in the mud gulch and waiting, lights off, to ambush Sarah's car. "They're going to kill us," he whispers.

They reach the juncture in the road where the bridge begins. They take the curve. In that instant Boris glimpses, through the swirl and the pour, a flash of silver and shining black. "There they are," he says, but as he finishes the words he knows his error. Through the downpour, no taillights this time, but the dual glint of metal and glass: the El Camino, its grille in a weird diagonal, a slight incline into the storm. And as Sarah moves closer Boris sees each successive detail, this and this and the next, alarming and nonsensical, like a rebus. First a single blown tire, sunk into the earth. Next the windshield, shattered. And the charcoal skid marks, ripped wounds in the road, a swath that leads to the bridge's curve and falls abruptly to the ditch. The torn shaggy clumps of grass. The spews of mud. The wreckage.

"Oh, my god," Sarah says. She stops completely and they sit staring, a ticking of seconds. Here, dazzled close in the lone headlight halo, is the enemy's car, broken. Boris traces the tire tracks, the bent, ragged rips in the grass. The car missed the curve, spun on the asphalt, and blasted head-on into the headpost of the bridge. The collision lifted it through the air, jackknifing it cab first into the ditch, totaled, into the wet thicket of underbrush. An "Oh, my god" again, but this time Boris isn't certain if it comes from Sarah or himself.

He flings open his door. Without speaking to Harriet or Sarah, he runs to the roadside, feet sinking in the puddles. Katydids hide in the weeds, braving the storm, and as he approaches they vault and bump his legs. There are branches, bits of metal and glass, rushes fringing the twisted hood, and window supports where the car has moored. The only accidents Boris has seen have been from the television screen, and he expects plumes of smoke, a runaway hubcap twirling on the asphalt. He expects the joke soundtrack of groaning trombones, the *boing* of a spring unsprung.

Sarah gets out and slams the door, shutting Harriet inside. Boris turns, and within the single headlight spear sees Sarah's face, made ghostly from the nightcream mask. *Her face was pale, beautiful, smoldering.* She hurries to the scene, and here the light's aurora illuminates her form, her shadow tossing a black parasol on the road behind.

Glass, everywhere glass, in and on and around the car, gemming the bubbles of mud. Boris stands two arms' lengths from the wreck, looking to where the ruined black machine has landed in the overgrown hummock of weeds. The front tires have exploded, the grille has smashed; the hood ornament has broken, one of the squirrel tails now torn free. The car has nearly folded, half on half, into itself. When Sarah comes closer he offers his hand to help her through the sludge. Together they lope down, the rain raging. He moves around the passenger's side; Sarah takes the driver's. They steady themselves, lean, and peer into the flattened tableau of the windshield.

The form pinned behind the steering wheel is Wayne, but the features don't look, not a bit, like Wayne's. A lunate cut swirls above his eyebrow, hemorrhaging across his face. His eyes are half open, even with the blood washing over them, and his mouth, lolling dumbly, drinks the streams of red. Below his chin, the steering wheel and column have crushed his chest. The skin and bones have collapsed with the slamming weight, and slowly, like a flower opening, the blood seeps and irrigates his T-shirt. Boris leans nearer, his head at the blasted windshield. He doesn't think about what he does, just leans into the wreck and examines the lettered logo on Wayne's shirt: NILSON AUTO BODY above; LAWRENCE, KS and a phone number below. Between, sopped through and slick, a transfer of a big-breasted vixen beside a sportscar. Between his thighs is an open vodka bottle and the rubber strip of one torn windshield wiper. The platinum shine of his belt buckle: WAYNE.

Next, in the carseat center, Ellis. The crash has pitched his body forward, splitting his face through the windshield—for a moment he tried to fly, a baby from a glass birth canal—and then pulling his body, flinging it, back inside. Softly now, Ellis rests his head on the dashboard, as though comfortably slumbering. Glass triangles and beads scatter on all sides, and one spiked crescent has embedded between his lips, nearly severing them, a flawless shape of silver like a sculpted jewel bitten free from a chandelier. Another piece lies lodged, fanglike, in Ellis's cheek. The cuts are deep and stream with blood, his blood most frightening of all: that something so dark should come from inside him, a swan crying black-red tears. Blood, making him seem more whey-faced than before. His eye-lashes look whiter as well, long and bent like bleached spider legs. Spreading through his hair, above his ear, is a rouge patch, like a valentine placed upon his head.

Boris swallows his cold, horrified breath and looks. Rex. Spotlit by the headlight, eyes closed, shoulders pressed against the seat. His face is serene and Boris wants to touch it but cannot move, cannot. Rex's hands rest at his sides, palms and fingers bleeding, studded with glass as though he had punched both hands forward, protest-ing, as the car began its wailing pirouette. His kneecaps spread blood through his denim pants: His legs, too gangly and long for the car's space, have saved him from the windshield, but have shattered against the thrusting wall of the car panel. Rex's spectacles have fallen from his shirt front. Boris sees them lying, unharmed, within a sprinkling of glass and pebbles next to Ellis on the dashboard. In his head he feels sweeping pressure, not fear or sadness but something deeper, nameless. He reaches into the world of the car, takes the glasses, and hides them in his jeans pocket.

The boys lie stilled yet within their stillness are somehow vigorous, like three carousel horses, statued in rear and flare. The engine has died, and although the radio continues to play, Boris only now notices its song: roaring, from a heavy-metal tape, a strange, distorted version of some familiar childhood tune. Sarah hears it too; she shuffles closer to Wayne's door. But the crash has bent and crinkled the metal, easy as foil, and the door, as though welded along the seam, won't budge. Boris moves down to door level, Rex's side, slipping in the turfy earth but pushing himself back to his feet. He tugs and tugs the handle, and on a third try wrenches the passenger's side free.

Rain bursts so fast it makes everything else seem slow motion. The car's interior light flutters on, sheeting the boys in its gray-gold jellyfish glow. Beneath it Boris sees even more blood, splashed across the instrument panel, dropping and dripping from the radio dials and the glove-compartment button and the little marijuana-leaf pendant that hangs by a chain from the rearview. Through this chain, Wayne has pinned a badge that reads, 1996 ALL THE WAY, and a single spatter of blood, pristine, has touched its W. Ellis's face rests below it, close-up now, the ragged, lacerated flesh of his lip and cheek. Red marble beads pulse steadily from the hole in his head. Red; black and silver shrapnel; red. And the curious gleam of engine coolant in mint-mouthwash blue, translucent pools in Rex's lap and spraying the wound that spreads, slowly but not slowly enough, across Wayne's chest. Boris can smell it. He can smell motor oil, spilled liquor, and the smoke from the boys' final joint; a peculiar, seared wood odor, the odor of pencil sharpeners at school. But heavier than that comes the primal battleground smell of blood, so strong that Boris tastes it when he swallows, feels it diving deep from his throat into his body. As he leans closer, his head only inches from Rex's body, he breathes the blood and oddly, queasily, sees the puddle on the dashboard trembling. Families of mosquitoes from the woods have woken from slumber—Boris remembers the cloud of them, only last night, beside Potter's Lake—and they intrude on the car and now swim in the blood.

Now Boris hears, behind him, a scraping sound. Harriet has scrambled out of the car, her shoes sliding on the road. Her arms crossed at her chest, her face cabled with strands of wet hair. "I can't see you," Harriet says, her voice like a child's. She swipes at her brow and says it again, louder, adding, "Kids, what's happening out there?"

"Get back where you were," Sarah yells, the angry force of her words cutting through the rain and scaring Boris. "Get back there now!" And as Harriet stumbles back, Sarah tries Wayne's door again. When it fails to open, she rushes around the front of the car to join Boris. She leans into the compacted space to shut off the radio song but flinches, gasping, when blood smudges her fingers. The music stops and a drumroll of thunder dies away. Now only the silvery industry clatter of rain.

On the floor at Rex's feet are stacks of pornography, magazines with bodies selected and cut free. There is a lipsticked mouth and tongue; a single scissored breast; one long fingernail parting the lips of a cunt. One model's face has been replaced by Sarah's photograph, head cut out and glued above her neck. Another model has become Sammi Snow. Beside them, atop the magazines, lie a votive candle and the wooden flute. Boris can still see, a crystal moment in his memory, the scene from the rocking pinnacle of the Zipper as Wayne and Rex bought the flute from the carny girl and led her off into the crowd. He reaches down, brushes the glossy spattered pages and Rex's foot—he notes a nugget of chicken feed in the eyelet of the sneaker—and picks up the flute.

Wind shifts the trees and rain spritzes from the break in the window, washing and diluting the blood. A mosquito lifts from the dashboard to light beside the glass in Ellis's cheek. Snuggled like an infant at Ellis's side is the cast; it shows the Magic-Markered GET WELL SOON and a lopsided smiley face. Boris can feel the rigid plaster crashing down, again, on his shoulder, his mouth. He whimpers softly, soft enough for Sarah not to hear. He stares at Rex, hoping, silently hoping, his eyes will open. Inside the light, owned by it, the details glisten: the black strands of Rex's hair, the white flecks of dandruff, the wax in his ear, coppery and crumbly dry like crystals of nougat.

Sarah puts her hands back into the car and leans for Rex, as if to hold him. Before she can reach the body, Boris plunges his hands forward too. He will not let her touch him first. They stand together, shoulders curved identically, their fingers pressing into the boy's broken body as though they can heal. They remain connected like this, connected to Rex and Ellis and Wayne, consumed at last by the horror and awe, all their differences and wrongs and rages dissolving, Boris and Sarah unmoving now, as though some mystery will reveal itself. The world has stopped for something to happen, and this is what has happened.

Gently the air begins to crack apart. Boris hears the soughing of the trees and the thunder, again, a litany. Through the descending storm a feather of steam rises from the car, at war with the rain. "I'll get the head, you take the feet," Sarah says, and he remembers the last time she said this.

And then they are maneuvering Rex free. His head butts Ellis's body and lolls him against the seat, blood pouring from the wound in Ellis's skull and splashing the cast. Boris fetters Rex's ankles with his hands, clutching his white gym socks. He pulls, delicately, until the fractured legs are outside the car. Sarah manages to slide her hands behind his back, curving them under Rex's arms. He is heavier than OSTIT but they stride, heaving and wet, up the ditch.

Walking backward, the high-top sneakers pushing deep into his forearms, Boris looks down at Rex, straight into his face. Rex is still beautiful. But now his face looks very, very tired, the face of someone after a long race or fight who now must stop to rest, to drink. Staring, Boris feels the rainwater trickle in his nostrils and a sadness, dense and clicking, from low inside his throat. He makes a swift chopping sob and drops his end. "No," Sarah says, yelling. Just that, and then: "Boris!" He swallows the sob and it feels like swallowing a plum. He picks up the feet and they continue until they reach the asphalt.

Gingerly Sarah rests Rex's head on the road and hustles to the VW. Boris drops the feet and sits, propping Rex's head against his thigh. The headlight blinds him, but he keeps his hand, soothing, on Rex's forehead. He hears the rain, but over the rain hears Sarah's keys in the front compartment of her car. *Click-click.*

They carry him to the trunk. From inside the car comes Harriet's voice, tiny. Saying his name, his, not Sarah's. Boris does not answer. He grunts as they lift, higher; grunts again as they fit his body into the space. Inside is a green rectangle of rug like the false grass on Sarah's golf course; a plastic babydoll, gored and crusted with ketchupy blood; a nest of maggots, remaining from the mannequin and spoiled meat. Boris holds his breath from the smell. He makes a fist, scoops the maggots away, tosses them into the rain. They lower Rex, together, into the trunk's cramped closet.

Before he gets back in the car he looks one last time at the El Camino, unrecognizable in its new wicked geometry. The cluster of battle-armor metal and chrome, the animal-tail trophy and bumper sticker, the shadow of Wayne's head. Sarah starts the car and drives, passing the bridge the boys had missed, continuing into the storm.

Quietly, Harriet speaks again. "Oh, Marshall," she says. "Oh, my Marshall."

Boris cannot see her in the backseat shadow, and he will not turn around. Instead he looks to Sarah, needing her to speak. "They went so fast; they thought we were the manager," Sarah says. Her mouth moves from behind her nervous hand but still he hears her words. "He's not dead yet. Not. It was him wearing the Old Spice. I know that smell and I could smell it. Wayne and Ellis, we can't help them, they're gone. But not him."

Blood covers Boris's hands and smears a swath along the seam of his jeans. It is Rex's blood. Back at Sunflower, kept safe in the bottom drawer, are Rex's things. Boris collects them, he owns them. The test tube of his piss, his fault-ridden term paper, a cinnamon wad of gum, the paperweight rock from his locker, the pink nub of an eraser Rex once chewed from a pencil and sidearmed into the trashbin.

Water spats from a crack in the passenger-side window and runs in streams from Sarah's. "You were right," she says. "He is handsome, isn't he? I never saw it before, but you were right." Blood drenches her hands as well, but this blood is real, unlike the raspberry-syrup blood. This blood doesn't bubble or run, unlike the blood pushing from the hole in Ellis's head or the split skin of Wayne's chest. Sarah opens her mouth again, but Boris looks away, drifting to the side window and the world that eases past.

The car hurtles forward. Sarah pumps the brakes, and after many, many minutes they come to a fork in the road. There are no lights, no houses, nothing on either side but water and trees and the blue-black gloom. Harriet murmurs again. "Quiet," Sarah says, taking a left turn, driving slower and slower. Then, with a frustrated bark, she slaps her hands against her face. "Where the hell are we?" she says. She scratches and rubs at the mud mask, wiping both palms on the steering wheel. "God," she says, "this *burns*," nearly screaming. The mask's residue is putty-gray but in the aqueous stormcloud light it seems another color, like the blood blotting the torn dashboard of Wayne's car. Everything looks like blood: the mask, the worn vinyl of the seats, the faded dye in Harriet's hair. Sarah tears at her skin again, and Boris realizes they are lost. Rex lies dying inside the trunk and the rain won't stop and they are lost. Boris begins, uncontrollably, to shudder, his hands and his neck and knees, the hairs shivering on his scalp. He holds Sarah's arm to steady himself. Inside her net of confusion and wide-eyed concentration on the road, she pushes him, violently, away.

Boris cries, softly. Sarah allows it, and he cries. He feels Harriet's hand, moving into the front seat. The old woman combs her fingers through his hair, just as he did with her in the motel room, less than an hour before. That was a different time, wasn't it? A different world?

"The rain will stop," Sarah says. "It'll stop soon, I know it." Right now she is supposed to say, *Don't cry,* supposed to touch him the way Harriet touches, but she doesn't.

Without warning she swerves the car. Boris looks up; she has turned into a narrow lane, her high beams throwing luster across the mass of objects in the near distance. There are piles of lumber and branches; broken furniture and cinder blocks and bricks; mountains of tires; rows and rows of wrecked rusted station wagons and tractors and trucks. They have come to a junkyard, an abandoned car cemetery.

"I can't see the road anymore," Sarah says. "We'll rest here. Just a minute. Just rest." But Boris feels a slowness in her words, as though she has some other purpose, as though she has been willed to come here. He feels the heat of the beautiful bleeding boy in front of him, and cannot look at Sarah, cannot argue that to stop now is to kill the one he loves.

The lane continues ahead and Sarah continues along it. Through the window cracks Boris smells the wet timber, the vermin. Puddles in the road are pools of blood, and the oak and cottonwood leaves clog them, pieces of skin and muscle and heart. Railroad ties on the left and the right, gradually closing in. The lane ends, and the car stops. Ahead of them is a school bus, brooding, blocking the way. The headlight drifts across it; the engine has been gutted from the bus's hood, and its yellow has faded with age.

Sarah shuts off the ignition and pulls the keys. "Harriet, stay here." She points to the handle on Boris's door and opens her own. He follows her back into the storm and stands, watching the ground, as Sarah leans over the front end and reopens the trunk.

GUTTERSLUT. FOSSLE. TRASH MOTHERFUCKERS. Boris has memorized Rex's handwriting and believes, even now, that the words, all of them, were sprayed, not by Rex, but by Wayne and Ellis only. Without speaking, Sarah motions him over. Again he begins to take the feet. He is still crying but to remain silent hurts worse. The blood from the wounds on Rex's knees has spread, a pair of starfish patches on his jeans. Gently, Boris touches a wound. He examines the blood on his finger, but the rain washes it away, so he lifts, straining, with Sarah. He feels the moist spill of blood, the ooze, on the boy's socks. Rex's eyes stay closed. There are threadlike trails on his left arm, scratches and cuts from the windshield. His hands drip blood and they contract and twitch, a network of tendons and nerves severed by metal and diamond-edged glass. Boris has dreamt of these hands, the long, strong farmboy fingers with their shabby cuticles and calluses. He realizes he will never hold them, no palms pressed tight and no interlocking fingers, never.

Sarah leads; Boris follows. The unwaning storm soaks their clothes, sucks at their feet, adds pounds to the body they carry. When she reaches the bus Sarah straightens, still gripping Rex beneath the shoulders, and kicks the door's thin vertical separator of rubber. It budges against her heel; they climb the three steep stairs.

Inside the bus, dust gauzes the windows and the black aisle and the seats, all two columns and thirteen rows. There is an alkaline smell of wet roots and worms. The driver's seat wears a luxury wrap, patterned cedar beads for comforting massage. In the seat behind it, a cardboard box holds empty Mason jars and vinegar cruets; two pink muslin roses with pipe-cleaner stems; a globe terrarium with a veneer of dirt and marbles and jacks and the empty shell of a turtle, brown and gold and locular. A collection like the

Suffering Box, Boris thinks. He hefts the weight onto his right side and reaches for one of the flowers, but Sarah moves back too quickly. Lips pressed together, she heaves and walks with syncopated steps. "To the last seat," she says, again as though she has planned it. Boris begins to lose his grip on Rex; he squeezes the sock harder, and blood leaks between his fingers to pap ankle-level on his pants.

The bus is an old one: the last seat stretches from one side to the next, not separated by the aisle, like the seat in a bus Boris remembers riding long ago. Its corners and edges are latticed with spiderwebs. Sarah motions to Boris. They push and pull at Rex, cautiously, until he rests, face up, on the seat. Above him is a blue rubber lever and a sticker reading EMERGENCY EXIT. His skin has paled to buttercream white—the color of Ellis's, Boris thinks—and he is wet all over, not only from the blood and the rain, but from sweat.

Sarah curls her hair behind her ears. Her labor over Rex has sullied her face with his blood, and a trail of it covers the mud mask on her cheek. Boris wants her to hold him, to take the seat in front of Rex and assure him that soon the storm will stop, they will find a hospital. But Sarah heads back up the aisle. She stretches her hand for the school-bus door and Boris, immediately swayed by fear, leaves Rex alone in the cobwebby dark and runs. Sarah is hurrying too, her hands parried against the hurl of water. Through the chop and the pour until they are back, slam and slam, inside the warmth of her car.

They sit staring at the water that popples the windows. Lightning rips in white filaments, and in the series of blazes Boris sees details from the cars around them, all beaten and battered. Here a relic Nebraska license plate; there a stack of mufflers; there a hood ornament's leaping leopard. All are burned and crashed and totaled automobiles, their interiors misted by the ghosts of accident victims, years past. Boris feels his stomach and chest churning sadness. He feels fear, pulsing, everywhere; there are no hands to hold, so he clenches his blood-pasted fists and crams them in both pockets. Then he hears it, even above the thunder. Once, twice, a low, tormented moan. He glances out the window to the other cars, to the salvage piles of garbage and timber. Harriet leans in from the backseat; shadow screens her face, but he can see the silhouette of her body, blue gingham dress, and funny frazzled hair, surfacing in the rearview. The moan comes again. Out there, apart from them, inside the bus, from the green vinyl seat. Rex, bewildered, calling out numb in the orderless language of pain.

"We have to go back," Boris says. He breathes a drop-shoulder sigh and says it again, his voice lowered, as though trying to convince Sarah and Harriet and all the ghosts haunting the world outside that no, no, he isn't crying.

—S.

One-two-three steps & I stood inside the bus again, I couldn't hear his moans but oh god the smell, the deodorant the soured cologne the sweat & all the blood, now a vomit stink as well. Outside the bus windows the world had gone hazy, unseen stars hanging upside down, only cobalt-black sky & the blacker clouds, exploding. Flashbulbed by the lightning whips were broken heaps of engines & hoods & seats, the junkyard, only natural we should anchor here, since I'd never fixed the car, it was destined to happen. I braced myself, shook water from my hair, moved toward whatever was next. Inside the bus I felt the creepy hesitance from when Harriet & I entered the carnival spookhouse in our clattering car, to keep going I imagined the screenplay's directions (Sarah takes a deep breath. Begins walking, slowly, down the aisle, approaching the back seat . . .).

In his dusty dark corner he appeared worse than before, he had begun to shake & sweat thick sweat, he had vomited, a yellowish mash down his throat & shirtfront. But what scared me most were his eyes, he had opened them, two burned holes in the wide wide white. They shivered in their sockets, when I stood over him they looked up but didn't focus on me, they drifted above, unregistering unrecognizing. Sprinkled on his shoulders were pieces of hair, chopped swatches from the windshield glass, on waking Rex must have fought & twisted, the hair coming loose to cover his blood-spattered shirt. His body was shaking still, not a nervous or scared kind of shake but a forth & back jerk, violent as a seizure. I bent closer, the vomit smelled a little like apples & a lot like booze, beside it on his shirt were more hairs but these were bloodied blond, glass-sheared from the towhead of dead Ellis. I brushed them away w/the pebbledust bits, everything scattered on the floor.

I tried to quell my fear, although my muscles felt frozen I moved to the seat & edged behind the space where he lay. Up so near I saw blood bubbling from his neck, a cut I hadn't noticed before. Here the freckles on his face—I recalled something Harriet used to say, The way to cure freckles is to scrub your cheeks w/buttermilk, Marshall would get freckles in the summer but not me, I would only tan.

One of Rex's legs had fallen off-angle from the seat, the kneecap shattered, it seemed red handkerchiefs were wadded in his hands but I knew it was only the bleeding still. Although I didn't believe it I said It'll be okay. Part of me wanted to say I want you dead like the others, I want you dead. But only part of me wanted to say it & I couldn't.

Then another moan, godawful loud & I went numb, had to keep speaking to quiet him down, to calm him, he was shaking all over in full heaving shakes & I knew he was dying. I thought about Marshall & things I'd said to him in the hospital, how I talked about the music we'd loved & the movies we'd watched. Only two months earlier I had stretched beside my friend & reminded him of our favorite "urban myths," now nudging Rex's head w/my thigh I repeated those stories. The one about the tin of crescent rolls that exploded in the station wagon's backseat heat, causing the driver to think a gunman blew her brains out. The one Marshall told where a man goes to a bar, gets picked up by a handsome doctor, waking some three days later w/an expert scar on his side & a miraculous missing kidney. Oh I talked about the bands we loved, the bands from the decade when we were Rex's age, for what seemed fifteen minutes, twenty, maybe half an hour I spoke to this boy that Boris loved, this boy we had followed through road & town because I wanted my revenge. I named so many bands, Ultravox, Blondie, Simple Minds, Visage, Altered Images, Japan, B-Movie, Psychedelic Furs, Adam & the Ants, China Crisis, Echo & the Bunnymen. I named the movies we loved too, Marshall holding my hand at Friday Afternoon Frights, I named Halloween, The Burning, Maniac, City of the Living Dead, Terror Train, Phantasm, Friday the 13th, Parts 1 & 2, Mausoleum.

Rex's hair looked deliberately put into place, as if dyed & fringed, the sort of New Wave cut Marshall & I would have given each other over a decade ago. I tried to pat it down, a piece of glass stabbed my palm, a perfect red ridge along the lifeline, I flinched fast but he had felt my touch, his body jerked again & even louder now he moaned. He put one hand out, blood crusted on the arms & wrists, I reached for it & trying again to calm him I held it tight. I lowered the hand to his chest &

held it, held. His breathing went shallow, quick inhalations like a baby's sighs. It felt not as if I were touching his skin but instead his very soul, if that could be touched.

Something shiny peeked from his jeans pocket, I snuggled myself between his seat & the seat in front, w/one hand still holding his arm I knelt on the floor. The shiny was the cellophane from a peppermint disk, I pulled & the candy fell to the aisle. Reaching inside the pocket I found three more peppermint disks & something else, a pencil perhaps, Rex gave another soft half-moan & I tugged the object from the pocket, I held it to what little light there was.

It was hard & thin & wrapped w/tissue paper, I ripped the paper but already knew what I'd find. A hypodermic needle. Pot I knew about, booze & maybe acid I knew about, not much would surprise me from Rex & his friends, but heroin? It didn't add up, heroin, I was hearing Rex cough & moan again, seeing him twitch & another peppermint trickle like rain or yes blood to the floor & then, then I knew the secret Boris didn't know. The secret more secret than the black-frame spectacles Boris took from Rex's pocket. I remembered a girl during my Sunflower days, insulin-dependent diabetic *the counselors called her, there were days she'd botch her shot or days she'd take too much, she carried candy or cans of pop for that instant sugar rescue. Now I knew Rex was diabetic, the candies were for possible onset of seizures, the wreck had taken control of his body, had unraveled his veins. Veins still soaring w/various drugs & alcohols but needing that additional essential drug to survive. Rex was dying & blazing inside the shock & blood loss & sweet need for insulin his seizures were coming harder & faster.*

I twisted both ends of cellophane, the peppermint candy spun free. Maybe Rex needed the sugar, but maybe I didn't want to give it. Maybe I wanted to see him die as the final step of revenge, maybe I wanted to know that none of them, not three not two not one, could cause us harm or fear again. But I had to help him, I thought of Marshall, quickly I pinched his bottom lip so the mouth opened easy as a puppy's. Inside was gum, a blueberry plug of the same the boys had wadded on Harriet's dress, I took it out. His tongue was tight & shock-

stiff w/the tip curling toward the back of his throat, I delivered the savior peppermint there. At that moment he wasn't Rex anymore, he became any one of a series of boys, lying here, needing me, Chuck Eidel, Suzanne's big brother Jerry, Victor Earl or Jan Skovgaard or Mickey Green or even perfect Howard Westenhoffer. I kept my fingers in his mouth easing the candy onto his tongue, making certain he would taste it, the sugar would work magic.

Suddenly his jaw clamped down & he bit, no easing or letting go. His body raged w/another seizure, back leaping, teeth vised together in superhuman strength. I tried to pull my fingers away but couldn't. His eyes rolled back in his head, in the gray dust-mote light I saw the bulbs straining their sockets, their stalks. W/out thinking I smacked at him w/my free hand, slapped his chest & shoulder, his cut hair & Ellis's hair snowing across the seat, the puddled vomit. I punched at him, struggling there in the tight cranny between the seats. His teeth broke skin & on one last hit I struck him full in the neck, my knuckles drumming hollow on his Adam's apple & the blood from his cut making a soft splatter that hit my shirt. His mouth opened, I pulled my hand away, he was choking. Then the seizure stopped & he lay exhausted.

I lifted my hand in front of me, it was bleeding, just as his hands, still, were bleeding. I stood again, stepped three steps away & listened as he made a single desperate hissing noise. The uneaten candy lay in the vomit on his chest, striped edges of red white red, but the chest didn't rise or fall w/the normal rhythm of breath. Soon the rain would stop, it had to, I knew I must run back to the car to summon Boris. Wayne & Ellis were dead & Rex was dying too. I thought of the words on my car, the girl on the shore. The face at the window. The bird in the house, the blood in the egg, the baby in the box.

In movies, before, death seemed so exciting, the scatterbrained class clown impaled w/arrows on his dorm room's front door, the murderous villain disemboweled & beheaded, thrown from the speeding locomotive, but it had lost its seethe & simmer, death ruined & made so, so real w/Marshall & now it had taken me even further, one step from what I thought was the barrier. Back outside the rain washed over my face, it *hadn't let up, not one fraction, I let it drench me until the mud mask was gone completely. Under the rain I thought about what had happened, what was still happening, inside the bus. I knew I could not tell lies again, could not exaggerate my stories, never. Before I'd wanted my life to be as exciting as the movies we saw, as the lyrics to our favorite songs. I wanted those days back but I couldn't have them, couldn't couldn't. The eighties were gone & Marshall was gone. No one wanted to listen to that music anymore, wanted to watch those silly overwrought overacted films. The eighties & Marshall, w/one final look at the bus & the dying bleeding boy inside it I turned, I headed for the car, ran faster than I'd ever run, on each slippery step thinking this: That nothing will ever be the same. That nothing will ever, & everything will never.*

—H.

The Beautiful Son
BY HARRIET JASPER

There was once an old woman who lived on a farm with her son. The old woman's love for the boy was so great that if all the drops of water in her pond were precious jewels, they could not outweigh it. Her love was so great, that if all the leaves in her stretch of wood were tongues, they could not utter it.

Over the years, her son had grown up tall and strong, but lately he had fallen terribly ill. Shortly the time came when he must stay in a room in the town hospital. Each morning the widow woke and sat patient until a girl, lovely as a princess, arrived at her door. The girl would accompany the old woman to the hospital where her son, terribly ill but still beautiful beyond measure, slept quietly in his white bed.

One morning at the end of summer the old woman woke and started about her daily business. She brushed her hair and washed her face and put food into bowls for her great many cats. Into her windows the sun was shining, and for variety she made tea instead of coffee.

Then the old woman heard the telephone ring. The lovely girl had yet to appear, and the woman counted fifteen rings before she answered. She knew what the words would be before she heard them. After she heard the words she hung up. Then she lifted the telephone again and dialed a number for someone else to come and take her, now, to the hospital where her son lay. The woman put on her wig and her scarf and her good shoes. Into the basement she shut the cats, and then she waited on the porch.

I walked alone into the rain. I stepped into the bus as Sarah had done before me. In the darkness I could hardly see. I heard a terrible noise. The noise was a wheezing and rattling sound like Marshall had made. I held my arms in front of me and slowly made my way up the aisle.

When she got to the hospital she went forth to the little downstairs shop. To herself she thought, "At times like these, one should buy a gift." She had come here once before, after the doctors had worked on her son's eye. She had bought her son a toy brown bear, and as she handed him the gift he smiled and very gently plucked the button of its right eye from its face.

It so happened, on that day, that the old woman saw more toys. She saw lions, ponies, seals, and many sizes of bears. She saw chocolate candies in splendid boxes of gold and wrapped baskets of fruit. "An apple a day," thought she; perhaps that would make her son better. But the apples were too hard, and she knew her son would not eat them. So the old woman bought a basket of soft yellow pears. Into the wastebasket she threw away all but one, the shiniest and healthiest of all. With this magic pear in her hand she slowly, gently, climbed the steps and went forth to the room.

Her son was in the room as before but surrounding him now were a doctor and two nurses, all dressed in white. When they saw the old woman arrive, they stepped away. She watched him there, on his bed, his eyes closed and his hands resting still at his sides. Yet her son did not move. Presently the doctor and nurses left the room, and she was alone with him at last.

Each time she came to see her son he seemed different. There on the bed he remained lying as always, but each time she beheld a little less of his muscle, sensed a little less of his mind, as though parts of him seeped out during the dreadful night. Today he did not seem her son at all. His skin was white as the wing of an angel. There was a big bandage of gauze on his wrist and the faithful bag of fluid beside the bed, leaking into him. The nurses had shaved her son's face, but in their effort not to nick or draw the rose-red poison blood, had missed wide patches on his chin and neck.

When he was just a little thing, barely as high as her knee, she would call him "silly goose." Now her heart shivered with fear, and when she opened her mouth not a sound would come. "I must be brave," thought the old woman. She touched her son's face but his eyes, which had cried through so much trouble and winced through so much pain, would not open.

I stopped when I saw the boy in the seat. He was choking and his eyes had rolled back into his head. His body vibrated like a machine. I wanted to help him. I knew there was nothing I could do because I'd seen this before and there was nothing I could do then. Before they'd operated on my breast I'd been sick for a long time; Robert had been sick before he'd passed on. But neither of us had behaved this way. It was Marshall who had died like this. And now this boy, this Rex, was dying like this.

The old woman put the magic pear up to her beautiful son's lips. He didn't move his mouth; she put her fingers to the lips but didn't feel even the slightest hint of breath. Against his mouth she pushed the pear to and fro, a wee bit harder this time, but again he did not move.

So the old woman began to eat the pear herself. She took a bite and then she took another, making a chain of bites in the yellow fruit. She chewed and chewed and bent low and then, desperately, tried to transfer the magic nourishing food to her son's mouth with a motherly kiss. But he would not eat, he would not move.

At last the old woman gave up and put the pear on the bedside table. Then she proceeded to scratch her son's back, in the same manner as she'd done when he was a little boy. She wanted to touch him all over; she had become so selfish. "He is mine," thought the old woman to herself. Her son was hers, she loved him so much, more than anyone. She wouldn't let anyone take him. Not the nurses, not the girl who looked so much like a princess, not God.

Standing before Rex in the bus, I remembered standing beside the magic bridge. It had been only hours ago but felt like days. I stood with Sarah and Boris, my princess and prince. On a slip of paper, I pretended to write my secret wish. But instead of writing I peeked at their wishes. Please by the end of the year let me be famous, Sarah wrote. Boris, I saw, wrote about the one he loved. And as both of them finished writing, I quickly scribbled one word—the name of my beautiful son, that and only that—on my slip of paper. I wedged the paper into the O of the bottle. Together we prepared to drop. "Three, two, one," we said.

Against his mouth one last time she put what was left of the pear. When still he did not move, the old woman knew the pear wasn't magic after all. She wrapped her arms around her son's small shoulders and lay down beside him. She heard a funny sound, like springs unspringing, and felt the bed make an awful shudder.

There was a moment of great silence. Silly goose, *thought the old woman, and leaned closer to him. Then she heard another funny sound, a slow dribble, the sound of leaking water. Many days earlier the nurses had fitted her son with a catheter of yellow rubber because there were many things he couldn't do himself, and presently the old woman knew what the sound was from. Into the rubber, for the final time, her son was releasing himself. "No," said the old woman. She made her grip go stronger. She pulled her son even closer and squeezed ever so tightly, but he didn't squeeze back.*

I knelt and put the dying boy's hand in mine.

He was gone. The old woman should have made haste to the hallway, to alert the doctor and the nurses. But this moment was theirs. With another she would not share it. In her arms she held him, rocking gently and gently rocking. The white room where her son had stayed so long was now drawing close. The light was fading and the old woman knew the sun outside, which had shone so brightly when she woke, had fallen behind a cloud. Suddenly she could not feel her body. She was no longer an old woman but a force, a strength enough for both of them. And although she knew he was gone, the old woman opened her mouth and spoke into the ear of her beautiful dying son.

"Breathe," said she. "You've been so sleepy, my baby, and now it's time.

"I'm here for you now," said she. "My baby."

"Let go, just take another breath and let go and then you'll sleep, my little one."

Breathe. Just breathe, yes, yes—Let go, I know you want to sleep, you've been so tired—

It's okay, let go, my baby—

My baby, my little one—

—B.

My turn it was my turn.

Mud sloshing my shoes as I entered. Stood in the lonely jungle of shadows and, after a silence, heard his dull ragged wheezing. Harriet whispering over him. Her first word, "Breathe." Then, "My little one." My head spun shy and I thought this is still happening, all of it. An embarrassed kick against a seat to alert her. Harriet turned and without another word walked back up the aisle. Both arms held out stiff as though moving through fire. Brushed past me. Left the bus.

Now alone with him. I hugged my wire-spiral journal at my chest. Ten steps, eleven. Became keenly aware of everything. Gouges and scars on the seats. Rain walloping the windows in drumbeat hundreds. A fly had edged inside and I heard it vibrating the air. Heard the planet spinning around me.

Tried to tell myself I wasn't scared but seeing him there changed everything. When I saw him I knew. What dying looked like. What the dying did and how it happened. Oh Rex. The glass and the blood. Skin creamy gray with bits of sweat like tapioca pudding. His eyes gone gray too, a mushroom color with eclipse pupils overtaking the green. Eyes that now and again drifted back into his head. Here was his sweat and drool. His vomit and tears and beetpulp blood. All spitting from the seat as he shuddered. Rex past pain in the intimate cocoon of his death.

Fear now my skeleton, inside my legs and stomach and shoulders and face. Here. Now. I had loved him so much for so long like I'd never loved another. Thinking maybe someday he would love me too and he could see it all. Understand how much I loved, how much I wanted. I dropped the notebook. Leaned down inches from his face and looked into his eyes. But no they registered nothing. The arterial blood threading from a gusset of glass still embedded in his throat. His hair damp and greasy. Bangs a dark forelock. All shellacked snug against his skull. Overlong ends curling into snail shells. My king my Rex. So much, I loved him so much. Into his ear I whispered, "It's me. It's Boris, remember me?"

I sat on the floor and put my hand on his stomach. Fingers in the blood and vomit but touching him once I couldn't stop. Ran my hands over his shirtfront. Put them inside the shirt and felt the ribs felt the hard collarbone. Gems and bits and dust of glass. Everywhere hot and wet. Route of hair below his navel and also wirelike hairs around his nipples. I had dreamed all this but never knew it. Now went around the ribs to the backside of his chest. At the small of his back, another thatch of hair soft as chamois. Rubbed my fingers there. Up up. Backbone ridges like individual metal bars of a glockenspiel. Now I was hugging him and shuffling closer on the floor laid my head down on his body. Waited for him to breathe. Finally he did. I fell in love with the breath. Hugged him with every force inside me hugging. Snuggled him tight but all I could smell was the vomit and blood. All I could feel, the hot sticky floodtide of his dying.

My head was too much weight and Rex began coughing. Heavy blood-burst heaves. His stomach a bag of sharded glass he needed to cough free. "I'm sorry," I told him. Moved my head and caressed his corded throat. His cheekbones and brows. Blood spattered my shirt and then my face. With each cough his eyes roamed in his head and the tongue lolled from his mouth. I touched his nose and lips and chin.

Then the seizure got worse. Lifting and crippling. Feet and bleeding hands in the air so I put myself upon him. As much as I could to pin him down. On the floor beside my knee was the fallen journal. An open page with my headline "If Rex Were Mine." Too dark to read the words beneath but I knew them by heart. If Rex were mine, our enemies would catch fire and burn. If he were mine, white lights would wink inside my head. If he were mine, the snow would make a sound as it melts. If he were mine, we would wake with animals circling our bed. If he were mine, I would blow warmth on his cold hands. If he were mine, the 17-year gap in my heart would seal. If he were mine, if he were mine . . .

Coughs thick with spit or blood or vomit and when the quivering didn't cease I panicked. Wondered would he choke. Put my thumb into his mouth, felt the teeth and tongue. Moved it around to clear it. Didn't care if he bit. Went nearer and with the mouth full open I looked inside. There a dulled pinpoint heat hovered, airy, like the flutter from a hidden candle. Some of the teeth anointed with blood. Wiping them clean. Even in darkness I saw two fillings flash on the back bottom left, one on the right, none up top. I'd thought of kissing him for so long now. His kisses sweet relished daydreams I kept locked safe. Aching my head until the best savoring moment. His kisses would faint inside my mouth. Practiced I had practiced for them. On my pillow, the backside of my wrist. Sometimes I left tooth-bruises thinking of him. Now never again.

No breath for almost a minute. Only his shaking body going slower and without breath. Then another cough thrusting poison in the air. A crushed gurgling sound and the exhalation bursting visible and almost black, the breath of a miner. I held him as though harnessed. Arms prickly with horror but tight around him and the fingers touching behind his back. No Rex I would not let go. Again I put my head on his chest. Blood in my eye I wouldn't rub away. Blood in my mouth I rolled on my tongue and swallowed.

Ear positioned over his heart. Precisely there, dropping anchor over the oozing red treasure. I had thought of this heart for so many days, days wanting to plant my love seedlike there. A song lay just beyond my memory. I thought and thought. Remembered the words. The final verse to a favorite song Marshall and Sarah used to sing. My beloved's seizure shaking my head and battling with my holding the tune but still I sang. With my ear on his heart I loved him so much singing as best I could for Rex.

> The first time ever I lay with you
> I felt your heart so close to mine
> And I knew our joy would fill the earth
> And last till the end of time

The last word went hoarse and still over his heart I looked into his face. His eyes shallowed from wild to soft. Lowered to focus on me but *didn't focus, not really. Rex's face became the face of a dreamer. Drifting from pain to painless as though through warm water. And somewhere some long-ago parent had told me when people die their souls gush forth. Breezy cold and palpable. Yes I felt it. Yes Rex I bent close beside and felt you. Departing now. Gone, leaving your shuddering polluted exhaust. Angry gone soul junking and reeling the sad shell of you. Here I was the chosen one. Witness to its last motion.*

In and inside that moment the storm didn't matter. Moon and dilated stars didn't matter. For that instant I forgot the bus and my friends and myself too. Only the process in front of me. The lesson. Enormous weight of it. All elements centered and falling in circles. Like a whirlpool on this bleeding shaking thing with the breathing stilling. Still and stiller and the heartbeat I could hear going slow and slower and stop.

Stop I stared into his eyes. Stop I wouldn't look away.

The quiet. Exalted quiet. Just out of my vision the world outside the window went twirling. The rain, entire sky, shifting sideways. On the floor. Me sitting with my hands on his bloody body unable to heal. Dead. Dead.

Governing the rain was that silence. Like a god-mouth held open. Silence overtaking the bus. Throbbing a steady rhythm, throbbing over the thunder that wrecked the sky. Over the wind and water, thin mocking silence on the thirteen window rows left, thirteen window rows right. One month ago we had trespassed on his farm. Maybe as a boy he'd wanted to be a fireman or astronaut or rodeo bronco-buster. Maybe just wanted the farmer life of his dad and granddad. To carry on the Jackson trade. Oh Rex I loved you and this is what happened. Rex. Suddenly fear opened like a cold chrome fist inside me and I stood and ran. Left him and fled back down the aisle. Dropped ragdoll into the driver's seat. Curled in it watching the rain hit the windshield. Rain hitting and hitting. Screams and weeping under my heart but I couldn't release. No not yet and still the rain hitting and hitting. Staggered half-breaths steaming gray auras on the glass.

Time could have been minutes or hours. Losing track but the rain still fell and the black remained. At some point in there my eyes stayed shut for a creeping ribbon of time and in a half-dream I saw things moving in the overhead driver's mirror. Unsure was I asleep or awake. Something white and ghostlike at the back of the bus moving closer. As it neared I saw it was Sarah's screaming white goose. Come to attack. Near and nearer and then it was black and no longer the goose. Altered to the Doberman from long past with its attached healed head. Come to bless me. Now no longer the dog but changed to Marshall, in the mirror I dreamed Marshall too. But before I could reach for him the dream changed again. Mirror clouding purple and then silver. It was Rex. My Rex healthy again, alive again. Oh his big goofy nose and shaggy coal-black hair. Red sneakers the red of blood shuffling closer. Leaping the seats agile as the day he'd leaped the librarian's partitioned desk. Magic Marker in his big farm-callused hand to once again scrawl his secret ONFIRE.

But no my Rex I had wandered away. Shimmying the vision from my body and brain I saw for the first time I was alone. Alone but with his cells swimming gold and brilliant inside me. His word still shining on my back. My hands clenched on the steering wheel. Dust gauzing everywhere and with one dizzying pull I stood again.

Go and get help. Yes I knew what I must do. But so alone the must do *shrank a whole world of difference from the* want to do. *What I wanted to do. Want. Now too much to think and I closed my eyes. A fog inside my head lifted. Responsibility gave in to want and everything around me went black. Going there felt like floating. Again I stood before the last seat of the bus. Only me and the boy before me. If he were mine* and at last he was. *His body colder and motionless. Eyes still open with no more sparkle just a filmy stare. Cuts on his head seeping blood into the right eye but the eye unblinking staring. Rex only a little dead but here and now and mine.*

Thumb in his mouth again. Scraped the blood out the vomit out. I knelt the way I'd knelt in churches as a boy. Put my mouth on his mouth and kissed softer more superior than the pillow kisses wrist kisses. No he didn't kiss back like I'd dreamed but this was Rex's mouth. Flicked my tongue inside teasing. Then planted it deep into him. His tongue sandpapery like a husk. Mouth gone sour and bitter metallic with old food and new blood. Me closing my eyes and stretching my tongue into every space of his mouth until I'd felt it all and then returning to the baby-breath sweetheart kisses. "Rex, Rex" as I kissed.

I lifted the tattered shirt to his neck. Not too high so I could still see his face. There it sopped up the blood and I rubbed my hands over his body, so much of his skin. The glass-scratches and the wiry hairs again. Saw his secret elmleaf birthmark below and leftside the Adam's apple. Kissed it. Kissed left nipple and right and kissed his button peachfuzz navel. Close by two moles two speckles of brown. Loving all of him and showing my love with my mouth.

In my hands was the limit. As far as I'd gotten, the basement all those years ago. Now I kissed his mouth again and nearing the limit said, "It's Boris, it's your Boris, it's only me." A surge of strength and crossing that limit I unbuttoned Rex's jeans. Unzipped. Took the folds of his fly in my hands and tugged them hard and harder with only a slight resistance. Rex wearing sky-blue boxers with a waistband bleach stain and making a single jerking motion I pulled them down.

Wild in the violence of death he had pissed himself. Soaked on the underwear and there in topaz beads inside the clump of hair. With my fingers I pinched and patted the hair. Reached for my notebook and pulled a page free. Sarah's handwriting, her story of the haunted house and the hellion boys. Mopping the piss as best I could and seeing her cursive words the way that felt but was scared too. Then his tongue pushed in, for a second I let it lick there and wadding the paper when mopping was done. I threw the crumpled ball behind me. Sarah and the boys and Pemberley mansion into the air behind me. No more, no one, only Rex and me.

His cock smooth and two shades lighter than the lingering summer tan on his stomach above and legs below. Uncircumsized with a swaddle of skin over the head and I pulled it back. Pasty from the drying piss. Single filament hair a deep thick black on the head and I pinched it away. Rex. His beautiful body naked now and yes still beautiful. So *long I'd wondered how this would be. Me staring at the Suffering Box photo torn from last semester's yearbook. Xeroxed and enlarged with Rex's face and me imagining what his body was like, what his cock. I put my hand on his cock and moved it up down. In my room at nights staring at his face. Expanding into nights I'd dream Rex stealing into my window. Letting me undress him. Me dallying until only his underwear. Then he would unveil it like a gift. For me and me only. Fingers entwining in my hair and his "I love you." This is what I dreamt sometimes. Now slipping into this dream I let my head move toward his cock. Remembered the man's mouth on me only one night back and emulated. A heavy vein on the underside, a curved blue rivulet only now no blood flowing. Pushed up against his whole body my mouth open. "It's your Boris." Whispered because I still truly believed part of him was in there somewhere. My tongue tip tickling tracing the blue vein. Then wrapped my mouth around him. Sucked him inside my mouth the head and foreskin and lowering my mouth down down. The smacking sounds and the drool spilling. Taking it all in my mouth and rolling my tongue on its wet. Soft he wouldn't get hard and I lapped at him hungry. Oh Rex. The first time with my mouth on a boy and yes the boy was Rex. But on my tongue the taste was worse than I remembered from the day I drank the piss and no sunny-side-up egg to disguise it. I tried not breathing the horrible swarmy smell. Moved one hand over his stomach and chest, the other under his balls touching fondling. Slobbering with him limp and dead inside my mouth like tender thawed meat. Lifting my head and painting my tongue on his balls pasting the hairs together tens and hundreds. Down lower. Fingers stroking the unchanging cock and my tongue teasing here there and down down to the perineum. No he wouldn't moan or squirm with pleasure. Licking I pulled his pants further down. The man had done this too, and it had felt good. Licking blowing love air on the secret skin. One more pull on his pants but I smelled the worse smell now. Saw the filth tainting black on my fingers. Felt its squeeze on my lips and tongue. My head shot up my mouth open. Yes too inside the final seizure he had shit himself. Oh Rex my Rex. Spitting and wiping my tongue on my shirt shoulder I found another page inside the journal. This one from Harriet's fable. Honey baby it's okay I will clean you up now yes. Lovingly I wiped the black muck with a page from the story of the old woman and beautiful son. Their garden and cats.* No magic lantern to shine or wish-granting genie to consult.

Tried to put my mouth back on him but felt the gag rising. Dead corrupt odor on my hands in my nose and mouth. My face back on the naked space of his chest. Sticking fast in the blood. That too was impure and I pulled one last page from the journal. Without thinking I wiped the blood. Tried best I could to wash the death from him. Blood already drying in clots. Tried to say "I love you" but couldn't. Brushing the page over his ruined skin. Too late I saw the page I'd taken was from my novel, my future prize. Stuck in this crippling blank second I knew the futility of what I'd wanted. What I'd dreamed. The Zombies remained together. No one could match the power of their claws and teeth, no one could outdo the force of their revenge.

Standing I spat again. Wadded the bloody page from the novel and stuffed it into my pocket. His eyes gone darker now, unwatching behind their milky gauze. Yes Rex I could smell you and taste you and see the very last second of you and yes you had ended you were dead.

Something inside me constricted with self-hatred and grief and I wanted to die too. So deep in awe I had been inside it, not in but inside, I could not see out. We all for our own reasons had been inside it. Blinded. And now only now the mystery was mine. The mystery was mine but no, I didn't want it anymore.

I thought back through years of regret and shame and discontent. All past moving through little by little until it seemed everything had been rehearsed for these stitched-together moments. My hands my face blazing hot, as though the smooth jade school bus seats had caught fire. Melting plastic, toasted foam. The sound of shattering glass. But the seats were not burning and the crushing noise was only the storm, wanting in. When would it end. Dappled here and there a translucent yellow like the light in my room at night. Light of Sunflower. Light on Carl's face as he sleeps. Glinting and sending the sheen from the tiny Bible key to open the Suffering Box. I went there. Could almost feel my hand inside the chicken wire. Touching pieces from my past. From Sarah's and Harriet's and Marshall's. Everything I'd collected from Rex.

Back I ran back all the way back to the driver's seat. Waited for the rain to signal it was time to leave. Give me some sign it was really over. Standing there but my body in the posture of a boy just stabbed full-hilt in the back and not yet ready to fall. Then I felt it coming. Tried to fight the sob but still it rose inside me, tightening my chest and throat. Swallowing didn't pinch it away. There it expanded a final time and went free. Something more than a sob, a sickening yell removing some elemental part of me and I slapped my hand across my mouth. Knew Sarah and Harriet safe inside the car could not hear over the rain but still cried hard behind my hand. Choking behind my hand. Cries cutting forth, screams that would not stop. Rex Rex. Lost in storm raging minutes I listened only listened to the sounds I made. Needled bright red and unreal. Thought if I could follow the sounds I would. No longer mine I followed them. Escaping the bus and slipping in the downpour. Tumbling and leaping every battered car in this abandoned junkyard. Rats were sleeping warm in their sand and cardboard hideaways but they weren't with me. Crickets in weeds and the leeches in their rotting puddles but not with me. Trash from decades past, tossed from kitchens and bathrooms of once happy families now split and swallowed up by history. Somewhere there were half-cindered letters written maybe by another boy without family. Love letters, wishes maybe. What is your greatest wish? And yes oh yes I wished for Rex. Now those wishes went floating deep downriver, taken swift by the current. Going going. Rex I wish you loved me Rex. Rain and rain and my sobbing screams cut short with my Rex wish falling falling into the liquidy dark. The water pushed fast and heavy but it felt warm and I went there. I went there alone and stayed for a long long time thinking maybe I'd feel warm without the pain of shame. But no. Only soft only alone. Remaining alone in soft and silent black.

20

When the time arrives it is Sarah who possesses the strength. She carries the resistless body from the bus, or rather drags it, uncomplaining. Bending over him, step by diligent step. The sun is throbbing and on each throb moves further up, up. Its light falters on her face and somehow Sarah manages to lift Rex into the trunk. Somehow she starts the car on first attempt; she recognizes all the correct turns and bends in the roads until, at last, the sad narrow bridge and its attendant wrecked El Camino come looming, soundless, before them.

Of course she knew what Boris had done. On returning to the car, he glanced at her only once, but inside his eyes she saw. And after the rain stopped, after the sun wedged above the eastern margin of the salvage yard, Sarah straggled back to the bus. She hid the peppermints, syringe, and wadded sheets of paper underneath random seat cushions. She tidied Rex's clothes; smudged the imprint of Boris's face from the blood paste on the dead boy's midriff.

Now an imperial glow suffuses the car. Harriet sits in the front seat; Boris, the back. Sarah parks in the ditch and does not ask for help. The trees in the far field seem planted strategically, each equidistant from its neighbor. She remembers her teenage fantasy with Marshall, how they vowed to enter the forest and live for days, to badge each tree with scarlet and gold yarn. She thinks of this, thinks of her best friend's smile, as she carries Rex. His hair is still damp and his chalky face regards the blank and empty heavens. One eye has pasted shut with blood but the other stares dully above as though expecting some resplendent vision or phenomenon.

Sarah tugs the body into the low ditch and opens the passenger door. She tries not to peer in at them; focuses instead on the swaying of the grasses, an enormous tree leaking black molasses. She and Marshall would have adored that tree. They would have lain under it for hours with board games and whiskey-spiked lemonade, revealing their fantasies and future hopes. Deeper and deeper into the woods the drenched limbs intertwine, light settling through in puddles, green varying darker to black. The trees and only the trees bear witness to what has happened; only they have seen the kidnapping, the absence, the defeated return. Sarah musters all her remaining strength and hefts the body. First she pushes the head inside, then the back and stomach, the hips with his unzipped jeans, urging him part by part into the car. The insects still swarm. The engine coolant has dried to blue puddles. Ellis and Wayne haven't budged but the blood from their lacerations and wounds has stopped pulsing. As Sarah swings Rex's feet onto the seat floor, she sees an image of herself: the tiny face they scissored from her picture, staring back.

Sweet cordial smell of the blood. The cast on Ellis's arm, the nexus of safety pins over the rip in his jeans. Wayne's R-rated T-shirt and brass belt buckle. She stares at their faces, lingering longer on Wayne: this boy who desired her, fancied a blazing power over her, dreamed of tunneling deep inside. He has been broken in half, annihilated. Sarah looks away. She scatters a palmful of glass over Rex's lap, angles one arm, leans his head against the seat. She snaps and zips his jeans. Later, the ambulance will arrive. Nothing will seem tampered with, nothing out of place. She slams the door on the three boys and, wiping her hands on her thighs, hurries back to the car.

Three miles of dusty road, after which the dust becomes gravel. Wrapping the sky, south to north, are the mackerel clouds. A horsefly sizzles in the bottom slant of the window, sketching lassos on the glass. The car radio still plays, but the station has faded and the speakers only send forth a damaged swollen noise. Littered at Harriet's feet are Sarah's brownies, gone crumbly and stale; the box of leftover chocolates; Harriet's tiger-beetle brooch, unpinned and removed during the night. The flute, smeared with dried mud and blood, where Boris dropped it. And the camera, abandoned, its shutter's persistent eye sealed conclusively tight, shut silent from the storm, the wreck, the deaths.

The rearview hovers above her, Marshall's crystal still dangling. She dreads looking in the mirror. At last she does and sees Boris staring through his window, squinting as though trying to focus the details of some faraway scene. He scratches a mosquito bite, rolls the window halfway down and, closing his eyes, breathes the hale daybreak breeze. Before Sarah can look away, Boris wriggles a hand in his pocket. He finds an empty roll of film; drops it. Then pulls out Rex's glasses. Sarah watches the road but keeps an inconspicuous fraction of her sight on him; slowly, he puts the glasses on. Boris sighs at the rushing air on his face. He opens his eyes, the world whirling past in a wet blue blur. He shakes his head as though, through the undefined angles and distortions of vision, he doubts what he sees. Perhaps he considers tossing the glasses out. Perhaps he considers crying. But Boris does neither. He seals the window with a single handle-turn and sits back.

Sarah attempts the day's first words. "I know I saw a farmhouse around here somewhere." Swerving left, she strives to memorize their alien surroundings. Here the road cracks into clodded segments, like the dismantled streets in Lawrence, and just as she prepares to turn around and drive elsewhere, Harriet points to the north. Beyond the windshield are cottonwoods and elms. The timber thickens and thins. There, where the trees narrow, are a tumbledown maroon barn, the blue-gray summit of a grain silo, and a small white house.

The sun shudders on the car hood; the air commands them forward. As Sarah eases into the driveway, Harriet nods at a red Massey-Ferguson combine, beached in the lonesome field like a lobster. "Look at that great big thing," she says, but her voice carries no hint of excitement. Close by, the figures of three men stand working, digging some sort of trench along the meridian of a cornfield. One holds a sack of sand; the others, two shovels. The corn-stubble stalks have been cut, spearing row after row of sharp black silhouettes against the morning sun.

The farmhouse is hemmed by square-clipped bushes, its doors and shutters fading candy pink. The roof wears new shingles; the brick chimney bruises the sky with a greenish curl of smoke and supports a weather vane of a grazing hog. When Sarah opens the car door, she even hears hogs arguing inside a pen between the corn crib and the barn. She heads for the house. A collie bellies under a barbed-wire fence, tail wagging, and trots alongside to the front porch.

The doorknob releases with a pop. An old woman, much older than Harriet, peers from behind the screen, white apron tied around her Sunday-best dress, paper napkin in her hand. "There's been an accident," Sarah tells the woman. "Do you have a phone I could possibly use?" Without a word the woman swings open the screen, utter kindness and trust, and welcomes Sarah inside.

Coffee is brewing; breakfast being fried. Ham sizzles in a skillet on the stove, four lean oval slices, their edges searing black. "Did anyone get hurt?" the woman asks. She widens her eyes at Sarah's hand. "Oh, dear, you've cut yourself. Are you okay? Is the accident near here?"

Drifting from the kitchen radio are hymns, hushed madrigals played before church. Sarah nods, and the woman reaches for the wall phone with her thin fingers. She unhooks the receiver; delicately dials the rotary numbers. She has made the kitchen her own: antiques, heirlooms, floral sachets. Behind her, on the walls, hang telltale photographs of children and grandchildren. They are grouped together by person, showing individual progress from child to teenager to adult. Each girl and boy, Sarah notices, has made it through. Each has survived.

"I'm calling Lindsborg hospital," the woman whispers. She connects and delivers the phone into Sarah's hand. There are greasy fingerprints on the mouthpiece and a sour undersmell of turpentine on the wall. Sarah leans there, waiting. Watches the dust drizzling through the sunlight; watches the orange cardboard FOR GRANDMA pumpkin thumbtacked above the table. But she does not watch the woman's face, not that.

The receptionist's voice stays composed, remote. Sarah knows that tone, feels memory tugging her like a rope back to all those other hospital visits, other apprehensions. The old woman tells the address, and Sarah backtracks the path she took from the wreck to the farmhouse. "It's pretty bad," Sarah says into the phone. "Just one car. Three boys. I don't think they're—" she stops a moment; looks toward the old woman. "They might not make it through."

She puts the phone back on its receiver. As she drops her arm, the black cord swings and spools into itself, a slender intestine. "They're sending an ambulance right away." Although she knows she should leave, Sarah moves to the table, sits in one of the four chairs.

On the radio, the soprano sings her hallelujah, and the music ceases. A news report begins: in Lawrence, police have brought a suspect into custody. The reporter familiarizes listeners with the details of the case . . . the victims, the crafty detectives . . . but before any more can be said, Sarah reaches and shuts off the sound.

Rising and suffocating now, the granular atmosphere of the

room, the silence. Something is baking inside the stove. A stick of butter has been centered on the table to thaw. "Right away," Sarah says, "that's what she told me." The house, she guesses, was built years before any of them, even Harriet, was born. The sink shows a tan-stained throat from year after year of dripping faucets. Out the kitchen window, the dilapidated barn bears the same color, and Sarah sees it is the very shade of Rex's dried blood, the blood of Ellis and Wayne sullying the El Camino seat.

The woman blinks at her, then treads to the stove, her fuzzed slippers making one-two scrapes on the fissured linoleum. "I'd yell for my husband," the woman says, "but he's out in the fields. Scheduled to be setting fire to the cornstalks and the chaff today. But what with all the rain, dear me."

The woman presses a spatula to the slices of ham and lifts her face to the filmy kitchen window. She pauses, staring, then spins to confront Sarah. "It was *you,* wasn't it?" she asks. She has seen their car, the missing hubcaps, ruined fenders. And the words, always the words. "It was *you* who had the accident."

Sarah stands again. She follows the woman's gaze and, as if for the first dreadful time, views the irremediable damage. And then she looks further. Looks through the car and truly sees. Past the scrapes and dents, past the windows clouded like paraffin, past the words. She sees three people inside: not two, but three now, immured and unmoving. Harriet in the front, yes, but two others, two, in the back. Perhaps shadows cast by the teasing sun; perhaps her fickle myopia, numbed from lack of sleep. But perhaps not. Perhaps there are three.

"My family," Sarah says. She swings the screen door open and steps outside. The old woman is speaking behind her, offering breakfast and well wishes and a bandage for her hand. But Sarah hardly hears. She follows this vision to the car; she is pulled along, willingly, by the vision's invisible governing string. In the trees, the cicadas wake and begin to sing. Their hearts are too big for their bodies and they sing: a love sound, pain sound, taking everything and everyone with it as it chops and slices the air. Sarah walks faster. She fixes her eyes on the car door handle and will not look inside. She will not turn her head for Harriet or Boris. She will not turn for Marshall. *He is with us now,* she tells herself. She gets into the car and shuts the door behind her and reaches for the key, shining razzle-dazzle within the light.

Somewhere music is playing and sirens are wailing. As she drives she thinks of this. Somewhere people are falling in love, dressing up, telling little lies. Somewhere, some other man plots his next horrible deed and others, somewhere, will mimic it. Yes, Sarah thinks, yes. Somewhere the boundless river funnels and crashes with the rains from last night, from the night before last, all the water they believed would never end. But the water ended and now it ferries their wishes, safe within the green glass, forever drifting with the wasted, undreaming bones of the dead.

In the rain-eroded field the men have grouped together, diligent in their effort to start the fire. Sarah looks there; feels the others looking too. She brakes in puddles at the driveway's brambled end and watches. Suddenly the men straighten. They leap back, applauding, astonished. At the core of their abandoned huddle, a spark flickers bluely. Then the fire eats the fuel, spreading quick and miraculous along the gasoline tossed across each cornstalk row. The farmhands drop the shovels and begin to run. The fire takes so fast it startles an armada of crows, their black bodies thrust burning into the cindered air, fire-feathered and screaming, yet all, unbearably, alive.

The fire is blood-red and tranquil, and Sarah, driving away, smells it. She blushes against its lovely swooning heat. Her family: Boris and Harriet and Marshall, all here, now, with her. "Look," Sarah says. Ahead lies the shimmering highway. At last it will lead somewhere; it will lead them home. The sky is cloudless. The road gleams beneath it, an exposed wet nerve from the earth's dark heart. They can almost hear it, thudding.